THE QUEEN'S ASSASSIN

MELISSA DE LA CRUZ

PENGUIN BOOKS

Penguin Books
An imprint of Penguin Random House LLC, New York

First published in the United States of America by G. P. Putnam's Sons, 2020
Published by Penguin Books, an imprint of Penguin Random House LLC, 2021

Visit us online at penguinrandomhouse.com

THE LIBRARY OF CONGRESS HAS CATALOGED THE G. P. PUTNAM'S SONS EDITION AS FOLLOWS:
Names: De la Cruz, Melissa, 1971– author.
Title: The Queen's assassin / Melissa de la Cruz.
Description: New York: G. P. Putnam's Sons, [2020]
Summary: "The Queen's Assassin is forced to take on a mysterious apprentice on his most
dangerous mission yet, pulling them both into a vicious web of secrets and lies"
—Provided by publisher.
Identifiers: LCCN 2019005524 | ISBN 9780525515913 (hardcover) |
ISBN 9780525515920 (ebook)
Subjects: | CYAC: Assassins—Fiction. | Kings, queens, rulers—Fiction. |
Apprentices—Fiction. | Secrets—Fiction. | Fantasy.
Classification: LCC PZ7.D36967 Que 2020 | DDC [Fic]—dc23
LC record available at https://lccn.loc.gov/2019005524

Penguin Books ISBN 9780525515937

Printed in the United States of America

Design by Kristie Radwilowicz
Text set in Adobe Caslon Pro

10
BVG

THE
QUEEN'S
ASSASSIN

For Mike and Mattie, always

Excerpt from the Scroll of Omin, 1.2:

A Comprehensive History of Avantine

LONG AGO, WHEN ALL THE kingdoms of Avantine were united as one under the great goddess Deia, and the mighty Dellafiore dynasty ruled over the land, there lived a terrible man named Phras.

Though he had some measure of wealth in his own right, Phras was deeply envious of his cousin, the king, who came from the Dellafiore bloodline on his mother's side and had much stronger magical ability. This envy ate at Phras's heart and mind until one day it consumed him entirely, and he murdered the king, taking the crown for himself.

Once in power, he erased all records of the Dellafiores so that in the future, the history of Avantine would begin with him, King Phras I.

But instead of winning the people's hearts, he became known as the Tyrant King, for he was a cruel man, paranoid and consumed by the desire to keep magical power to himself.

With promises of riches and power beyond their ken, the Tyrant King amassed a great and powerful army, which he sent out into the land to collect every scrap of the mystical, sacred texts they could find—from recipes for potions and poultices to spell books and arcane tomes filled with dark magic and demonology. A council of his most loyal followers compiled a single document from them. These became known as the Deian Scrolls, the fount of all magical history, information, practice, and use.

No one in the kingdom was allowed access to the scrolls save for the group who had put them together, who called themselves Aphrasians, after their king. Through their efforts, King Phras learned the secrets of the darkest magic in the universe, and ruled as king and sorcerer. The Aphrasian order served as his magical soldiers and were given the castle of Baer to use as they wished. It was there that they founded their abbey.

Meanwhile, magic was decreed forbidden to the common folk, especially for the wise women, who were considered a great threat to the king and his men.

Brave witches saved as much magic as they could, which they passed on secretly. Thus the Hearthstone Guild was formed. In the early days, the Guild was simply an underground organization dedicated to preserving common and household magic; only later did it become a society of assassins and spies.

The surviving Dellafiores went into hiding. Extinct, it was said. The bloodline had died out. They were forgotten, as were the myths about mages and demons.

Over the course of his three-hundred-year rule, numerous revolts broke out against the Tyrant King, and in the wake of the tumult of his death, Avantine fractured into different kingdoms, all vying for power: Renovia to the west; Montrice to the north; Argonia to the south; Stavin to the east.

Baer Abbey lay to the west, and thus the Aphrasian monks fell under Renovia's rule. While they were subject to their king or queen, over time their power grew so great that their leaders began to disregard the monarch and act on their own accord; after all, many of them were high-ranking aristocrats themselves. The Aphrasians believed they were subservient to no one, collecting tithes and levying taxes as they pleased. There were rumors that they kept Renovia locked in an endless cycle of wars with its neighbors, selling magic to the highest bidder and fanning hostilities while feigning loyalty to the crown.

Thus did the Aphrasian monks maintain control of the Deian Scrolls for centuries, doling out wisdom in bits and pieces as they saw fit, forcing commoners to consult them for all sorts of spiritual and physical ailments, wearing a mask of obedience before royalty as they pulled the strings of the puppet monarchs.

That is until the Tyrant King's descendant, King Esban, toured his lands and saw the effect that lifetimes of high taxes and spiritual oppression had on his people. He decided enough was enough—magic and knowledge belonged to all. He vowed to end the Aphrasians' reign of terror once and for all.

So rather than follow in his forefathers' footsteps, King Esban chose to follow the peace treaty and not to attack Montrice in retaliation for their anger at his Montrician bride, as his advisors counseled. Instead, he declared war on the Aphrasians and descended upon Baer Abbey. After a lengthy battle, the king's army prevailed, but did so at great cost. In an act of selfless bravery, King Esban gave his life for his kingdom.

Despite his sacrifice, the Deian Scrolls were not found. They disappeared along with the tattered remnants of the Aphrasian order.

King Esban's widow, Queen Lilianna, has been searching for the scrolls ever since. They are the only remaining collection of Deian magic, aside from knowledge that was passed down from the Guild, and from grandmother to mother to daughter.

However, the Guild's knowledge is just a fraction of the magic contained in the scrolls, and without them, the Queen, and the Kingdom, *of Renovia remain vulnerable to threats lurking outside the country's borders, as well as those within.*

But the queen thinks only of her country. She will stop at nothing to find the scrolls, for they are the key to her family's protection . . . and her country's salvation.

✢

Renovia

IN THE TIME OF KING ESBAN
AFTER THE BATTLE OF BAER

"THE KING IS DEAD! LONG LIVE THE QUEEN!"

A frail elder from the village of Nhainne began the chant from where she stood, hunched at the back of the crowd, her left hand grasping a worn walking stick. She raised her free hand to point one crooked finger toward the palace and shouted again, louder this time, voice scratchy and breaking from the effort: "The king is dead! Long live the queen!" At first the others gathered were afraid to speak of the sovereign's death prematurely, as to do so had been a treasonous offense under former monarchs, but the old woman had weathered too many seasons to fear the truth. She lifted her stick and brought it down with a bang as she said it once more, with all the breath she could muster: "The king is dead! Long live the queen!"

A small child joined next, and the crone's words began to spread the way wind gains force in a storm. Faintly and then all at once, until all the people around her were shouting: "The king is dead! Long live the queen!"

It became a demand. The people of Renovia wanted answers.

Villagers had flocked to meet the Renovian army—what was left of it, at least—as they dragged themselves on the dirt roads toward home the evening prior, ragged and barefoot, shoulders slumped despite their success, often with a fellow soldier in even worse shape hanging on beside them. The soldiers confirmed that, yes, their beloved king, who fought by their side in battle against the Aphrasian monks, had indeed been killed.

AND SO RENOVIANS BEGAN to gather at the perimeter of Violla Ruza soon after daybreak, a scattered few at first, then more and more, waiting for an announcement. But the sun was already high in the sky and still they heard nothing. Surely, the palace would issue an official statement, as was tradition when a monarch passed, or at least give some indication that the rumors were true—and that the kingdom was secure. A Montrician invasion was a Renovian's greatest fear, although an attack from Stavin or Argonia was not incomprehensible. Peace treaties were often broken.

But their hopes were met with silence. The white stone palace and its jagged turrets loomed over them, still and eerie, and the royal banner of Renovia flew high over the tallest spire long after the sun dipped behind the building and below the horizon. It was never lowered. Nobody knew quite what to make of this—was King Esban actually alive, or was his queen simply unable to accept his death? Or worse—had the Aphrasians seized the crown?

The next dawn arrived and there was still no word. Yet news of the king's demise and the Aphrasians' defeat continued to travel from town to town, swelling the crowds gathered around the palace. The hordes began at the grand iron gates and overflowed into the surrounding fields as the mourners grew by dozens, then hundreds. Some rode in on horseback or on bumpy harvest wagons filled with family and neighbors. Others arrived on foot. They tied scraps of white and purple cloth to the castle gates and carried baskets of freshly cut flowers from their gardens—lilies for the queen and lilacs for the infant princess—which they arranged in bunches along the edge of the grounds. Their king's sacrifice had given them the dream of a better future, free of the Aphrasian order; all their hope now lay with the regent queen and his heir.

The mood was strangely festive, if solemn. Everyone arrived in their best hats and dress for the occasion, so there were bursts of blues and reds and yellows amid the traditional funereal white. They looked less like mourners than a rich garden in full bloom. Old friends were reunited; children ran between their parents' legs, chasing one another around in circles. After all, it was rare for so many from so far to gather together, and they had the longed-for defeat of the treacherous Aphrasians to celebrate even though victory had come at a great cost.

Still the survivors reveled in recounting King Esban's valiant final moments for the crowd, all swearing they'd witnessed it with their very own eyes: how after taking on an entire company of men by himself, their great king was cut straight through with a longsword, at the top of a knoll, a magnificent sunset ushering him into the next world. And how, within seconds of the king's death, the Aphrasian monk who felled him had met his own end, thanks to Grand Prince Alast, the king's younger brother, who lunged toward the monk, his blade shining in the setting sun, slicing through the traitor's neck.

When the last of the Aphrasians retreated, fleeing into the

woods surrounding the abbey, the strongest of the king's remaining soldiers gathered their fallen, including the king himself, onto makeshift wagon beds and hitched them to the few horses they could find.

A parade of the departed, led by their slain king, was en route to the capital city's catacombs. All those they passed could see King Esban was well and truly dead.

Yet the palace remained silent . . .

ON THE FOURTH DAY after the Battle of Baer, late in the afternoon, Queen Lilianna finally pulled the edge of the curtain aside from one of the high arched windows in her private quarters. Ever since the news reached her of her husband's death, her place of refuge had become more like a tomb, lit only by a single candle. Even the jangle of the metal curtain rings was jarring. Her head throbbed. Sun spilled into the hushed room, casting a stream of light across the marble floor. The queen flinched, squinting until her eyes adjusted to the bright light, then peeked out at the agitated crowd congregating below. Her gaze settled on a cluster of men near the gate. One of them was shouting. Those surrounding him nodded along in agreement. He gestured wildly toward the castle, punctuating his words with flailing arms and pointed fingers.

"I need to speak to my people, Holt," the queen said. "Assure them that I am their true queen, even if I am not from Renovia."

She'd hardly slept since her husband led his army for Baer Abbey to quash the Aphrasian uprising. Nor had she left her lavish rooms. This was precisely what she'd feared when he set out. She'd implored him not to go, but Esban insisted the men needed their king. It was his duty. He was, above all else, a man of honor, a leader in the truest sense. But now he was gone, and she was left behind to pick up the pieces.

Still, despite private grief and public turmoil, Queen Lilianna managed to remain as poised as always. Her ebony hair remained perfectly wrapped in a high braided bun, and her deep purple satin dressing gown flowed effortlessly from her shoulders to her slippered feet. Only her face betrayed her fatigue: usually traced in smoky kohl, her eyes were bare and swollen from crying; her deep brown skin was wan and dull. Silver trays of food sat untouched on her tea table. She'd only nibbled at the corner of a single slice of bread the night before in order to appease her counselors before banishing them from the room.

All except one. Known commonly as the King's Assassin, Cordyn Holt was the crown's personal advisor and commander of Renovia's security forces—as well as the king's dearest and most trusted friend. As such, he'd been tasked with guarding Queen Lilianna while King Esban was away. Holt was the only person the queen had allowed in her presence since news of Esban's death was delivered by Grand Prince Alast on the evening of the battle.

The moment Alast left, Holt had positioned his imposing frame near the room's double door, where he intended to stay as long as his queen needed him.

"Holt, I must speak to them," she pressed.

"Too dangerous," he said, hands clasped behind his back, strong chin lifted high with authority. "If you step out onto the balcony, you will be exposed. We don't know who's out there."

Eyes wide, she turned to him. "You told me those wretched rebels had been purged. That the Aphrasians were finished."

For the most part, he thought. He kept his expression as neutral as he could. "Yes," he said carefully. "But there are almost certainly sympathizers remaining. There always are."

She snapped the curtain shut, drowning the room in darkness again. "Then my husband died for nothing?"

Holt sighed, shifted his feet. In a rare moment of weakness, his confidence faltered a bit. "It was not for nothing. The loss we have suffered is a great one. But the realm is secure, at least for now. There is still a kingdom left to inherit. That is far from nothing."

She stepped away from the window. "And what of the rest? Where are the scrolls? Were they recovered?"

He stammered, "We don't—unfortunately, no, Your Majesty, we don't have them." He kept his hands behind his back and his eyes on the ground to avoid agitating her any further. "Yet," he added.

"What do you mean you don't have them?" she shouted. Holt clenched his square jaw. He reminded himself that she was still recovering from a complicated delivery just a few weeks earlier.

"Without the scrolls these monks aren't 'purged.' They've only been set back!" She began pacing the plush cream rug, violet waves of fabric fluttering around her. "They'll keep coming for me. They're relentless. As long as I'm alive, I'm in their way. Am I to be a prisoner here forever? What use is living in a kingdom of fear, under constant threat?" Holt had never seen her so out of sorts. He was unsure whether she was even speaking directly to him anymore. "They've already attempted to kill me once. That we know of! And there are rumors of other plots . . . They'll never stop coming. Never. How long until they get to the baby?" She stopped pacing to stare at him, as if she expected an answer. He didn't have one to give her.

Just then, an urgent wail erupted from a canopied cradle near the queen's chaise. She hurried over and lifted the baby to her breast, shushing her softly. Without turning back to face Holt, she said, "He will never know his child."

"I'm sorry, Your Majesty." He paused, then added, "I understand."

At that she looked at him, clear-eyed, focused, almost as if a spell had broken. "Of course you do," she said, softening her tone. She walked to the window again and drew back a corner of the drape to peek out at the crowd, still cradling the baby. An ivory silk receiving blanket trailed over her shoulder and down her back. "What shall we do now?" she asked him quietly.

He didn't respond right away. What could he say? There were never guarantees, especially not in a time of war, and the rebels had been relentless in their pursuit of the royal family, determined to eliminate the rulers as well as any possible heirs. Holt could offer only to do his best to protect her and the child. And his best—a plan he'd been mulling over since the assassination attempt early in the queen's pregnancy—was something she probably would not want to consider just yet. If ever.

They stood in uncomfortable silence for a few seconds; Holt considered the situation. The Renovian army had returned victorious, but weak. They'd sustained a great many casualties. Their king was dead. Several key Aphrasian leaders had been killed, but the survivors had fled, no doubt taking refuge with supporters, most likely in another kingdom. But which one? Stavin? Argonia? Montrice?

Worse, they'd taken the Deian Scrolls—and all the ancient magical wisdom they contained—along with them.

The queen took a deep breath and glanced out behind the curtain again. In the distance, she spied a merchant selling white mourning ribbons from his cart. People were tying them to sticks and waving them in the air, a traditional symbol of both sorrow and hope, meant to help lead the departed souls home.

"If I cannot address my subjects directly, then you will make the announcement in my stead. The king is dead. We must move forward," she said. Then added, "Whatever that means now."

Holt bowed slightly, relieved. "Of course, Your Majesty." If the queen was finally willing to accept the kingdom's new, precarious situation, this might be his best opportunity to broach the issue they had been arguing about since first declaring war on the monks. He considered his next words carefully before making his case.

As Holt outlined the shape of his plan, the arrangements he had made, and the precautions he'd already taken, the queen's visage hardened to match her steely gaze. She didn't like any of it, of course. But she recognized she had few alternatives now, and little time to waste deliberating.

Queen Lilianna turned her head toward the window, though she couldn't see out from where she sat. Nevertheless, they could still hear the crowd's chants growing louder from below: "The king is dead! Long live the queen!"

At last she spoke. "Yes. I will agree to the arrangement," she said. She looked at Holt just as the shock of her words flickered across his face. He knew his plan was a risky one and had expected more resistance from her.

The queen held up her finger. "One caveat," she added, emphasizing every word. "I will agree . . . but only by blood vow."

His face fell. Of course, she *would* want more than promises and words. While he was duty-bound to protect her, he had dreaded such a demand. But some part of him knew it would come to this, and his position and loyalty meant he had no choice in the matter.

His only concern was safeguarding the kingdom's future. And so he nodded his assent, though doing so sealed his own fate. The vow meant there would be no possibility of escape—not until it was fulfilled, anyway—and a painful sacrifice on his part as well.

After all, magic always requires balance. An eye for an eye—or a son for a daughter.

The queen laid the sleeping infant, tightly bundled so that all Holt could see of her was a bit of golden skin and brown hair, back in her cradle. Then she strode across the room to the table near him and picked up an opaque bottle. She poured a bit of pink wine into a heavy crystal goblet, set it down, and raised a golden knife.

Her eyes fixed on Holt, she began chanting: *"Sanguinem reddetur votum. Sanguinem reddetur votum."* The mantra grew louder and faster as she pressed the small dagger across her wrist, drawing a line of blood. As it spread down her arm, Holt saw that it wasn't red—it was deep blackish blue, like the midnight sky during a full moon. He tried to hide his surprise at the color, but he couldn't stop himself from staring. She did the same to her other wrist, still repeating the words: *"Sanguinem reddetur votum."*

When she was done, Queen Lilianna closed her eyes and held her hands low over the goblet, palms lifted up toward the sky as her royal blood pooled in them, threatening to drip between her fingers. Then she turned them over, allowing her blood to spill into the wine, creating plum-colored swirls that spun as she chanted, *"Sanguinem reddetur votum. Sanguinem reddetur votum. Sanguinem reddetur votum."*

Kneeling, Holt offered his open palms to Queen Lilianna, closing his eyes as an image of a motherless one-year-old boy came to mind.

The queen took his rough hands in hers, pressing her thumbs to his wrists to feel the beat of his blood coursing through his veins. The skin on the queen's wrist had already smoothed over, as if it had never been cut at all. "Say the words after me," she ordered. "I, Cordyn Holt . . ."

"I, Cordyn Holt, Guardian of Renovia, devoted servant to the House of Dellafiore," he repeated as she continued, "hereby pledge my life—and that of my heirs—to this promise: Defend the crown and restore the sacred scrolls of Deia to their rightful purpose."

"Is this your vow?" Queen Lilianna asked.

"This is my vow," Holt said.

"Until it is done?" she asked.

He paused. Then nodded. "Until it is done." Holt felt slightly ill as the declaration left his lips, almost as if the words had been removed from him by an unseen hand rather than given freely, a punch in the chest almost—but before he could grasp it, it was gone.

The queen released his hands and handed him the goblet. He accepted it, willing himself not to hesitate, and drank of her royal blood.

With that, he was bound. As was his son.

— I —

Renovia

Eighteen Years Later

✠

Chapter One

Shadow

Something or someone is following me. I've been wandering the woods for quite a while, but now it feels as if something—or someone—is watching. I thought it was one of my aunts at first—it was odd they didn't chase after me this time. Maybe they didn't expect me to go very far. But it's not them.

I stop and pull my hood back to listen to the forest around me. There is only the wind whistling through the branches and the sound of my own breathing.

Whoever is following me is very good at hiding. But I am not afraid.

Slivers of light penetrate the dense foliage in spots, shining streaks onto the blanket of decaying leaves and mud under my boots. As I slice through thick vines and clamber over rotting logs, speckled thrushes take flight from the forest floor before disappearing overhead. I pause to listen to them sing to one another, chirping elegant messages back and forth, a beautiful song carrying warnings, no doubt, about the stranger stomping through their home.

Being out here helps me clear my head. I feel more peaceful

here among the wild creatures, closer to my true self. After this morning's argument at home, it's precisely what I need—some peace. Some space. Time to myself.

My aunts taught me that sometimes when the world is too much, when life starts to feel overwhelming, we must strip away what's unnecessary, seek out the quiet, and listen to the dirt and trees. "All the answers you seek are there, but only if you are willing to hear them," Aunt Moriah always says.

That's all I'm doing, I tell myself. Following their advice. Perhaps that's why they allowed me to run off into the woods. Except they're probably hoping I'll find *their* answers here, not my own. That I'll finally come to my senses.

Anger bubbles up inside me. All I have ever wanted is to follow in their footsteps and join the ranks of the Hearthstone Guild. It's the one thing I've wanted more than anything. We don't just sell honey in the market. They've practically been training me for the Guild all my life—how can they deny me? I kick the nearest tree as hard as I can, slamming the sole of my boot into its solid trunk. That doesn't make me feel much better, though, and I freeze, wondering if whatever or whoever is following me has heard.

I know it is a dangerous path, but what nobler task is there than to continue the Guild's quest? To recover the Deian Scrolls and exact revenge upon our enemies. They can't expect me to sit by and watch as others take on the challenge.

All the women I look up to—Ma, my aunt Moriah, and Moriah's wife, my aunt Mesha—belong to the Guild; they are trained combatants and wise women. They are devotees of Deia, the One Mother, source of everything in the world of Avantine, from the clouds overhead to the dirt underfoot. Deia worship was common once but not anymore, and those who keep to its beliefs have the Guild to thank for preserving the old ways. Otherwise that knowledge would have disappeared long ago when the Aphrasians confiscated it from the people. The other kingdoms no longer keep to the old ways, even as they conspire to learn our magic.

As wise women they know how to tap into the world around us, to harness the energy that people have long forgotten but other creatures have not. My mother and aunts taught me how to access the deepest levels of my instincts, the way that animals do, to sense danger and smell fear. To become deeply in tune with the universal language of nature that exists just below the surface of human perception, the parts we have been conditioned not to hear anymore.

While I call them my aunts, they are not truly related to me, even if Aunt Moriah and my mother grew up as close as sisters. I was fostered here because my mother's work at the palace is so important that it leaves little time for raising a child.

A gray squirrel runs across my path and halfway up a nearby tree. It stops and looks at me quizzically. "It's all right," I say. "I'm not going to hurt you." It waits until I start moving again and scampers the rest of the way up the trunk.

The last time I saw my mother, I told her of my plans to join the Guild. I thought she'd be proud of me. But she'd stiffened and paused before saying, "There are other ways to serve the crown."

Naturally, I'd have preferred her to be with me, every day, like other mothers, but I've never lacked for love or affection. My aunts had been there for every bedtime tale and scraped knee, and Ma served as a glamorous and heroic figure for a young woman to look up to. She would swoop into my life, almost always under the cover of darkness, cloaked and carrying gifts, like the lovely pair of brocade satin dance slippers I'll never forget. They were as ill-suited for rural life as a pair of shoes could possibly be, and I treasured them for it. "The best cobbler in Argonia's capital made these," she told me. I marveled at that, how far they'd traveled before landing on my feet.

Yes, I liked the presents well enough. But what made me even happier were the times she stayed long enough to tell me stories. She would sit on the edge of my bed, tuck my worn quilt snugly around me, and tell me tales of Avantine, of the old kingdom.

Our people are fighters, she'd say. *Always were.* I took that to mean I would be one too.

I think about these stories as I whack my way through the brush. Why would my mother tell me tales of heroism, adventure, bravery, and sacrifice, unless I was to train with the Guild as well? As a child, I was taught all the basics—survival and tracking skills, and then as I grew, I began combat training and archery.

I do know more of the old ways than most, and I'm grateful for that, but it isn't enough. I want to know as much as they do, or even more. I need to belong to the Guild.

Now I fear I never will have that chance.

"Ouch!" I flinch and pull my hand back from the leaves surrounding me. There's a thin sliver of blood seeping out of my skin. I was so lost in my thoughts that I accidentally cut my hand while hacking through shrubbery. The woods are unfamiliar here, wilder and denser. I've never gone out this far. The path ahead is so overgrown it's hard to believe there was ever anyone here before me, let alone a procession of messengers and traders and visitors traveling between Renovia and the other kingdoms of Avantine. But that was before. Any remnants of its prior purpose are disappearing quickly. Even my blade, crafted from Argonian steel—another present from Ma—struggles to sever some of the more stubborn branches that have reclaimed the road for the wilderness.

I try to quiet my mind and concentrate on my surroundings. Am I lost? Is something following me? "What do I do now?" I say out loud. Then I remember Aunt Mesha's advice: *Be willing to hear.*

I breathe, focus. Re-center. *Should I turn back?* The answer is so strong, it's practically a physical shove: *No. Continue.* I suppose I'll push through, then. Maybe I'll discover a forgotten treasure along this path.

Woodland creatures watch me, silently, from afar. They're perched in branches and nestled safely in burrows. Sometimes I catch a whiff of newborn fur, of milk; I smell the fear of anxious mothers protecting litters; I feel their heartbeats, their quickened breaths when I pass. I do my best to calm them by closing my eyes and sending them benevolent energy. *Just passing through. I'm no threat to you.*

After about an hour of bushwhacking, I realize that I don't know where I am anymore. The trees look different, older. I hear the trickling of water. Unlike before, there are signs that something, or rather someone, was here not long before me. Cracked sticks have been stepped on—by whom or what, I'm not sure—and branches are too neatly chopped to have been broken naturally. I want to investigate, see if I can feel how long ago they were cut. Maybe days; maybe weeks. Difficult to tell.

I stop to examine the trampled foliage just as I feel an abrupt change in the air.

There it is again. Whoever or whatever it is smells foul, rotten. I shudder. I keep going, hoping to shake it off my trail.

I walk deeper into the forest and pause under a canopy of trees. A breeze blows against a large form in the branches overhead. I sense the weight of its bulk, making the air above me feel heavier, oppressive. It pads quietly. A huge predator. Not human. It's been biding its time. But now it's tense, ready to strike.

The tree becomes very still. And everything around does the same. I glance to my right and see a spider hanging in the air, frozen, just like I am.

Leaves rustle, like the fanning pages of a book. Snarling heat of its body getting closer, closer, inch by inch. I can smell its hot breath. Feel its mass as it begins to bear down on me from above. Closer, closer, until at last it launches itself from its hiding place. I feel its energy, aimed straight at me. Intending to kill, to devour.

But I am ready.

Just as it attacks, I kick ferociously at its chest, sending it flying. It slams to the ground, knocked out cold. A flock of starlings erupts from their nest in the treetops, chirping furiously.

My would-be killer is a sleek black scimitar-toothed jaguar. The rest of the wildlife stills, shocked into silence, at my besting the king of the forest.

I roll back to standing, then hear something else, like shifting or scratching, in the distance. As careful as I've been, I've managed to cause a commotion and alert every creature in the forest of my presence.

I crouch behind a wide tree. After waiting a breath or two, I don't sense any other unusual movement nearby. Perhaps I was wrong about the noise. Or simply heard a falling branch or a startled animal running for cover.

There's no reason to remain where I am, and I'm not going back now, in case the jaguar wakes, so I get up and make my way forward again. It looks like there's a clearing ahead.

My stomach lurches. After everything—the argument and my big show of defiance—I am gripped with the unexpected desire to return home. I don't know if the cat's attack has rattled me—it shouldn't have; I've been in similar situations before—but a deep foreboding comes over me.

Yet just as strongly, I feel the need to keep going, beyond the edge of the forest, as if something is pulling me forward. I move faster, fumbling a bit over some debris.

Finally, I step through the soft leafy ground around a few ancient trees, their bark slick with moss, and push aside a branch filled with tiny light green leaves.

When I emerge from the woods, I discover I was wrong. It's not just a clearing; I've stumbled upon the golden ruins of an old building. A fortress. The tight feeling in my chest intensifies. I should turn back. There's danger here. Or at least there *was* danger here—it appears to be long abandoned.

The building's intimidating skeletal remains soar toward the clouds, but it's marred by black soot; it's been scorched by a fire—or maybe more than one. Most of the windows are cracked or else missing completely. Rosebushes are overgrown with burly thistle weeds, and clumps of dead brown shrubbery dot the property. Vines climb up one side of the structure and crawl into the empty windows.

Above the frame of one of those windows, I spot a weathered crest, barely visible against the stone. I step closer. There are two initials overlapping each other in an intricate design: BA. In an instant I know exactly where I am.

Baer Abbey.

I inhale sharply. How did I walk so far? How long have I been gone?

This place is forbidden. Dangerous. Yet I was drawn here. Is this a sign, the message I was searching for? And if so, what is it trying to tell me?

Despite the danger, I've always wanted to see the abbey, home of the feared and powerful Aphrasians. I try picturing it as it was long ago, glistening in the blinding midday heat, humming with activity, the steady bustle of cloaked men and women going about their daily routines. I imagine one of them meditating underneath the massive oak to the west; another reading on the carved limestone bench in the now-decrepit gardens.

I walk around the exterior, looking for the place where King Esban charged into battle with his soldiers.

I hear something shift again. It's coming from inside the abbey walls. As if a heavy object is being pushed or dragged—opening a door? Hoisting something with a pulley? I approach the building and melt into its shadow, like the pet name my mother gave me.

But who could be here? A generation of looters has already stripped anything of value, though the lure of undiscovered treasure might still entice adventurous types. And drifters. Or maybe there's a hunter, or a hermit who's made his home close to this desolate place.

In the distance, the river water slaps against the rocky shore, and I can hear the rustling of leaves and the trilling of birds. All is as it should be, and yet. Something nags at me, like a faraway ringing in my ear. Someone or something is still following me, and it's not the jaguar. It smells of death and rot.

I move forward anyway, deciding to run the rest of the way along the wall to an entryway, its door long gone. I just want to peek inside—I may never have this chance again.

I slide around the corner of the wall and enter the abbey's interior. Most of the roof is demolished, so there's plenty of light, even this close to dusk. Tiny specks of dust float in the air. There's a veneer of grime on every surface, and wet mud in shaded spots. I step forward, leaving footprints behind me. I glance at the rest of the floor—no other prints. Nobody has been here recently, at least not since the last rain.

I move as lightly as possible. Then I hear something different. I stop, step backward. There it is again. I step forward—solid. Back— yes, an echo. Like a well. There's something hollow below. Storage? A crypt?

I should turn back. Nothing good can come from being here, and I know it. The abbey is Aphrasian territory, no matter how long ago they vacated. And yet. There's no reason to believe anyone is here, and who knows what I might find if I just dig a bit. Perhaps a treasure was hidden here. Maybe even the Deian Scrolls.

I step on a large square tile, made of heavy charcoal slate, which is stubbornly embedded in the ground. I clear the dirt around it as much as I can and get my fingertips under its lip. With effort, I heave the tile up enough to hoist it over to the side. Centipedes scurry away into the black hole below. I use the heel of my boot to shove the stone the rest of the way, revealing a wooden ladder underneath.

I press on it carefully, testing its strength, then make my way down. At the last rung I jump down and turn to find a long narrow passageway lined with empty sconces. It smells of mildew, dank and damp. I follow the tunnel, my footsteps echoing around me.

I hear water lapping gently against stone up ahead. Could there be an underground stream? The passage continues on, dark and quiet aside from the occasional drip of water from the ceiling.

At the end of the corridor a curved doorway opens into a large cavern. As I suspected, an underground river flows by. A small hole in the ceiling allows light in, revealing sharp stalactites that hang down everywhere, glittering with the river's reflection. The room is aglow in yellows and oranges and reds, and it feels like standing in the middle of fire. This space was definitely not made by human hands; instead, the tunnel, the abbey, was built up around it. There's a loading dock installed for small boats, though none are there anymore.

Then I see something that makes my heart catch. I gasp.

The Aphrasians have been missing for eighteen years and yet there's a fresh apple core tossed aside near the doorway.

That's when I hear men's voices approaching from the corridor behind me.

✥

CHAPTER TWO

Shadow

"WHO'S THERE?" A GRUFF VOICE calls out from within the tunnel. It echoes: *Who's there? Who's there? Who's there?*

Frantically, I search for somewhere to hide. *They heard me!* But the tunnel appears to be the sole way out and I can't go back the way I came. There's only the river below. The voices whisper to one another from inside the tunnel as I slide off the edge of the dock and into the water, trying not to make a splash. I hear clanging as the men run toward the stream, their boots shuffling on the ground as they turn around looking for whoever was there.

"Got away," one says. His voice is deep, gravelly. It's the same man who called out before.

"Could be you're hearin' things again," says the other. Higher-pitched, scratchy. Younger than the first, I think.

"Is that so? Then who moved the stone?" the first replies. "More like they jumped in the river."

The second scoffs. "Then they're dead for sure."

His words are prescient as the flow of the river drags me along, turns a corner, and slopes down, the current picking up speed. I try to retain control but the water swallows me. I struggle to push myself above the surface and gasp for air. *They were right, I won't make it.* The undertow is too strong.

I kick as hard as I can, barely keeping my head out of the river, which is splashing against my face and into my nose and mouth. I can't keep the water out and also let air in. *Don't panic*, I tell myself. *Never panic.*

I spot a heavy branch sticking out of the water. I reach for it and fail, falling back into the current. I should never have come here. I'm going to drown. *I'm going to die.*

Also: *My aunts are going to kill me.*

No, no! I absolutely refuse to give up! My arms and legs shove me on as if being controlled by an outside force. I manage to propel my body toward another floating branch and grab on to it.

Water washes over my head again. I keep my eyes closed and hang on to the branch with all my might. When my head emerges, I try to suck in air but immediately begin coughing. Wheezing. There's water in my lungs. My nose and throat are burning. The men at the abbey can probably hear me splashing now but I hardly care. I just want to make it out of here alive.

There's a light ahead. The mouth of the cave. I hear banging noises from behind me, where the men were at the shoreline. It sounds like some kind of battle, as if the men I'd heard back there were suddenly attacked. My breathing is returning to normal, though I still feel the sting in my nose and chest. If I hadn't come across the branch . . . or if my leg had caught on one under the surface . . .

I emerge with the river. I look around and see I'm on the other side of the abbey now. Right near the hill I saw in the distance earlier—the site of the great battle. I feel the oppressive weight of death all around me, even within the earth itself.

The branch runs up against some rocks near the shoreline, beneath an ancient weeping willow. My arms are weak. Shaking. I have to get out of the water. I can take refuge in the tree. Its full, low-hanging branches are spread out around its wide trunk, like curtains. A good place to hang on, stay concealed.

Please just this one thing, I beg myself. *Get out of the water.* Gritting my teeth, I lift my upper body until I'm lying across the top of a stone. A horse whinnies from beyond the hill; a man shouts. Another man grunts again and again, as if he's punching someone. I rest a moment to catch my breath and listen to the brawl beyond the hill. The men are still struggling against some interloper, but it means they're not coming any nearer to me, so I swing my right leg up onto the rock and hoist myself out. The heavy boots I'm wearing definitely weren't helping me in the water.

The sounds of struggle subside abruptly, as if someone's won. Dripping wet, I crawl over to the willow and hide beneath its curtain of leaves. It's quiet now. They may have left—or killed one another. Either way, not my concern.

The sun is already setting; one of my aunts would definitely have started looking for me by now.

There hasn't been any other sound from beyond the hill for some time now. I don't like it here. Unlike the ruins, this place bears the stain of death. Violence. Its energy is an invisible fog. I place my palm against the willow's sturdy trunk to brace myself so I can stand.

A powerful shock surges straight through me.

Suddenly, I can see a soldier wearing the Renovian colors, bleeding out into the earth. Another soldier with a missing arm, leg snapped upward into a terrifying pose, is groaning. *I want to go home,* he cries. *I want to go.*

One man is almost fully submerged in the river, only his legs sticking out. And countless others are strewn about in the same condition, or worse. Everywhere. The dead. This is the Battle of Baer, playing out before my eyes. I can smell the stench in the air and hear the death groans, but it isn't real. I'm not there; this is just an illusion, a place memory. One so powerful that those with the sight can see it if they try. Even if they don't try. Aunt Moriah said sometimes such visions find the seeker, rather than the other way around.

I have been seeing visions since I was ten years old.

Then I look up. And there he is. King Esban.

I recognize him from his chiseled profile on Renovian coins. A striking figure, like the fabled shipbuilders of the north countries: tall, broad shouldered, bearded, golden hair flowing from under a dented silver helmet. Noble and brave, just as the stories say, but with kind eyes. They never mention that.

I feel the urge to go to him but I can't move. I know what's about to happen, and I want to call to him, to warn him. But when I try to yell, nothing comes out.

A man charges toward him, sword raised above his head. He's wearing a gray Aphrasian robe and their unmistakable black mask. The king is steady. Metal meets metal with a clang. They struggle, the rebel monk pushing the king back; the king shoves him off with equal force. The monk aims his right leg directly at the king's stomach, but Esban steps away so the kick lands off its mark, barely grazing his hip. He stretches his arm back and swings the sword at the rebel with all his might. The monk dodges the strike. The king is furiously red, chest heaving, teeth bared. He lunges at the monk again.

They go on like this. It seems that neither can win. The other soldiers haven't even noticed the skirmish on the mound yet. I try to scream, *Help him!* But I can't, because as real as it seems, I'm only watching. Witnessing the past.

I look back up.

The rebel is on the ground. The king walks over to him and lifts his sword. For a brief moment I hope King Esban will win this time. That the past can change. But the monk rolls and swipes the king's leg out from under him. He stumbles, falls. He's about to get up when it happens.

The monk drives his sword straight through King Esban's chest.

I yank my hand away from the willow. I start gagging, retching. I haven't eaten all day, so all I bring up is bile. Tears are streaming down my face. This is what my aunts meant when they told me to *be careful for what you wish.* For the answer might not be the one you seek. I wanted danger and adventure as a Guild apprentice, and alas, I seem to have found it.

I stand to leave. Based on where the sun hangs in the sky, I've a little time left until complete darkness. I'll dry off as I go, as long as I'm moving. Good thing it's still warm at night. I won't freeze to death, at least.

I walk away, just as something slams into me. I'm knocked straight onto my back, totally winded. For a frenzied second I expect to see the jaguar again—but no, there's a man standing over me.

Gray robes. The dreaded black mask of the Aphrasian order covering his face. The mask that's given children nightmares for centuries. The monk raises his sword.

This is no vision.

This is all too real.

This must be who was following me earlier. The smell is the same—of rot and death. I was right, there *was* a predator on my trail, one who is intent on killing me. I am too shocked to move.

I shut my eyes and cross my arms over my face, anticipating the blow.

But someone comes out of nowhere, swooping over me and knocking the assailant away, running a sword through his belly.

I open my eyes. A hooded man stands over my attacker, whom he has impaled to the ground.

As he leans over to inspect the dead man's pockets, I catch a glimpse of my savior.

I'd know that face anywhere. It's Caledon Holt.

Scruffy beard over deep olive skin, messy brown hair falling over his eyes. He's nineteen, not much older than me, and already the Queen's Assassin. The Guild's golden child. No other commoner in Renovia knows who he is, or exactly what he does, but my mother and aunts are part of the Guild, so they know, and I know what they know.

I dash away while he searches the monk. I don't know what he's doing here. I don't understand what just happened. But I do not want him to see me; he could remember who I am and drag me back to my aunts, telling them where I'd gone. That I was nearly killed. My mother will hear of it and I will never be allowed to leave the house again.

So I hide, even though I doubt he'd recognize me. I'd only met him at his father's funeral, but I'm still well aware of who *he* is. My aunts keep close tabs on him. They admired his father, Cordyn, greatly.

I watch him from behind a nearby bush. He turns back to the monk and peels off the mask. The man beneath is golden haired and handsome, with a huge pink scar across his cheek, from when he was attacked years ago while avenging his king.

I gasp. But when Caledon looks up, I've already disappeared into the brush.

The rebel monk who tried to kill me was Alast, the Grand Prince of Renovia, King Esban's younger brother.

Chapter Three

Shadow

I COULDN'T STAY. AS SOON as Caledon unmasked the Grand Prince, a group of the queen's soldiers appeared out of nowhere. When I finally return from Baer long after dark, my mind is awhirl.

As soon as I step onto the gravel walkway by the herb garden, my legs start to give out beneath me. It's tempting to just collapse and sleep outside where I fall. But I make it past the apiary yard, with its rows and rows of beehives, and approach the house. It's dark aside from a pale yellow glow in one window—my aunts' bedroom. They probably did a locus spell to find my location, and have been following my trek home ever since. *Could have sent a horse.* I suppose they think making me walk home is a punishment I deserve.

Even though they probably know I'm home, I still slip inside the back door of the cottage and tiptoe through the kitchen. It's almost the middle of the night.

I climb the stairs to my cozy attic room as quietly as I can, avoiding the seventh step because it creaks loudly enough to wake a bear from hibernation, and finally flop onto my fluffy bed, managing to kick off my boots and nothing else. I'll regret it in the morning when I have to wash the dirt out of my bedding, but for now, I care about nothing but lying here undisturbed.

But I can't ignore what happened today. Visions of Caledon and the grand prince flash in my mind. The prince was trying to kill me! And he was wearing an Aphrasian mask. Did that mean he was a traitor to the crown? I owe Caledon a debt of gratitude I could never repay—and yet, I can't tell anyone he saved me! Still, guilt pulls at me—what if Caledon is punished for killing the prince? I have to do something. I have to say something.

The house is unnaturally silent, which means my aunts are listening to my every move. I tense, waiting to hear their footsteps on the staircase, but they never come.

Finally, I hear them whispering in their bedroom. I try to eavesdrop but I'm too tired to make much of an effort. Besides, the obstruction spell they cast over their room usually keeps me from hearing anything they say in there anyway. I wonder what, if anything, they already know about where I've been, and if they think my return means they've won our earlier argument. That I'm resigned to give up on the Guild.

As exhausted as I am, sleep will not come now. The events of the day repeat in my mind over and over again: Caledon Holt; the Grand Prince Alast; the argument about my future that led me to venturing off toward Baer Abbey in the first place. The mysterious pull toward it, the visions from the willow tree . . . I wish I could tell my aunts about all of it, except then I'd have to explain that I'd been to the abbey and admit the danger I was in.

Despite the flurry of thoughts crowding my mind, at some point I do drift off, because next thing I know, I'm waking up to the sounds of roosters crowing and pots banging downstairs. Aunt Mesha is making her morning oatmeal. My stomach growls. I hope we have molasses for it, and not just honey. And fresh cream.

I pull a pillow over my head. I'm not sure if my aunts went to bed at all; I hear their voices drift upstairs. They think I'm still sleeping, though—they're not making much of an effort to cover their words.

I hear Aunt Mesha say, "We can't let her—"

But Aunt Moriah interrupts her. "If she goes anyway, then what would we do? Do you want that?"

"Is it really our responsibility that she—?"

"How can you say such a thing? You know that it is!"

I hear a spoon being stirred angrily against a teacup before being slammed down on the table. "It has been quite a few years since we were her age, but if you recall, little can be done once a young mind is determined . . . Maybe if . . ." Aunt Mesha's voice trails off.

I roll over and push myself out of bed. My arms and legs ache something awful from the day before. My neck is stiff; my shoulders hurt. I have tiny scratches all over my hands. I'm afraid to check my reflection. I'm sure I look even worse than I feel. And I'm supposed to go into town today to sell honey too.

They're going to ask questions when I go down to the kitchen. I could tell them about the jaguar, I suppose, but not the rest. They'd certainly never believe I *accidentally* found myself at Baer Abbey, and that I was *accidentally* attacked, and that it was pure coincidence that Caledon Holt, whom I've so openly admired, happened to be there at precisely the right moment. How can I make them believe it was all by chance? They will most certainly think I tracked Caledon down in an attempt to persuade him to take me on as a Guild apprentice. There's no other reasonable explanation for my actions.

Avoiding the small mirror on the wall, I peel off my filthy shirt and torn black pants—completely ruined—and attempt to wash up a bit, using what's left of the clean water I brought up the day before. I comb out my long hair as best I can, removing a few twigs and leaves as I do so, and wrap it in a low bun. That feels better. I pull a clean linen shift over my head and step into a soft brown skirt, then lace my leather bodice over it. Presentable enough. I tie on an apron and slide clogs on my feet.

My aunts stop talking when they hear me clunking down the wooden staircase. I hear spoons stirring in cups, and an egg crack, then sizzle as it hits the pan.

"Good morning," I say, coming through the doorway.

Neither returns the greeting. My aunts stare at my face before glancing down at my hands. Then they exchange a look with each other. They don't seem angry. I'm not sure how to read their mood, actually. Worried, for sure. Also frustrated. Perhaps a little sad? They definitely haven't slept much—both are wearing nightclothes and Aunt Moriah's hair is still wrapped up. Aunt Mesha has her usual loose braid hanging down her back, the way she wears her hair day and night.

I go about my morning routine as if nothing has happened, waiting to see if either of them will speak, or if the incident will just blow over and be forgotten. I choose a chipped teacup from the shelf and sprinkle dried herbs inside. My aunts continue to watch me, and I pretend not to notice. I add a generous dose of turmeric to the cup, for the aches. I grab a mitt, pull the kettle off the fire, and fill the cup, then replace the kettle.

I begin to wonder if I should wait for the tea to steep here or if I should take it outside when Aunt Moriah finally says, "We need to talk, child."

Aunt Mesha springs into action, fussing with canisters, opening and closing them as if looking for something. She settles on the honey jar, begins adding dollop after dollop to her bowl of oatmeal. Her hands are shaking.

I nod before taking a sip of the too-hot, still-watery tea. I don't want to offer any information or ask any questions that may lead to subjects I don't have any desire to discuss right now.

"Mesha? Do you want to . . . ?" Aunt Moriah begins.

Aunt Mesha slams down the honey spoon. "Oh! Absolutely not, and you know that very well."

"What is going on?" I ask. Their behavior is starting to alarm me. I can sense this is about more than where I disappeared to yesterday.

"Well . . . ," Aunt Moriah says.

Aunt Mesha bursts into tears. "I just don't understand how this all happened so fast!"

"Calm down, Mesha. You're scaring her."

"Honestly, yes, you both are," I say. Something terrible occurs to me. Are they marrying me off? Some of the tea splashes from the cup. I put it down on the table and wipe my hand on my skirt.

Mesha wipes her face with her apron. "We received this today, a letter from your mother and orders from the palace. You are to take your place by your mother's side at court."

I read my mother's short note and the official document.

To Maiden Shadow of the Honey Glade, Nir,
in the Kingdom of Renovia

HRM Lilianna, Queen Regent of Renovia,
requires your presence at the court of Violla Ruza

I wanted my mother to call for me, but not like this. I had told her as much during her last visit. I had told her to send me to the Guild. I know I've been spirited at times, but over the years I've been a compliant daughter, always willing to listen and learn, and this is how I'm treated on the cusp of adulthood—with complete disregard for my own wishes? I am eighteen years old. I am old enough to marry, to have a life of my own.

Then it occurs to me: That is exactly why this is happening now.

And I cannot defy orders from the queen.

"We are so proud of you," says Aunt Mesha.

"Your mother is so proud of you," says Aunt Moriah.

I'm sure they think it's a wonderful honor to accompany my mother at court. Every little girl's dream. Except I'm not a little girl. And going to court has never been my dream. I long for dangerous assignments, to be out in the field, to be a spy just as she was when she was my age. But my mother wouldn't know that, because she's always been more concerned with living her life at court than getting to know her only daughter.

"But I don't want to go," I say.

"You're not leaving yet. Your mother says we have a week to prepare," says Aunt Mesha.

Aunt Moriah puts her arms around her wife and turns to me. "Let's not talk about it any more. Shadow, darling, go outside and check on the mint plants, would you? I'm worried those pests got to them during the night again."

I grab my hot tea and walk out the kitchen door toward the back garden. The mint is fine, of course. They simply want privacy so they can talk about me. I take a seat on our old stone bench and blow on my tea to cool it off while I think about the summons, as well as what happened last night. I still don't know what to make of it—or what to do about it.

Summoned to the palace. Certainly the girls in town, always copying the nobility's latest hairstyles and necklines—they wouldn't hesitate for a second. They'd think me a fool for even questioning it. Admittedly some small part of me would revel in seeing their expressions when the honey girl turns into a courtier. But the amusement would be brief.

I'm meant for so much more. Now I know some things even my mother doesn't know, that the Guild doesn't know. There are still secrets at Baer Abbey. The Aphrasians are not as weak and scattered as believed. Though Caledon is guilty of killing the grand prince, he is not a murderer, but a hero. He saved my life. The court needs to know. The queen needs to know.

And suddenly it occurs to me that it's not such a terrible thing that I have been called to Violla Ruza.

CHAPTER FOUR

Caledon

THE RUMBLE OF HOOFBEATS ALONG with the jangle of the royal equines' riding bells rustles Cal from a deep sleep. His head is throbbing, his mouth bone-dry. He licks his cracked lips but it doesn't help much.

Three sharp knocks at the door. He doesn't answer. More knocks. He groans. The knocking becomes banging. "Persistent this morning, aren't we?" he finally yells toward the door. Then he sits up, aching, shoulders and neck stiff and sore, and forces himself out of bed. He's still wearing his clothes from the night before, dirty boots and all.

The abbey ruins, the skirmish with the monks, the shock at uncovering the traitor's true identity, the strange girl whose life he saved, everything rushes back to him. Worse, the sunlight glaring through the front window means he slept much later than he meant to.

When he opens the door of the smithy, a baby-faced page—can't be older than twelve, if that—hands him a scroll sealed with the royal mark of Renovia. Cal croaks out a rough thank-you. Without speaking, the boy bows curtly and returns to the carriage waiting on the cobbled street.

After locking both bolts on the door, he crosses the room to the wooden stool in front of the hearth. It's his favorite place to sit and reflect, usually while stirring something hearty over the fire. His best work has been plotted here. Last year he'd had the idea to impersonate a cook in order to infiltrate the estate of an Aphrasian sympathizer in Stavin—that one was almost too easy—with direct access to the entire food supply, no less. And just this past summer he mastered an Argonian accent and memorized full monologues in order to get close to another would-be usurper by starring in his most beloved play.

He slits the scroll open with his knife and unrolls it.

HRM Lilianna, Queen Regent of Renovia,
requires your immediate presence at court

Short, but not sweet by any means. It is stamped and signed in ink by Queen Lilianna herself. Cal curses at the late hour. He meant to get there at first light, to be the one to tell the queen what happened at the abbey. But after battling a number of renegade monks, saving the girl, and killing the grand prince, he had collapsed in his bed the minute he returned. Now he has no idea what story she's been told by the soldiers who'd come upon the aftermath. He had been surprised to discover the queen's royal guard so far from the palace, but he appreciated their help in rooting out the remaining Aphrasians in the area.

Cal had gone out to Baer yesterday just to rule out a hunch. He didn't want to get his hopes up, but he felt like maybe—*maybe*—it could lead to the fulfillment of his obligation to the queen. Maybe he would find the scrolls hidden away in one of the hills behind the abbey.

The scrolls are the center of his existence. He will fulfill his father's pledge even if it means his life. Until then, this is the only life that he knows, and he will not rest until the scrolls are found and returned to the queen.

Except sometimes he and the queen do not agree on the best way to search for them. Cal leans forward with his elbows on his knees, rests his face in his hands. How will he account for last night? He'd explicitly ignored the queen's orders by going to the abbey. He was supposed to be on his way to Montrice by then. Yet while he was gambling with privateers in an Argonian shipyard last week, they'd mentioned a Renovian fisherman who purchased a small shipping vessel to move river freight, which immediately reminded him of the river running beneath the Baer Hills. Which is why he decided to follow his hunch and head out to the abbey instead. It's a good thing he did, too, or that girl would be dead right now.

He imagines talking to the queen this afternoon: "Well, Your Majesty, the bad news is, the Aphrasian insurgency is alive and well. The worse news is that your brother-in-law, the grand prince, is part of it! The good news is, I caught him. The bad news is, I slew him before I knew who he was. In my defense, he was dressed like a rebel and was about to stab an innocent girl."

The queen is most certainly aware of that fact, though. About the grand prince's murder, not the girl. Why *was* Alast going after that girl anyway? He can't fathom why she was wandering around that old battlefield. Most of the villagers steer clear of it, believing it cursed.

But he doesn't have time right now to dwell on who she was or what she was doing there. He'll have to come back to her later.

Cal gets up and paces in front of the fireplace, considering the situation. The crown's network of spies have known for a while that the Aphrasian sect is on the rise again. Reports are that they're gathering strength, waiting for the right moment to strike and take down the queen, who only rules as regent after all, in order to replace her and Esban's daughter with what they believe is *their* pure magical bloodline.

However, the Renovians have no idea where the rebel monks are based—some say they operate out of a tavern in the capital city. Others are certain it's a farm in rural Argonia or somewhere in Stavin. The queen is convinced they are being funded by Montrice, that her former home is conspiring against her. While the two countries are supposed to be at peace, Montrice has sent an unusually large number of soldiers to the border. Many Renovians fear invasion is coming.

Cal had a different theory about where the Aphrasians might be.

What better place for the resurrected Aphrasian rebellion to assemble than Baer Abbey itself? Everyone assumes it's empty, since its consecrated grounds are soiled and the structure itself destroyed. But the castle is equipped to store years' worth of provisions deep within its labyrinthine vaults. Plus it's unlikely anyone would happen upon it, and the few who live in the town of Baer are unfriendly to strangers, and that's before the dangerous trek through the woods to reach the abbey's gates.

He became convinced the monks had simply taken up residence in their old quarters, but he didn't tell anyone he intended to explore the abbey, least of all the queen. Better to keep his mouth shut entirely and avoid any possibility of that information spreading around. People at court love to talk, and there is a complicated system in place that barters in petty secrets and nepotism. Cal loathes court life and does his best to avoid it.

Of course, before the search for the scrolls, Cal has a more immediate concern: Will he be rewarded or punished for killing Grand Prince Alast? Cal doesn't know what the queen will do. He's been at her service, officially, only a few years. She trusts him, but he wonders who else may have her ear, and whether they worked for the grand prince. Someone could already be refuting his story for all he knows, or spinning some other kind of tale—that he framed Alast in order to benefit himself; that *he* is actually the secret Aphrasian monk—it could be anything.

If the grand prince was involved with the Aphrasians, anyone at court might be. The man has—*had*—an impeccable reputation. He was well-respected. Trusted. Beloved even. A hero. He had avenged Esban's death. There wasn't even a hint that he was the filthy traitor in their midst. By any account he was fiercely loyal to the queen and his niece, dedicated to Renovia. If you'd told Cal yesterday that he'd be killing the grand prince by nightfall, he'd have laughed.

Cal scans his memory, trying to recall anything he'd overlooked before: a conversation, strange behavior from anyone at court— did he ever notice Alast whispering with another courtier during a dinner party or disappearing at a royal event?—anything that would shed light on the prince's role within the Aphrasian order? Or anything Cal himself might have said that could be twisted, used against him by enemies? He can think of nothing. No one has acted out of character. Which means little.

A terrible thought comes to him: What if Alast had been in the process of fulfilling a secret assignment for the queen—what if the farm girl was actually a spy? And Cal, playing the hero, had killed him in the process.

He gets up and begins pacing. Crumples the summons in his fist. Throws it in the fireplace. *What's done is done,* he tells himself. He can't go back. There's no way to fix it. His stomach clenches and his headache turns sharper, slicing through his left temple like a knife. When's the last time he had something to eat or drink? He begins to pour what remains of yesterday's drinking water into a mug, then decides to finish it off straight from the clay pitcher instead. He grabs a chunk of stale bread and shoves it in his mouth. The chewy texture feels good in his jaw, gives his aggravation a physical release.

The not-knowing makes it all worse. Best to head to Violla Ruza at once, he decides. The sooner he faces the queen, the sooner he can stop worrying. He hates worrying. Worrying is wasteful. He prefers action. So he moves quickly.

Cal's only furniture is a bed and a simple wardrobe his father built, where he hangs his few items of clothing. The rest of his things—a couple of books, the blades he inherited from his father—are kept in a locked trunk at the foot of the bed.

He could have more if he wanted—the queen pays him well—but Cal believes the fewer possessions he has, the better. As much as he likes it here, he's never allowed himself to get too comfortable, too settled. He has to live for today, not some uncertain future. Plus, a lot of clutter means a lot of possible evidence lying around, a lot of baggage. He may need to abandon this place with only a few minutes of notice. As the Queen's Assassin, he never knows where his work may take him, or for how long, or even whether he'll return. And if he doesn't, who might rifle through his room after he's gone?

It's not as if he has anyone to leave his things to, either.

Perhaps it's better this way. His father didn't know that he'd never return when he left to track a conspirator that night five years ago. That he'd never see his son again. Leaving him orphaned and alone.

Growing up without a mother was hard enough, but losing his father, the only parent he ever knew, the one who cared for him, put meals on the table for him, and comforted him when he cried out in the night, who showed him how to lace up his boots and catch a trout, who had to fill two roles—one for Cal and another for his queen—that loss took something out of him that he never expected to recover. It's something he prefers not to think about.

Cal begins to dress in his finest pants and shirt, but decides humble is better for this meeting. He needs to appear as contrite as possible. He settles on his cleanest day clothes instead—simple brown pants with a matching jacket and a white shirt. He throws on a leather hat the queen gifted him a few years ago when he came of age and was officially hired on as the royal assassin. To remind her that she likes him. That he does his job well.

He leaves out the back door of the building and mounts his sorrel mare, Raine. She neighs, happy to see him. "Sorry, girl, no apples today," he says, rubbing her forehead. Raine pulls her head away and paws at the ground. Cal laughs. "No tantrums. I'll get you a treat later. Right now we have places to be."

The two of them have been inseparable since he rescued her as a foal. Raine is the one thing Cal allowed himself to get attached to over the years. She'd been left tied to a tree on the side of the road one summer evening. He found her there, skittish and afraid, as he rushed back from the palace to his workshop, right as a storm was brewing. *Too bad horses can't talk,* he often thought. He wanted to know who her prior owner was and why she was left behind. In any case, it doesn't matter now, because he believes she was put in his path for a reason. She was meant to be his companion. Two lonely orphans together.

He waves to the milkmaid selling butter out the back of her wagon, and the tailor standing outside his shop on the corner. To them, he's nothing more than the young blacksmith of Serrone, often commissioned to do work for the palace. In the few years he's lived there, he's never had any trouble with his neighbors. Never got mixed up with the local tavern vagrants or chased after anyone's daughter. He keeps to himself. And intends for things to stay that way.

❦

CHAPTER FIVE

Caledon

WHEN CAL ARRIVES AT THE castle, a footman leads Raine to the stable. He heads to the entrance hall, which is lined with portraits of kings and queens from Renovia's past. There is one of King Esban with his brothers, Almon and Alast. The three of them were said to be as close as brothers could be, and yet, the youngest, Alast, was an Aphrasian all along. There is another of Esban and his queen, one of the crown princess as a baby, then their ancestors going back all the way to Avantine. There is even one of King Phras: a grim, gray-haired man with a neat beard and hawkish nose and aspect.

At the very end of the hall, near the doorway that leads to the queen's reception room, is an imposing, full-length portrait of King Esban. Cal takes a seat on a cushioned bench to wait to be called inside, and his gaze keeps drifting back to the portrait of the king. Little wonder the king intimidated people. The man was as large as a bear.

His father talked about the king often. Cordyn Holt's own father, Cal's grandfather, was the renowned cook of the royal kitchens, his talents so valued that his lowborn son was given the honor of sharing a tutor with the young princes. Cordyn became closest to Prince Esban. They were playmates, and later, after Esban was crowned king, Cordyn became his personal advisor.

Cal's father told him that though Esban was fierce and uncompromising in many ways—mostly when it came to causes he believed in—he was far from the unreasonable tyrant the Aphrasian traitors painted him to be. He had no interest in taking the ancient knowledge of the Deian Scrolls for himself, as they claimed. Once they were in his possession, his plan was to share their knowledge with the people, to better their lives after centuries of oppression and suffering. Sadly, he never had the chance.

King Esban was nothing like the monarchs who came before him. He'd only inherited the throne because his elder brother, Almon, died suddenly while visiting a grand duke of Montrice. They'd been out hunting and were on their way back to the duke's estate when young King Almon fell from his horse in the middle of the field. He was rushed to his room at the manor house, but nothing could be done for him. Other guests at the manor reported that he'd been covered head to toe in a bright red rash; that his face and hands swelled like a melon before he finally suffocated.

As soon as Esban was crowned, a rumor spread that he had actually poisoned Almon. That he'd plotted to kill his own brother in order to enact a heretical agenda against the Aphrasian monks, the only rightful guardians of the Deian Scrolls. In truth, the monks were terrified of King Esban because he didn't turn a blind eye to their corruption. As rightful leader of Renovia, he was the one man who still had the authority to convict them of treason; he could also disband the order entirely if he believed their duplicity ran too deep to mend.

Aphrasian insurgents printed broadsides and spread them throughout the kingdom's towns and villages, representing King Esban as a dishonest and greedy man with a vendetta against tradition. "The new king demands the scrolls returned as he wishes to hoard the knowledge of Deia for himself," read one pamphlet Cal's father had kept. "Once in his control, he will use its magical power against us."

Never mind that the opposite was true. Once he was king, Esban and his council had begun working on expanding access to magical training by dismantling Aphrasian monasteries and establishing new centers of learning for the people.

King Esban wanted Renovia to be more than strong; he wanted it to become the most prosperous, advanced kingdom of all the lands, a beacon of arts and sacred knowledge. But for that to happen, the king understood that the privileged, like himself, had to relinquish some control. By the end of his rule, he had done more to advance equality than any other Renovian leader: He lifted levies; eliminated trade barriers at the borders so that rare spices and textiles became more widely available; instructed monasteries to open their doors to those in need—the sick, the hungry.

But that hadn't been enough to quell the public's suspicions; at least not with Aphrasians spreading unrest through their campaigns of lies. Some people flocked to the sect rather than embrace change, convinced that Esban would soon unleash his true plan. According to them, he would gain the public's trust, then, with the abbey disintegrated, hoard the scrolls and use his power to tyrannize the kingdom alongside his foreign-born bride.

If only King Esban had pushed back against the monks from the beginning. But he believed his actions would speak for themselves, that the people would know him through his works and see that the claims about him were false. That he would triumph by deed alone.

That was his greatest mistake.

Eventually the Aphrasians weren't satisfied with simply dethroning Esban. They plotted to assassinate the king and his pregnant queen, overthrow his advisory council, and place one of their own on the throne instead.

But the king's spies, led by Cordyn Holt, had infiltrated the sect and warned him before the Aphrasians could strike. Royal military forces descended upon the abbey, taking them by surprise on the eve of their planned attack, and put an end to the plot and the sect.

Or so they thought. Cal sighs. Now he knows the truth. The Aphrasians are far from finished. If anything, they had been able to turn the grand prince to their cause. A man so loyal to the queen that he never even married or had children of his own. It was said he devoted his life to the protection of the crown princess.

Cal leans back against the wall. A palace page eventually appears to greet him, and then vanishes again behind a doorway. Within moments the boy returns and leads Cal into the queen's receiving chamber.

There is no delay once she is informed of his arrival. This means she has been waiting for him.

Two guards grab the gold scroll handles on either side of a pair of ten-foot-tall arched mahogany doors. Despite their size they swing outward silently.

A long plush runner—flawlessly white—stretches from the doorway into the otherwise empty room, stopping just short of the monarch's dais. Cal removes his shoes in the receiving hall, takes a deep breath, and steps forward into the doorway. He is ready.

The guard to his left belts out, "Caledon Holt!"

Cal nods to the guard, who doesn't look back at him.

"Step forward." Queen Lilianna's steady voice, still lightly accented from a childhood spent in Montrice, fills the entire room.

She is seated at her throne, flanked by floor-to-ceiling windows on either side, black hair twisted into a thick bun above a simple circlet of intricately carved gold leaves. She almost looks like part of the room's décor. Her elegant white gown, trim embroidered with leaves of golden thread to match her crown, cascades from her lap and spreads out around her bare feet. She's been wearing the mourning color for eighteen years, marking herself a permanent widow. Not purely out of mourning, Cal's certain, but also to ward off potential suitors.

But today she's not alone. A girl sits on her right, also clad all in white, with a tall, ornate silvery-white wig propped on her head. She wears a white, feathered eye mask, trimmed in diamonds, over a heavily made-up face. Smoky black kohl is visible under the mask and her lips shine with burgundy gloss. Her mouth is set in a bored expression, slightly pursed—she looks down at her matching nails, long and shining in the light. Cal does his best to hide his surprise to see Lilac, the crown princess.

Her appearances are rare—she hasn't been seen much since she was born, except on special royal occasions, like the queen regent's birthday or the anniversary of the king's death, and sometimes not even then. Rumor around the palace is that Queen Lilianna is looking for a suitable match for her daughter before she comes of age and takes the throne, in order to unify Renovia with an ally and keep it safe from the growing threat of the queen's former home, which also happens to be the kingdom's closest neighbor. It was rumored that before her marriage to Esban, Lilianna was betrothed to the King of Montrice, but eloped with Esban instead. Their marriage disrupted the growing peace between the two kingdoms, and in the nearly two decades since Esban's death, relations have grown so strained they are at the brink of war once more.

The princess considers him with her piercing gaze. He slides his gaze elsewhere.

The queen doesn't speak right away. Cal tries to appear calm.

"Leave us," the queen orders. Her guards bend at the waist and back out of the room, shutting the doors softly.

"Your Majesty . . . ," Cal begins.

The queen holds up a hand. "There is nothing to say," she tells him. His heart sinks. He knows he's ruined. "You have slaughtered a prince of the realm."

"Yes," he says. "But—"

"Silence!" she growls. She pauses before continuing. "Regardless of what he was, first and foremost, he was my husband's brother. Royal blood."

Royal traitor, Cal thinks. He looks at the floor again. Does this mean he will be put to death, or merely imprisoned? *Which is worse?*

"Look at me," the queen commands. He wills himself to obey, though looking directly at her fiery eyes always terrifies him. Today, however, they are hooded, almost sorrowful. She continues. "Despite the sin you have committed, the fact remains . . . Alast was a traitor, an Aphrasian." She stops speaking. He waits for her to continue.

"I have been told by the royal guard that you also saved a girl's life."

Cal nods. "The grand prince appeared intent on killing her. Why, I cannot say. She looked like a local farm girl to me."

The queen's hands are shaking. "In your defense of the girl and the murder of the Aphrasian traitor, you have done the kingdom a great service," she says at last. "You have more than likely also saved your queen from assassination."

Relief washes over him. He bows. "It's my honor to serve, Your Majesty," he says. He will not be punished after all.

"However," she says, "you cannot remain in Renovia. Word is spreading, even into the distant villages, that the grand prince has been murdered, but they do not know that he was a traitor to the crown. We must keep it that way. We cannot let the Aphrasians know what we know. And we cannot reveal to the public the real reason for Alast's murder. The people are volatile enough as it is."

"Yes, Your Majesty."

"Unfortunately, you were caught by my soldiers on the scene and so I intend to send you away before anyone finds out the truth about Alast's loyalties or attempts to retaliate against you," the queen says. "A mission which will take you far from Renovia as well as benefit the crown. It must be conducted with the utmost secrecy; every precaution must be taken. I will not be able to come to your aid if you are caught. Do you understand?"

He bows slightly. "Yes, Your Majesty." He can't believe how well this day is turning out. As soon as he leaves, he's going to get a celebratory drink and warm meal at the Brass Crab. Why not? He deserves it.

"Good. As you know, my advisors have reason to believe that the King of Montrice—or someone near him—may be plotting war against Renovia. And there are whispers that Montrice is involved with the rise of the Aphrasians. An alliance, founded on mutual enmity of Renovia. You must infiltrate the inner circle of the king's court first, and discover whether this information is accurate."

"And if I confirm the king's involvement?"

She frowned. "You are the Queen's Assassin, are you not?"

"Yes, Your Majesty." Cal bows, his heart racing.

Cal reels inwardly. Killing a traitor, a spy, or a criminal is one thing—but killing a king? That's regicide. If he fails, or if he's captured, Montrice will have his head, without question. It will be straight to the gallows.

He had been intent on going back to Baer Abbey, to see if his hunch was correct, if the scrolls were hidden there. This will only delay that attempt, and someone else might stumble upon them or take them to another hiding place. Still, he must do as the queen commands.

"Who knows?" the queen adds, reading his expression like a book. "Perhaps the scrolls are in Montrice."

He doesn't believe for a moment that they are. But he just bows again. "Yes, Your Majesty."

"One more thing," the queen says. Cal turns back to face her. As he does, he catches the princess's eye. She returns his gaze with a level one of her own.

The queen continues. "In order to provide cover for you, and to appease the aristocracy for your crime, you shall begin your mission with imprisonment at Deersia. Meanwhile, the Guild will continue gathering intelligence regarding the situation up north. When ready, I will send a soldier to deliver your weapons and release you to begin your journey to Montrice. But until that time, you will remain at Deersia."

The princess whips her head toward the queen in surprise but quickly looks forward again.

Deersia. The prison no captive ever leaves. He'd rather take his chances locked in a room of Aphrasian aristocrats. Cal opens his mouth as if to speak, but finds no words. Finally, he manages to spit out, "I'm not sure I understand."

The queen bangs her staff against the floor. "Guards!" The doors fly open and the two men reappear. The princess turns away. Queen Lilianna points at Cal, all traces of friendliness gone.

"Escort the traitor to Deersia. Immediately!"

⚜

CHAPTER SIX

Shadow

NOBODY IS PARTICULARLY INTERESTED IN buying honey or beeswax salves, nor am I interested in selling them today when I arrive at the booth and say hello to Aunt Mesha. There's far too much on my mind. So I wander off to browse the marketplace flower stands instead, still fuming over what happened earlier that morning with Ma. I'd slipped into the palace to tell her what happened at Baer Abbey, but all we did was argue about the summons. *No, of course you must do your duty. You will take your place at court.*

My mother is as unmoving as my aunts, and once I am settled at Violla Ruza, it is clear that I'll be monitored night and day. There'll be no running off when there are guards and courtiers—spies— everywhere at all times.

How can you not want this? she asked. My mother assumes I am like other girls. She doesn't know me. Even if she did, it's clear she doesn't particularly care what my wishes are. I don't want to be a courtier, no matter how prestigious the position. I want to hone my magical powers, become as deadly and dangerous as she used to be, before she settled down to oversee and placate the nest of vipers at court. I want to train. If I go to the palace, it will be as an assassin. Not as a doll. Or a pawn.

The justice bell begins to toll from the palace tower and the sudden *clang* jolts me from my thoughts. I turn to look up the road. All around me townsfolk are abandoning their wares, their shops, their friendly chatter, and they swarm into the streets. Even though I'm as curious as they are, I roll my eyes. They're vying for a glimpse of the prison transport so they can be one of the first to view the offender. They'll exchange stories about it for days: *Oh yes, I was there. I saw the murderer with my own eyes. I was shocked. Well, I wasn't surprised whatsoever.* Even the kindly shopkeeper, who just moments before was carefully arranging fresh-cut blooms in his wife's elaborately hand-painted ceramic pots and vases, turns his attention toward the main thoroughfare instead. I purchase one from the old woman, a small plant pot in white, decorated with lush grapevines, purposely trying to seem indifferent to the commotion around me.

This isn't the first time I've witnessed a transfer. It never seems to matter who appears in the cart when it emerges, either; the crowd is always ready to condemn. It's alarming, really, how quickly nice people become ravenous, bloodthirsty. Children young enough to hide in their mother's skirts throw half-eaten food or handfuls of dirt at the prisoners; they spit toward the rickety cart as it rolls down the main thoroughfare.

The mob prefers to see justice administered swiftly rather than fairly. When I was younger, their furious scowls and screaming frightened me. I would cling to Aunt Mesha and close my eyes. She told me the people want to see someone punished, because order comforts them more than justice. They need to believe that the good are always good and the bad are always bad, and that they themselves err on the side of good. Few understand that there's a wide space between the two, where nearly all of us fall.

My aunts warned me of this many times—be wary of the sway of others, they told me. Find your own path and stay upon it. Don't allow yourself to be pulled in another direction, even if you must walk alone. "Do the most good" is their favorite saying. The *most* good. I like that because it allows for, well, some of the not-so-good too. Sometimes a bit of that is necessary.

But this—the angry horde—is not doing any good at all. Did no one wonder if they could be wrong? Question the lack of public trial? My eyes fall on a tiny girl who can't be more than three or four years old. She watches silently, wide-eyed, one thumb in her mouth, her other hand grasping her father's. He's paying little attention to her; his focus is on the spectacle around him. Raucous laughter drifts through the air, somehow adding an even more sinister edge to the hisses and taunts. She looks terrified. But in a few more years, she'll likely be throwing dirt alongside all the others.

The cart comes closer. I can see him now.

Like everyone in the crowd, I know who the prisoner is, but I can scarcely believe it.

The official story from the palace is that the grand prince was murdered by a local blacksmith, Caledon Holt. There is no specific mention of where the grand prince was found. It happened during a botched robbery, said one. An evening of high-stakes gambling at an out-of-the-way tavern that led to an argument, or perhaps an ambush, said others. He's being sent to Deersia to await trial and will surely be executed.

But I know the truth.

Caledon is not a traitor, but a hero.

He should be at the head of a parade, feted and beloved; instead he is being led from the capital of Renovia in chains.

Why did the queen do this? *Why?*

This is all my fault. Maybe if I hadn't been at Baer Abbey, he wouldn't have needed to rescue me or kill the grand prince.

The cart draws nearer. Now I regret buying this ceramic vessel. I can't carry it right now, and it won't fit in the cloth bag slung over my shoulder, which is heavy enough already, filled with tiny jars of the salves I was supposed to sell. I see a young girl standing alone just a few paces from me. She carries a basket with a loaf of fresh bread and some fruit.

"Excuse me," I say.

She looks startled. "I paid for this," she says. "Ask him." She points to the fruit vendor.

I hold out the pot. "No, no, I'm to deliver this to your mother. Can you take it to her for me?"

"Oh! Yes," she says. I hand it to her and she puts it in her basket.

"Enjoy!" I say, already walking away. I pull my hood forward around my face and disappear into the crowd, trying to edge closer to the road. If I stand tiptoe, I can see Caledon in the back of the cart. He sits with his back straight, defiant. I follow his piercing gaze to the palace balcony, where his eyes are locked on the queen. No hint of emotion shows on his face. Hers is much too far away to make out, even if it wasn't obscured by the drape of her veil, but I can tell she's holding her usual perfect posture, hands clasped in front of her long white dress. Still as a statue.

I wonder if Caledon is afraid. I would be. Deersia is a dangerous, lonely place. Most who enter are never seen again, even before they make it to trial. Few men are willing to take jobs at the prison—

it's considered a punishment just to *work* there—so it's become customary for royal officials to relocate their troublesome staff to the fortress. The threat of a stint boiling linens or flushing pans at Deersia is a useful deterrent. Parents are known to threaten their sons: "Behave, or it's off to Deersia with you!"

Caledon's situation is especially precarious. He is charged with murdering a royal. Those who loved Prince Alast will no doubt seek revenge, and there are likely to be a few of them working at the prison. And though Caledon is known only as a local blacksmith, there have to be some, especially at Deersia, who are aware of his true occupation. He's sure to have enemies in Renovia's underworld. They'd probably like nothing more than to be the assassin's own executioner.

The guard notices Caledon looking up at the queen, so he yanks him to the floor of the cart by his chains. The crowd cheers at the spectacle. "Impertinent bastard," the guard sneers. "Keep your eyes to your filthy feet." Queen Lilianna disappears behind white curtains in a flurry of fabric. A maid shuts the balcony door after her and draws the drapes.

Seems she can't even bear to observe what she's done.

My head pounds with a sudden surge of anger. I don't know how he can stand it. How can he keep from lashing back at the guard, at the people? I doubt I could be so stoic. Fury boils up in me just from watching it happen.

Caledon saved my life, without the slightest hesitation or consideration for his own well-being. For that, I am eternally in his debt. And he's in desperate need of a friend right now.

Then, the spark of an idea comes to me. Maybe, if I help him, if I prove myself worthy, he'll train me himself. I won't even need to join the Guild if he can teach me what he knows. My mother and aunts will be angry, at least at first, but once they see how well I do and on my own, they'll be proud.

The cart approaches. It's about to be directly in front of me, and in that moment I decide.

I push through the crowd, elbowing people aside. One woman jabs me back and curses, but I just rush to the side of the cart and grab on to the wood slats. Caledon and I make eye contact, but he looks away quickly, probably thinking that I'm about to spit at him like the rest.

I have to think fast. I wish I had time for a note, but obviously that's not an option. I reach into my bag and root around for something. A jar of salve won't do—he'll have nowhere to put it.

At the bottom of my bag I come upon crushed flowers wrapped inside a handkerchief. My mother gave it to me during her last visit a few years ago, when I turned fourteen, but it will have to do. I shake the dried flowers into the bag and thrust the handkerchief through the bars. "Take it."

Caledon glances down at the handkerchief, then scoots back and opens his hands, which are tied behind his back. His fingers close around the fabric before he slides it up his sleeve. "You're not alone," I add impulsively, letting go of the bars just as the guard looks in my direction. I'm not sure what I'm going to do or how I'm going to do it, but I have to help him.

I back away, holding my hood across the bottom of my face, and slip through the back of the crowd. I walk a few yards, following the road, then stand on the front step of the Brass Crab to watch the cart move on. Caledon stares at me as it goes, eyebrows knit together in confusion. I can't tell for sure whether he knows I'm the girl from the abbey.

His gaze roots me to the spot, and the world around me drifts away into the background; there's only the road ahead, and Caledon. We remain this way—watching each other—for a long, long time, until the cart finally disappears over the hill.

❧

Chapter Seven

Caledon

THE JOURNEY TO DEERSIA IS grueling—and painfully slow. The brittle cart bumps relentlessly over deeply rutted roads as it winds its way into the foothills of the border mountains. Before they've even reached the halfway point, Cal's legs are already sore and bruised, his arms and shoulders ache from being held behind his back, his wrists chafe raw against the rough restraints.

For the first part of the trip he resists the urge to fight or flee. Even if it wouldn't be difficult to escape from the tightly (but poorly, he notes) knotted ropes and overtake the guard and the driver, he cannot. He has been given an assignment and he must see it out.

The two men don't speak to him. They hardly speak to each other, either, and when they do, it's about nothing useful—just boasts about women, gambling, more women. So Cal has plenty of time to consider what happened with the strange girl in town. Who is she? Why did she give him . . . ? What did she give him? He struggles to grasp it in his fingers again. Just a scrap of cloth? Or is it a message from the Guild? He tries not to curse aloud; he's pushed whatever it is even farther up his sleeve.

Is she his replacement? Could the Guild have already chosen the new assassin? He feels a burst of irritation at the thought. He hadn't considered the possibility of someone taking his position so soon. And then immediately: No, he is not so easily replaced. More likely she was simply a messenger. Finally, he manages to get ahold of the edge and yanks the fabric down into a ball in his hand. He doesn't want the guards to see that he has it. He squeezes it but doesn't feel anything sewn into the material.

Maybe he'd seen her around town before? He tries to remember. She looked so familiar, and yet he couldn't quite place her. Had she been selling sunflowers in front of the haberdashery last week? No, that girl had lighter hair, pinker skin, a bright yellow shawl. This one wore a merchant's dress in muted colors, tans and browns, and a hooded linen cape. With a long, thick chestnut braid over her shoulder, woven with a lavender ribbon. Cowlicky curls framing her forehead. Big brown eyes, skin the color of amber honey.

The girl at the abbey. She also had dark hair, he thinks, though he can't exactly remember seeing it. Maybe it's her black hood that he remembers, not her hair? He didn't get a good look at her face that day. She was gone almost as soon as he showed up to save her life. And look where that got him.

The fortress of Deersia—formerly Castle Deersia, used by the earliest members of the Dellafiore dynasty—looms in the fog up ahead. The tall gray structure, as ragged and menacing as the mountains around it, sits on the highest point for a mile in any direction, with sheer cliffs on three sides. It appears to grow naturally from the rock itself, and that's by design; the base of the castle was carved out of the very mountain on which it sits, making it as indestructible as its surroundings. The Dellafiores intended this to be a reminder of their power—as natural and awe-inspiring as the earthly creations of Deia Herself. Only the upper levels were constructed by human hands, with stone quarried at the foot of the mountains and dragged up the skinny road or hoisted up the sides with pulleys. It cost a fortune, in coin, years, and labor, not to mention lives. Almost every family in Renovia has stories of ancestors who died while building Deersia.

The road is the only way to access the building. Or leave it alive. Caledon's heart sinks into his gut. The prison was chosen for the most difficult captives. How long will he be stuck here? When will the queen send for him?

The ride uphill feels longer than the entire trip did up to that point. Parts of the path are so narrow the cart turns slightly on its side. Cal's stomach lurches each time it sways. He decides to close his eyes the rest of the way.

They come to a stop in front of the entrance, where a shabbily dressed man holding a lantern waits for them. A large iron ring full of keys hangs from his belt. The guard flips down the back of the cart and yanks Cal out, tossing him onto the ground in front of the gates. "Now get up," the guard says.

Cal doesn't say what he wants to say; he bites his tongue instead.

"I said get up," the guard repeats. Cal struggles to stand. His right foot is numb and his legs are wobbly from sitting on them for so many hours. When he begins to rise, the guard pushes him down with his boot. "Try again," he says.

Would it have been so bad to let the prison guard in on the plan? Cal thinks. It's going to be a long stay, even if it's only a few days, as he hopes.

The keeper at the gate steps forward and addresses the guard.

"All right, Edmun. Enough. Plenty of time for all that." They both chuckle.

Once Cal's finally to his feet, the guard takes out a blindfold and wraps it around his eyes. From there he's dragged all the way through the fortress, the guard on one side and the keeper on the other. He trips, purposely, to slow down the guards and get some idea of what's around him, but they just continue to yank him along until he manages to get his feet back under him again. "You know that's not helping, right?" he says. They don't respond, just pull harder. He decides it's better to keep his comments to himself after that. Instead he listens for other prisoners. There's surprisingly little noise aside from the raspy breath of his captors and their feet shuffling against the floor. He knows he can't be alone in the fortress. They must be keeping him in an isolated wing.

He concentrates on memorizing how many steps they take before each turn, and whether they turn left or right, to create a crude map of the prison in his head. They go up at least four flights of stairs, the last even steeper than the others. They are so high up that he can feel a slight sway in the building from the wind. The air is thin too; the guard stops to catch his breath. They must be in one of the tall, skinny turrets. At least he'll have a nice view.

They jerk him to a stop. He hears metal keys clanging together and the creak of rusty hinges, a thick door sliding open against the uneven floor. The guard pulls the scarf down from Cal's eyes, leaving it dangling around his neck. He's in a cell with a tiny barred window that looks out beyond the cliff, past the Renovian Sea, all the way into Montrice. "Best room in the house!" the keeper says. "Got a privy and everything!" He whistles.

That's the last thing Cal hears before the heavy iron door slams shut. The bolts click into place. A bar slides into place across the door.

"You forgot something," Cal says. He slips off the wrist ties easily—he could have done that from the start if he'd wanted—and removes the scarf they left on his neck. "Don't worry, I took care of it," he calls out. There's no reply, just the jingle of keys and the echo of footsteps as the two men retreat into the depths of the castle, leaving Cal very much alone in the turret, empty aside from a basic sleeping space, a rough wool blanket, and a lone bucket in the corner.

The handkerchief. He pulls it back out of his sleeve and smooths it on the ground in front of him, eyes searching every bit of it for some kind of message. Nothing. He turns it over. Nothing. He picks it up to look closely. There may be tiny writing, or even a code of tiny dots, anything. But there is not. It's just a handkerchief that smells of a floral perfume.

He stuffs it back up his sleeve in case he missed something or needs it later. Then he balls up the scarf to use as a pillow and lies down on the hay-strewn floor near a stream of moonlight from the tiny window. There's nothing else to do now. Except wait.

CHAPTER EIGHT

Shadow

WHAT FELT SO RIGHT IN the moment feels more and more foolish as the days go on. I took a big risk approaching Caledon during the prisoner transport like that, and to what end? I'm stuck here, while he's all the way at Decrsia. Even if I could get there, it still wouldn't do him any good—women are absolutely prohibited from setting foot on the grounds.

From the moment I returned home to the cottage, the plan to ship me off to Violla Ruza continued to move forward. Less than a week. That's all I have. In six days, my life, as I know it, will be over. All my sensory training will be useless. Nothing will be expected of me once I officially arrive, other than looking pretty and following orders. I know this because I have occasionally accompanied my mother to court, and there is so little to do there I almost die of boredom.

I'm putting breakfast dishes away when I hear a heavy knock at the door. My stomach lurches—was I reported for the handkerchief? Did someone see me slip it to Caledon?

Another knock, more insistent. I wonder if I can get away out the back door.

Aunt Moriah shouts, "On my way!" to whoever's knocking as she rushes to the door.

"Wait!" I yell, but before I can stop her, she's already opening it. I take a few steps toward the back door and peek through the window over the kitchen sink. I don't see anyone out there.

"It's Missus Kingstone, dears." I look toward the front door and see her drop into a quick curtsy.

"Good morning," Aunt Moriah says, bobbing down as well. "Please, come right in." She calls into the kitchen. "Shadow, time for your fitting."

Missus Kingstone has been coming to the cottage for four years, to give me lessons in court life and outfit me for the times when I am called to join my mother. I'm not surprised she's here since I'm supposed to leave for the palace so soon.

I wipe off my hands and reluctantly join them in the sitting room.

Missus Kingstone is plump, with a plain, but kind, face and frizzy gray hair tucked under a white cap. She wears simple clothing of high quality. The stitching is immaculate. Her skirt falls almost to the floor, neither too long nor too short, swishing perfectly as she walks, and her sleeves gather into small stiff ruffles at the wrist without any drooping. If anyone needed proof of her skill or her exacting standards, it's evident in her own clothing.

"Hello, Shadow! How are you, my sweet? Let's get to it, shall we?" she says to me, clapping her hands together. "We don't have a moment to waste!" She puts her large basket on the floor and begins taking various instruments out of it, including a small square of wood.

"Missus Kingstone is going to make your new gowns," Aunt Moriah tells me. "For the palace."

"Of course," I say.

"Stand on this, would you?" the seamstress orders, pointing to the wood block. I step onto it, feeling somewhat ridiculous, as I do every time I am called for a fitting.

But time passes quickly. Missus Kingstone is swift and efficient. Maybe a bit *too* efficient. She pushes and tugs at me like I'm a doll. Measurements are taken for every single part of my body, even my fingers, to make new gowns and precisely fitted elbow-length gloves.

Every piece of clothing she puts on me—samples that she pins and re-pins endlessly—starts to feel like another layer of confinement, piling on top of me to weigh me down and keep me from being able to flee. She stuffs me into a mock-up corset as well.

"A satin one, lined in whalebone, was ordered for you," she says.

"I hope it's not like this one. It's laced far too tight," I tell her as I attempt to pull it away from my body in order to breathe. She looks at me as if I've spoken utter nonsense and doesn't reply *or* loosen it.

Fabric swatches are brought in too. They're pinned onto parchment pages in a heavy massive book: red like a shiny apple, a matte mauve taffeta, deep blues, and light pinks.

"Which colors do you prefer, dear?" Missus Kingstone asks me, holding up the book. From her friendly tone, I know she assumes I must be thrilled about the silks and laces, but I can barely muster an opinion. Mostly I give her a tight smile, point at one or the other. She pats my leg. "Nervous, are you, dearie? Don't be, you'll be perfect," she says, more to my aunts than to me.

My aunts match the woman's cheer and fuss over the beautiful material, but I can tell it's forced. Their exclamations are high-pitched and overdone; a show. "Oh!" they coo. "Would you look at this one, Shadow? Absolutely exquisite!" They never speak that way. It's as if they're lying to my face. I'd rather they say, "Shadow, we know this isn't what you wanted, but there's nothing we can do about it. It's out of our hands. So just pick the fabrics and get this over and done."

When the seamstress finally packs up her cart and heads back into town to begin making my fancy, unwanted finery, I help my aunts clear the table. Aunt Moriah tries to initiate conversation. "I adore that blue on the tea gown. It was a good choice. Reminds me of winter nights, when the moon is full—"

"I don't want to talk about it," I snap. From the corner of my eye, I see her exchange a knowing look with Aunt Mesha, who opens her mouth to speak but shuts it when Aunt Moriah shakes her head slightly.

"I'm going outside," I tell them. Neither responds.

I stomp down the pebble path away from the cottage. I sense a hare chewing on bark before he sees me coming. They're always out here trying to get into the vegetable garden. Usually, I slow down so as not to scare them, but at the moment I don't care. He freezes, then hops off toward the field.

I clench my fists so hard my nails dig into my skin. I'm going to miss all this. The gardens, the beehives, even selling honey at the marketplace and bickering with my aunts.

But my future is no longer mine to decide. Resignation washes over me in a wave, so I start back toward the cottage. Everything—from the cozy house itself, with its patchy roof and the peeling picket fence around it, to the lanterns lit in the kitchen, and all the grounds surrounding it—seems shrouded in my sadness. I'm reminded of something I overheard my mother say to my aunts when

I was younger: *A dramatic little thing, isn't she.* I remember it exactly that way: a statement, not a question. Over what, I don't recall, though I believe it was about a meal I didn't want to eat. Something so simple, so common that children do, and my mother's response was, "A dramatic little thing, isn't she."

The memory fuels my indignation for the next minute or so as I walk up the cobblestone path to the house. I'm snapped out of my self-pity when Aunt Moriah's voice drifts out of the kitchen: "If the boy can't do it, then what?"

"I don't know. I really don't know," Aunt Mesha says. "I wish I could say otherwise." And then something muffled.

" . . . not what Cordyn wanted. Not at all," Aunt Moriah is saying. They're talking about Caledon's father, the former Queen's Assassin. I hear cupboards opening, closing. Dishes being put away.

"It *would* come down to Montrice, wouldn't it?" Aunt Mesha says. "But who?"

More muffled talking. But clearly, no blocking spell. Maybe they didn't want to take the time. Or forgot. Ever since they announced my departure, my aunts have seemed more and more distracted. I stop walking and listen more carefully.

" . . . another Montrician spy has been discovered . . . sent up to Deersia this week . . ." Tidbits of their hushed conversation float on the air and I can feel my heart start to race.

Another prisoner is being sent to Deersia. That means another prison transport will be traveling up there very soon.

"It's all much too dangerous," Aunt Mesha agrees. "And we're supposed to send her anyway, as if none of this is happening? We could be dealing with anything. Anything! There's no knowing what evil the Aphrasians are capable of unleashing. Shapeshifters, demons even."

I can't see inside the house, but I can picture Aunt Moriah's frustrated hands emphasizing her words, and then smoothing back her blond hair when she's finished speaking. I'm certain she is closing her eyes and shaking her head at that very moment.

"Oh, Mesha. This again? The king is dead and has been for centuries!" says Moriah. "Those are just fairy tales meant to scare children."

"We can agree to disagree," Mesha says. "Until I'm proven right, of course."

"Well, for our sakes, I hope not," Moriah says, putting an end to the conversation. "Shadow should be back any minute anyhow."

After that all I hear is the sound of pots being put away and water from the kitchen pump filling the sink. I've never heard them speak this way before—I always thought such creatures were old wives' tales—myths born from whispers and shadows in the forest. I wait, hoping they'll say more about monsters, or about the prisoner. My mind races. There will be another prison cart headed to Deersia . . . where they are keeping Caledon. Suddenly, a plan begins to form in my mind . . .

I stay outside long enough to keep them from knowing I eavesdropped, and then walk up the porch steps loudly and open the back door.

"Feeling any better?" Aunt Mesha asks me.

I just shrug. I don't want the energy buzzing through my veins to be mistaken for newfound willingness.

"Maybe we all need a good night's sleep," Aunt Moriah says. She sets a cup of chamomile and cream in front of me. "What do you say we all turn in early and start fresh again in the morning?"

I just nod and sip the tea.

———•———

I TOSS AND TURN well into the early hours of morning, thinking about what I overheard. At some point I must fall asleep, though, because the next thing I know, my mother is standing over me at the side of my bed. Her back is to the open window so that the moon glows in a vibrant yellow ring around her. She is dressed in Guild black, her face obscured in the darkness of her hooded cloak. Before I can react, I feel her gaze lock on me. I can't see her eyes, but their intensity sears my soul. When she finally speaks, her words settle into me like the warmth of a hearth. "Follow your path and fulfill your destiny, Shadow."

After that it's morning. My eyes flutter open; the sun is shining through the window. And I decide that this time I *will* follow my mother's command.

CHAPTER NINE

Caledon

NIGHT TURNS TO DAY, AND then to night again. And again. Soon enough Cal's imprisonment has lasted nearly a week. To him it feels more like a year. The days drag on and on endlessly. Mornings are spent doing push-ups and pacing the perimeter of his round cell, what he has come to assume is a converted bedchamber in the fortress's east turret. He considers stuffing his wool blanket with hay to create a fighting dummy so he can keep in shape, but he's reluctant to make his sleeping conditions any worse than they already are, especially since he's no longer so certain this will be a short stay.

There are no books to read, and no letters arrive in the post. He has no idea what's happening outside the prison walls, no way of knowing when he will be released. It's maddening.

He examines the handkerchief over and over again. Holds it up to the bit of sunlight that streams in the tiny cell window every morning, in case there's something he missed, perhaps a secret message written in milk or lemon juice—but there's nothing.

Maybe the handkerchief itself was the code, and her words: *You're not alone.* He may be reading too much into the encounter—she could have merely been a sympathetic bystander. But there was something familiar about her . . . When—*if*—he finishes the task in Montrice, he decides he's going to find her.

In his isolation, he tries to keep his mind nimble. He runs over the list of courtiers at the palace. It's impossible that the grand prince was acting alone. There are surely other traitors at court, and what good is Cal if he's trapped behind bars? He can't do his job here. There aren't even other prisoners nearby he can extract information from. That may be for his protection; but it could also mean Queen Lilianna is keeping him isolated to protect others. He doesn't want to believe that, but under duress his mind is going to dark places.

Cal scratches a mark into the wall for every night he sleeps on the cold floor, on top of the increasingly filthy hay. *Good thing I didn't wear my best clothes to Violla Ruza.*

Though he tries to keep the thoughts away, at night Cal's mind wanders to his father. When sleep finally comes, Cal dreams of him. They're usually sitting in front of the hearth back home together. Sometimes Cordyn speaks to Cal, though when he wakes he can't remember anything the man said. Sometimes all Cal sees is the back of his head, looking up at it, like he's a child again, following him on a crowded street, scared they'll be separated and he'll be lost.

Cal wakes and sighs. If he wasn't bound to Queen Lilianna, he wonders what his life would be like now. It certainly wouldn't include a stint at Deersia. But there is no escape from a blood vow; he's learned that the hard way.

It first happened after his father was killed. He was only thirteen.

Rash and angry, old enough to desire freedom but young enough to feel orphaned, abandoned. He knew about the vow by then, of course, but he figured he could flee from it; perhaps, if he hid from it long enough, it would die with him instead of being passed on. At least, that's what he thought.

He'd packed up a few necessities, or what he considered necessities at the time, laughable to him now, the perishable food and inadequate footwear. But he'd made it pretty far, farther than he'd ever gone away before. Then the headaches began.

He shook it off at first, faulted hunger and the long days of walking, but they grew more intense with every mile he traveled from Renovia. He stole fresh meat off a butcher's slab and cooked it up in the woods, drank fresh water from a crystal stream, spent an entire day resting his feet, and still, the piercing throb in his head would not cease. Next came the nightmares. Those were vague enough when they started, visions that vanished from his mind as soon as he startled awake, but soon became worse—something chasing him, and he'd run and run, but no matter how much he ran it was always right on his heels, ready to grab him. He'd wake up drenched in a cold sweat. After the worst dreams he'd find himself far from camp, disoriented from sleepwalking. When he didn't heed these warnings, the shapeless threat on his heels turned into an actual monster, and then one night he was visited by an angry vision of Queen Lilianna herself. When he woke, he found himself perched on a cliff—ready to dive into the inky depths below.

He returned that very morning. The blinding pain, the visions— it all subsided as he drew closer to Renovia. Cal had learned his lesson. He never attempted to abandon the vow again.

Cal's silent days at Deersia are punctuated by three meals shoved quickly through the doorway. He has no human interaction aside from the gruff words—"Breakfast!" "Dinner!" "Supper!"—yelled through a narrow slot in the door.

The food at Deersia is terrible—typically some kind of gruel, or if he's lucky, a porridge of peas with a hard square biscuit made of crudely milled, cheap flour and a bit of salt—and on more than one occasion, a few grubs—but he eats most of it anyway, to keep up his strength. He's eaten worse to survive. The trick is not to look at it or think about it much. Consider it a sort of medicine, awful but necessary.

He draws a simple map of the prison interior on the floor so he can push hay on top to hide it. He's not sure he'll need to use it, but it gives him something else to focus on. Makes him feel like he has some control.

He does his best not to think of the momentous task that lies beyond his release.

And if I confirm the king's involvement?

You are the Queen's Assassin, are you not?

Regicide. The thought chills him more than his current imprisonment, though his circumstances are already enough to drive a man mad. How long must he wait? The queen promised that she would send for him, but if she does not, he will take matters into his own hands.

Cal spends hours at the barred window, observing the mountains and tracking travelers as they pass through roads in the distance, making note of any who have a routine. He scratches a crude calendar of sorts low on the wall where he sleeps and uses symbols to mark patterns, a *D* for the local draper who delivers flour and ale and other kitchen necessities at the beginning of every week, *G1* and *G2* to mark the various guards and their shifts, and so on. Far off in the distance Cal can see townspeople on their way back and forth from the marketplace and to worship.

From each meal he saves half the biscuit, when he gets one; if the porridge is fresh and filling enough, he'll save the entire thing. He stores them in a pouch he fashioned from the blindfold scarf. He'll need hardtack on the road should he have the chance to flee. A bit of water is all it takes to make them palatable, and palatable is all it takes to ward off starvation when decent meals or fresh meat are difficult to find.

Each day he tears a bit of the wool blanket, rolls squares of the rough fabric into tubes. He stuffs handfuls of hay inside. Since he has no needle or thread, he ties them closed with thin strips of the fabric. These can be set on fire easily, which might be useful for many reasons.

At night Cal wraps the remains of his blanket around his shoulders like a shawl and curls up in the corner with his knees against his chest to retain body warmth. Not ideal, but it works well enough. The smaller the blanket gets, the colder the nights feel, functioning as a sort of countdown. He decides that once he's run out of blanket, it's time to go.

He puts himself to sleep recalling tales from his childhood. His favorite was the one his father used to tell him about Omin of Oylahn, the origin of all magic, blessed by Mother Deia Herself. According to legend, Omin was the most powerful mage who ever lived, a master of both the physical and ethereal arts, and served the ancient Queen Alphonia during the time when Renovia was still a tiny, weak dominion of Avantine.

Nobody knows who Omin's parents were—if they were even

human. At that time, people still spoke of the fae folk, before their kind either went into hiding or became extinct. Omin was found as an infant in the woods, so some stories said the great mage simply sprang from the dirt itself, a creature too divine to be human and too human to be a spirit.

"Of course," Cal's father would say, "this is just a story, and stories are always a little bit true and a little bit false; we just don't know which is which."

Young Cal chose to combine them all and believe that Omin was both human and fae—a being part heaven and earth—and that version satisfied him.

He can still hear his father's deep, melodic voice, recounting the same scenes over and over from memory. Omin was an unknown orphan, a nobody, and grew up to establish a mighty kingdom, to become a great monarch with a loving family, loyal liege lords and knights, adored by thousands. Cal closes his eyes in his prison cell and pretends he's six years old, when life was simple, before he knew what the future held for him and before he was left adrift and alone in the world. Those days, his father would tuck him in under his mother's faded quilt and Cal would listen to the story, picturing each heroic character as he drifted off to sleep.

He does this now and recalls the words he always heard last:

The lesson, my son, is that we alone, no matter how skilled or how smart or how rich, are but spokes, and cannot move the wheel alone; only together can we do that.

CHAPTER TEN

Shadow

By mid-morning tomorrow I'm supposed to be officially on my way to Violla Ruza in a carriage provided by the queen. *Supposed to be.*

I have my own plans for transportation, my own destination—the prison transport to Deersia. If only I were a boy, then maybe I'd have a better chance of carrying it out. Or if I could just get my hands on an official work order from the palace . . . If I think about the obstacles ahead, what seemed so promising at first will begin to feel close to impossible.

Missus Kingstone visits with two of the completed gowns for a final fitting, a regular day dress and one for my first evening at the palace. She's had her whole team of apprentice seamstresses working around the clock this entire week. The rest, she tells me, will be delivered to the palace ahead of my arrival.

One of the gowns is pale pink and frothy, full of frills and lace and bunches of fabric, with round puffy short sleeves. "Stunning!" Missus Kingstone claps her hands with delight when I model it for her and my aunts.

I turn to the full-length looking glass she brought for the fitting. I look absurd. Like a feral cat forced into a wedding gown.

My aunts don't look convinced either, but they play along. "Yes, stunning. Quite a sight indeed," Aunt Mesha says, holding her hand to the side of her face. Aunt Moriah has a similar reaction: "I agree—can't say I've ever seen anything like it."

The other dress isn't much better, but at least it doesn't make me look like a bowl of strawberry mousse. I like the color, which is a pale, almost silvery, blue, and the long draping sleeves make it sleeker—and a little less reminiscent of a noblewoman's overly manicured poodle.

Regardless, I don't intend to wear any of these gowns if I can help it. But I'm quickly running out of time, and no matter which way I look at it, I still don't know how I'm going to make my plan work.

When the seamstress finally says goodbye late in the afternoon, my aunts begin saying things like, "You know, we will still see you, and you can write, and if there's any problem . . ." All the assurances seem to be more for them than me, though. They can't complete a single sentence without getting teary-eyed, though they try to conceal it. I'm pleased to see that they don't want me to go. That they're nervous about it.

After a light dinner (none of us have much of an appetite), they begin testing my knowledge of palace etiquette while we wash up the soup bowls and put them away. I'm subjected to an endless stream of pointless questions with even more pointless answers. "When does a formal meal end?" and so on. (Answer: when the queen is finished eating—whether the rest of the dinner guests are finished or not.)

We've gone over palace etiquette this way every night, such as who is obligated to bow to whom and which of your dinner neighbors you should turn and speak to first, or when you shouldn't speak to anyone at all. I'd learned of many of these confusing rules before, in training manuscripts from my aunts' library (three small shelves in the sitting room, and another of my own in the attic), so I am already familiar with much of it, though judging by how many I answer incorrectly, a refresher is sorely needed. Even if it is a waste of time. I should be learning something useful—combat, magical energy management—anything other than which fork is for seafood and which is for salad.

"I don't want to spend tonight being torture—er, tutored," I tell them. Though I don't say "my last night here," the words hang in the air.

Aunt Mesha places her apron over the back of a chair. "I have an idea," she says.

A few minutes later we're all crowded onto my bed, the way we used to when I was a little girl and had trouble getting to sleep on my own. Aunt Moriah and Aunt Mesha take turns voicing characters from my favorite childhood storybook, a collection of legends from all the different lands of Avantine. Most are said to date from the Deian era, before the kingdoms fractured. Instead of tales about great kings and battles and enemies, they are about people, even animals, and how they sometimes do good things and sometimes do bad things, but in the end they always do the right thing.

My aunts read the entire book, cover to cover. By the time they're done with "The Adventures of Landy," about a girl who pretends to be a boy and sails a great ship across the sea to save the prince, I'm half asleep. I feel each of them kiss me on the forehead before slipping out the door and down the stairs.

I close my eyes for a few minutes but sleep won't come. This is it. I have no time left.

I can't stop thinking about what's coming, so I climb out of bed.

My new gowns are hanging from hooks on the attic wall. They look strange and out of place in my simple room. *The same way they look on me*, I think.

Beneath the dresses is a small trunk that holds matching pairs of satin slippers for each outfit and a variety of underthings designed to squeeze my body into an unnatural shape. A for-all-intents-and-purposes *immobile*, unnatural shape. One can hardly sit in these clothes, let alone run or kick or, well, breathe. I suppose that's the privilege of the rich.

There's a box in the trunk as well, but I didn't have an opportunity to look at its contents until now. I retrieve it and sit cross-legged on the wood floor, placing it in front of me. Inside I find a smaller, hinged rectangular box, nearly flat, lined in velvet. It contains a set of gold and diamond jewelry I'm to wear when I go tomorrow: a pair of diamond stud earrings, each gem the size of a large pearl, and a glittering multi-strand collar necklace to match, as well as a wide diamond bracelet to wear over my arm-length white gloves, and two diamond rings—one designed in the shape of a flower, with emeralds as petals, and the other set with a huge square Argonian emerald, the rarest sort, surrounded by more flawless round diamonds.

I try the necklace on in front of the mirror. The weight of it chokes me. How will I wear this? It feels like it's clinging to my throat. I unclasp it quickly and place it back in the velvet box.

The only other thing in the small box, aside from the jewelry case, is a black leather pouch filled with gold coins. Presumably this is mine to spend as I wish, since there are no instructions included.

I spill the coins out on the floor. I hold a bunch in my hand, just to feel the weight of them. All are fresh-minted, shiny. Generic profiles of the late king and his widow are etched on one side; the royal seal—a Renovian rose surrounded by three circles to symbolize eternity—is on the other.

The idea arrives as swiftly as a bolt of lightning.

Heart pounding, I bring one of the coins to my desk and take out a stick of sealing wax. I warm it over the fire and when it melts enough, I drip some on a torn bit of paper. Then I smash the coin onto the wax, carefully lifting it out with my fingernails. It leaves a perfect mark.

The order I received from the queen is in the trunk. I rush to grab it and carry it back to the desk so I can compare the official seal with this one.

They're nearly identical. Sure, the official seal is cleaner and a touch bigger, but at a glance, the average person would not notice. A sloppy seal could simply be the result of a hasty hand. A distracted guard wouldn't take the time or effort to worry about it, not for this.

The only difference is that my wax is red. The royal wax is purple. *Only* the royal wax is purple.

I look around, trying to find a solution. My eyes land on the inkstand. I drip some wax onto paper again, then open the top of the jar and dip the end of my pen into the dark bluish-black ink, then let a drop fall onto the melted red wax. I swirl the ink into the wax, quickly, so it doesn't set, and as it blends together, it becomes purple.

My heartbeat quickens and happiness bubbles into my throat.

I want to scream. I want to dance around my room. It worked. It worked!

I place a fresh sheet of paper over the queen's order. Dip the end of my pen into the ink again. Carefully, I trace the letters: HRM LILIANNA, QUEEN REGENT OF RENOVIA. Then the next line: REQUIRES YOUR PRESENCE. Under that, in my best formal cursive: *as Stable Hand at Deersia.*

After I make more purple wax in as close a hue as I can, I use a gold coin to forge the royal seal. This is a serious crime, and I know it. But then that vision of Mother flashes in my mind, the one I had in my dream the other night, and determination crystallizes in my veins. I must live my own way . . . or not at all. *Follow your path,* she had said.

I intend to do just that.

Next problem: Women are prohibited from the prison grounds. In "The Adventures of Landy," the heroine figures out ways to disguise herself. I glance around the room, chewing on my thumbnail. Gowns and frippery everywhere. I have black pants and something that could pass as a boy's jacket well enough, but I don't think that will suffice.

My eyes fall on the bedsheet.

I pull it off the bed and tear a long strip from the bottom so that I have a generous length of soft linen. I stand in front of the mirror and tie that around my chest to flatten it, turning sideways to consider my new shape. With the right shirt, I think it will work fine. I use an even longer one to thicken my waist so I look less curvy, which also helps me shift my walk from my hips to my shoulders. My voice and face could probably pass for those of a young boy, but my hair might be a problem. It isn't unusual for boys to have long hair, but mine is longer than any stable hand's I've ever seen, and thick. I also have a habit of twisting it with my fingers and fussing with it in ways that could give me away.

A heavy pair of silver shears sticks out of my sewing basket. My heart skips a beat as I glare at them.

I take a deep breath. I don't think of myself as a vain person, but my long, thick hair is as much a part of me as my brown eyes or the trio of freckles on my left hand. I pick up the scissors. I set them down again. But I know I have no choice—I have to do this.

I yank my hair back into a ponytail, pick up the shears, close my eyes, and chop it off in one swoop. I open both eyes and run my hands through what's left. I'm a little shocked, and a little saddened.

But the worst is done, so I trim the rest. Closer to my head, but still a little shaggy, leaving some curl at the nape of my neck and at the top. *Like a boy who needs a haircut.*

I get dressed in black pants and a loose tunic with a tighter shirt underneath and put my sturdiest boots at the side of the bed, ready to go. I have the forged work order and all the coins in a pouch at my hip. I'd leave now but I don't want to spend too much time out in the dark. If I wait a few more hours, the rising sun will provide enough light for a journey.

All the potential problems with my plan repeat in my mind over and over again, endlessly. It's impossible to quiet my nerves. I review my preparations, certain I'm forgetting something, though everything seems to be in order. As soon as I get to Deersia, I'll find a way to help Caledon escape, and he'll be so grateful, so impressed with my bravery and cunning, that of course he will take me on as his apprentice.

At the first sign of golden light at the horizon, I jump up and lace my boots. When I get to my bedroom door, I stop to take one last look at the dresses hanging on their hooks, at the girl I could have been. It may be my imagination but they look a little forlorn.

I creep down the stairs, edging as close to the wall as I can to avoid those creaks. I hear Aunt Mesha snoring. Moriah is a quiet sleeper. They're going to be absolutely furious when they wake up. In the end I hope they'll be proud of me, though.

Before I slip out the back door, I leave ten gold coins and a short note on the kitchen table: *You know that I need to do this. Tell my mother I am safe. I love you both.*

CHAPTER ELEVEN

Shadow

I MAKE IT TO SERRONE—TORSO bound, hair shorn, clad in stable hand's garb—just after the sun rises. The crisp morning air chills the back of my bare neck. I hadn't thought to bring a scarf.

The palace looms over the village. I feel as though it's watching me. Like it knows I am escaping, and does not approve.

The Brass Crab is closed and won't open for hours, which is a good thing. The proprietor buys honey for mead all the time. I'm certain he would recognize me. Otherwise there are few people up and about. I see the baker through his shop window; he doesn't look up or notice when I walk by. The glove-maker's wife sweeps the walk in front of his workshop and though I pass less than a yard from her, she offers no more than a polite nod of the head.

I was nervous coming into town, but it turns out young men don't garner much attention at all. It occurs to me they probably believe I'm a page or errand boy, the background of their daily routine and nothing more.

After the row of shops, there is the town square, where I set up our market stand a few times a week. From there the main road forks left toward merchants' homes and farms beyond; it forks right toward other towns in northeast Renovia. And it continues straight to the palace. The stables, along with the prison tower—a temporary holding cell for housing the accused before they go to trial—are situated on the west end of the property. That's where I need to go.

Before stepping any closer to the castle grounds, I pause. If I go back right now, I can fix everything. My hair can be covered with a wig. I won't miss the royal carriage that has been sent for me. It's not too late to change my mind.

Except, it is. My decision has been made, and I know that this is what I have to do, risks and all.

I follow the ancient stone wall, once tall, now a ruin barely to my waist, that runs through the grassy field toward the stables. Once there, I linger alongside the building, collecting piles of hay. I need to look like I belong.

A couple of boys show up for work, their breath steaming puffs in the frigid morning air. One of them shoves the other, both laughing. Birds land in the grass searching for their breakfast. A mourning dove sits on a fence post; it coos back and forth with others hiding in the trees of the garden.

Shortly after, two transport guards stomp across the grounds, heavy leather boots squelching in the damp lawn. The birds scatter. The men disappear into the stable building, likely to check on the horses and the transport wagon. Stable hands will feed the animals first, then check their shoes and prepare their bridles and reins before hitching them to the wagon. Only when everything's in order and the wagon pulls out onto the gravel path will the guards board the prisoner. He'll take the same route through town as Caledon.

I have to time my appearance exactly right. If I approach them too soon, they may expect me to do work I don't know how to do, or they might want to check up on my story before departing. They're more likely to accept it if they don't have much time to think about it.

My hands are dirty, so I smear some of the grime on my face. That will help disguise me. One of the guards shouts out to the other and my stomach feels as if it's leapt into my throat. I take a few deep breaths. Slow, deliberate, like my aunts always tell me to when I'm upset or scared.

Once they've inspected the transportation, the guards return to the castle, following the winding garden path rather than cutting across the lawn. They turn left and enter a creaky back entrance that leads down into the cellar dungeons.

A whip cracks. Hooves clop. Two chestnut horses come out of the stable, dragging the wagon behind them. A stable boy pulls the wagon up on the path to pick up the prisoner, as predicted. He jumps down and walks over to the horses, strokes their backs.

Minutes later the guards reemerge, holding the prisoner between them, the Montrician spy. The guards load him into the cart—or rather, they shove him onto it.

The driver snaps the reins. "Hyah!" The cart lurches forward.

I hesitate for half a breath before running out of the garden toward the cart, yelling, "Sir! Sir!" and waving.

The cart slows and the driver scowls at me. "What is it, boy?"

"Sorry I'm late, sir," I say, my voice raspy. I should be pretending to be out of breath from running, but the truth is that I'm simply terrified. "I've just received this." I'm brandishing the forged work order.

"What's this?" the older and heftier of the guards says.

I hold the paper up to him. I hope that he will read it from a distance since he's in a rush.

No such luck. He snatches the paper from me and opens it, spends a moment glancing it over. My entire body tenses. If he questions me, should I run away, or take my chances on answering and defend the order? After what feels like forever, he sighs. "All right, then," he says to me, and then to the other guard, "Looks like this one's comin' with us." He mutters, "Not that anyone bothered to tell me before today."

Relieved, I climb onto the back of the wagon and settle on a crude bench, grasping a wood slat for balance.

"What do we need with another stable boy? All's they do out there is make trouble," the second guard says.

The other shrugs. "How about I go in there and ask somebody, then?" he says, motioning toward the tower.

My pulse quickens. I know he's just being sarcastic, but still. Every minute we stall is another minute I could be exposed. The faster we leave, the better. *Go, go, go,* I repeat over and over in my head.

"Bah," the second guard says, waving him off. "We're behind as it is. Let's go."

As we start moving, I can't help but smile a bit. My disguise— and my forgery—are a success. So far.

I MANAGE TO FALL asleep for a while, sitting up against the side of the wagon with my arms folded across my chest. When I wake up, we're far from Serrone. Far from the rolling green fields. The terrain is much rockier now. The sickly sweetness is gone; the air is dull with dirt and dust.

It's late afternoon, almost evening. I shift my body, trying to find a more comfortable way to sit, which is, of course, near impossible. The prisoner is talking with the guards. He's facing the front of the wagon with his back to me. Their voices are low, so at first it's hard to make out what they're saying over the *clip-clop* of hooves and rattle of wheels.

"Maybe you'll get lucky," one of the guards says. "Plenty of vacancies up there, I hear."

"Yeah. I'm sure that can be worked out," the other says, nudging the first guard with his elbow.

What are they talking about? Work what out? Then the prisoner says: "If he's anything like his old man . . ."

A chill races up my spine. They're talking about Caledon. I lie back again and cover my face, pretend to sleep. They continue their conversation, seemingly oblivious to my presence. Most of it is garbled by the time it reaches me, but if I concentrate I can hear their words under the rumble of the wagon and the rutted road: *Queen Lilianna, Aphrasians, Prince Alast, hotheaded kid.* And then, *Wasn't expecting the boy, though. Certainly complicates matters.*

It hits me—this is all coming together perfectly. The spy is going to Deersia to kill Cal. And the guards are in on it. A conspiracy. Nothing else makes sense. Prisoners are prohibited from addressing the guards, especially in such a casual manner. Why else would they have this hushed conversation? They're delivering an enemy spy directly to the Queen's Assassin while he's a sitting duck. No better way to eliminate him—when he's less able to defend himself.

Well, I'm not going to let that happen. Little do they know, reinforcements are on the way.

BY THE TIME WE make it all the way up the mountainside road to Deersia, it's dusk. The fortress looms above me, dark and foreboding. Its highest towers are shrouded in fog. Now that I'm here, I'm not sure what to feel. From a distance it looked, well, regal, elegant—but up close, I see the crumbling mossy stone for what it is. A neglected structure housing neglected human beings.

I expected to feel nothing; this is just another building after all, like so many others I've visited. But I don't. Maybe it's the castle's history. People locked up, treated worse than animals. Executed. It leaves an ominous cloud around the place. I fear the return of my visions.

A wave of goose bumps sweeps my spine when I set my feet on the ground. My response must show on my face because one of the guards says, "Impressed, are ya?" I ignore his comment.

The guards take the condemned man out of the wagon. They lead him to the front gate by each arm. I start to follow them inside, but then one turns to me and says, "Where'd you think you're going, boy?"

While I search for a believable reason to go inside the fortress, he says, "The stables are across the yard." And points.

With little choice, I turn and head in that direction. I won't be able to see where Caledon is being held. At least not without some wheedling. This is going to be more complicated than I hoped.

As I approach the stables, I hear raucous conversation inside. It sounds like the stable hands are taking turns telling jokes. One speaks and the others laugh. Their language is rougher than I'm accustomed to. Not that I'm so delicate—just not used to it. I stop at the entrance and take a deep breath. If the stable boys don't accept me as one of their own, my entire story could fall apart.

I push the door open. There's a group of boys, around my age and younger, sitting together. They all turn to stare. They stop laughing and talking. "Who the hell are you?" one says. From his demeanor and central place in the group, I guess that he could be their leader. He's sitting on a crate, perched above the others, who gather around him on the ground in a circle.

"Um . . ." I search my mind. I hadn't thought of a fake name. How careless. My first mistake.

"So very nice to meet you, *ummm*," another says.

One of the others chimes in. "It happened. I finally met someone too stupid to know his own name."

"Of course I know my name. Doesn't mean I need to tell *you*," I snap.

The first boy asks, "And what do you want?"

"I was sent to work," I say. The boys look at one another in confusion. Would they have been informed of a new hand on the way? I hope not.

"None of us is leaving," he says. "So you can bugger off."

"Yeah. None of us is leaving," the other chimes in.

"You don't have to," I say. The boy on the ground mocks me again, repeating *you don't have to* in a high-pitched voice. My cheeks flush.

"Well, thank you for allowing us to stay, honorable sir," the leader says to me before bowing dramatically. Others laugh. I think I'd rather be locked up alone in a cell at this point.

"That's not what I meant," I say, trying to keep my voice low and level. I can't let them know they are getting to me. Most of all, I just want to go to sleep. My body hurts from being jostled around in the wagon all day long. My throat hurts; I'm thirsty. My water skein ran out hours ago. They all stare at me, waiting. I lift the skein, showing the boy on the crate.

"The well's out back," he says. Then he adds, "We sleep in the loft."

I look up where he's pointing. Seems like there's plenty of room. I'll find a spot as far away from the others as I can.

"But you can sleep there." He points to a filthy corner. Some of the other boys snicker.

I don't respond. I won't give him the satisfaction. Besides, a secluded corner is preferable. I walk away and go out to fill the pouch. I hear them begin talking as soon as they think I'm out of earshot.

I linger outside, listening. Once they determine it won't be so bad to have someone lowly around to burden with their grunt work, I return inside, heading for the corner where the leader said I could sleep. There's hay nearby, so I gather some to make a bed and lie down, grateful to collapse into a heap on the ground. I do wish I could remove the linens I've wrapped around my body; I'm itchy and it's difficult to find a comfortable position. But I have absolutely no privacy. And the wrapping does offer more warmth.

Though I haven't said another word, I guess my mere presence did ruin the fun, because within moments the stable hands disperse for bed, almost all climbing up into the loft. Only one stays behind, in the opposite corner of the barn. If he's separated from the others, then he's my best bet for an ally. I wonder why he's relegated to the floor like I am—maybe he was the last new addition? I'll try to learn more about him later. In the meantime I need to figure out how to get to Caledon. After I get some rest, that is. My eyelids are heavy. All the sleepless nights combined with today's adventures have caught up with me.

The first day was a success; still, I'm determined to make this visit to Deersia as short as possible. I won't be able to hide for long.

❧

CHAPTER TWELVE

Shadow

I SPRING AWAKE, READY TO fight. I'm being attacked.

The leader of the pack is standing over me, holding a small pail, doubled over with laughter. My face and hair are soaking wet. As are my clothes. I'm lucky there was just water in the bucket.

"Wakey-wakey!" he says. His minions are watching from a distance. "Time to shovel dung, plebe," he continues. "Follow Jander. He'll show you what to do."

Jander turns out to be the boy who slept in the other corner. He looks at me sheepishly and shrugs. Standing next to him, I realize how small he is, and young. He must be eleven or twelve at most. I wonder how he ended up here, and why the others treat him so poorly.

"Are you going to take off your shirt?" the bully asks me.

"What?" I blurt out. I realize I'm standing there with my arms wrapped around my wet torso. The linens under my shirt are loosening.

"He's afraid we'll see how soft he is," one of the other boys offers. They all laugh and begin adding their own insults.

"His soft widdle baby belly," another calls out.

I clench my jaw and control a jolt of fury. I'm tempted to go after them. Pummel them until they beg forgiveness.

Jander turns toward the horse stalls, so I take a deep breath and follow him. I'm more than happy to put some distance between myself and the others.

It's not a terribly cold morning, but my wet clothes make me shiver. Jander disappears around a corner and returns seconds later with a folded wool blanket, which he holds out for me. It belongs to the horses, but it's clean, so I don't mind. I wrap it around my shoulders. "Thank you, that was very kind of you," I tell him. I think I see a bit of a smile around his lips before it evaporates.

Cleaning the stalls is easy work. I never did so many at once, but I'm accustomed to taking care of animals. I reach down to grab hold of a wheelbarrow when a wave of guilt rushes over me. I left my aunts with all the work. No doubt they're furious that I've gone— but I'm not worried about furious. What upsets me is imagining them distraught or terrified, not knowing if I'm all right. Selfishly, I hadn't considered that side of it. And I must stop thinking of it now. I bite the inside of my cheek to distract myself.

I bite down again, hard, and think of Caledon and the Guild. "Not too bad, huh?" I say to Jander, referring to the clean stalls we've already done. He nods but doesn't look up.

We shovel out the manure and replace the hay for each horse while they're being exercised in the field. With two of us, it doesn't take too long.

Jander doesn't speak, but I don't know if it's because he's shy or because he's mute. I realize I haven't heard him talk at all to anyone.

"So, how long have you been here?" I ask him. He just shrugs. I try again. "My name's . . . Shadow," I say, holding out my hand. I don't want to start out by lying to him. He hesitates but then shakes my hand weakly before going back to shoveling.

By the time we finish, my clothes are almost completely dry. Things could have gone differently this morning—I'll have to be a lot more careful from now on. If I'm caught, not only will I lose the opportunity to rescue Caledon and get to the Guild, I'll face charges of trespassing, forgery, and treason—all punishable by death.

We each take a wheelbarrow full of manure and push it out to the gardens. I see a few prisoners wandering the gated castle yard and try to see if Caledon is among them. I don't see him. They all look bigger and older than he is.

"An hour a day," a guard says. He noticed me looking. I hadn't even seen him standing by the fence. "We're not barbarians."

I nod. Did disapproval show on my face? I stop myself from telling him that I never accused him of such. The less I talk to anyone, the better.

We dump the wheelbarrows and head back to the stable for another load. When we return to the garden, the prisoners are gone. I need to find a way to warn Caledon about the Montrician prisoner.

The rest of the first day isn't too awful; Jander leaves me to go do whatever else he does, and I avoid the pack of stable boys—especially their leader, who I discovered is named Luce—and keep busy weeding the gardens. As long as I look occupied, nobody bothers with me. I look for a way to snoop inside but can't find an excuse to go into the building.

When the sun starts to set, I hide in some bushes behind the stable buildings and wait, the wool horse blanket keeping me warm. I don't want to go to bed until the rest of them do. I wonder if there's someplace better I can sleep. But the only options I can think of don't sound any safer than staying where I am.

The final beam of sunlight disappears over the horizon when the truth dawns on me that I didn't think this plan through. I hadn't considered exactly how dangerous Deersia is. On some level, I suppose I knew, but it wasn't until actually getting here that I realized it will be near impossible to get out again. The road down the mountain will be bad enough without a posse of armed prison guards chasing us. I have to think of a way to find Caledon, release him, and leave without being detected, which means we'll need a long head start. So we'll have to leave at night. That solves one of the three problems, but not the other two.

I don't have much time to figure this out either. The longer I'm here, the greater the chance I'm going to be exposed. Lessons with my aunts never included acting—I have barely a clue about how to seem like a boy. And soon I'll have a fourth problem on my hands—what my aunts liked to call "Deia's monthly gift." I have supplies but it's better if I'm not here when it starts. Tomorrow, I need to focus solely on finding Caledon.

Once I hear the boys snoring in the barn loft, I go in and find a dark corner to curl up in. I toss all night, worried that Luce will get up before I do. But I'm determined to get outside in the morning before anyone has a chance to douse me with water again.

When I get up, it's still dark, closer to night than day. I go behind the stable into the tall grasses and squat down, listening for anyone nearby. The boys relieve themselves wherever and whenever, but obviously that's a problem for me.

I sneak out of the grass and go to the water pump to splash some water on my face. I don't have a tooth stick or even a clean cloth to wipe the fuzz that's accumulated on my teeth. I've never felt so grimy in my life. I've always had access to fresh baths and mint pastes to freshen my mouth, and though I didn't grow up with dressing maids and fancy silks, I guess I'm more accustomed to certain comforts than I realized. I cup my hands and swish some water around in my mouth, spit it out into the grass. That relieves the worst of my dry mouth but doesn't take away from the dirty, itchy sensation that's spread all over me, from my scalp to my feet.

Then again, the dirt and stench probably help with my disguise anyway, so perhaps it's not such a bad thing after all. Stable hands are hardly squeaky clean.

The others are up now and dressed for the day, walking up to the castle to get food in the dining hall. Guards eat first, then servants. That's the usual way of it. My stomach growls. I didn't eat at all yesterday. I don't want to go in with Luce and his crew, but I can't skip another meal. I let the pack disappear inside before I follow. Hopefully, they'll grab their food, eat quickly, and be on their way out before I even sit down.

I turn at the sound of footsteps behind me. It's Jander. He stops walking when I look at him. "It's okay," I say, waving him toward me. I stand there and wait. He joins me on the path. His gentle nature is an unexpected surprise here at the prison. I'm not sure what to say to him, so I decide to stick to yes or no questions. "Hungry?"

He nods. Now we're getting somewhere. "You like it here?" I ask him. He shrugs. "Have you been here long?" I try. He shrugs again. His timidity reminds me of the stray dog who started coming around the farm one summer. It was clear the dog had been abused—the evidence was all over him—so he was desperate for affection but also distrustful. Eventually he came around, though, once he knew we weren't going to hurt him. Maybe Jander is like that, too.

I try once more. "They mean to you?" I say quietly. This time he doesn't respond right away, but then he nods. How awful. "How old are you?" I ask, but he just shrugs again in response. A terrible thought occurs to me. "Do . . . do you know how old you are?" I say. He shakes his head. I don't want to push any more, so I stop asking questions.

We get inside and walk to the dining hall, which seems to be one of the only rooms still being used for its original purpose. There's a queue for food. At the front, two men are doling out bowls of porridge with bread.

We get in line. Luce is already sitting at a table with a few of his minions; the others are getting their food. They haven't noticed us yet. But when they do, it happens quickly.

Luce knocks Jander's porridge bowl, spilling it to the floor.

Without thinking, I lunge at Luce. His eyes widen as I knock into him, slamming him to the ground. He gains the upper hand quickly, flipping me over so he's on top of me. He punches me in the side of my face. I try to knee him in the groin, but someone pulls him off me. I sit up, scrambling backward. My shirt is torn, almost exposing the wrap. I try to hold it closed.

The guard who pulled Luce off me is the same one who escorted the Montrician spy the day before. He's scolding him: "I told you! Leave that boy alone!" The guard lets him go and turns to me. "I knew you'd be trouble," he says. "Let's go. You're coming with me."

I dig my boots into the ground. "Where?" I'm not about to follow anyone around here unless I want to.

He is taken aback by my question, but he answers me anyway. "Kitchen duty."

At least that gets me inside the castle. Progress! I look around for Jander and spot him by the open stable door. I point to him. "He was fighting too. It's only fair."

"You're giving orders now, huh?" the guard barks at me. But he takes one look at Jander and gives in. "Fine. He's good at washing floors."

I nod to Jander. He comes out from the doorway and follows the guard. I step behind him, glaring at Luce. He glares back. Then, finally, he smirks and disappears into the barn.

But I'm the one who gets the last laugh. Wonder who will shovel manure for them now?

CHAPTER THIRTEEN

Shadow

THERE ARE ONLY THREE MEN and one boy in the kitchen, but there's so much going on that it feels like at least twice that many. There are two enormous cooking hearths, each with two massive black pots bubbling, and a bread oven. More pots of various sizes line the walls, though they're probably rarely used. I'm sure this kitchen hasn't prepared grand multicourse feasts in quite a long time.

The cooks are sweaty, their shirtsleeves rolled up past the elbow and white caps holding their hair back. One of them frantically scrubs out bowls, stacking them beside him on the butcher block counter to dry. Some of the bowls still have bits of food left in them. The wheeled cart from the dining hall is next to him, full of dirty dishes. Another cook is peeling potatoes, and the other is chopping them. He fills a bowl, runs it to the pot, dumps it all in, then returns to chopping at the table.

The head cook notices Jander and I are waiting for orders, so he grabs a mop from the pantry doorway and hands it to me. "There's another around here somewhere. The hall needs a good wash. Go to it."

Jander and I find another mop and pails and begin cleaning the dining hall. The cook wasn't joking—the floors haven't been cleaned in a rather long time. The initial swipe of the mop leaves muddy smears, but under those layers of dirt is a gorgeous mosaic tile floor. Were the windows clean, the floors would be glittering in the sunlight. As we uncover more and more of it, I see that the tiles make a giant floral pattern, blue and red blooms with green stems and leaves, against a black background.

I keep cleaning, and as I do, I begin to doubt this whole scheme. What am I doing here? Why am I at Deersia? Am I even helping Caledon or just hurting myself?

I jump back and shout, "Ouch!"

Jander looks at me quizzically. "Just a shock," I tell him. But that's not true; it's the weeping willow at Baer all over again. The feeling of lightning runs up my spine and down my arms. It's overwhelming, and a bit scary, but curiosity floods me before fear can take hold.

I hunch down and run my finger along the emerald stem of a bright red rose, admiring the tile's craftsmanship. I get another shock and press my finger against the flower and hold it there. Maybe a vision will give me information, help me find Caledon.

The dining hall, except the dining hall from long ago, wavers into focus. The tiles are brand-new, glossy and perfect, not a scratch or chip anywhere. A blurry figure sits at the head of a grand table set with white cloth and gold dishes. The figure . . . is it human? I take a deep breath in and the image gets clearer. Human, yes. With waist-length silver hair, wearing a long-sleeved, full-length white tunic and an emerald gem around his neck. Violet eyes bore into me with a fiery intensity.

I pull my hand up and the vision disappears. Jander is still mopping the far end of the hall, and everything is dingy and plain again. My mind races. There was something strangely familiar about that figure. Was I imagining that they looked straight into my eyes? When I saw King Esban at Baer, no one there seemed aware of me watching.

I need to know. I'm not sure if I can make the vision return, but I have to try.

So I press both my hands against the floor and close my eyes, willing myself, with every bit of my heart and mind, to return to Deersia's past again. *I want to see. I want to see . . .*

It works. In a flash, the entire floor stretches out around me, glistening and new, sparkling in the light coming through the brand-new panes of glass. I'm awed by the beauty of it—a floor, of all things. Though, really, it's a work of art.

There's an eerie silence. Almost a void of sound. Then footsteps approach, thunking, echoey. A gust of air blows my hair and I look up—a silver-haired mage with violet eyes gazes down at me. Omin of Oylahn. The founder of Avantine.

I hear a voice in my head. Omin is speaking to me.

Follow your path.

That's all I hear before I'm yanked backward to the dirty floor of the dining hall.

Jander is standing there, looking concerned. "I'm okay," I say. "Really, I'm okay." He mimics throwing up. "No, no," I say. "I'm just tired. I was daydreaming." He doesn't look convinced, but he lets it go.

Follow your path, Omin said. Does that mean I am on the right one? Is this where I'm meant to be? It was the same message I received from my mother—the one that sent me here.

It takes all morning and many fresh buckets of water pumped

from the kitchen well outside, but we finish the room without incident. I can't stop thinking about what I saw. *Who* I saw.

But I can think more about it later. I need to find Caledon.

When we're done, I stand back and admire our work. It's not quite as stunning as it was in the vision, and we couldn't get to every nook and cranny with all the tables in the way, but compared to how it looked at breakfast, it's a dramatic transformation.

JANDER AND I ARE sent to the kitchen to assist the cook. A guard pops his head in while we're working. "Renold? I was wondering if it'd be possible for me to start my rounds a little earlier tonight. I was hoping to join the card game in a few . . ."

The cook frowns.

"I can take the food to the prisoners," I say. "Then we don't have to rush to have the food ready, and he can go to the card game."

Maybe I might even be able to find Caledon.

The cook chews the offer over for a second or two. "Well, I suppose I can't see why not," he says. He tucks the errant hairs back under his cap.

The guard claps his large, rough hand against the doorway. "Excellent," he says, beaming. "The route is easy. I have the east wing and the turret. Takes no time at all. None at all."

Not long after, I'm pushing a tall, shelved cart piled with trays through the damp halls. It's a far walk from the kitchens, so I was worried about the food getting cold, but I've learned that the prison staff gets the freshest food and the prisoners get week-old pea soup that's been simmering for days on end and yesterday's leftover biscuits. I feel guilty giving it to anyone.

I've also learned that it's nearly impossible to see who is in each cell. Trying to get a good look inside not only makes me appear suspicious, it slows me down way too much. I'm supposed to deliver food to a row of cells, return to the kitchen to refill the cart, then deliver to another row, and so on. If I gape at every single prisoner, it will take me all night. I'm only to slide a tray under the door and keep moving.

Still, I do what I can to catch a glimpse. Most prisoners are immediately ruled out—too old, too big, too bald, and in one particularly remarkable case, far too hairy. But a couple of them look like they could possibly be Caledon, around the right age or size. I'll have to come back later somehow to check them again. Maybe I can do the morning deliveries too. I'll have to find a way to fill in for the other side of the castle, but I'd locate Caledon within the next few days if I do that.

Then I have a terrible thought: I haven't seen the Montrician spy since we arrived. For all I know, Caledon has already been killed.

Once I finish the ground floor, I return to the kitchen to refill the cart. Mister Renold seems surprised to see me. "Back so soon, huh? Sure you got 'em all?" he says. He stops chopping potatoes to bend down and take a look at the bottom shelf of the cart.

I shrug. I thought I was moving too slow—I guess I didn't have to hurry after all. Good to know I can take my time and get a better look inside the cells. Makes me wonder what usually takes the guard so long to finish his rounds.

"Careful, now. Or we're gonna have you doin' this every day," Mister Renold says with a wink.

He doesn't know I wouldn't mind that at all. But I don't want to seem too eager, so all I say is, "Yes, sir."

As soon as the cart is filled, I push it out the door. In my rush I hit a bump in the stone floor and almost tip the entire cart. Mister Renold shakes his head. "Careful there, boy!" But he looks amused, watching me go.

There's a ramp leading to the upper-level cells. Before Deersia was a prison, it was a castle fortress, and the ramps were for transporting cannons and other large artillery. Convenient, but a bit steep for this purpose, and I have to go slow or risk bowls of slop sliding off the tray and pouring onto my feet.

A man with long, straight, dishwater-colored hair sits on the floor of the first cell, rocking back and forth and murmuring. Not Caledon. He looks toward the door when I slide the tray under it, then goes back to his rocking. The second cell isn't Caledon's either; it's an older man asleep on a small, sagging cot. The third and fourth fare no better.

It's not until I reach the fifth cell that I get a glimmer of hope. As I slide the tray into the cell, I catch a glimpse of tousled brown hair. Looks like it could be Caledon's. He's a bit thinner than I remember but that's to be expected.

I try to peer through the food slot for a better look, but I don't see anyone now.

The cell's makeshift bed is empty. I try to see into the corners of the cell, thinking he moved out of sight to protect himself. He won't know I'm there to help him. I look toward the right side of the room.

Two huge eyes stare back at me. I let out a yelp and flinch. There's wild cackling on the other side of the door. I stand, heart racing, and try to look in again. That couldn't be Cal . . . could it?

A face pops up in front of mine again. Then disappears. I force myself not to look away until I know whether it's Caledon. If it is, I have more trouble on my hands than I thought.

Then I hear the food tray bang against the opposite wall. I look inside the cell, careful not to expose much of my face in the door slot, just in case.

There's a boy sitting on his haunches, rocking back and forth. The tray is lying upside down by the wall where I heard it crash. He isn't looking at me now. But he's not Cal. He's barely more than a little boy, maybe thirteen years, or a couple more if he's small for his age.

He catches me looking and opens his mouth, letting out a piercing screech. I leap backward and grab the cart, hurrying away as quickly as I can.

Though I'm frustrated that I can't find Caledon, I'm relieved that wasn't him.

When I return to the kitchen again, only the kitchen boy is there. The cook is in the dining hall setting up for tomorrow's breakfast. He puts two trays on the cart. "These are the last two. They go up in the east turret," he says. "You'll need this." He hands me an old iron key on a large metal ring. As I walk through the kitchen doorway, he adds, "Try to cover your mouth while you're up there."

I nod. Deia forbid Caledon is there. I take the cart all the way to the end of the east wing. There's a locked door. I assume that's the way I'm supposed to go, and sure enough, the key fits. The door opens. Behind it there's a winding staircase leading up into the turret. I'm going to have to leave the cart and carry the trays.

Walking up that many stairs, while balancing a soup bowl on a tray with each hand, is exactly as hard as it sounds. I take each step slowly and pause often. Pea soup on my clothes would definitely require a bath and I can't risk that.

My feet ache. I'm going to sleep soundly tonight. I wonder where that will be. Not that I care. I could sleep on these stone steps right now.

I get to the top of the first set of stairs and find a curved hallway with one door. The first room in the turret. I slide the food under the door. I don't hear anything. I don't think anybody's in there. But there's no way to see inside unless I get down on the floor and I'm not going to do that. I'm not spending any longer here than I absolutely must.

I keep going. I come to another set of stairs. It's a lot easier with only one tray to carry. And it's a shorter climb. But I'm tired and I just want to be done with this. Between looking for Caledon and navigating the Luce issue, not to mention the anxiety of covering up my identity, I'm exhausted.

The top floor is pretty much identical to the one below it. There's another door with a food slot. There's a curved hallway. But unlike the floor below, there's a wall at the end of the hallway where the stairs would be.

I slide the tray under the door. As I turn to leave, I hear a noise. Moaning. I wait. There it is again: *Ugghhh.*

I go to the door. "Are you all right?" I feel foolish. Of course he's not all right. But what else could I say?

No response. The moaning gets louder. He's in a lot of pain. "Can you hear me?" I ask.

"Yes," he squeaks. Then more groans.

"Are you . . . hurt?"

"Sick," he replies. But it comes out as: *siiiiickkkk.*

I bend down and try to see through the opening where I slid the tray. I can't see much, especially with the tray partially blocking my view of the room. I spot some movement on the left. A swatch of brown fabric. A body lying curled up on his side, back to the door.

"I see you," I say. "Is there anything I can do to help?" He just moans. "I'm going to send for a doctor," I tell him.

"Nooo," he replies forcefully. Then more weakly: "Water."

"Sit tight. I'll get you a doctor."

"Water!" He gets more insistent. Then he goes back to rocking and groaning.

"I'm sorry . . . I can't do that. I can't come in. And you may be contagious. But I can try to get someone who can help you."

"Not contagious," he says. "Happens all the time."

"Then you still need help."

"Thirsty," he begs.

I'm absolutely certain I am not supposed to open any cell door, let alone enter one. But he seems harmless enough—he can't even get up to reach his water. How can I let this poor man suffer? Who knows how long it's been since he had anything to eat or drink?

For all I know, this key only works on the ground-floor entry to the turret anyway. I'll just try it. If it works, if it unlocks the door, I'll hand the man his water and head right back out the door. Besides, he's a human being, a *sick* human being, not a rabid animal waiting to pounce, and I'm not exactly defenseless either.

I slide the key in the lock and twist. It clicks. I push the door open. The man is lying on old straw that's been stacked against the wall, covered up to his ears by a blanket, though his feet and the bottom of his legs stick out. He's still groaning and rocking back and forth. At this rate it doesn't seem like he'll last long enough to see a doctor. But I don't see any obvious boils or sores on his exposed skin, and he doesn't look particularly sweaty or flushed, so not feverish. Must have something gnawing away inside him, like one of the countrywomen Aunt Mesha treated years ago. A tumor. She suffered in much the same way at the end. And that's not contagious.

I pick up his water mug and carry it to him. "Here you go," I say, crouching down and holding it out. The prisoner rolls over a bit to take it from me.

His hand reaches out. I offer the cup. Suddenly, he's flinging himself toward me and his hands grab my wrists before I'm able to process what's happening.

The mug crashes against the ground.

In a flash, he has my arms pinned behind my back and holds a sharpened stick at my neck. I stifle a scream as I recognize him at last.

CHAPTER FOURTEEN

Shadow

"CALEDON HOLT! I'M HERE TO help you!" I try to break free from his grip but he's too strong. "Stop! You're hurting me!"

"You're not the usual guard," he says in my ear, pulling my arms tighter. He looks me up and down. "You're not even a guard. Who are you? Why are you here?"

"Aren't you ill?" I ask. He doesn't show any signs of the disease he was supposedly suffering from minutes ago. He yanks my arms tighter behind my back.

"Ouch! Ease up a little." I try to pull away from him but he only strengthens his grip again. "I've been looking for you. I'm here to get you out."

He doesn't respond right away. Or let me go. Seems like he's trying to understand what I've said. This is not the dashing rescue I'd hoped it would be. If anything it's already a disaster.

He pulls me with him over to the doorway and looks out into the hall. "Who's with you?" he asks me.

"Nobody. I'm alone. The guards are playing cards tonight. That's why I delivered the food. I was trying to find you. They're full of ale, totally oblivious. I know where we can get horses."

Caledon looks puzzled. "What do you mean?"

"I told you. I'm here to get you out."

He laughs. "Is that right?"

"Yes."

"And I'm supposed to believe that she sent *you*?"

"She who?"

"*She who?*" He laughs. "Who are you working for?"

"Let me go and I'll show you."

"That's not going to happen. So either you start talking or . . ."

"Queen Lilianna sent me," I finally tell him. That's the only "she" he would believe.

"Prove it."

A wolf howls off in the distance. We both turn our heads toward the window for a moment. But we'll worry about the wilderness later; for now I have to manage to leave this cell in one piece. "Let go of me and I can. I have a royal work order."

"A work order? Is that how we operate now?"

I'm unsure whether he's referring to the palace or the Guild, but either way, simply being included in Caledon's "we" thrills me. Still, I didn't expect him to question me this way. I suppose it was foolish to believe my arrival alone would be cause for celebration. Lucky for me, I have the paper. "It's in my pocket," I tell him. He squeezes my wrists with his right hand and reaches into my back pocket with his left. My whole body tenses. "Other side," I say. If he decides to search me for weapons, that could be rather awkward . . .

He pulls out the paper and opens it with one hand. "This is fake. A decent one, but fake all the same."

The fact that he knows that instantly makes my stomach turn. The only reason I wasn't caught straightaway is because the guard in the wagon was too dull-witted to notice. "We don't have time to argue. Because there *is* someone in this prison who was sent here to kill you and it's not me."

He looks me up and down. That revelation didn't get the reaction I wanted. "No, she wouldn't send you. Who are you really?" He pulls on my wrist and twists it. "A spy?" he demands, scrutinizing my face.

"No!" I pull away from him. He lets me go this time. He does believe me, then. I snatch the paper out of his hand and put it back in my pocket. "I told you! You're wasting time. The queen sent me to you for training. Getting you out was my first assignment."

"You're to be my apprentice?" He looks confused. "She knows I work alone."

"Look, there's nothing else I can do to prove it, but if you want to get out of here—"

"Well, first of all, how about giving me your name?" he says. "Since you already know mine."

"Caledon," I say, stalling for time.

"Name's Cal," he corrects. "No one calls me Caledon but my father and the queen."

Reluctantly, I answer him. "My name is Shadow of the Honey Glade. My aunts Moriah and Mesha are part of the Guild." He may not know me, but his father knew my aunts well. I wait for some kind of recognition, but none arrives.

"Shadow. Awfully unusual name for a boy, isn't it?"

That's all he has to say? He clearly doesn't remember me or my aunts. My face burns red. "Maybe because I'm not a boy."

Then I see it—his face lights up for the first time. He reaches into his pocket and pulls out a dirty scrap of fabric, holds it up for me to see. A bit worse for wear, but it's the handkerchief I gave him in Serrone. "Do you know anything about this?"

"Of course I do. I gave it to you," I say, and his face changes. "Why?"

"You saved my life once. And now it's my turn to save yours."

CHAPTER FIFTEEN

Caledon

"THAT WAS *YOU*?" HE SAYS. "At the abbey?"

She nods. Cal's mind is reeling. He can't reconcile the memory of the strange girl from Baer Abbey with the one in Serrone and the person standing before him now. They were all so different. One a mysterious black-clad combatant, one a demure merchant girl, and now . . . This is who the queen chose as her messenger? Why not send a man from the Guild? The girl's absurd disguise would barely pass the Guild's standards . . . It doesn't make sense to him, any of it, but Queen Lilianna must have her reasons. She always does. And the girl did give him the handkerchief: *You're not alone,* she said.

He can see out of the corner of his eye that she's still shaking. *She's terrified,* Cal thinks. And he doesn't fault her for it. That all could have ended much differently. She's clearly a novice, but if she's from a Guild family, she knows exactly who and what he is. He feels sorry for threatening her, but he couldn't have known. She'll get over it. She'll have to if they're going to get out of here. "Explain the forgery, then."

"I told you, I had to convince the queen I was worthy, so I had to do everything myself. Now we need to go," she says. "Listen— I hitched a ride here on a prisoner transport carrying a spy from Montrice. I overheard him talking to the guard, about you and the Aphrasians and Alast. He's somewhere in this fortress. I think he's here to kill you."

A Montrician spy. Of course their enemies have made their move after hearing of the grand prince's murder. Cal thinks quickly, weighing whether he should stay to take care of this new threat before leaving.

"I know where we can get horses," she says. "I've been working in the stables."

"You mentioned that." This is not what he expected when Queen Lilianna said she would send someone for him. But Shadow knows about Montrice. She managed to infiltrate the prison and find him, so he supposes it *has* to be her. But he can't shake the feeling that something isn't right, though he can't be sure if he's not thinking clearly because of his confinement. "We should deal with the Montrician agent first," he finally says.

She walks in front of Cal without addressing what he's said. He follows her into the hall. "Where is he?" Cal asks.

"I haven't seen him since we got here. But he's already imprisoned. It's a waste of time, don't you think? Why pick a fight we don't need?"

He's about to argue, but she's not wrong, and they need to make their escape soon if they mean to leave undetected. He decides to agree for now.

They descend the tower stairs. "There are two guards stationed at the front," she says. "But they seem to get bored and wander off a lot. And there's that card game in the dining hall tonight . . ."

He nods; he's been keeping tabs as well, and he memorized the map of the castle he'd made when he first arrived. "This way," he says as he leads them out toward the back.

The sound of out-of-tune instruments playing disjointed songs floats into the dark hallway. "Good," she says. "They'll never hear us over all that racket."

Curious girl, he thinks to himself. The way she's taking charge, it's almost as if she thinks she's the one saving him. Entertaining as it is, he supposes she *is* sort of rescuing him, even if he could have overtaken the guards and been on his way out of Deersia on his own. But his orders were to wait. Regardless, he's rather enjoying the charade.

They back up against the wall and inch toward the dining room. Cal nods at the swords leaning against the wall outside the entrance. Shadow nods in agreement. They will take them.

She studies the open doorway and closes her eyes for a moment. Then she opens them and urgently waves her hand down. They both crouch just as a guard walks into the hall. The man glances in their direction but doesn't see anything amiss. He turns and heads the other way.

Shadow puts her hand over her heart and exhales softly. Cal's not worried, though—amused is more like it.

They continue sliding along the wall until they get close to the door.

Now they just need to slip past the doorway without being noticed. Shadow gets down on her hands and knees and peeks into the room. Then, in a flash, she's on the other side, grabbing a sword. Cal stays low and moves next to her, then chooses a blade for himself.

They move quickly through the hallway until they reach a side entrance off the kitchens. Cal's about to open it but Shadow puts up a hand to stop him. He rolls his eyes and tries not to sigh. He can tell no one is there. He'd hear boots stomping. As he pushes the door open, she grabs his arm, for all of a sudden he's face-to-face with the guard who'd left the dining hall earlier.

Without thinking, he drives his sword through the man's stomach, then yanks it straight back out. The man's exclamation gurgles in his throat, arms flailing wildly. Cal steps away as the man collapses.

Shadow's breath hitches.

Cal walks through the doorway and continues on the path leading away from the building. He is clearly out of sorts from day after day of insufficient food and movement. If she hadn't warned him, it might have been him lying crumpled on the floor with a sword through his belly, blank dead eyes wide-open in shock. He looks back. It won't be long before someone finds the body. But they don't have time to hide it.

He shakes off the thought, and they creep down the path toward the stables. Shadow leads them around the side. "The stable boys sleep in the loft, so try to stay quiet. We'll take the horses closest to the door and head straight down the path to the main road. We should make it all the way to Alvilla before anyone notices." The village is far enough away to make a safe haven.

He nods. They creep inside the barn, trying not to make any loud noises or sudden movements that would startle the horses.

They begin to saddle up when a whiny voice calls out from the far end of the loft. "Hey! What do you think you're doing?" An angry blond boy is peering down at them over the loft rail.

"Luce," Shadow snarls.

In the time it takes her to yell, "Go! Now!" Luce is already climbing down the ladder. He gets about halfway, then jumps the rest and chases after them.

Shadow has already mounted her horse and started for the lane leading to the gate, but Luce catches up to her and pulls on her leg.

Cal leaves his horse and runs after them, then tackles Luce to the ground. But the boy kicks him hard in the ribs and gets up first, so Cal grabs Luce's ankle and twists his leg so hard that he slams to the hard-packed ground, belly-first. Cal gets to his feet; so does Luce. Both are covered in dirt from the stable floor. Cal is breathing heavily, annoyed at how winded he is; it should be easy to get rid of this snot-nosed stable boy. Then Shadow runs up, grabs Luce by the back of his shirt, and drags him away.

Luce turns to lunge at Shadow but misses.

"Go back to bed," Cal calls to Luce. "I don't want to have to hurt you."

Luce laughs and turns back to Cal. "You're gonna hang for this," he says, then looks to his right and grabs a pitchfork from the wall. He aims it at Cal, walking toward him. "Be a shame if I impale you to the fence first, though. Deprive everyone of the public show—"

Luce is caught on the word. He rises a couple inches off the ground, feet dangling. Shadow has him by the back of his shirt. She grabbed and twisted the fabric so it's choking him. "Should have gone back to bed," she says. Luce drops the pitchfork and struggles to release the shirt from his neck.

Shadow walks a few feet, up to the fence, and tosses Luce over the side. There's a squishy plop and splash as he lands in the pigsty.

Applause erupts from the loft. A row of faces is staring down at them, laughing.

"It's not funny!" Luce yells, his voice cracking and hoarse, only making them laugh harder. He tries again: "Oy! Go get 'em!" One of the boys oinks in return. More follow, until a chorus of oinks and squeals bounces off the stable walls. They're far more interested in the humiliation of their ringleader than the escaped prisoner—or they don't want to end up in the pigsty alongside him.

Cal and Shadow get back on their horses. He tries to suppress a grin—he enjoyed watching her throw that kid into the slop. So this is what it's like to be rescued. He could get used to this. He wonders what else she can do, but there's no time. Her antics with the boy have drawn too much attention already. It won't be long before the guards realize something is going on outside.

Cal grasps the reins and rides on after her, through the castle gates and toward the mountain trail that will lead them away from Deersia.

It's a good thing the moon is nearly full tonight, he thinks. *Or we'd never make it down the mountain.* It feels as if the universe is conspiring to help them. He gives silent thanks to Deia for that.

They stay close to the inside of the trail, near denser foliage, trying to stay somewhat concealed as they approach the gate. "Even if Luce already alerted the guards, it's dark and they're too drunk to bother coming after us tonight. More likely they'll put out a notice for us first thing in the morning, and by then we'll be long gone," Shadow says. It sounds like she's trying to convince herself more than him.

"Don't be so sure," he says. He murdered the grand prince. He's a high-profile prisoner. Valuable enough to chase no matter the time of day.

They slip through the gate without a problem. Shadow has the key ring, and there isn't a guard in sight. But Shadow doesn't look pleased. "What is it?" he asks her.

"I don't know," she answers. "Something doesn't seem right."

Cal shrugs. "Like you said, they're all out by now. There's nothing to worry about." That's what he *says*, because that's what he hopes.

They get about half a mile down the road before discovering there *is* something to be worried about, after all.

CHAPTER SIXTEEN

Shadow

MY HEART IS BEATING SO hard in my chest, and my arm aches from tossing Luce into the pigsty. But we managed it! We escaped from Deersia! I have Caledon Holt riding beside me, and freedom is within our grasp—until we see a group of prison guards standing in the road ahead, right after the bend, as if they've been waiting for us.

I pull on the reins and my horse rears up, belting out a piercing neigh. Next to me I see Cal gripping his reins and leaning forward, digging his heels into the side of his mount. "Keep going!" he yells. We can charge right through them; they're on foot. They'll have to move or be trampled. And they'll never catch up without something to ride.

Grabbing on tight to keep steady, I lower my upper body and prepare to bolt forward, following Cal as he runs through the guards, except one of them is able to grab his foot and pull him from the horse. They struggle on the ground, the guard attempting to overpower him but failing. Cal lands a punch directly on the guard's cheek, but he barely pauses before coming back at Cal.

Then Cal gets a burst of energy. A low growl erupts from him and he charges forward, knocking the guard onto his back. The two guards on the road start toward us. Cal yanks the guard's sword away and pierces him in the heart. But there are more, and they soon surround him. Cal takes another down, and another; he is fearless and relentless and frightening in his speed and skill, but they keep coming.

Someone appears on my left and grabs my leg. I swing my sword at him but miss, as I'm losing my balance; I slide off the side of the horse, which is now in great distress, pawing back and forth in the dirt. I hit the ground, landing hard on my left arm, which softens the blow to my head and torso but does some serious damage to my elbow. A lightning bolt of pain shoots up my arm. I flinch and yelp in agony—I can't help it—then immediately pull myself up, trying to favor the sore arm as much as possible.

I take a clumsy swipe at the guard with my sword, but hurt and winded and taken by surprise, I miss again. He catches my wrist and twists. I drop the sword. I try to shake him off but he grabs my other arm and twists it behind my back.

"Let me go!" I struggle against him but he yanks my arms again and immobilizes me. Nearby, Cal is faring no better—he lies face-down on the ground, his arms stuck behind his back as well, the guard's knee pressing into his spine.

We're trapped. This was an utter failure.

Worse, we're both in deeper trouble than when we started.

We have to get out.

That's when I remember a story Aunt Moriah told me once, about how she learned to conjure a power inside herself stronger than she ever dreamed she possessed. She'd been backed into a corner by an assailant, but her fury propelled her onward in that moment—perhaps I can do the same.

I close my eyes and concentrate, directing all my energy inward, willing my power to consolidate in the pit of my stomach. I feel it, hot, gaining strength. The guard is pulling me. But my feet are planted in the ground. I imagine them becoming one with the earth, growing roots, staying put. Stronger than any man. The guard is getting frustrated; I can hear him yelling, demanding I obey, but he's outside of me somewhere, as if I were underwater and he were shouting from above. It's muted here, and tranquil.

And I control what happens. Not the guard.

I ask the energy to come through me now. I feel it as a white-hot orb, quivering, ready to be unleashed. Legs solid, rooted, I prepare to knock the guard across the road.

I picture the orb; I release it. Everything in slow motion, with force, like moving through water . . .

But instead of attacking the guard, I'm knocked forward, slammed into the ground. I gasp to breathe, air sucked out of my lungs. *What just happened?*

The sounds around me waver back into focus. Voices are suddenly booming; leaves rustling more like crackling; animals hooting and chirping and howling, all bouncing off my pounding head.

I'm yanked to my feet, but my legs give out under me. The guard pulls me again and drags me along while I shuffle and scurry to get my bearings.

The guard laughs. "Tricky little witch, are you? Didn't expect that, I bet." He laughs.

My vision is blurred, but becoming clearer. I zero in on something I hadn't noticed before: He's wearing a shiny black plate over his chest. Not full-vest armor, just a diamond-shaped piece of dark metal sewn into his uniform. No, not metal, it looks almost like black liquid flowing directly under the surface.

Is it some sort of shield? It has to be; it repelled my magic.

"Hang on. They're slowin' us down. Let's throw 'em on the horse," one of the guards says about me and Cal. "I'm not carrying this kid all the way."

"Fine," the guard with the black shield responds. He lifts me up and tosses me, stomach down, onto a horse. They think we're too weakened to put up much of a fight. Two of them walk in front and lead the horses; the other two walk behind us. I move my head enough to see Cal on the horse next to me. His wrists are tied behind his back, as are mine, but if I can regain enough energy . . . maybe I can try again.

I try to see if the other guards have the same protective plate on their chests, but it's too difficult to see. The shield deflected a force of energy directed at a specific person, but can it deflect a natural spell? Can it stop a weirding call? There's only one way to find out.

Besides, what were Deersia prison guards doing out in the woods anyway?

This doesn't make sense. We were far from the main gate, which was bolted shut, and almost all the guards were busy at that card game. So why were they here . . . ?

That's when the truth hits me.

These are not Deersia prison guards.

CHAPTER SEVENTEEN

Caledon

CAL REFUSES TO GO BACK to that squalid cell. Even if it means dying. For now, though, he'll pretend to be cowed and shackled. Let them think they have him while he formulates a better escape plan. But it's hard to think. He is light-headed and slung over the back of a horse, which is jostling him around like cargo, making his ribs ache. He can't even use his arms to adjust his body or steady himself.

His hands are tied—quite literally. Shadow keeps trying to tell him something, motioning her eyes toward the guards, but he doesn't understand what she's trying to say. If only she would just let him focus for a minute. He can admit she's better trained than he'd thought, but she's far too eager and impulsive. He hasn't survived all this time by not knowing when to step back and think before acting.

She's mouthing something to him—he can't make it out. *Uprising? Off*—something? *Afraid of them?* The caravan slows, and one of the guards walks his horse up closer to her as she rolls her eyes back in her head and begins muttering gibberish, as if she were severely injured and disoriented. Cal stays still and shuts his eyes as much as he can while peeking through a tiny sliver, enough to know if the guard comes toward him, but not enough to look fully conscious. The guard studies Shadow before stepping back behind the horses again, next to the other guard, apparently satisfied that she's not a threat.

Maybe he can slide off the back of the horse, kick the guard—if he's really lucky, he can kick one into the other, and together they can take the other two? But can he count on her to carry her own weight in this attack?

Shadow still has her eyes closed, and has started mumbling under her breath. *What's she doing?*

An owl hoots. Wings flap overhead. Another hoot. Owls begin to descend from the skies. Shadow opens her eyes to look. Then she closes them again.

This time, a wolf howls; then another, a whole pack, it sounds like. Cal wishes he had his full strength; he'll need it to get them out of these woods alive if there are nightwolves out here.

The guards unsheathe their swords, look around nervously. "Better move faster," one yells. The horses hesitate, lurching back a bit before being spurred forward.

There's a chorus of flapping wings and howling, and the howling is getting closer. Shadow's face is scrunched in concentration and she continues to mouth something over and over again. The horses keep moving, but slower and with increasing reluctance.

Cal realizes what she's doing. Somehow she's communicating with the owls and wolves, maybe the horses too. He's heard of this kind of magic, but never seen it done—he didn't think anyone could do that anymore.

Shadow might not be so bad to have around after all. He wonders if she may even be able to teach him a few things. Despite many attempts to learn over the years, Cal was never gifted in the magical side of Guild training. He's like his father in that way.

The owls dive down out of the treetops, swarming around the horses.

The guards bat them away, to no avail. The owls screech and peck, and the howls are getting closer. The horses rear and Cal is tossed from the saddle. He rolls to the ground.

In the chaos, Cal sees his chance. He yanks on his restraints and leaps to his feet. He looks for Shadow but doesn't see her.

Owls are still swooping overhead, and the horses bolt. The men scream, and through the commotion he catches sight of her sleeve and fights his way to her side.

Shadow is standing stock-still in the middle of the melee, her eyes closed and lips moving, even as a guard holds a blade to her neck.

"SHUT UP, WITCH!" he growls.

Cal lunges for the dagger when she suddenly opens her eyes and looks right at him. "NO!"

He balks.

Shadow falls limp, still whispering, and the guard strikes, but Cal disarms him so fast that the blade merely grazes her skin. Before the guard can react, Cal has turned the blade on him. But just as Cal begins his fatal strike, Shadow stays his hand.

Cal stops, confused.

"Don't," she says, and he knows she has seen him deal too much death this evening.

It is what I do, he wants to tell her. *I am the Queen's Assassin.* There is so much blood on his hands he is surprised they are not always red and dripping. He is the queen's will, the throne's hangman, protector of the crown of Renovia. He sends men and women to death before they even know their lives are in danger.

But the owls are taking care of it for now—a great horde of them is clawing at each man. There's a rumble of creatures prowling through leaves and branches coming toward them. This time it's Shadow who pulls Cal into the brush, and they hide just as a pack of snarling nightwolves bursts out of the trees onto the path, only the silver glint of their eyes visible in the darkness. Their hunger is ferocious and tangible. The guards' screams echo through the woods as they run and the wolves give chase.

"You called them," he says, catching his breath. "The owls and the wolves."

Shadow shrugs. "I was trying to finish the spell, and you almost got in the way."

"You're a mage." He can barely keep the awe out of his voice.

"My aunts are. They taught me a little."

Someone else runs down the path. A kid. Looks like a kitchen hand. "Jander," Shadow whispers. The boy turns his head and looks directly at them. Then runs away quickly.

Another guard follows behind, grabs the boy by his shoulders. "Where'd they go?" he demands.

Jander shrugs.

The man curses. He shakes the boy. "Well, don't stand there. Find them!"

The boy nods and motions excitedly to the path. He points. The guard looks that way. "What is it?" the man asks. "You see them?"

Jander nods again and points the other way, away from where Shadow and Cal are hiding.

The guard shoves him in the back. "What are you waiting for? Go!"

Jander begins running away on the path, kicking up dirt all around him. The guard mounts one of the remaining horses and clops away after him. Cal and Shadow wait to be sure all is clear. In the distance they can hear the sounds of men shouting, horses whinnying, a cacophony of hooting and snarling.

"You know that boy?" Cal asks Shadow when he's sure there's no one nearby.

"Yes . . . but . . ." She looks off in the direction the boy fled. "Never mind. It doesn't matter." They are quiet again, unsure if they should leave their hiding spot yet.

"We should go before the guards return," he says.

"About the guards. I was trying to tell you earlier. They're not from Deersia. They're Aphrasians."

Cal's heart drops into his stomach. Of course. He should have noticed it sooner.

"I realized it when one of them blocked my magic. He had some kind of armor on his chest. A small piece but it was enough to reflect it back to me. That's what knocked me out."

"Are you certain?"

She narrows her eyes. "Yes, I'm certain. I could feel it. And I don't think they were taking us back to the prison. Look how far west we are."

She was right; if they were being brought to Deersia, they would've been back by now. They hadn't gotten far. But he'd been so occupied with escaping that he didn't realize they were headed elsewhere. "I've never heard of anything like that before. A magic repellant."

"I *know* that's what happened." She sighs and rolls her eyes.

"Not saying I don't believe you," he says, noting just how quickly she grows defensive. "Good thing I was here, then," he says with a grin. "To help you out when your magic couldn't."

Instantly, he knows he should've kept his mouth shut.

She shakes her head, lips curled in disgust. "You know . . . ," she begins scolding him. But she quits speaking and abruptly puts a finger to her lips. He nods.

Hooves are clopping down the path.

But when the horses finally come into view, they are riderless. Standing before them are the two steeds they took from the prison stable.

"I wasn't sure they got the message through all the noise," she says.

Cal is impressed. Shadow just might end up being useful to him after all. They each pick up a sword from the ground and mount the horses. He still hears noises in the distance, but less screaming. Did the wolves finish off their captors? He hopes so. "We'll take the south road," he says.

Shadow pulls her horse in front of his. "Yes. But when we come to the descent, stay alert. You might need to 'help me out' again," she says, her voice thick with sarcasm.

"That's not what I meant . . . ," he begins to say. But he supposes that *is* exactly what he meant. He considers trying to explain, but it doesn't matter, as he's speaking to her back.

CHAPTER EIGHTEEN

Shadow

AFTER EVERYTHING I'VE DONE FOR him—the risks I've taken—and he acts like he's the one coming to *my* rescue. *He'd still be sitting in that cell—or dead—if it wasn't for me.*

What an arrogant lout Caledon Holt, Great Master Assassin of Renovia, has turned out to be. I'm almost tempted to go back to my aunts' farm and then on to the palace, where at least I can live out my days in comfort and warmth. But I can't even pretend to want that. If I'm being honest, that's still less appealing than sticking out the journey ahead with my knight in shining armor, Sir Full of Himself.

So what if he saved my life a few dozen times this evening?

The man is a terror with a sword. It's clear he could have escaped Deersia anytime he wanted, so why didn't he? Was he truly waiting for the queen to send for him?

We don't speak the entire way down the mountain path. Besides, we have to focus on managing the horses' steps. I'm just glad we're taking the road down and not the reverse. Going up to Deersia under these conditions would be even more daunting. And exhausting.

We're both relieved when we make it to the foot of the mountain, and so are the horses. I can feel the tension leaving my horse for now—as I rub his head. "Good boy. Good job."

"I have to apologize," Caledon says finally. "I was skeptical at first but now I see why Queen Lilianna sent you for this."

"I appreciate that," I say stiffly.

He stares off down the road. I can tell he's mulling something over. Then he looks back at me and says, "So do your orders include accompanying me to Montrice?"

"Yes," I say, because I want nothing more than to share his mission.

"Huh." He hesitates again. I know he still isn't sure he can trust me.

"I am to aid you in any way I can, which includes traveling to Montrice," I insist, as I cannot be left behind.

He nods and he must decide that he can finally trust me or that he won't get rid of me so easily. I try not to look relieved. "Montrice may be funding the Aphrasians and helping them regain power. They may be plotting to invade Renovia."

I nod, letting him continue.

"The queen believes a Montrician conspirator is aiding the Aphrasian monks, and we need to find out who it is and ensure that person isn't a threat to Renovia ever again," he says grimly.

"Understood."

Caledon nods. "Good. In that case, let's get moving."

WE RIDE ON AT a steady pace for a while, each absorbed in our own thoughts. Even though I just traveled this way not too long ago, it all looks different. More menacing. Every large stone or tree looks like the ideal hiding place for an ambush of guards or thieves; I don't like being out on this wide-open road either. We can be seen from miles away.

"Once day breaks, we should head into the Black Woods," I say, motioning toward the forest ahead. "There's a road cut through there that should lead all the way into Montrice." I know this only because I read it in one of my aunts' books. I don't tell him that, of course. "It's tricky but will be less traveled. And easier to find cover."

"I don't like it," Cal says. "That's the first place they'll look," he adds. "Anyone would take the first opportunity to get off the road. It's the obvious move."

Not sure if he meant that as an insult, but it felt like one. "Even if they do, we'd still have a better chance of getting away. Where are we going to hide out here?"

"We won't have to hide. If we don't stop, they can't catch up. Crossing the woods will take longer."

Ridiculous. How has he even survived this long? It's common sense—it's almost like he *wants* us to be an easy target. "Queen Lilianna sent me in the name of the crown, and I say we go into the woods," I say, hoping I sound more confident than I feel.

"Unbelievable," Cal mutters.

We go on quietly for a few more minutes. Cal rides up right next to me. I stare ahead intently, ignoring his presence.

"It's vital we work together," he says. "Arguments will only slow us down."

"We wouldn't argue if you didn't contradict everything I say. Hold on, I mean if you don't want to *hear* anything I have to say. You think you have all the answers already!"

He shakes his head. "You should follow my lead!"

"But you interfered with my spell-casting!"

"Was I supposed to let him hurt you? You said it yourself, I was *helping* you."

"What if I didn't need help? I got us out of there, didn't I?"

"But . . ." His voice trails off and I feel somewhat triumphant.

After some silence he says, "Fine, we'll do it your way. We'll take to the woods."

It's not quite the triumph I was hoping for, but at least it's a start.

THOUGH IT'S DAWN AND the sky is clear, as soon as we enter the forest it's as pitch-black as the middle of the night again. The treetops obscure the bit of sun that was just beginning to peek above the horizon. I instantly regret insisting we go this way, but I'm not about to admit it. There's nothing to be afraid of, anyway, and I maintain it makes more sense to stay off the main road. If a missing-prisoners bulletin goes out, a farmer could see us and either report it or attempt to detain us for the reward. That's a headache we don't need.

I can tell Cal is thinking the same thing—that maybe the forest *was* a mistake—but for now, he doesn't say anything. We're forced to slow down due to the darkness and the condition of the path—the horses have to step carefully over half-buried branches and deep ruts. I can feel the eyes of the hidden wildlife watching as we go by. The horses are on edge. Out of nowhere something large flaps right past my head, spooking the horse and making it rear up. I stop to calm him. "Shh. Shh. It was just a bat."

Cal snorts.

"The horses are tired. I think we should stop and rest them when we get to Alvilla," I tell him.

"Of course you do," Cal says under his breath.

My nostrils flare. "It's close to the border. And we can't push the horses that hard. What do you think we should do?"

"I think we should have taken the main road and gone straight into Montrice. And now that we're here . . . I *still* think we should go straight through."

"Do you? Or are you just saying that because you want to disagree with me?"

"Look, I don't think it's a good idea to stop in town. People will be looking for two fugitives."

"But we need to stop in Alvilla. For the horses," I say, even though that's not quite the truth. The truth is I'm hungry and tired and I need to rest. Casting that spell took a toll on me, but I don't want him to know how weak I am. I don't want him to win.

Cal shrugs in response. We don't speak again for a while.

A bit farther on I hear something. "Wait." I put up a hand as I try to make out what it is. It may just be something wild, but I need to be sure. I listen intently, beyond the sounds directly surrounding us, into the distance. "Horses," I say softly. "And armed men."

"Looking for us?" Cal asks me.

I focus on the sounds, but it's too far to hear clearly. Not that we need to. Armed men don't usually enter the woods at dawn. This is my fault. We're being followed just like Cal said we would be.

Worse, they have tracking dogs. I can hear their barking more distinctly as they draw near. We can't outrun them once they pick up our scent. They'll just keep coming and coming until eventually . . . I close my eyes and try to think, and then I hear something else. A great rumble coming from the other direction.

"We need to outpace them," Cal says.

"I have an idea," I say, opening my eyes. "Follow me."

If I'm right, there's a crossroads ahead. If I'm wrong, we're in real trouble.

"We can't ride too fast; I don't want to risk making too much noise. The guards may not pick up on it, but the dogs will," I tell him. We go at a steady pace but I hear the dogs getting louder, closer. I also hear the thundering noises getting louder from the other side. I begin pleading: *Please let this work. Please. Please. Please.* It has to.

Finally we come to the crossroad in the woods. "Which way?" Cal asks.

"Straight ahead," I answer. "But not yet. Wait."

"Why?"

"Trust me," I say, as much to myself as to Cal. I close my eyes again. From one direction, I still hear the guards approaching; from the other, the commotion I'd heard barreling toward us. "On my word, we bolt down the path."

He assents.

We get ready as if for a race, bent low, prepared to bolt. The two forces get closer and closer . . . there's a clamoring of hooves, boots, and steel behind us; the dogs are coming right around the bend, and a clash of a horde booming from the other direction, just as loud and unstoppable. Cal doesn't need my extrasensory strength to hear either one anymore.

Nearer still. Cal looks at me, his eyebrows knit together. I shake my head. He doesn't look convinced but he doesn't move either. The dogs are so close. They can definitely see us at this point. Cal looks like he's about to go with or without me.

"Wait!" I shout over the noise. The clamoring gets louder. "Now!"

We take off down the road just before the dogs lead their masters right to us—just as a stampede of deer charges across the trail directly in front of them, blocking their path.

I hear men yelling and dogs barking furiously. The deer stampede continues, giving us the distraction we need to get away. The confusion should mask our scent and throw the dogs off our trail.

Once we've put enough distance between us and the hunting party, we slow the horses down to a trot. I don't hear our pursuers anymore. "That was close." I start laughing and can't stop. I'm so relieved that it worked.

But if I'm looking for praise or thanks, there will be none from him. "Best to get where we're going without any more excitement," Cal says. "I'd like to survive the rest of the way, if you don't mind. We'll ride until we get into town."

"You're welcome," I say, unafraid to hide the annoyance in my tone.

Cal says nothing. Just clops on ahead of me.

❦

CHAPTER NINETEEN

Caledon

ALVILLA IS A TINY BORDER village nestled in a valley, the last proper town before crossing the invisible line between Renovia and Montrice. It's typically populated by a mix of local farmers, shop-keepers, trade merchants, and diplomats, as well as some unsavory types; a place accustomed to outsiders and unusual people. So nobody pays much mind to two strangers on horseback.

Cal is still uncomfortable, however. There are too many people around for his liking. Out of habit he reaches to pull a hood up over his head, then remembers he doesn't have one. *Maybe I can buy one in town,* he thinks. *Too bad I can't get cleaned up properly first, though.* He's in desperate need of a hot bath.

He's still a bit angry at Shadow for insisting on taking the forest trail. Even if she rescued them from her own mistake, they could have been captured or killed. The closer they get to leaving the relative safety of Renovia, the more irritated he feels.

He should probably get rid of her. Leave her behind somewhere and continue the journey alone. She can go back to Renovia. He'll send a message to the queen that the girl was a liability. Except it seems Queen Lilianna wanted the girl to be with him, for whatever reason. He'll have to deal with having a shadow—ha!—for at least a while longer. He'll just have to be more assertive, stop allowing her to make decisions she isn't qualified to make. Sent by the crown or not, Montrice is *his* task—*he* is the Queen's Assassin. She may have been ordered to release him from Deersia, but she isn't equipped to deal with the Aphrasian traitor.

Shadow seems to know exactly where she wants to go. She leads them directly to a tavern in the middle of town. They dismount and tie up the horses; there's a water trough for the animals, and they can keep an eye on them from one of the tavern's front windows.

They walk inside and sit down at a small table. A man holding a dirty rag in one hand shouts at them from across the room. "The missus will bring out some salt meat and ale for ya. Four coppers apiece." He disappears through a door in back.

"Thank you kindly, good sir!" Shadow shouts back, a bit too jovially.

Cal leans toward her. "Do you have any coin? Because I do not."

"I do," she says, avoiding his gaze.

"Why don't I believe that?" Cal says. "Look, if you were given coin for the trip, we should save it for Montrice."

When she doesn't answer him right away, he says, "We should leave."

"But I'm hungry," she says with a frown.

Cal sighs. "I might have something to eat," he says, motioning to the drawstring pouch under his shirt in which he'd carefully collected food scraps for his escape. "Or we can catch something if need be."

"Those moldy old biscuits you've been dragging around with you? Very kind of you to offer, but no thank you." She sits up straight and shouts toward the back room: "A loaf of your freshest bread alongside that salted meat, good sir?"

"Beats stealing," Cal hisses back at her. "You want more people chasing us? Because *I'm* not a beggar. Or a thief."

"Ouch!" Shadow puts her hand to her heart. "Of course I can pay for the food," she says, rolling her eyes. "Why would you assume I'm going to steal it?"

He frowns. It's because he never has any coin of his own. Since she hired him from the Guild, Queen Lilianna rarely sends him off with any—too easily robbed and would attract too much attention. She sets up places for him to stay and the like instead. Of course, now that he thinks of it, he has neither Her Majesty's coin nor largesse at hand. "You truly have coin?"

She shrugs.

"Let me see it, then," Cal says to Shadow. He isn't about to be fooled into eating a meal that won't be paid for.

She reaches into the side of her trousers and pulls out a small leather pouch from a hidden pocket. She loosens the top and shows Cal a handful of shiny gold coins inside. Just one of them is more than enough to pay for this meal, and the next three after that. He raises his eyebrows and calls out toward the back room: "Make that two loaves of bread for the weary travelers, please."

Eager as he is for his first real meal in over a month, it is still infuriating to think that the queen lavished so much coin on this green apprentice. The queen was never so generous with him— certainly not before an assignment was fulfilled, either. But at least they will be able to eat.

BELLIES FULL OF MUTTON and fresh bread slathered in creamy butter, they step back onto the wood-slatted sidewalk. Cal is practically delirious with happiness; he can't remember the last time he ate so well, the memory of Deersia porridge is too strong. "Maybe it wouldn't be a bad idea to spend the night here. Rest up some," he says. "Then head into Montrice early tomorrow." The luxurious meal has altered his outlook considerably. If she has coin, why should they suffer? The thought of a real bed, even an old lumpy one in a tavern lodge—not to mention the possibility of a bath—is so enticing that he forgets he's the one who didn't want to stay in Alvilla to begin with. "We can make arrangements for our introduction to Montrice."

"Wonder if that inn down the road back there has any vacancies?" Shadow says. They'd passed a two-story wattle-and-daub building on the way into town.

"Not sure that's a place for a lady," Cal says. "If you know what I mean."

She scoffs at that. "I'm not some delicate flower . . ."

"Clearly," he says, then puts his hand up to quiet her. "Hold on." He sees a man tacking a sign to a fence post. When he's finished, he walks back inside his shop—a print shop. The two of them approach the fence to read the sign up close:

NOTICE
ESCAPED PRISONER

ARMED AND DANGEROUS

MAY BE TRAVELING WITH HOSTAGE

DO NOT APPROACH

ALERT DEERSIA AUTHORITIES IMMEDIATELY

There are two crude charcoal sketches on the poster. One shows a man with an exaggerated upturned nose and bulging eyes over a wild mane of uneven hair and a patchy beard. Underneath the drawing it says, CALEDON HOLT, ARMED AND DANGEROUS. "Terrible likeness," Cal says, frowning. "Ears are all wrong." The other drawing shows a handsome young boy with chiseled features and wavy, tousled brown hair, one eyebrow cocked, smiling mischievously: IDENTITY UNKNOWN.

Cal looks at Shadow and then at the picture and back at her again. "Surely they can't be serious. Did you give them this description yourself? Because—"

"Shame," Shadow says, shaking her head. "They gave you way too much beard. Yours is actually a bit shorter and gnarlier than that. Otherwise, though . . ."

"You continue to amuse," Cal says. He looks inside the shop. The printer is still operating the press; he's making more posters. Soon they'll be hung all over town.

"Guess we won't be staying," Cal says, noticing a young mother and her two small children staring at them from across the lane.

This time, Cal and Shadow agree. The sooner they get out of Renovia, the better.

❦

Chapter Twenty

Shadow

ONCE WE'RE SAFELY OUTSIDE THE village limits, we decide we'll make do with camping overnight in one of the nearby hill caves before tackling the last stretch into Montrice. The most direct route over the border, a narrow passage between two mountains, is visible in the distance.

"We'll be too exposed in the gully. I think we should take the high pass," Cal says.

"But the gully would be *much* faster," I reply. "I thought that was what we wanted—to get off the road as quickly as possible?"

Cal exhales loudly.

I hear rustling nearby. I pull back and motion for Cal to move away from the clearing. We steer the horses off the trail behind a dense thicket. From there I'm able to see what caused the noise ahead of us.

About a dozen Aphrasian monks, wearing their telltale gray robes, are gathered around a clear blue spring, resting their horses. We almost wandered straight into them—and a fight.

These aren't the same men who were attacked by the owls and the wolves, but perhaps they are from the same company.

Cal peers through the trees. "Do you recognize any of them?" I ask him. He shakes his head no. "Let me look," I tell him. He has the best vantage point where he's standing. He moves aside to let me get in next to him. Our faces press close together so we can both see at the same time. His beard is scratchy against my cheek.

At first I don't know who any of the men are, either. None of them look familiar. An older gentleman with a haughty air is ordering them about.

"Wait here," I tell Cal.

He grabs my arm to stop me. "What are you doing?"

I look down at his hand and he removes it. I make a point to smooth my sleeve where he grabbed it. He rolls his eyes at the gesture but I pretend not to notice. "I'm going to divert them. Then you will escape into the high pass. I'll meet you there."

"No." Cal shakes his head. "No, you will not. I'll figure out what to do."

"Really? You agreed that we should go through the woods."

"Just so you'd stop badgering me about it. And that nearly got us killed."

My face immediately scrunches in disgust. "And you've never made a mistake before? I do happen to know a thing or two. I was also raised by the Guild."

His gaze hardens on my own. "What exactly do you suggest?" Cal says. I know he's humoring me, but I'll take it.

"I'll distract them. You go on to the high pass. I'll find you there."

Cal shakes his head again. "That's the same plan! If they attack, you won't be able to fend them off alone."

He may be right. Then again, maybe not. In the short time since I left home I've discovered that I have far more strength and power than I ever knew. Plus I'm determined to prove him wrong. "Let me worry about that."

"Impossible. You can't fight that many men. Or outrun them. Even if you managed to get away, you'd lead them straight to us. I'll check the other side and see if there's another way around. Wait here."

I look up into the trees that surround the spring. While Cal wastes time coming up with another plan, I decide to go ahead with my own.

CHAPTER TWENTY-ONE

Caledon

WHERE'S SHADOW?

Cal looks around but doesn't see her anywhere. He almost yells out to her, but he stops himself; the monks might hear.

A chunk of leaves falls on his head from above. He looks up. A glimpse of fabric and skinny arms flash by him. Shadow is maneuvering through the thick trees, as adept as a predator, trying to get closer to the spring.

Cal curses under his breath. "I told you—"

"Too late," Shadow whispers down from over his head. "Just get ready."

"We weren't finished discussing this," he hisses back.

"I was," she says, then hauls herself up to another branch.

She has gumption, he has to give her that. She just doesn't know when to rein it in. Cal draws his sword and watches, waiting to see what she's going to do. All is calm, and then a sudden silence descends: Birds stop chirping; even the breeze seems to halt.

Seconds later something whizzes through the air. There's a *thunk*, and one of the monks' horses rears up and whinnies, followed immediately by another thunk and another frightened horse, and then they're all rearing and whinnying and running, scattering in every direction. The men, alarmed and confused, begin chasing after them, yelling for them to stop and come back.

Stones begin flying at the men now, too; three of them are hit, falling to the ground. A couple of the men draw their bows and begin shooting arrows toward the trees, trying to strike their hidden enemy. Shadow.

Without another thought Cal runs out from behind the trees and leaps into the fray, swinging his sword. The men turn their bows toward him. An arrow flies by his head. He knocks the bow from the man's grip and aims his sword for the man's neck, slicing it open. The man crumples to the ground. Yet another appears beside Cal and takes aim at him with a sword. Cal spots another archer and sees him draw his bow. He ducks, hitting the ground just as the arrow whizzes by, striking his attacker instead. It feels great, flexing his fighting arm again. The others have given up on the horses to join the battle; they charge toward Cal, yelling at the top of their lungs. Rocks are still flying through the air, and a couple of them hit their target. Meanwhile, Cal drives his sword through the back of a monk; a large stone finishes off the other, clocking him squarely in the face. The last three monks run off into the woods, one bleeding from the side of the head, where another of Shadow's stones got him.

Their leader jumps onto a horse and begins riding away—with Cal following close behind. But before he can loosen his bow, the man is hit by a stone, jerks back, and tumbles from the horse's back. The horse continues galloping.

Cal runs up to him and lifts his sword. Until he realizes that man is already dead. Shadow's aim was excellent—too excellent. The fall broke his neck. The mangled heap on the ground can't respond to any questions now. Cal curses. Shadow has the brute force part under control, but if she's going to become a properly trained apprentice, she'll have to learn the finer points—and fast.

Cal hears a high-pitched shriek. Horrible visions pop into his mind, and he runs to where Shadow had been hiding up in the trees.

His fear is correct. Shadow is lying facedown on the ground, eyes closed, right arm curled under her. Blood seeps from her clothes.

The guilt sears through him in a flash. *I never should have let her do this,* he thinks, though he knows there was nothing he could have done to stop her. All she wanted was to fight for a good cause, and he's given her grief over it every step of the way. He was supposed to work with her, be responsible for her, and he fought with her instead. She was brave and resourceful, and had the makings of a good assassin. Now she is lying in the dirt. He falls to his knees beside her. "I'm sorry," he chokes out. "I'm so sorry." If he could do this all differently, he would. He's failed in his duty.

Then Shadow's eyes pop open. "Hey, it's not that serious. It's just my arm."

"Oh. I thought you . . ." He looks at her arm. She's hurt, but not nearly as seriously as he first thought. He pulls away, embarrassed about his outburst. She slides the injured arm out from under her, wincing. "Can you move it?" he asks. She wiggles her arm a bit. There's a large gash and a lot of blood, but it looks like it will heal if they take care of it. And it doesn't appear to be broken. She begins picking herself up off the ground.

"Let me help you," he says. He puts her good arm around his shoulder and pulls her into a sitting position.

She puts her hand against her stomach and takes a few deliberate breaths. "Got the wind knocked out of me is all."

"Why didn't you tell me you were going to do that?"

"You didn't exactly give me a chance, and you were supposed to run."

"Yeah." He raises his eyebrows.

Shadow is subdued. "I'm sorry—"

But Cal doesn't let her finish her sentence. "Let's get you fixed up," he says. He leans down and reaches under her knees and arms to pick her up.

"It's okay. I can walk," she says. But when she takes a few steps, she's limping.

"Here," Cal says. She doesn't say no this time. He scoops her up and carries her the rest of the way to her horse, her arms grasping his neck tightly.

❧

CHAPTER TWENTY-TWO

Shadow

WE MAKE OUR WAY UP the high pass, leading the horses carefully over the rocks. Cal asks me if I'm okay, if I'm in too much pain. If I need to stop and rest awhile. I assure him I'm fine, but he still offers for me to ride along with him. Again, I tell him I'm fine. In the span of one day, he's gone from dismissive to overly attentive. But that's my fault, at least partially. I guess I might have encouraged it back at the clearing. I really was hurt when I fell, but I could have gotten up sooner than I did—it's just that his sudden anguish was too enjoyable. Before that I'd have guessed his response to me falling out of a tree would have been a shrug and a "served her right."

At the same time, I'm irritated that he seems so affected by my fall, although I can't quite put my finger on why.

"Did you grow up in Serrone?" Cal asks me, breaking the quiet of our silent truce.

"Right outside of it, in Nir," I tell him. "I live with my aunts on a farm called the Honey Glade. After they ended their active service in the Guild, they began running bee colonies and raising herbs. They make poultices and such that they sell these days."

"Ah. Sounds nice, actually. Peaceful." He gets quiet, and for a moment the only sound is the hooves clicking on the trail. Then he asks, "And your parents?"

"My mother is part of the Guild and she serves at the palace, so she isn't around a lot." Eventually I'm going to have to tell him the truth—how I'm currently running away from her and the plans she'd made for me—but I'll worry about that later. Maybe if he finds me worthy he'll speak on my behalf to the Guild, maybe even help change my mother's mind. I urge my horse away from the cliffside.

"And your father?"

"My father . . ." I don't know what to tell him about my father. Partly because I don't know much myself. "Not much to say; he died when I was young." I don't often have to discuss my family with strangers and it's making me uncomfortable. "How about you—how did you end up working for the queen?" I know most of this background already, but I'm desperate to take the focus off me and curious to learn what version of his story he'll share.

"Long story," he says. "Boring. I don't like to talk about it."

"Your father was Cordyn Holt, right?" I push him. "King Esban's assassin."

"I said I don't want to talk about it," Cal snaps. He adjusts how he's sitting on the horse.

"Hardly anything to be ashamed about," I assure him. Why ask me about my family if I can't ask about his?

"I didn't say I'm ashamed. I said I don't want to talk about it."

"All right. You don't have to," I say. "I was just curious. I'm sorry I upset you."

His shoulders relax a little and his expression softens. "You didn't know."

His words make me feel even worse, because I did know, just not that he would be touchy about it. I shake off the guilt and change course. We have a mission ahead—and I have plans of my own to attend to . . . "Let's discuss exactly what happens when we get to Montrice."

"I'll get to work making contacts, to get an audience in the king's chamber . . . ," Cal says, barely glancing my way.

I scoff in response. "If anybody is going to infiltrate a royal court, it's going to be me."

"You? Why you?" His eyes are incredulous, but I see a slight smile playing at the edges of his lips. He's amused, but I am not.

I look him up and down. "You clearly have no manners. Sure, your brooding and arrogance will make you quite at home with Montrician royalty, but they won't be enough to gain the connections we'll need at court. Do you think you can just slash your way to the king? That they would let you even get that close?"

He reflects on that. "You may have a point. I suppose you could bat your eyelashes; I hear honey is more effective than vinegar."

I take a deep breath in and sigh, lest I lash out at Renovia's deadliest assassin while already injured.

He shrugs. "But in the end, neither force nor flirtation will lead us to King Hansen. In Montrice, it's purely who you know that wins you favor and success. We need a powerful courtier to introduce us. That's all that matters in their world." He stops his horse to look at the view. We are high up on a ridge, and from here all we can see are valleys, streams, and forest. We are alone in the wilderness, far away from villages and towns, let alone a palace and courtly life.

"Yes," I say, scanning the treetops. "I am well aware of the conventions of Montrician society, which is why I—"

He interrupts me by making a slashing movement across his neck. He drops his reins and his horse whinnies. "If we are caught, it's over. There's more to being an assassin than tracking and weapons. Espionage is an art. You need a wide range of skills learned through experience and perseverance. I learned that lesson early on, and it was . . . well, let's say it was a far cry from your Honey Glade."

My nostrils flare. "Yes, I know." My voice comes out as a low growl and it takes everything within myself not to lunge at his taunting face, claws bared.

"Fine, then. I'll save my tricks for someone who deserves them," Cal says. "Can't make someone learn something they're not ready for, I suppose."

My face twists with disgust. "*Deserves?* Care to explain what you mean by that?"

"I don't like to pull rank, Shadow, but you were sent to—"

"Be your apprentice," I say. Here I am, about to embark on an adventure under the tutelage of *the* Caledon Holt. It's all I've ever wanted—and yet all I feel is frustration and fury. Maybe I should have gone to the palace after all . . . I doubt any life would be as infuriating as one shackled to this pompous buffoon. I dig my heels against my horse's flank, ready to gallop ahead so I don't have to look at him.

I let my horse run for a while, and leave Cal behind.

Then I hear him galloping up next to me, pulling up so we are riding side by side.

"What?" I say.

He scrunches his eyebrows and blinks a few times. "Apprentice. Right. Then let me remind you that it is I who am the captain of this ship, so it is I who will issue the orders. For now, I'd like to keep my head. I'd even like for you to keep yours. It would be a shame to lose such a pretty face. And yours isn't too bad either." His eyes are shining in merriment.

I clench my jaw and shake my head. "You are definitely . . . something." I wonder if there's a shred of truth in his words . . . but I refuse to be distracted by flattery, especially when it is of a back-handed sort.

He looks at me out of the corner of his eye. "Funny. I feel the same way about you."

I turn my gaze away toward the trees so he doesn't see my cheeks flush pink. From a distance, wolves begin to howl, and I'm thankful for the distraction.

"We need to stop soon," Cal says. "We won't make it across the pass before nightfall."

It's the second time we agree.

CHAPTER TWENTY-THREE

Caledon

WITHOUT SHADOW, CAL HAS TO admit to himself—though he won't admit it to her—*we wouldn't have made it back there.* He knows he wouldn't have stood a chance against that many men alone. The problem is, while he's come to the grudging realization that she may be useful, it's clear that as much as she might admire him, she also finds him deeply exasperating. So he isn't quite willing to allow her the satisfaction of being right so she could hold something over him.

After an hour of searching, they locate a cave where they can sleep for the night. He'd expected her to say she doesn't want to stop, maybe to prove something to him, but she agrees straightaway. Good thing too, because if she doesn't get some rest, they'll be in jeopardy. The echoing howls of the nightwolves likely helped her decision. Neither of them was looking forward to facing that pack again.

They're relieved to have found a cave not too far from the road, especially one so dry inside. When they settle in, Cal sets to building a fire, using one of the scraps of wool from his blanket, and a flint from Shadow. Then he tends to Shadow's arm. She's reluctant to let him at first. "It's fine. Much better already," she says.

"No, it's not. It's worse than I thought," he says, touching the area around the wound gently as he inspects it.

She abruptly pulls back, away from his hands.

"It would help if you stopped yanking yourself around like that," he chides.

She rolls her eyes a little but allows him to continue his examination. He gingerly cradles her arm in his lap and tries to assess the damage by the glow of the flames.

"Mage blood," he says, noting the blue-black color.

She nods, trying to be modest about it. Blue blood is prized in the kingdom.

"The gash was deep. It may feel better but that doesn't mean you have full use of your arm yet. And you'll need it for us to survive these woods. So we need to stop and let this heal before we go any farther. No matter how long it takes."

She pulls her arm from him again, but slowly this time. "I told you, it's just a scratch. I've had worse."

"Take it from someone who knows, Shadow. It's more than a scratch. Listen, I don't want to have to cut that thing off for you if it rots. I've done it before and it is not pleasant. The flesh is one thing—I can get through it easy enough—but the bone is another. I'll have to use a sword to cut it off. I'd prefer very much that you keep your arm instead. I'm sure you do too."

Shadow suddenly looks ill, and Cal wonders if maybe he overdid it. "We won't let that happen," he assures her. "But you do need to let it heal."

She nods. "Fine—but we can't afford to sit around. The longer we wait, the more likely someone catches up to us."

Cal is glad he's persuaded her to agree to his plan—even as he makes new plans of his own. The queen should have known better than to send him such a novice. Once they get to Montrice, he intends to part ways with her. He has never taken on an apprentice before. The work he does, he does alone. He can't keep worrying about her recklessness—not to mention her injuries; it will only distract him.

He gathers some herbs, clay, and fresh water from a mountain spring near the cave and brings it back to set Shadow's wound. The salve always worked for him; every scrape and cut his father treated with it healed seemingly overnight. It should do the same for Shadow.

Once he mixes it, with Shadow looking on curiously, he has her sit, leaning against the rocky wall. He kneels next to her.

She winces when he touches her arm this time, proving that it does hurt much more than she admits. He's glad they didn't try to push on through the night. As soon as he applies the paste, she exhales. "Better already, isn't it?" he asks her. She nods, eyes closed.

He wraps her arm with some large gunnera leaves and tells her they'll see how it looks in the morning. She nods again and he takes a seat next to her, leaning his head against the wall. It may be the toll of such a harrowing day, but with the soft moonlight on Shadow's face, he notices how elegant her features are, the length of her neck, the delicate slope of her cheek; suddenly he's not sure how he ever thought she was a boy.

"Are you sure you want to do this?" he blurts out.

She frowns a bit but keeps her eyes closed. "I'm not sure what you mean."

"Accompany me to Montrice." He thinks maybe he can convince

her that leaving is her idea. That would make all of this much easier.

She opens her eyes and turns her head to look at him. "I don't just want to; I have to. Like I told you, the queen herself ordered me to come with you."

"Right, I'm to take you on as my apprentice. It's just . . . I'm not sure you fully comprehend what you're getting yourself into."

"Of course I do," she scoffs.

"Do you? Because it requires quite a sacrifice." He shifts his body weight and adjusts his legs.

She glances at him out of the corner of her eye. "What sacrifice?"

"You say you want to train as an assassin. Well, this is who I am. It's all I have." He stops talking and looks down at his hands. "I don't have a home or a family. When I'm not working at the smithy as a cover for being in Serrone, I spend most of my time on the road, sleeping outside in the wilderness. To get the work done, I must always pretend to be someone else and sometimes I wonder if I'm getting too good at it. Because there are days when I don't even remember who I really am. And yet, I know *what* I am. I am an assassin, a death dealer. I don't know if I would choose this life if it hadn't already been chosen for me."

Shadow is silenced by his sincere tone and sobering words.

"You'd choose to live a life devoted to killing whoever you're ordered to kill?" He thinks back to how she'd stayed his hand when he'd held a dagger to that soldier's throat. "A life where your own could end at any moment?"

"I think that's been established," Shadow says, motioning around her. "I do, I choose this." When her gaze meets his, Cal sees the challenge in her eyes.

"What about . . . marriage? Children?"

She shakes her head and looks away from him, crossing her arms across her chest. She shrugs. "Your father had both, didn't he?"

"And it was a mistake," Cal says. "One I won't repeat. Your mother is part of the Guild. Tell me, how often was she around?"

There's an awkward silence after that. The fire crackles outside the mouth of the cave.

"I don't intend to get married or have children either," Shadow says. "That's exactly what I'm trying to escape."

Cal turns to her, but she refuses to meet his eyes. There's a determination in her expression that he's quickly grown to recognize. "I understand," he says.

They don't talk about it any more after that.

IT ISN'T LONG BEFORE Shadow falls asleep, the events of the day—the past few days—obviously wearing hard on her. Cal spreads his legs out by the dwindling fire. He tries to close his eyes and sleep some himself, but he can't. His mind is racing.

He's worried about what will happen when they get to Montrice. It's not going to be so easy to get rid of Shadow after all. But they need to get there in one piece first. Then he'll make his final decision.

He's about to stand when Shadow's head falls onto his shoulder. He's still for a moment, wondering what to do. He should get out of the way, move her so she can lie down. He pulls his arm from where it's stuck between them and places it around her. This way, he can shift to the side and lower her to the floor slowly. But as he begins to move, he finds he's drawn to her warmth, and a thought occurs to him, unbidden: When was the last time he let someone so close to him? When was the last time he fell asleep next to someone else? And there's Shadow's arm to consider too. Maybe it would be best to leave her be and let her lie on him.

He returns to their original position and adjusts his arm to support her injury. He moves slowly, careful not to startle her. Somehow, he doesn't want her to move away quite yet.

CHAPTER TWENTY-FOUR

Shadow

I WAKE CURLED UP ON the cave floor. I sit up slowly, expecting to be stiff and sore, but I don't actually feel too bad. I slept well, considering the conditions, and Cal's salve is doing wonders.

I find him outside gathering sticks for our fire. I clear my throat. "Good morning."

Cal's shaved his scruff and washed himself in the stream, and looks much healthier than the day before, almost like a new person. "There she is, our lady of perpetual sleep!" he says, smiling broadly.

I bristle at the dig, but recall that I lobbed similar ones at him before. "Why didn't you wake me?"

"There's only so much that salve will do. Sleep will heal that arm faster," Cal says without looking at me. He works on organizing the sticks. "And I was enjoying the peace and quiet."

My nostrils flare. "Well then, I've given you that. Don't you think we should get moving? We've lost a lot of time already and—"

"It will be awfully hard to play the part of a noblewoman with a gaping wound on your arm," he says, motioning toward my injury.

It does look pretty bad when I take the leaves off. Aside from the gash, which runs the entire length of my arm and is dark blue and angry-looking, there are bruises on both arms and my legs, and probably elsewhere as well. I can feel sore spots all over my body. But he doesn't know about those. "How so? I can wear long sleeves."

"There are also scratches on your hands. And a bruise on your cheek. Women of high birth don't walk around like that. How would you explain yourself? There aren't many opportunities for that type of injury when you spend your days getting laced into elaborate costumes and sitting for tea. Everyone would want to know how it happened. They'd want a story. It would draw quite a bit of unnecessary attention."

He's going to lecture me about the behavior of highborn ladies? "What do you know about how noblewomen behave? Besides, I'll just say I fell while riding, or something like that."

"It will draw attention no matter what. Attention we do *not* need. You want to be my apprentice, that's your first lesson: Don't draw attention. Our very existence will cause gossip as it is. If you give them anything else, even the slightest tidbit, they'll run with it. Make up all kinds of stories. Start asking questions." He locks his eyes on mine. "And by the way, I know plenty about how noblewomen behave. I was raised at the queen's court. As I recall, you're the one who grew up on a farm."

I blink a few times. He's right, of course, and I can't argue otherwise. "And what of it? Are you saying I'm too *common* to play the part of a noblewoman?"

Cal puts his hands up. "Nobody could ever say you're common." He laughs at his own remark.

I feel my jaw clench and decide to change the subject. "Maybe we should head out to the spring to catch some fish for breakfast."

"I still have biscuits," Cal says.

"I'll consider one of those stale biscuits once we're on the verge of starvation. I don't even know where those things have been, nor do I want to." He doesn't respond to me. He continues picking up sticks, and sets to work rekindling the fire.

I want to say more, but I know I shouldn't pick a fight. As much as I hate to admit it, I need him until I'm recovered and there may be things I can learn from him. "I'm going to go wash up," I say, turning to walk down to the spring.

It's a short distance before I find a semi-secluded spot where the pool cuts behind some trees. I'm glad for the privacy, but before I can dip a toe in, my aunts' faces appear in my mind, distorted as if they're watching me through glass.

They're using the orb to look for me.

I quickly blink them away and the vision of them scatters. Though they saw me, I doubt they can pinpoint where I am. I don't want them to catch up with me and drag me back home, or worse, to the palace, but I can't help being pleased that they're searching for me. As guilty as I feel for the worry I'm sure I've caused, it's nice to remember they care so much.

When I'm certain they're gone from my mind, I finally strip off my dirty clothes. The shirt is tricky, though, and unfortunately I can't ask Cal to help me. I slip out my good arm first, carefully peeling the garment over my head, then down the injured arm. It's still sore, but the wound has become more pink than blue, so it's healing well. I wrap my arms around myself until I get all the way into the water, just in case Cal is watching.

The water is cold. I shiver but force myself to walk in up to my chest. It's bracing at first, but soon the clear water feels amazing. I lean my head back and soak my hair. I reach up to touch it, expecting to find long hair spread out around my head. I almost forgot it's so short. No soap, so I just scrub my scalp as best I can. That alone makes it feel better.

I put my head back in the water and listen to the muffled sounds below, water running gently in my ears, the soft swaying of aquatic plant life and small trout, turtles zipping through mazes of their vines.

Out of the corner of my eye, I spy Cal to my left, sitting on a rock near the shore, fashioning a long, thin stick into a fishing pole. At first he isn't paying any attention to me—he seems determined to find us a decent meal. But then he glances up and catches my eye. Though we are frozen for a mere moment, the warmth of his gaze washes over me like a wave. He raises an eyebrow, a challenge, and I decide I don't care. Let him look.

I slowly make my way back behind the trees and drag my clothes into the water and scrub those off too, laying them out on a few large rocks. Hopefully they'll dry in the sun while I swim for a while longer.

When I put my damp clothes back on, they're cold, and stick uncomfortably to my thighs and torso. Cal is still fishing; I can hear splashing noises as he wades deeper into the water. I walk back to camp and add wood to the fire so I can crouch close to it to get warm. Cal returns a few minutes later holding up a good catch, several shiny silver fish hooked on his line.

I can't help but smile.

He roasts them over the fire and we eat them with the biscuits from his bag. "They're fine. A little crunchy, but fine." He shrugs.

I hate to admit it, but he's right. The biscuit is awfully hard, but not too bad if I let it dissolve in my mouth a bit before chewing. With the smoky flavor of fresh-caught fish, it's practically a feast.

After we finish eating, Cal picks up a stick and begins using it to trace a circle in the dirt. He stands back and looks at it, then tosses the stick aside. "Grab your sword, Lady Shadow."

"Why?" I ask, suspicious. Even though it's amusing to be called that, I'm not quite sure what to make of the invitation.

"Time for practice," he says.

I laugh. "I don't need practice."

"Aren't you supposed to be my apprentice?"

"Yes, but—"

"Then you need practice. You've been lucky so far, but you can't rely on throwing rocks and hiding in trees."

"You forget you're speaking to a mage. And what about the dire emergency of letting my arm heal?" I say, teasing.

"If you knew anything about sword fighting," Cal says, "you'd know that in a situation like this"—he tosses me a sword—"you're supposed to use the other arm." I catch it in my left hand.

I suppose I asked for this.

"Now, when using your nondominant arm, you want to . . ." He comes at me, swinging the sword. An attempt to take me off guard. But I come right back at him, holding him off. His eyes widen when I do.

"Clever," he says, stepping away. "I thought you hurt your dominant arm."

"I did." I grin.

He narrows his eyes.

"I'm trained to use both." I shrug, though it hurts my arm a bit.

We skirmish for a while, and he teaches me a few moves and counterattacks, and even with my injured arm, I'm able to pick up the lessons. He's a good teacher, surprisingly patient, and takes the time to explain the thinking behind each parry. "Once you have a foundation, it will come naturally," he says.

He proposes a duel to show him what I've learned, and even though I fight my hardest, he disarms me in a flash, and holds two swords at my chin. He is quick, deadly, and merciless. I saw it during our escape, but his arrogance these past few days has distracted me. It's been too easy to forget the man I am dealing with. I can't help but tremble at sword point.

"Hey," he says, drawing them back quickly. "It's just a game."

I take a deep, shaky breath. I thought I was good enough for the Guild, but if this duel is any indication, the truth is maybe I'm not. Maybe I'll never be the fighter that he is.

He throws the swords down. "That's all for today."

His weapon hits the ground and I find I can suddenly breathe again. I've come back to myself. "Okay. Your turn."

"My turn? For what?"

"Lessons. If we're going to be posing as aristocrats from Argonia, then you have to learn how to behave at a royal court."

"As I've already explained, Lady Shadow, I've spent a lot of time at court. I'm already well-versed in the art of bowing and keeping my mouth shut."

"Ha! But have you read *Crumpets and Cravats*?"

"Sorry, no, my missions for the queen don't leave much time for novels."

"Well, when you're an aristocrat, nobody expects you to keep your mouth shut. Quite the opposite. The more interesting you are, the more they'll like you. But the art of communication is about so much more than talking. For example: What does it mean when someone bows to you, but they only bend at the waist?" All those lessons with Missus Kingstone are turning out to be useful after all.

"Easy. You outrank them but you're only titled, not a royal."

He's right. "That was just to get you warmed up. How about . . . ? Oh, I know. You're invited to a masked ball. A woman—a countess, let's say—is standing across from you. She flicks her fan open, twice, then puts it away. What does that mean?"

"What does that mean?" he echoes. He thinks for a moment and then shrugs. "That she has no use for her fan."

"It means she's irritated with your presence and wants you to go away." I want to enjoy my victory, but the smile on his face is perplexing.

"Excellent!" he says, and begins to laugh.

I rap his knuckles, as learning the complicated language of a woman's fan is a serious endeavor. "Here's another. I'll keep it simple. Same woman. But this time, she takes out her fan, flicks it open once, fans herself briefly, then closes it in her right hand."

"She's saying, 'Bring me a glass of water, peasant.'"

"No, of course not! That's two flicks and a twist."

"You don't say!"

Now it's my turn to laugh. "I was joking!"

He blinks.

"Actually it means she's open to conducting an affair with you." I wiggle my eyebrows for comic effect. "Probably happens to you often."

"So you admit you find me handsome, then?" He smiles, and the sun hits his dark eyes so I see there are gold flecks in them. He knows how handsome he is; he must. It is one of the qualities that make him so good at his trade. No one could suspect that someone so handsome would also be so merciless.

I turn to put away the remains of our meal so he won't see me blushing. "No, of course not. I mean, not that you aren't. I'm sure a lot of people think so."

"Do they now," he says. I can feel him smirking.

"You're pretty fair yourself," he says as he walks away. I pretend I didn't hear, but I'm smiling anyway.

CAL'S HERBAL PASTE IS like magic on my arm—it's almost back to normal in a single day—but we decide to spend one last night before continuing our journey. It's safe here, and we both need the rest. We use the morning to continue our sword-fighting lessons, and in the afternoon we catch a few more fish. Cal goes off to bathe at the spring while I stay back at camp and prepare our meal. He returns with his hair wet and his skin glowing, and I can only imagine how the courtiers will swoon when he arrives at the court of Montrice.

Today he hasn't been half as irritating, which I find rather irritating.

Once it's dark, I curl up near the fire, drowsy and content, wishing we could spend a few more days here just like this, with nothing to worry about but training and catching fish.

Cal settles in across from me, his gaze trained on the fire. I haven't had a chance to study him like this before, without worrying about being caught staring. He has a small scar near his left eyebrow, and a dimple in his right cheek that only appears when he smiles.

We watch the fire in silence, the two of us sprawled in our make-shift beds of leaves, next to each other. "Do you know any stories?" he asks. The expression on his face is so earnest, I know he can't be teasing me.

"Do I know any stories," I repeat, and pull my knees to my chest. My mind begins to wander, and before I know it, I'm telling him the story of Renovia, the one my aunts used to tell me at bedtime, when we were warm and safe in our cottage in the Honey Glade. It's their favorite story, about the mage Omin and a queen and the love between them that established the ancient kingdom of Avantine, glorious and grand and full of magic and light.

I let myself get lost in the story, imagining my aunts gathered around me in bed. They seemed so big when I was so little and the way they spun this tale always left me in awe. At the end of it, Cal looks up at me. He is studying me the way I had studied him. "I know that story too," he says. "You tell it well."

Then without saying another word, he lies back and turns away so I can no longer see his face.

"Good night," I say softly.

A moment passes before he responds. "Good night."

CHAPTER TWENTY-FIVE

Shadow

WHEN I OPEN MY EYES in the morning, I find myself curled up against Cal, my head on his chest while his arm is wrapped around my shoulder. I must have rolled over in my sleep. I don't move for a moment; he's so incredibly warm, and I'm so comfortable. Eventually I try to shift away without waking him, but when I look up at his face I see that his eyes are open. How long has he been awake, knowing I was in his arms? He doesn't appear to be perturbed by the situation. The thought bristles—perhaps he assumes I am just like any lady who waves her fan at him. Or maybe he was just being kind. It is very cold on the rocky cave floor.

"Look," he says, and motions to his hand on my arm. His voice is as warm as the rest of him, still deep and scratchy from sleep.

"What is it?" I ask, looking down.

"The wound is nearly gone," he says, turning it over. He runs his finger down the length of my arm where it was sliced open when I fell. His touch is so gentle that it sends shivers all over my skin.

We look at the wound together. There's still a pink line where the cut was, but it's almost completely healed over, and the bruises have faded away as well. "You were right," I say. "Your father's salve is miraculous. It's even better than Aunt Mesha's. Don't tell her I said so."

"Never," Cal says, raising his hand as if he's swearing an oath.

"I suppose that means we're ready to move on now," I say, getting up from his embrace. I wrap my arms around myself, but they are not even half as warm as his.

He doesn't seem to notice my absence; he's already intent on what lies ahead. "Yes, breakfast first and then we can discuss what to do once we get into Montrice."

Fish was never my favorite, but somehow it has become one. Freshly caught as before, it is divine, even without seasoning. We eat five between the two of us, barely speaking until we've consumed every last morsel.

Cal works a stick between his teeth after eating. "We need a plan. The problem is, I don't know exactly what I'm planning for, so we will have to change course as we come upon obstacles."

I nod, thinking of the forged work order and how I chopped my hair off before running away from home. *Running away from home*—that's exactly what I did, so of course they used the orb to try to find me, and they cast a locus right away, no doubt. Except that spell couldn't reach as far as Deersia, let alone beyond it. *Has Ma been informed of my disappearance?* I wonder. If only I could communicate with them somehow, let them know I am safe. After all, if I am with Caledon Holt, it's probably the safest place to be in all the kingdoms.

"I've only been to Montrice once, and that was some time ago. The people are friendly enough, but false words mask true intentions. Don't forget that."

I assure him that I'm naturally distrustful and he smiles once more, his dimple winking at me. I try not to look directly at his face; it's too distracting. I remember what he told me earlier, that the queen believes someone in Montrice—someone powerful—is working with the Aphrasians to overthrow the Renovian monarchy.

"What I don't understand is how the grand prince was an Aphrasian. He was so devoted to the royal family," I say.

"A loyal façade hides the worst kind of traitor," Cal says.

I shift uncomfortably. "And I thought we were at peace with Montrice."

"Well, it has been about eighteen years since they last tried to assassinate the queen. I suppose that means we're due for another conflict."

"I'll never understand that. Why can't people be satisfied with peace? It's as if they do everything possible to avoid harmony between the kingdoms." The thought of another war with Montrice infuriates me. Such a useless loss of life. Innocent people used as pawns to carry out the whims of the aristocracy.

"You know that and I know that, but we aren't the ones who benefit from war. We're the ones who suffer so that others gain," Cal says darkly.

"Why do what you do, then? Why work for the crown at all? You have the smithy. Couldn't you do that instead of being in the queen's service?"

Cal doesn't speak. Then he sighs and rubs his face with his hands. "Because I have to."

I can tell he has more to say, so I let him talk.

"My father made a blood vow to the queen. But he died before it was satisfied. So it passed on to me. Now I must satisfy it." A blood vow? I've only heard of them from the old tales my aunts read to me. It seems so . . . barbaric. Evil even. The blood in my veins runs cold at the thought.

"Why did he do that? What do you have to do?" I think of the path my mother and aunts set for me. I veered off it on my own, with no consequence so far. But a blood vow—if the stories are right, then Cal's very life has barely been his own.

"After the Battle of Baer, the queen fell apart. She wouldn't govern. She wouldn't leave her rooms. She wouldn't even lower the palace flag to confirm the king's death. My father was there to protect her, but he couldn't do that for long if she wasn't able to perform the most basic duties. The kingdom would look weak, it would be invaded, and that would be the end of us. There'd already been an attempt on the queen's life soon after her pregnancy with Princess Lilac was announced, which sparked the Aphrasian Rebellion in the first place.

"The only way he could rouse her from her grief was by promising her the Deian Scrolls. She insisted on a blood vow, so he made it. He was foolish and shortsighted, I guess, but the kingdom was on the verge of collapse. One victorious battle meant nothing if the queen let it all fall to pieces. He intended to return the Deian Scrolls to her long before I came of age, but that never happened. So now I must."

"And if you don't?" I ask, my heart in my throat.

"If I don't, it passes on to my children and theirs . . . until it is finally done. Until the scrolls are returned to their rightful place. But I refuse to pass it down to my children. I will have no children." His jaw is set and his eyes are stormy.

"You can't abandon the vow?"

At that, a rueful smile. "A blood vow is deep magic. There is no escape from it. Not that I haven't tried."

Of course he has. I would. "Is that what you were doing in Baer

Abbey that day?" It suddenly dawns on me that we've never spoken of the first time we met.

He nods. "I thought there might be a chance they were hidden there, that my father had missed something. And what were *you* doing at Baer that day?"

"Nothing, really. I was exploring, I guess."

"Did the queen send you? Because I wasn't even supposed to be there."

"No. Queen Lilianna did not send me to Baer. The truth is, I didn't mean to be there at all." Yet something had pulled me to the ruined castle, something deep in the earth had led me there. The visions choose the seer; that is what my aunts taught me.

"So, you were out for a walk and just happened to end up there."

"Pretty much, not that it matters now." I don't appreciate his skepticism, but the truth is, I did lie to him to get where I am right now. "What matters is what happens next."

"Next is Montrice. We need to find a place to stay, and buy new clothes. If anyone asks, we're brother and sister. Taverns are typically the best places to find information, particularly when you want to know who the criminals are. Or better yet, who the criminals work for."

"And if this discovery leads all the way up to King Hansen?" I ask.

"Then he will be taken care of," Cal says softly.

I feel chills, and am suddenly nauseous with fear. Cal will protect Renovia at all costs. There is nothing he will not do for his kingdom when the time comes. Without fear and without regret.

He is the Queen's Assassin. And no one is safe from his blade.

A Comprehensive History of Avantine

On the Origins of Omin of Oylahn

LONG AGO, WHEN ALL THE *kingdoms of Avantine were one, the region of Renovia was a backwater, a swampland, a hopeless swath of fallow earth sparsely populated in most places and dominated by warring clans in others. The oldest child of the oldest child of the oldest family in the land was unlucky enough to lead the chaos, for however long they could until they were ousted—either by murder or fatigue— and replaced by the next oldest child in line, and so on. Clan leaders bribed or blackmailed the monarch in return for favor and to maintain control over their own territories.*

However, Avantine's new queen, Alphonia, only thirteen years old, wasn't satisfied with the struggling realm she inherited, especially since surrounding kingdoms had begun taking advantage of Renovia's weaknesses and invading its outlying communities.

Alphonia may have been a child, yet she was older than her sister had been when she was crowned at age ten but died soon after from consumption, and both were older at accession than their father had been before them, though he had lived to the ripe old age of twenty. And thirteen years, then as now, was old enough to know her own mind— and young enough not to know that maybe she really didn't.

So Alphonia, at just the right age and station to insist on having things exactly as she wanted them, and fortunate enough to possess the right temperament for the task, called for the smartest, wisest, strongest, and wittiest to join her at court.

They arrived in droves: aristocrats, beggars, traders, thieves, alchemists, farmers, lutists, bakers, mapmakers, and all others you can imagine. From these the girl queen chose the best of the best of each, then gathered them together at a feast. She told the chosen that they were the founding members of the new court of Avantine, and gave them rooms in the castle.

Quite pleased with herself, she then called for women from each clan, and gathered them together for a feast of their own. She told them about her sister, whom she missed very much, and her parents, whom she barely knew at all, and asked them about their loved ones. No one had ever asked them this before, so they didn't know what to say, because killing and being killed was the way it was and always would be.

"It doesn't have to be this way," the girl queen said. "Instead of fighting one another and scrambling for the leftover odds and ends, we can band together and thrive."

The clan mothers doubted the new queen, and went back to their lands, and back to the way things had always been.

Except one thing had changed. They couldn't stop thinking about what the queen said. They had been introduced to the idea of something different, and there is no putting back an idea.

Meanwhile, Queen Alphonia had the best of the best at her disposal and not the faintest idea what to do with them after that.

"Our talents are wasted here," they said. "If something doesn't happen soon, we're going home."

The girl queen wasn't sure what to do. It was her first official crisis as sovereign, and she had no one trustworthy to advise her.

She was ready to give up. But before Queen Alphonia could dismiss the best of the best from her palace, there was a booming knock on the castle door.

At the door stood the strangest, most beautiful being Alphonia had ever seen, a silver-haired mage with violet eyes, neither female nor male, but both, as all the most powerful mages are. They wore a long white tunic and an emerald gem around their neck.

"I am Omin of Oylahn," the mage said. "I heard you called for the best."

"I did," said the queen. "But I'm afraid that time has passed."

"No," Omin said. "The time has not even begun, because the time was not right, and now that I am here, it is."

And so it was that magic came to Avantine.

It is said that mages came from the Oylahn, a land beyond the Montrician Mountains, an impassable landscape no Avantinian had ever crossed; however, the girl queen never asked of Omin's origins, or if she did, that knowledge was never recorded.

The women of the clans soon returned and agreed that they were tired of the way things were. Omin trained the group Alphonia had assembled and taught them the ways of Deia, which were already ancient even in the ancient time. As the years wore on, the Deian order served the kingdom well. The greatest scribes collected the wisdom of Omin and Alphonia and spent years handwriting the Sacred Texts of Deia, and the greatest artists illustrated them, and the greatest philosophers studied them, and the greatest teachers taught them, and the greatest students learned them.

In time the queen and Omin married, and had a daughter, and that daughter was named Dellafiore, and Dellafiore had a son, and that son took his mother's name in her honor, as the first of their new house.

Thus began the story of the Dellafiore dynasty.

— II —

MONTRICE

CHAPTER TWENTY-SIX

Caledon

BEYOND THE MOUNTAINS, MONT, THE capital city of the Kingdom of Montrice, rises to greet them. In the sun's glare the city's harsh gray structures look like part of the natural landscape, jutting up aggressively behind an intimidating stone wall that stretches miles in each direction. But as they ride closer, they can see the carved-out details in the buildings, deep-set windows, arrow loops and battlements on every roof in case of attack.

"Not very welcoming, is it?" Shadow says.

Cal nods. "Mont is a city accustomed to war." Most windows that he can see, especially near the edges of the city, are gated with iron bars—decorative, but also functional. Armed guards patrol the perimeter, on horseback and on foot. A wide gated entrance at the north side of the city, usually open, is shut tight. Cal frowns. They're not going to be able to walk right in after all.

"What should we do? Find another way in?"

"No," Cal says. "Stealth is too risky at the moment."

Shadow looks down at her clothes and then at Cal. She's still wearing her stable-hand uniform, except the shirt no longer has sleeves thanks to the incident with the Aphrasians, and Cal has been wearing the same clothes since he left to see the queen. They have been washed in the river, but are ragged and worn from their journey out of Deersia and into the black woods. "Except we don't look like we belong here. We look like nothing but trouble."

"We look as well as we are going to look," says Cal.

"Do I still look like a boy?" she asks.

He shakes his head emphatically. "No one would mistake you as male. Your deception was successful at Deersia only because people see what they expect to see."

They approach the gate. A man stands inside the guard tower. Cal clears his throat. "Gates were open last time I was here," Cal says to him, using the neutral dialect of Avantine.

The man replies, "Times have changed, especially concerning Renovians. Beware of them, shady folk."

Cal nods. "Horrible city, Serrone, full of barbarians," he says.

"From where do you hail?"

"My sister and I are from Argonia," he tells the guard. "Just passing through Mont on the way to our grandfather's estate in Stavin."

The guard narrows his eyes.

"Of course, we have coin to spare," adds Cal, and Shadow takes her cue to bring out the pouch full of gold.

"Much coin," Shadow says, smiling slyly.

THEIR PASSAGE INTO THE city secured, they ride into town. People everywhere stop to stare at them, even pausing mid-conversation to watch them go by. Their dirty, plain clothes mark them as poor or foreign or both, especially compared with the elaborate dress around them. Behind Mont's impenetrable fortress walls lies a city of vanity and finery.

Mont's women, and some of the men, wear dramatic, garish makeup and huge hooped gowns of ornately embroidered fabrics with headdresses so large that the streets feel even more crowded than they already are. It's difficult to see around them, even on horseback. One woman's headdress is so big that it requires wire supports from her shoulders. The men and women wear similar fabrics, but rather than wide, swishing gowns, most of the men have long, narrow tunics over tight pants and heavy boots. Over their tunics, they wear chest armor, and all are carrying weapons, as if they're ready to go into battle at any moment. Cal notices that even the women in the grandest gowns have daggers sheathed at their hips as well. The Montricians have become far more fearful since he was here last, though that was some time ago—two years? And he was only in the city a day or two, picking up a message from one of the queen's operatives.

"Try not to stare; it's considered rude," Shadow says out the side of her mouth. "You really should read *Crumpets and Cravats*."

He's about to retort when he realizes she's only teasing him.

They pass a marketplace, where vendors are selling imported produce at shockingly high prices. In the town square, skinny, barefoot children in linen shifts throw copper coins into a huge fountain. An old man sits hunched on the edge of it. A ten-foot-tall statue looms over them. "King Hansen himself." The man nods when he sees them staring.

The statue depicts a generically handsome young man wearing a crown and fur-lined royal cape, one arm raising a sword, the other holding a shield. He looks about the same age as Cal, nineteen or so.

"It's good luck to make offerings to him," the old man adds, motioning to the children. Shadow scrunches her nose in disapproval. Cal doesn't like it either. There's something . . . lacking about this place. Shallow. Elaborate statues celebrate an unaccomplished young king while children use what little coin they have gambling on fountain wishes. Coin that will surely end up in the king's pocket.

"You're not from here, I take it," the old man says.

"No, sir, we're looking for an inn," Cal says. "Do you know where we can find one?" Shadow hands the man a silver coin.

"Follow me." He gets up slowly, straightening out his back. Cal can almost hear it creaking and cracking. The man begins walking on the road, shuffling his feet.

"May I offer you my horse?" Cal asks. The old man waves him off.

He leads them a few streets away, stopping in front of a two-story wood-and-brick building in a more modest neighborhood. The sign out front reads: STARLIGHT INN, LINDEN GARBANKLE, PROPRIETOR.

They dismount on the side, where there are low-walled stalls to keep the horses overnight. The old man holds out his hand as if to shake Cal's. "Well. I suppose this is where I leave you."

"We appreciate it," Cal says. The old man reaches out and grabs his forearm to shake it.

"Don't worry about a thing," he says. He looks pointedly at their clothing. "Garbankle'll take good care of you. Best place in all Montrice for a couple of ruffians to stay undetected."

"Not sure what you mean," Shadow says. "We're—"

"Garbankle has no love for the authorities but a great love of money, you understand? I know you'll think of a way to improve diplomatic relations between our two fine kingdoms."

Cal shakes his head, his courtly Argonian accent impeccable. "But I told you, we're not—"

"Bah!" He waves his hand at him. "I been around long enough to know a crook when I see one. And you gave me a Renovian coin." He winks.

Shadow stammers, trying to protest, but the old man says, "Don't worry about me. I lose no sleep over law and order. The crown, it comes and goes. Or the one wearin' it does." He begins shuffling away.

"Can I give you a ride back to . . . ?" Back to the fountain? Home? Cal doesn't know what to say, but he wants to offer the man some kindness in return for his aid. "A ride back?"

The old man just waves his hand behind him again. A few seconds later, he rounds the corner, out of sight.

They tie up their horses and prepare to enter the inn. If Shadow is nervous, she hides it.

"Let's get our story in order," Cal says.

"I know what to do," Shadow says. "Follow my lead." Without waiting for him to respond, she walks inside.

"So sorry about that, Mister Garbunkle . . . erm, -bankle. Don't mind my brother. If he seems out of sorts, it's only that we're dreadfully road-weary! My brother can't control his temper, that boy! Again, my apologies. I agree you said nothing wrong whatsoever— I would've assumed the very same if I saw two people like us walk into my place of business." Shadow smiles widely at the suspicious-looking innkeeper, who leans over the bar to take a better look at them.

Garbankle squints at her, but doesn't respond.

Shadow continues. "You see, we've come all the way from Argonia. Dressed as beggars, as you can tell, to repel thieves. As one does. It was so dire out there, I was even forced to cut my hair to disguise myself. What a trial *that* has been! We're simply traveling through Mont on our way to Stavin, thought we might pay a visit to the vizier while we're here, if possible, pay our respects . . ."

Cal nudges her. She realizes her mistake immediately. Why did she say "pay our respects"? To whom would they do that? She's lost hold of her story.

"Pay our respects to the vizier's father. Who . . . knew our grandfather. You see, we've inherited my grandfather's estate, so we must hurry on to Stavin. Backley Hold. Is what it's called. The house, that is. I assume you know it?"

Cal closes his eyes. She's repeating the plot of an old Renovian fable. He hopes the man doesn't know it.

The innkeeper shakes his head from behind the weathered wood counter. He opens his mouth as if to speak, but Shadow just continues talking. "Well now. That's quite surprising. It's home to one of the largest vineyards in the triangular kingdoms. Maybe you'll recognize our name, instead?" She glances to a vase of white lilies on the counter. "Mine is Lady Lily . . . I mean Lady Lila Holton. This is my brother, Lord Callum." She blinks, waiting.

Cal gives the man a curt bow and then sticks his nose in the air, trying to look haughty. The innkeeper shakes his head again. Shadow looks to Cal and follows his lead, lifting her nose a little higher in the air. "Hmm, where was I? Oh yes. The, um, Holtons, our family, are always happy to pay our bill in advance. In fact, we insist upon it." She roots around in her money pouch and pulls out a gold coin. "I imagine such a fine establishment charges . . . fifty a night for room and board and stabling of our two fine horses? We only carry Renovian currency, as we just came from there. But this should cover two. And a half. Please, keep the half. On *be-half* of the Holtons!"

Cal almost chokes. *Fifty a night? For this? More like fifty a month, at best!*

"Imagine that, got it right on the first try!" the innkeeper says, snatching the coin from her hand. "You do know your room and board. Must be a frequent traveler."

She smiles politely. "Mm-hmm."

"Lucky for you I got one room I save just for special noble guests like yourselves. You and your, uh, brother here can take room seven. I'll go ahead and show you up." He grabs a key from the wall behind the counter and walks ahead of them. Shadow turns to Cal and flashes him a self-satisfied smile. He won't deny that she's a decent storyteller, but he also knows the innkeeper never would've bought that ridiculous yarn if she hadn't grossly overpaid him.

They follow him up a few well-worn stairs and down a dusty hallway. There are no sounds from any of the other rooms. They must be the only guests.

He stops in front of a door. "As you two are flesh and blood, there won't be any impropriety, right?" he says, sticking the key in the lock.

"Well, I never!" Shadow says, feigning outrage.

"You'd be surprised," the innkeeper says. "Or maybe you wouldn't." The door swings open. "Make yourselves at home," he says, before handing the key over to Cal and shuffling back down the hall toward the front desk. On his way he calls over his shoulder: "Washtub's out back."

Inside the room there's a small round table with one chair and a single bed. Cal wipes his hand across the table and leaves a long smear in the dust. Shadow sticks her head out the door into the hallway and calls out, "Excuse me, Mister Gorfinkle. I believe there's been a mistake."

"No mistake," he yells back over his shoulder. "Take it or leave it."

She shuts the door. "I gave him fifty a night for this?"

"I couldn't stop you." Cal sighs. He looks out the dirty window. Their view is the gray brick wall of the building next door. "Hopefully we won't be here long. And you're not paying for the room so much as his silence."

"Right," Shadow says. She sits down on the bed, then falls back. "A real bed. A hard one, but a real one, at least."

"No time for a nap. We have things to do."

"Yes. We should inquire about proper attire for Lord and Lady Holton of—what did I say it was called?"

"Backley Hold."

"Backley Hold! Is there a quill around here? I should write it down."

"I'll remember for you," he says, and holds out his hand for her, a true gentleman.

She takes it. His hand is warm in hers.

He bows to her. "Shall we, my lady?"

"I believe we shall," she says.

BY THAT EVENING LADY Lila and Lord Callum are outfitted in simple, yet far more suitable, clothes whipped up by Mont's finest—and most bribable—tailor. Anything can be bought in this city, for the right price. And somehow Shadow's purse seems to be bottomless.

Cal even made an appointment with the barber next door. He's already bathed and dressed in a sharp new black suit, in the Montrician style, of course, when Shadow comes out of the back room of the shop where a seamstress was helping her into a new gown.

He doesn't look up from the broadside he's been reading. He's discovered that political treatises are illegal in Montrice, so clever satirists use fictional characters to stand in for King Hansen and his council. Cal's totally absorbed in the tale, about a greedy, spoiled little boy who takes whatever he wants from anybody he wants, when Shadow clears her throat to get his attention.

A beautiful figure is standing a few feet in front of him. For a moment he can't quite place her or where he is. Then Shadow smiles and holds out the skirt of her new dress. "What do you think?" The sound of her voice takes him back to himself.

He looks at her as if for the first time.

The seamstress has pulled her growing hair up off her face with a thick band, decorated with glittery leaves and vines around the top of her head. The gown is a pale greenish-blue, with iridescent layers flowing from a fitted empire bodice, and covered in pale gold-and-silver floral embroidery.

"Just a little something I had lying around," the seamstress says. "It was just waiting to be fitted to the right person." She smiles and stands back to admire her work. Then glances disapprovingly at the choppy hair around Shadow's ears. "The wig will be ready tomorrow."

Cal blinks a few times. He hardly thinks a wig is necessary; she looks perfect exactly the way she is. He tries to find the right words but can't. Finally he manages: "I think . . . I believe Lady Lila is going to be quite popular."

Shadow waves him off. "Don't be silly."

There's an awkward moment until the seamstress breaks the silence by clearing her throat and announcing, "We accept coin of all realms."

Each of them receives a set of day clothes and evening wear, which Shadow pays for with the coins in her pouch. Their old clothes are thrown in the burn pile out back. They are too ragged to save, though Cal feels a bit melancholy about it. They're all he has left of home, and he had rather grown accustomed to Shadow in her shirt and breeches.

WHEN THEY RETURN TO the inn, Garbankle is still leaning behind the front desk. He's tearing up a notice about new Montrician tax codes. "I'll be sure to let the vizier know distinguished guests are in town," he says as they pass by. They smile at each other.

In their tiny room, Caledon and Shadow stand around uncomfortably, one of them on each side of a double bed that barely looks big enough for one. Somehow, being under a roof and inside four walls feels quite different from sleeping near each other in the cave. "I'll take the floor," Cal says.

"That's not fair to you," Shadow says. She clasps her hands in front of her and begins to fidget with her fingers.

"It's not a problem," Cal insists, despite the fact that he was secretly thrilled at the idea of not sleeping on a cold, hard floor. "I don't want you to be uncomfortable. You've just recovered from a rather serious injury, remember?" he adds. "And I'm fine there. I'm used to it."

But she shakes her head. "We've both slept on that frozen ground; you are as tired as I am. We will share the bed," she says with a finality that brooks no disagreement.

Cal shrugs and points to a screen in the corner. "You can change. I'll step out of the room if you like."

Shadow gathers up the bottom of her gown and clomps over to the changing screen. "The seamstress made me quite a matronly night shift, so there is no need."

While she's taking off her dress, Cal removes his boots and slides under the covers. He tries to keep his eyes on the wall, but somehow, he can't help glancing to the corner of the room where Shadow is changing. He can see her silhouette through the screen and looks away, abashed. He remembers seeing her walking out of the spring in all her glorious form. She had not been embarrassed to be seen then, and he'd admired her spirit. It was not all he'd admired, of course, but he was a gentleman.

"So tomorrow," she says, interrupting his thoughts. "The vizier." She steps out from behind the screen and the shift is as matronly as promised, but made of linen so fine as to make everything underneath it visible even in the low light.

Cal coughs and averts his eyes once more, trying to find a safe space for them to land. He has been alone for so long, he had forgotten how much he enjoyed female company. But while there had been many girls in Cal's past, he's never met one like her. The vizier, right, they were talking about the vizier.

"The vizier is our key to the palace," Cal says after he has composed himself.

Shadow climbs onto the other side of the bed. He feels her leg brush his as she slips between the covers, and senses the slight pressure from it in every part of his being. He is a fool who should have slept on the floor.

"Can we discuss it in the morning?" she asks, voice groggy as she turns to the wall.

"As you wish."

She doesn't move again, so he assumes she drifted off to sleep. After the day they've had, she must have been exhausted. Cal is too, but the knowledge that Shadow is so terribly within reach gnaws at him, pushing sleep farther away with each passing moment.

Shadow of Nir, from the Honey Glade, a beekeeper, a maiden of the farm.

He remembers how she nestled up to him in the dark cavern, and how she didn't move away when she awoke to find them so entwined. He wishes they were back there a moment, huddling for warmth, instead of in a cozy room with so much air between them.

At last, after a very long while, he falls asleep.

❦

CHAPTER TWENTY-SEVEN

Shadow

LINDEN GARBANKLE KEEPS HIS WORD. The following afternoon Cal—or should I say *Lord Callum*—and I are summoned to tea at the vizier's grand town house in the city.

We don our new finery and borrow the innkeeper's carriage to take us to the side of town where the nobles live. The carriage is close quarters, and my wig, a towering concoction of curls, is heavy on my head, so wide that it practically brushes Cal's cheek. The entire journey I'm hyperaware of every inch between us, every jolt of his arm against mine.

Last night, in his sleep, Cal rolled over from his side to mine, and his arm draped itself around my waist, his legs over mine, his nose in my hair, his chin resting on my neck. I felt his warm breath on my cheek, but instead of moving away, I burrowed even closer to him, my back against his chest, my hand on his arm, pulling him closer. In answer he tightened his embrace, so that we lay cleaved to each other, the hot center of him against my body.

When I shifted against him, I swear he moaned a little.

I didn't want him to wake up. I didn't want him to realize what he was doing, or what was happening between us. I didn't want him not to want this.

What am I doing? He is the Queen's Assassin and yoked to a blood vow. He's sworn never to have a family, never to have children. Just a few days ago I thought he was the most arrogant, irritating boy ever to live.

I must find a place in the Guild, and I cannot allow anything—even him—to distract me. If I am to be a spy and an assassin, I cannot have emotional attachments.

When we woke up, we were huddled on opposite sides of the bed. So far it's been an uncomfortable morning, and while nothing has been said about last night, it feels as if something has shifted between us. There's a new shyness, as if we hadn't just survived a harrowing prison escape together and spent days camping in the woods.

He's been quiet all day, and when my arm falls on his, he practically flinches. Perhaps last night was just my imagination. Perhaps nothing happened between us, and I am merely delusional.

"What?" he asks, sounding annoyed.

"What?"

"You keep staring at me; do I have dirt on my face?" he asks.

I shake my head. The tailor made him a midnight-blue Montrician-style day suit, more fitted than what I'm used to seeing men wear in Renovia, with leather shoes rather than tall boots. The jacket is long in the back, shorter in the front, and the vest has similar gold-and-silver embroidery to my gown. He's had a closer shave, so I can see his face even more clearly, that strong jawline and chiseled nose, knife-sharp cheekbones. He's had a haircut too—thankfully they didn't take it all off, but they did clean it up so that it falls perfectly around his eyes. Besides the obvious physical changes, he seems different somehow, distant and more detached.

It's like a handsome stranger is suddenly sharing my space.

I try to keep my attention focused out the carriage window. There's a clear dividing line where the struggling areas, with their modest dwellings, become stately manor houses. The homes' iron gates and barred windows make me think of the children at the fountain, giving money that should have been for food toward the vain hope of luck instead.

A tall footman opens the door before we even finish our approach up the steps, then whisks us into a small parlor off the main hall. He offers us large cushioned chairs and then disappears into the house to inform his master that we've arrived.

The walls are lined with animal heads—hunting trophies, which represent species from many different lands: boar, bears, foxes, a type of striped horse, and a scimitar-toothed jaguar like the one that almost took my life. A narwhal horn. A giant rare pink sea star, easily three feet wide. Strange fish—antennae-like eyes and rainbow scales—mounted on plaques. Everywhere I look I find more: a small winged rodent posed under a glass dome sits on a shelf; a framed montage of butterflies hangs near the window.

I already don't like this vizier, this collector of dead things.

The door flies open. A short, bald man strolls in, followed by the footman, who closes the door. The footman remains by the entrance, his arms clasped behind him, awaiting further instruction.

The vizier is draped in furs—so many furs that I become confused trying to count them. At least two of them match the fur of the heads on the wall. In fact, one of them still has a head *on* it. A mink, I believe. I try not to think about that. Or look at it.

He reaches up to shake Cal's hand. I notice he wears amber rings on almost every finger. The largest one, on his left thumb, has a petrified wasp suspended in it.

I hate wasps. Once a swarm of them invaded our beehives and wiped out most of the colonies. They are predators masquerading as something they're not—something friendly.

Cal nods his head and presents himself. "Grand Vizier," he says. "A pleasure to make your acquaintance."

"Lord Holton," says the vizier, shaking Cal's hand. "The pleasure is all mine."

He offers his hand out to me—"This must be the lovely Lady Lila!"—and I offer mine in return, but he doesn't shake it, he pulls me toward him and kisses me on each cheek—with sloppy, wet lips. He smells like mothballs and rose water. I try not to gag. His entire persona is overwhelming. Something about him puts all my senses on alert—and rather than just experiencing the underlying sounds and feelings around me, I get the sensation of something being drawn out of *me*. As if he's inspecting me. Sizing me up. When he backs away, I have to force myself not to wipe my face. The last thing I want to do is offend him. But I don't have to be his friend; I don't even have to see him again. I just need to stomach him long enough to get access to the king's courtiers.

"Imagine my surprise. We have so few visitors in Montrice," he says. "And even fewer who've journeyed all the way from Argonia." His voice is friendly, but I sense the challenge behind it. He wants to know what we're doing here; if we're even who we say we are.

"We're only passing through," I explain. "On our way to see to our grandfather's estate in Stavin."

"Yes. So I've heard. An inheritance, is it?" He gestures for us to sit.

We take the chairs offered to us previously; he sits on a larger one across from us. He uses a little step to climb onto it. Once settled, he's sitting higher than we are. He places his hands on the armrests as if trying to look regal. He stretches out his stubby fingers and begins tapping them against the wood. I get the feeling he's trying to draw attention to his rings.

"Our grandfather's estate." I keep my answers short. I don't want to encourage too much prying, or draw the conversation out any longer than it needs to be.

"Backley Hold," Cal adds. "Have you heard of it?"

"Hmm . . . yes, yes, of course I have. In fact, I believe I attended a hunting party there in my youth. Lovely place. So sorry to hear about the elder Lord . . ." He waves his hand around in circles, as if he's trying to conjure up the name.

"Holton," Cal and I say at the same time.

"Lord Holton, yes. Fine fellow. It's been quite a while since I've seen him, so he wouldn't have remembered me anyway, you know. Tell me, what favor do you require?"

Both of us are taken aback by his sudden bluntness. "Favor?" I say. The footman opens the door. A maid walks in carrying a silver tray. She sets it down on the table next to the vizier, curtsies, and leaves. The footman closes the door and returns to his position.

"Yes, of course. I assume you're here for that reason. Tea?"

We don't respond, but he places a porcelain teacup and saucer in front of each of us anyway. Neither of us moves to pick it up. The vizier takes a sip of his, places the cup back on the saucer—it spills a little—then turns his attention back to us. He folds his hands in his lap and waits.

"No favor," says Cal. "But perhaps an introduction."

"To court?" asks the vizier, looking skeptical.

Cal nods.

I lean forward. "It's just that we've brought a gift for King Hansen, if he'll do us the honor of an audience." I reach into the hidden pocket of my skirt and pull out the diamond ring with the large Argonian emerald in its center that I have been carrying for so long. I thought it might be useful on my journey.

Out of the corner of my eye, I can see Cal looking at the ring, then at me, and then at the ring. I hadn't mentioned it and I'm not looking forward to the questions I know are coming. I didn't tell him about it because I hadn't intended to use it until right at this moment. I can tell that expensive, shiny gifts are the type of thing that impresses the vizier and earns his favor.

The vizier's eyes widen. He sits up and leans forward to get a close look at the ring. "Well, well. How wonderful. A beautiful piece."

"I've brought a little something for you as well, if you'll accept," I say. I pull the smaller, slightly less valuable diamond-and-emerald ring out of the pouch and hand it to him. "Argonian mined and set, of course."

"Of course, of course," he says, putting it on his pinkie finger. It only fits halfway. He holds up his squat little hand to admire it in the late-afternoon light shining from the bay window. "It'd be my honor to speak with King Hansen on your behalf."

There's another knock on the door. The footman opens it, and another steps inside. He approaches the vizier, bends down, and whispers something in his ear.

He nods at the footman before turning back to us. "Will you please excuse me?" he asks. He scoots off the chair and hops to the ground, then leaves the room, followed by the footman. The door shuts behind them, leaving Cal and me alone in the creepy room.

"I don't like him," I tell Cal.

"We're not here to like him," Cal says, his expression unreadable. "We're here to get into the palace. And we're that much closer already."

CHAPTER TWENTY-EIGHT

Caledon

"ARENʼT YOUR AUNTS HEALERS? THEY sell salves and teas and such?" Cal asks Shadow when they are alone. He tries to sound casual. He gets up from the chair to get a closer look at the vizier's house of horrors. He leans toward one of the deep bookshelves, only to discover that the tiny jars lined up on it are filled with preserved primate ears.

First a pouch full of gold coins and now Argonian emerald rings—is Shadow a thief? What kind of name is Shadow, anyway? His earlier suspicions about her resurface in an instant. Who is she really?

Shadow busies herself with brushing nonexistent debris from her dress. "Yes, and . . . ? They weren't always. In any case, they do well for themselves."

He stares intently at one of the fish—a dragonfish, according to the label. "Remarkably so, apparently."

She folds her hands in her lap and glares at him. "What are you saying?"

He shrugs and crosses his arms against his chest.

Shadow bristles in her elaborate dress, flouncing her ruffles. It almost brings a smile to his face but he keeps it grim. What else is she hiding from him?

"Honestly, how I acquired the rings is none of your concern," she says haughtily. "But I suppose you can't help making assumptions, questioning everything I say—you know why? Because . . . because you're a hypocrite." She looks pleased with herself for saying it.

This time, Cal does bark a laugh, but it only provokes her more.

"You are!" she nearly shouts.

He shushes her; she lowers her voice but continues. "You question everything about me and yet tell me nothing about yourself!"

"I have hardly been so circumspect," he says. "You are the only one aside from my father and the queen who knows about the blood vow."

For a moment she looks chastened, but soon sits back against the chair in a huff and crosses her arms. "Just because you don't know any Deian healers who can afford Argonian emeralds doesn't mean they don't exist!"

He knows better than to respond. She's clearly hiding something and trying to deflect. He's just glad the tension between them is broken. He'd rather have her annoyed than distant . . .

Even if it doesn't answer his question about the riches she's carrying around.

Is she upset about last night? He was very much awake when she pressed herself against him, and it had taken all his discipline to hold himself back, when she was so pliant and soft and close, and he was more than ready and willing. He'd thought about properly rolling her over so that she was under him, so that they could . . .

Hold on. Did she know what she was doing? What she was doing to him? Why are they acting as if nothing happened last night? He can't take his eyes off her all day, even as he can't help but notice she spent the entire morning being utterly hostile to him.

Maybe that's best. They are unsuited for each other, clearly, and neither of them is keen on marriage or a family. She is bent on joining the Guild, and he had made himself believe that the comforts of hearth and home are not his to have until he delivers the Deian Scrolls back to their rightful owner. She is not meant for his bed, or his heart. Yet there is no scarcity of coin, and neither of them thought to let two rooms at the inn. Perhaps he should suggest it, although the thought pains him.

Shadow busies herself by studying the glass vitrines while Cal broods. Not too long after, the door flies open.

"Ah, I see you enjoy my little sea monsters," the vizier says, voice booming. "My shipmaster is out on the Silvren Sea as we speak, procuring a merman." He claps his hands together. "Enough of that. Dinner. Tonight. Please! Join me."

"We'd be honored," Cal says quickly.

"Just a few friends," the vizier says. He runs a disapproving eye down Shadow's dress and then over Cal's jacket. "Do let me know if you need to borrow something else to wear."

A FEW HOURS LATER, Cal and Shadow are seated at the vizier's glittering dining room table along with eighteen overdressed members of the Montrician aristocracy, all of whom are pointedly ignoring them. Which is absolutely fine, as they themselves are barely speaking to each other.

The meal began at least thirty minutes before, and the guests haven't been served the main course yet—although platters of roasted duck, broiled venison, sauced hen, and fried pork have been set at the table. Cal has been to grand banquets before, but it has been a long time since he's been able to feast like this. He's stuffed full as it is and yet more keeps coming. Even the most formal meals weren't this elaborate back home. Shadow was smart; she paced herself from the beginning, only eating a bite or two of each. She obviously knew what to expect. He wishes she'd tipped him off. Maybe he should read *Crumpets and Cravats* after all.

Now the waiters are bringing in a plate with some sort of fish over a bed of asparagus. For the first time ever, Cal just wants a feast to end.

He notices how Shadow pushes food around her plate to make it look like she's eaten more than she has, and he follows suit. The whole charade makes Cal resent these people even more—what a colossal waste this dinner is. He pictures the children at the fountain, wonders if there's a way he can sneak some of this food to them. Maybe Shadow can spare some stolen jewelry from her bag. Or whatever else she might have stashed in there.

The vizier stands up and claps his hands. Voices taper off as people lower their forks and turn their attentions to him.

"As you all have noticed, we have new guests with us tonight." Heads bedecked with feathers and enormous fabric concoctions swivel in Cal and Shadow's direction. It's about time they acknowledge the couple's presence. He continues. "Please allow me to introduce, from Argonia, the Honorable Lord Callum Holton and his sister, the elegant Lady Lila Holton." He claps his fingers into his palm; his guests do as well. "The Holtons have graced us with their company, but only for a short time, for they are en route to Stavin, where they must collect the substantial estate of their late grandfather. I had the pleasure of spending some time at his, erm, Bucklam Park house many years ago, and to my astonishment, the elder Lord Holton remembered our brief acquaintance as fondly as I, and willed to me this very fine Argonian emerald ring." He holds out his hand to display the ring Shadow gave him that afternoon. The dinner guests ooh and ahh. One of the women claps politely and others follow, tapping their fingertips into their palms.

Though they're still irritated with each other, Cal looks to Shadow so he can catch her eye at the vizier's phony story involving their supposed grandfather and the hilarity of his "Bucklam Park" remark. But her face is turned away from him, and she ignores him even when he nudges her with his foot.

"Yes, thank you, thank you," the vizier says, bowing slightly. "Please make the Holtons feel welcome, and enjoy the rest of your meal. I believe we still have a few more plates before dessert." He sits down and arranges a napkin on his lap.

Now's Cal's chance to get Shadow's attention. But the woman seated on her right addresses her first.

"I see you packed lightly," the woman is saying, looking up and down at Shadow's new gown.

Cal feels a flash of anger. How dare she be so rude? Shadow is beautiful, much more beautiful than the overly primped ladies of Montrice. They remind him of plucked chickens in satin and diamonds. He keeps his attention on his food to avoid saying something he might regret. Last time he rushed to Shadow's defense, she was angry with him for interfering. And anyway, this is what he tried to warn her about. Montrice's nobility is known for their vanity.

The woman continues, smiling wide. "No doubt you didn't expect a formal dinner invitation while traveling. Don't get me wrong, I *completely* understand. But older is wiser, and that's why no matter how my husband hounds me to stick to only five trunks, I don't listen. I would die—simply *die*—if I had to meet a monarch in last year's afternoon gown."

"Mmmm . . ." is all Shadow says back. Cal wonders if the woman understands how close she is to being throttled.

"I know for a fact it's not your fault anyway, dear. There isn't a single wimple to be found in Argonia, let alone proper pannier hoops. I've seen it for myself. Such a . . . *relaxed* people. I really admire that about Argonians. They just don't pay any mind to the fashions or what anybody else thinks of them."

A woman to Cal's left hears this and leans over him to join their conversation. Up close he can see she's much younger than he first thought, around his age, with a pretty face under all the thick white makeup the noblewomen wear. "This type of social disaster has happened to all of us, Lady Lila. Don't you worry about a thing. I can help you get everything you need—a lovely wimple, a court gown, furs . . ."

Shadow begins to protest, but the woman holds her hand up to stop her. "It's my pleasure."

"Thank you," Shadow says. "But I'm afraid we don't have an invitation to the palace."

"Of course you do," the lady says. "Why do you think you're here? This is how the vizier evaluates your worthiness, and judging by that speech, I think it's safe to say you're in." She winks.

Cal and Shadow share a glance at last.

"Oh! Silly me, I forgot to introduce myself. I'm Gertie, the Duchess of Girt. Everyone calls me Duchess Girt, which I suppose is better than Duchess Gertie. The lady to your right is my dear friend, the Duchess of Aysel; her husband, the duke, is beside her. Mine has, unfortunately, passed."

"I'm so sorry," Shadow says.

Duchess Girt waves her off. "Oh no. Don't be. I prefer spending my meals alone so I can converse with eligible bachelors." She forces out a high-pitched giggle.

Cal has the urge to plug his ears.

"So, if you know any eligible bachelors . . ." She glances at Cal. "I like the handsome, brooding type. Sort of like your brother here. In my experience it's the quietest ones who have the . . ."

Cal hides a grimace. But perhaps the duchess's interest in him will be useful, as women's attentions have been in the past.

A glass clinks. The vizier stands to get everyone's attention again. Cal is relieved for the interruption. He notices a small step as the vizier gets up this time; he's standing on another stool. The vizier, swaying a bit, says, "After dessert, please join us in the library for libations." *He's up to his neck in libations already,* Cal thinks.

The duchess turns back to them. "Where was I? Oh, I don't remember. Here, I have it!" She reaches across the table to grab Shadow's hand with her pale, thin one. Her nails are long, filed sharp, and painted the same shade as her red rosebud mouth. "You two are coming home with me. Yes, yes, don't protest; it's been decided. Where are you staying?"

Shadow tells her and the duchess looks confused. "I don't think I've heard of it? No matter. From now on you're both staying with me." She releases Shadow's hand and pats it, as if Shadow were her pet or a child. Cal sees a flicker of annoyance cross Shadow's face.

"I'll send for your things. This way we can get the lovely Lady Lila all ready for the king. I think she'll clean up rather nicely. And perhaps I can do something with her little brother too." She runs her eyes up and down his body, stopping to raise an eyebrow right in the middle. Then she looks around for her footman, snapping her fingers when she sees him. He rushes over and she begins relaying a list of tasks: *Collect the lord's and lady's things; see to it that their rooms are ready at the house . . .*

"Excellent," says Cal. "We would be honored to stay at your residence."

Shadow looks alarmed, and when Duchess Girt turns to her other side, she whispers in Cal's ear. "You don't mean for us to stay with that strumpet?! And what about our horses? We can't bring them with us."

Cal pretends to be absorbed in the food on his plate as he answers her from the side of his mouth. "We'll pay Garbankle to keep the horses until we need them. Meanwhile, she is a duchess, a high-ranking courtier to the king, which means we will be part of the inner circle. And we need to be appropriately dressed to be welcomed at court. We don't have time to get a new wardrobe otherwise. It sounds as if we'll have a much nicer room, and I, for one, won't miss the bugs, will you?"

"You won't miss a pest in your bed, if that's what you mean," she retorts angrily.

He looks up from his plate and catches her eye. It's the first time they've spoken about last night. "No, that isn't what I meant at all," he says sincerely. He would spend every night at that flea-bitten inn if it meant he would lie next to her again. But of course he doesn't tell her that, as much as he wants to, and as much as he wants to know how she feels about all this.

Shadow saws into her meat, the color high on her cheeks. "It doesn't matter. Sleep well, my lord."

CHAPTER TWENTY-NINE

Caledon

DUCHESS GIRT'S ESTATE SITS ON the far side of Mont, just outside the city proper, one of the old homes that was built before the city walls went up, and many years before the Long Wars with Renovia began. It's surrounded by a tall spiked fence, painted white over black wrought iron—as evidenced by a few flaking spots—and a thickly wooded area to the rear of the main building. A wide gravel lane leads from the gatehouse up to the actual residence, lined on each side with towering trees that shade the drive.

The duchess seats Cal between her and Shadow in the cramped carriage. While riding to the estate, she keeps finding reasons to touch his arm, his leg, to get closer to him. He smiles broadly at her while inching as close to Shadow's side as he can, which causes a cascade of completely different feelings. While in the past he would gladly manipulate the duchess's attraction to him if he were alone on this task, he is not alone. To make matters more awkward, it appears Shadow is trying as hard to get away from him as the duchess is to get closer.

The house itself is little more than a huge brick rectangle covered in windows, a strangely utilitarian architecture considering its pretentious resident. All of Montrice's architecture appears this way, though, created with defense taking precedent over decoration. *Strong buildings made to protect a weak people,* Cal thinks. Renovia, he realizes, is quite the opposite: a powerful populace who surround themselves with beautiful, ornate structures.

The carriage grinds to a halt in the paved circle at the front of the house. Two footmen wearing deep-red uniforms stand outside the front entrance. One of them rushes forward to open the carriage.

The other footman holds out his hand for Shadow; Cal climbs out after her. The duchess follows, gripping the footman's hand tight and a bit longer than strictly necessary. "Good to see you again, Danier, darling." Cal notices that Danier smiles at the duchess in a way that would be considered highly impudent from a servant in Renovia.

They walk up the stairs out front and through the double-doored entry into the foyer. It's not quite what Cal expected—less pink and feathery than he'd have guessed the duchess's home would be . . . it is far more traditional and stern. There are black-and-white-checkered tiles throughout the front hall, with walnut paneling covering the walls from floor to ceiling. Against that backdrop, the footmen look more like part of the décor than actual people.

"Hellooo," Duchess Girt calls out. Two white fur balls scurry up to her feet, yapping, their nails clicking on the tiles. "Oh! Mommy's babies." She picks them up; little pink tongues pop out from under all the white fur and begin licking her face. "You missed your mommy! Yes, you did!"

"The duke is in the library, my lady," the footman tells her. He stands still, hands behind his back, staring ahead.

"Thank you, Danier, darling," she says. And to the tiny dogs: "Let's go see Daddy, shall we?"

"I thought your husband passed away?" Shadow blurts.

Cal is wondering as well. *Who can she be referring to?*

"Passed awa—oh!" She laughs. "Oh dear, no. I meant he passed on the *dinner invitation*. The duke has no interest in idle gossip and nonsense. Or at least that's what he calls it; it's not nonsense to the rest of us, now is it?"

"No, not at all," says Shadow, glancing at Cal.

He can't help but notice how a sigh—almost of relief—escapes Shadow's lips. Perhaps she's jealous, Cal realizes, and the thought consumes him. The idea sparks something in him, but he can't risk the distraction and pushes it aside.

FROM THE FIRST GLANCE Cal can already tell the Duke of Girt is nothing like his wife. He is a good deal older, with a quiet manner, withdrawn where the duchess is outgoing and loud, and clad in much simpler clothes than the other Montrician nobles Cal has met so far. He is vaguely familiar, and Cal wonders whether he has met the duke before, but cannot place him. The duke keeps his dark hair—no wig—held back in a low ponytail. His suit, also black, is finely tailored but simple and unadorned except for a fine platinum pocket watch and a simple ring with a black stone on his fourth finger. Like all aristocrats, he is heavily perfumed—perhaps even more than most. Cal has a desire to hold his nose. Still, despite the unassuming demeanor, the duke isn't particularly friendly or welcoming.

When he sees two strangers enter the library behind his wife, he doesn't hide his irritation. Without acknowledging them, he looks at her and says, "You are aware we have an entire hunting party invited to the estate this weekend?"

She doesn't address what he said directly, and nuzzles the dogs in her arms. "Darling, this is Lord and Lady Holton of Bruckley Villa. They were guests of the vizier. They're only here for a short time, and Lady Lila has misplaced all her luggage and she can't be brought in front of the king in . . . in that." She sweeps her arms out toward Shadow. "I offered to fix her dilemma and outfit her . . ."

The duke begins shaking his head and throws his hands in the air to quiet her. "Yes, yes, yes, fine. Whatever you need to do. Just don't tell me any more about it." He focuses his attentions back on the papers spread across his desk, grumbling under his breath.

She smiles, satisfied. "We'll leave you to your work, then." The duchess hands Cal a puppy. He accepts it with some reluctance. "Let's see to your rooms," she chirps. The puppy in her arms cocks its head and considers Cal. Or maybe it feels sorry for him.

"Lord Holton can borrow a bow from the armory, I suppose," the duke adds.

"For the hunt? Of course," the duchess says. "Are you familiar with a bow, Lord Holton?"

"Of course," says Cal, still holding one of the dogs.

The duchess leads them to a grand split staircase, freshly waxed mahogany lined with a handwoven wool runner. She stops at the first door in the hallway to the right, closest to the stairs. "This one's for you, Lady Lila," Duchess Girt says.

"Your Grace is too kind," says Shadow, entering the room.

"Do you have everything you need, sister?" Cal asks her, not quite ready to be alone with Duchess Girt.

"Absolutely," Shadow says from behind a tiny crack in the door. "Don't let the bedbugs bite!" She slams the door closed in finality.

The duchess walks ahead of him, carrying a lantern. The wall sconces are not lit. There are no sounds aside from his boots on the tile and the swoosh of the duchess's skirts. His room is on the other end of the long hallway, at least ten doors from Shadow's. They stop in front of a doorway.

"The other guests are all in the opposite wing," the duchess says with a sly look on her face. "I thought you'd prefer being away from the commotion. So many people wandering about. Poking their noses into everything. Watching. Isn't it so much better to be alone?"

"Yes, that's true, I prefer being alone," he says. "In fact . . ." He yawns dramatically and places the puppy down on the floor between them, hoping she takes the hint. While her attraction to him might be useful, it is clearly upsetting Shadow for some reason, and there are always other ways to infiltrate the court.

The duchess fumbles for the key, the other puppy perched precariously in the crook of her arm. "Here it is!" she exclaims. She unlocks the door and pushes it open. For a moment he's uncertain if she's going to walk in front of him or not—she moves as if she's about to, but then steps back.

He grabs the opportunity and steps inside the room, immediately beginning to shut the door behind him. "You are too kind, Your Grace," he says. "The evening has quite tired me out. I bid you good night."

The door clicks shut as her mouth opens to say something. He hears her on the other side of the door: "Good night!"

Then the sound of another door opening and Shadow's voice

calling from down the hallway: "Duchess! Oh, I'm so glad to have caught you before you go downstairs. If I may, do you have a candle? I can't seem to find one in here. Oh, and if it isn't too much bother, would you send up a lady's maid to help unbutton my dress?"

No doubt, if they were still sharing a room at the inn, it would fall upon him to do the honors. He is a stupid, stupid man.

The dogs both start barking, their yaps traveling down toward Shadow's room. The duchess's voice follows them as she answers Shadow's request. "Oh yes, my dear, I can take care of that for you, of course!"

Cal's room is clean and comfortable, from what he can see with only the dim night sky in the open window, but he doesn't care to inspect it just now. He really is exhausted—it hits him fully, all at once, the weeks of being on alert morning and night.

He sits on a chair to remove his boots, then climbs onto the wide, fluffy bed. His body sinks into the soft cotton bedding. Newly laundered, smelling faintly of rose water and fresh air from hanging to dry outside the wash building. No creaking old bed frame, no sagging middle of the mattress. This one is stuffed full with fresh down. He was right about it being far better than the room they had at the inn.

Except for one exception, and the loss of her presence makes the room as quiet and unforgiving as his cell in Deersia prison.

Alone in the silence, his thoughts return to last night at the inn . . . Her silhouette behind the screen and under her linen shift. The warmth of her next to him. The way she burrowed herself against his chest, their bodies entwined in sleep. Just last night his hand curved around her waist, and her hair rested against his cheek.

She is the most maddening girl he's ever met, defiant, stubborn, and impulsive. She doesn't listen to reason and is much too reckless with her person. Shadow has also made it quite clear that she has no desire for romance or a family and doesn't care a whit whether he likes her or not . . . and yet. He finds he can't deny the truth. He hopes she cares at least a little bit, that he is right, that she might be jealous of the duchess.

He falls asleep imagining what would happen if he got up, walked down the hall, and knocked on her door . . .

❧

CHAPTER THIRTY

Caledon

B<small>Y THE TIME</small> C<small>AL WAKES</small> up and goes down to breakfast, the duke's hunting guests are already finished eating. The men have moved out to the gardens to smoke cigars. Footmen and butlers clear their empty plates and scattered utensils. He chastises himself for missing his chance to make inroads with the other titled lords, to gain a little more knowledge about the Montrician court. At least Shadow is still sitting there, sipping hot tea, and the duke and duchess are there as well, waiting politely for her to finish.

The duke looks exactly as he did the prior evening, but the duchess looks like an entirely different person. Her face is clean, with only a touch of gloss on her lips. She wears a simple pastel day dress, and her golden hair is free of the elaborate updo and extensions, pulled away from her face with pearled combs but otherwise trailing down her back and around her shoulders in loose waves.

Shadow catches him looking, and he immediately feels remorseful for having even noticed the duchess, who perks up considerably when she sees him. "Did you sleep well, my lord? I do hope you're hungry. We made sure to wait for you. Toast? Tea?"

Cal takes a seat next to Shadow. He's still not hungry after last evening's feast, but he says, "Tea and toast would be wonderful, thank you." It is only polite.

"Were the accommodations to your liking?" Duchess Girt asks him, bright and friendly.

"Very nice, thank you." Waitstaff appears to pour him a steaming cup of strong breakfast tea. There's a faint orangey scent to it; his appetite returns. Like a comfortable bed, it's been ages since he's had good tea.

"Bit quiet, though?" She puts her elbows on the table and gazes at him. "Lonely?"

"Er, no, it was fine, thanks." He pays intense attention to sweetening his tea in order to avoid looking at her. Still, her attention is much preferable to the stony glares Shadow is throwing his way.

Meanwhile, he can't help but notice that the duke is anxious to leave and only feigning patience—he clears his throat and snaps the paper he's reading every few seconds.

"Good-looking young man like you shouldn't be used to spending nights alone." The duchess takes a bite of her toast and chews slowly. "I'm sure that's a rather rare occurrence."

"Perhaps. One *does* tire of traveling companions, however," says Cal, taking a dig at Shadow, who has yet to acknowledge his presence or bid him good morning.

Shadow picks up her teacup. "May I have a fresh cup as well?" The server steps forward to pour her one too. She grabs a sugar cube with the tongs and has her revenge soon enough. "My brother is lonesome for his lady," she says. "Oh, has he not mentioned it?"

"Mentioned what?" asks the duchess, looking alarmed.

Shadow titters coyly. "My dear brother, do share with the duke and duchess the news of your engagement!"

"Engagement?" the duchess says before taking another bite of toast. She can't keep her eyes off Cal.

Cal raises his eyebrows. Strike and parry. "Pray, tell them, sister."

"Oh dear," Shadow says, placing her hand over her heart. "Was it still hush-hush? Have I spoiled the surprise?"

Cal tries not to smile. Shadow seems determined to keep him away from the duchess, for reasons that he hopes are in his favor. He takes a sip of his tea. "We'd intended to announce together, of course. As we'd met quite by accident."

"Do tell the story," says Shadow.

Cal taps a finger against his cup. "It was almost as if she just appeared in my room one day, out of the blue."

"Oh! Who is she?" cries the duchess.

"A lady I met in Renovia," he answers, as Shadow's cheeks burn. "In a castle."

"Renovian," says the duchess with distaste. "What is she like?"

Shadow is about to answer when Cal cuts her off. He looks right at her when he speaks. "She's the most beautiful girl I've ever met. Brave, courageous, and loyal. In all the kingdoms of Avantine I have never met her equal."

"And how did you propose, brother? Seeing that you had sworn off marriage and children to look after Mother's estate," says Shadow softly.

"Ah, but she too had vowed not to marry," Cal answers. "So we promised to be unmarried to each other, but together, forever."

"What an atypical arrangement," says Shadow, not quite meeting his eye.

The duchess was fully agitated by now. "Sworn off marriage and children? How strange! What kind of engagement is this?" She takes an aggressive bite of toast.

"A promise between two souls," he says, but he only has eyes for Shadow.

"A promise can be broken," Shadow replies.

"Not mine," he says, so quietly that he's not sure she can hear him.

"Nor mine," she says, which means that she did.

They catch each other's eye, and Cal wants nothing more than to reach across the table for her hand and pull her to him. But they are at the Duke and Duchess of Girt's table, and must conform to propriety.

THE SNAP OF THE duchess's fan brings them back to the present. The duchess flicks it open once more with a snap of her wrist and begins airing herself. Then she closes the fan in her right hand, her eyes trained on Cal. She knows exactly what she is doing and what she has signaled. "Dear Lord Holton, it certainly doesn't sound like any kind of engagement to me," Duchess Girt drawls. "Besides, the only reason to get married is so one can have affairs."

The duke is oblivious to all of this. He seems to regard himself as above everyone else, even—and maybe especially—his wife. Like they're all children he's tolerating until they're sent back into the nursery with the governess. He continues to read the previous day's news, paying no mind to the way his wife gushes over Cal. Maybe he really doesn't notice. Or maybe he hopes someone will take her away from him, or at least entertain her for a while.

He wishes he and Shadow were alone, so they could talk more openly. He tries to catch her eye but she is resolutely studying her plate, as if her breakfast were the most interesting thing in the world.

A loud bell clangs outside. The duke throws down his paper. "Hunt is on. Come on, Holton." The duke and duchess rise from the table, and there's a clatter of activity as servants rush behind them, gathering dirty cups and plates. The duchess bustles away and the duke marches out after her. Cal follows, except Shadow holds him back. "A word, brother?"

He nods and they find a quiet alcove. "Yes?"

Her eyes are dewy and her cheeks flushed. It looks as if she wants to say something important, but all she says is, "Be careful, on the hunt."

"Is that all?" he asks.

She nods.

"I assure you I shall return in one piece, my lady," he says, and bows.

CAL JOINS THE OTHER men gathering near the stable, hunting dogs milling about between them. He chooses a bow and quiver from the duke's collection even though he has no intention of using it. He has always detested the sport.

The duke introduces him. "Lord Holton of Argonia." The duke's friends murmur appropriate greetings. This is the center of the aristocracy and Cal has been accepted as one of their own, a foreign lord who has won the duke's approval.

Hours pass on the duke's hunt. Cal lags behind the men with his borrowed bow and borrowed horse. The boar they're chasing holds no interest for him, but then he overhears a conversation that does. "Renovian problem," someone says. He rides up to try to get closer so he can hear them better.

"They'll take us if we don't take them first," says a second voice.

"Don't disagree."

"Montrice cannot fall."

"War is inevitable."

But before he can hear more, the dogs begin running and barking furiously: They've found the boar. They corner the animal in some dense hedges. It cowers there, squealing. The sound is horrendous. The men rush forward, praising the dogs: "Excellent work, White-foot" and "Good job, Jak."

Cornering an animal with dogs is not hunting, Cal thinks. But at least it's nearly over and they can soon go back to the house. He's eager to talk to Shadow about the day and the snippet about Renovia he overheard.

The men all move aside to allow the duke to ride through and approach the boar. He dismounts and removes a dagger from his boot. "Lord Holton," he says.

All the men look at him. Cal is taken aback. "Yes?"

The duke twists his wrist and holds the dagger out, handle toward Cal. "Please, do the honors."

"Your Grace, I thank you, but that isn't necessary. It is your hunt, after all."

But the duke motions with the dagger again. "I insist."

There's no way out of this. Cal jumps down from the horse and walks toward the duke. He takes the dagger. The duke watches him as he moves past the dogs toward the scared boar. It lets out a snorting squeal. The dogs begin barking again.

"Quiet!" the duke yells at them.

Cal looks at the boar, shaking and pawing at the dirt. To those who worship Deia, causing an animal fear before killing it makes it inedible. It becomes cruelty for sport, rather than survival, and interferes with the balance of energy. Cal may not be an incredibly religious man, but he still has respect for Guild customs.

The duke is challenging him. He wants to see Cal's response to this task.

"Well, get on with it!" the duke shouts. The other men laugh.

"Deia take you," Cal whispers to the boar. He closes his eyes and quickly slides the dagger across its throat, killing it immediately.

"We're feasting on boar tonight, gentlemen!" the duke announces.

As Cal walks by him to return to his horse, the duke mutters to him: "Excellent hand with that dagger. Had a lot of practice?"

"On a different kind of hunt," Cal replies with a grim smile.

The duke snorts.

"THERE WAS NOTHING AT the inn." The duchess is standing on the staircase landing when Cal returns from the hunt. She's changed into an afternoon dress, light pink, with a long brocade jacket over it. The jacket has bell sleeves and a high stiff collar that frames her face. Her hair is pulled into a soft twist. She's pretty, he admits, and in another lifetime, perhaps he would have appreciated her attentions; but there is business at hand, and he's still aggravated from the hunt. The duchess is the last thing he wants to deal with.

"No trunks, no wardrobe—it appears all you had are the clothes on your back," she says.

"Of course," Cal says. "We traveled lightly. No time for a lot of baggage." He nods and begins walking past her.

She turns as if to follow. "No, it appears not. Where in Renovia did you say you called? I have many friends in Serrone."

He stops, one foot on the stair. "You know, I can't quite recall the names . . . My sister usually keeps track of these things."

"Ah. Yes. Your *sister*."

He doesn't like the way she said that. He turns and regards her coldly. "If you'll excuse me, I do need to get cleaned up."

The duchess taps her forehead with her hand and says, "Silly me, yes, of course, I'm so sorry. Do get out of those filthy clothes! I have to go take care of something in the meantime. It's supposed to be a surprise, but, well, oh, I just can't keep it to myself! It's too exciting."

Cal doesn't like these games of intrigue but the only way to get her to go away is to play along. He tries to soften his expression into something friendlier. "Perhaps I can spare a moment."

She leans forward and puts her hand on his shoulder. "Don't say a word . . . and if you do, I'll know who told! But"—she pokes his arm—"I have the perfect match in mind for your sister." She pulls her hand away and smiles broadly.

"A match?"

"Well, since you are affianced, it is only right that she is married off as well, don't you think?" asks the duchess. "A beautiful eligible maiden like her isn't set to be an old maid."

Cal coughs. "I am sure Lila will appreciate your concern. Where is my dear sister, if I may ask?"

"Oh, I've sent her away with the maid for a dress fitting. As I told her the other day, she can't meet the king wearing *those* clothes. So she won't be back in time for dinner. Will most likely be quite late before she returns. You'll probably be asleep. Do be sure to get some rest tonight," she drawls. "Tomorrow is the king's weekly audience."

With that, she turns on her heel and walks down the hallway, waving herself with her fan.

Her words hit him like a slap. The duchess is no fool. She has not only ensured that he won't see Shadow that evening; she is also intent on matching her with someone else. The thought brings an ache to his chest.

But there is nothing between them—only unspoken embraces in the night and veiled conversations at breakfast. They have made no promises to each other, and likely never will.

Perhaps it's best if Duchess Girt does find Shadow a suitable gentleman. After all, what can Cal give her? He does not even have his life to offer; it already belongs to the queen.

CHAPTER THIRTY-ONE

Shadow

"YOU WILL GET HURT, IF you flirt, with Duchess Girt," I sing to Cal after I fling the door open to let him inside my room. "Thought of that one last night. Couldn't wait to sing it to you," I say, with forced cheer. Without him around yesterday, I was able to clear my head. Whatever might have been between us is over—it has to be—and the strange conversation at yesterday's breakfast was just the last part of it.

Caledon Holt is the Queen's Assassin and I am meant for the Guild. We are here to uncover a conspiracy and learn if Grand Prince Alast was working with our enemy kingdom against the Renovian throne. I cannot believe that he was a traitor in the first place, even though I saw him try to kill me with my own eyes.

Maybe if I make light of our hostess, Cal will lose that intense look in his eyes whenever he catches mine. I can't bear it anymore.

"You are merry today," he says as he shuts the door behind him.

"Why shouldn't I be? We are to meet King Hansen today; isn't that what we're here for?"

Cal walks over to the window and leans on the sill. "It's not as simple as that."

"No, I suppose not," I admit. "It's not as if he'll let us into his confidence right away."

"He might," Cal says slowly, as if something has just occurred to him. "Especially if he takes to you."

"Takes to me?"

"You asked to be my apprentice. Seduction is part of the job," he says with a shrug, as if he hasn't just offered me up to the royal palate like a cut of fresh meat. "It is an easy way to gain trust."

"Like you and Duchess Girt, I presume?" My good mood sours.

"Exactly."

"She is certainly quite taken by you," I snap.

He returns my gaze levelly and I break my promise not to look into those dark eyes of his. "It is an advantage, Shadow. And we use every advantage we have to fulfill the task at hand. It is what they teach us at the Guild. What you will learn if you are permitted entry."

"Then I will make certain to arouse the king's ardor!" I cry. "If that's what you want."

"What I want is immaterial; this is about the security of the kingdom," he says.

"Is that all you care about? Oh, why do I even ask!" I turn away, shaking.

"Shadow!"

"Just go away," I tell him.

Cal moves from the window so that he's standing right in front of me, and I put up my hands to shield my face, just as he takes my wrists in his. He lowers them so he can look right into my eyes. His own look wild, desperate.

"Shadow of Nir, Maiden of the Honey Glade," he says, his voice low and husky. His hands are rough from the road, but his touch has always been gentle. My wound is gone; not even a scar remains. "Renovia does not claim all my heart."

"Caledon Holt," I say. "What do you want from me?"

"I want...," he begins to say, but he never finishes as there is a short rap on the door. He releases me so quickly that it catches my breath.

A lady's maid walks into the room. "The vizier is ready for you, milady, milord."

"We will be down shortly," Cal tells her as I search around for my satin shoes. I find them near the bed. They're awful, pinching my toes and rubbing against my heels until they're raw, but it's what's expected. I am a lady of court now, and the irony that this would have been my life if I had stayed in Renovia doesn't escape me.

He doesn't finish his sentence and I find I don't care to discover what he meant to say. Cal is right, I am here as a spy and must employ every weapon in my arsenal, including, it seems, my femininity.

We're quiet for a moment while I check my hair in the mirror and straighten my borrowed gown. It was a little big in some spots and too tight in others but the duchess's seamstress took care of it. I fret about the neckline, that it's too low, and fuss with ribbons around the waist.

"Ready?" asks Cal. He doesn't say anything about my obvious discomfort in the gown nor does he finish what he began to say before the maid interrupted us.

I nod. He has ordered me to catch the king's fancy and I only mean to satisfy. I am his apprentice, and I learn from the best.

———————

WE ARRIVE WITH THE duke and duchess for the king's weekly audience. There are at least a hundred people in the great hall and almost as many armed guards as there are courtiers. Cal scans the room, reading and remembering each face. Is the Aphrasian conspirator here among these obsequious aristocrats? Or is it the king himself?

King Hansen has already begun receiving visitors by the time we arrive. The senior guard bellows out names; once that person is announced, they approach the dais. I have no idea how the order is decided. One after the other, Montrice's aristocrats are beckoned forward. I hear "Duchess Aysel," whose name I recall from the vizier's dinner party.

Duchess Girt speaks close to me, pointing at one group or another: "Those two traveled a hundred miles to be here today and probably won't be seen. They are putting on airs—but they lost everything, including the family seat, to gambling debt, yet they retain the title, so here they are. Over in the corner—now that's a juicy one. The Earl of Neri's second wife, the one with the horrible yellow gown? She's been having an affair with the grand duke, the king's uncle." The lady in question turns sideways, her gown protruding in front of her. "The swollen belly? Well. You know where I'm going with this—but you didn't hear that from me." The duchess nudges me and winks, her enormous bouffant wig bobbing along with her head as she does.

The senior guard stands at the top of the step again. "Lord Callum Holton of Backley Hold, and his sister, Lady Lila Holton."

The others watch as we walk toward the throne. Cal offers me his arm. It feels almost like we're walking down the aisle at a wedding. My cheeks flame from the idea even though Cal can't possibly know my thoughts. I wonder if he has the same one, though, because he seems to deliberately avoid glancing in my direction.

When we reach the dais, the guard puts his staff across our path to stop us, then he steps sideways. Cal bows; I curtsy. "Your Majesty," we both say.

King Hansen, slouched in his padded silver throne, barely nods at us. He looks impossibly bored. Like his statue, he's handsome. His hair is fair, as is his skin. He is nineteen years of age and came to the throne when his father died after a long illness. Hansen has the physique of someone who jousts and rides for sport. Or for the mirror. From his floral perfume and the gold entwined in his lace cuffs, he reeks of vanity and pompousness. I almost expect him to pick up a looking glass and gaze into it right in front of us.

"The vizier tells me you're visiting our great kingdom?" the king says.

"Yes," Cal answers. "We're headed north into Stavin."

The king nods and says to Cal, "A lot of good hunting in Stavin." Cal agrees.

"Do you like fishing?" the king asks.

"Fishing? Yes, I've done a bit of that lately," says Cal, without looking in my direction.

The king nods approvingly. "I spent quite a bit of time fishing at the summer palace last year. One of my larger lakes is there. Truly blissful. The trout were amazing. I'm quite looking forward to next year. I intend to spend the entire season, rather than just a month. Breeders are working on restocking the lake for me already. I want them nice and big by the time I get there. Otherwise, what's the point?" He pauses.

"There is none, Your Majesty," agrees Cal, and I swear I can see an imperceptible lift in one of his eyebrows.

The king nods to the vizier, who steps forward to usher us away. No! Wait, it can't be over so soon.

"Your fields and valleys are beautiful, Your Majesty," I blurt. How am I supposed to get the king's attention if I don't even address him?

"Have you seen much of the country?" The king looks in my direction as if noticing me for the first time. His eyes lazily take in the shape of my dress and wander over the low neckline of my gown. I am on display, and available for the plucking should he so desire.

I smile. "Not as much as we would like."

The king considers that. "Do you plan to be in Montrice at the end of the week?"

"Yes, Your Majesty," says Cal, even though we have no idea if the Duke and Duchess of Girt would extend their hospitality to us for that long.

"Excellent," says King Hansen. "Then you will both join me on the royal hunt."

"We would be honored, Your Majesty," I say as Cal agrees.

King Hansen nods. We bow and curtsy again. The vizier steps forward and says, "Thank you, Your Majesty," and leads us away.

He is even more excited than we are. "Such a great compliment!" he exclaims. "A royal hunt! And guests of mine—this is good for us all. One must always be concerned with staying in the king's favor." He titters nervously. "Excellent job, Lady Lila. Your charms made quite an impression on His Majesty. Did you see how he looked at you?"

I certainly did, and it was unnerving.

"The king is rumored to marry soon, after turning down many suitable maidens, which makes this all the more fascinating, don't you think?" asks the vizier.

In my opinion, *fascinating* is not the word.

CHAPTER THIRTY-TWO

Caledon

ANOTHER HUNT, AND SHADOW IS invited this time. The royal hunt, as is customary, has provisions for the ladies to participate. Duchess Girt spent all morning after the meeting with King Hansen instructing us on proper etiquette. Demanding a guest slaughter the prey is noticeably absent from her lessons, but Cal doesn't say anything about how the duke behaved at the last one. The other day, he told Shadow what he'd overheard among the Montrician lords during the hunt. The lords are certain that war is coming to their lands—but when? And how?

For now, Duchess Girt is preoccupied with outfitting both of them. Because they are her houseguests, the duchess has taken a special interest in their appearance. The way Cal and Shadow look reflects directly on her and the quality of the company she keeps.

And the way the duchess feels about Cal and Shadow directly affects their ability to fulfill his task in Montrice.

That's how Caledon finds himself back in a tailor shop. Being measured and draped in one fabric after another, all indistinguishable to him. Duchess Girt takes it upon herself to monitor the situation this time, though, which he welcomes since her presence prevents the tailor from asking too many questions. The basic story about Lord and Lady Holton worked the first couple of times, but now that they've run out of things to discuss, the nosy little man is starting to probe further.

"I want him to have the most traditional Montrician hunting attire," the duchess tells the tailor. "But perhaps with just a touch of Argonian flavor. What do you say, Lord Holton? What sort of details do you miss from home?" She looks at him expectantly.

Thankfully, Cal is up to the task. "Well, Argonian hunting jackets always include a small green rose on the lapel, typically embroidered, to represent the defeat of the Stavinish invasion that ended the Twenty Years' War."

"Would you require a green rose on the lapel, then?" the tailor asks.

"Certainly," Cal answers. "And one for Lady Holton as well. But the women never wear a green rose. Make certain it is a yellow one."

"You are so sweet to be concerned about your sister," says the duchess as she leans back against the chaise and fans herself, watching him.

BACK AT THE GIRT estate, the duchess presides over dinner that evening with the kind of giddiness Cal had previously seen only in children eagerly awaiting a much-desired gift.

"The Vicar of Rivefont will attend, though he is staying at the vice minister's house, as usual, and the vizier, naturally, and . . ." She rattles off a long list of names. Cal's thoughts begin to wander as he watches one of her dogs wrestle with a stray chicken bone at her feet. Then she says, "And Ambassador Nhicol of Renovia will attend with his husband, Mathieu . . ."

Shadow kicks Cal under the table.

The duchess continues talking. "They will stay here, of course, since their country house is a bit away, and we have the room."

"Did you say the Ambassador of Renovia is staying here?" Cal asks.

"Yes, he was home in his own country but just returned to Montrice for—what was it—a missing piece of art? Something valuable." She looks at the duke.

He startles and looks up from the book he's reading. "What was that?"

"Oh, never mind. What do *you* think the ambassador is looking for, Lord Holton?" She bats her eyelashes at him.

Cal has no idea. But he does know he must keep away from the ambassador, who is sure to recognize him as the lowly blacksmith who killed the grand prince and escaped from Deersia.

"Who can say?" says Cal. "But are you wise to host the Renovians? I think only of your safety, Your Grace."

"Oh! You are too sweet. Worrying about me. There is still peace between the two kingdoms, is there not? Besides, we are well protected here." She looks over at her husband, who doesn't seem to be aware of anything that's happening around him.

"We are quite friendly with the ambassador. I cannot wait to introduce him to my distinguished guests. But it will have to wait, I'm afraid, because they're due to arrive late in the evening. I'm sure they'll want to retire immediately. But breakfast tomorrow— it will be a treat! The cook will prepare a special batch of scones."

The duchess continues telling them her complete breakfast menu, but Cal tunes her out. He has to figure out how to avoid being introduced to Ambassador Nhicol and the Renovian entourage.

CAL EXPLAINS THE DANGER he's in while Shadow paces the room. Her pink dressing gown, a gift from Duchess Girt, billows out behind her as she goes, so it looks like it's chasing after her, trying to keep up. She's taken her wig and jewelry off, so her wavy dark hair, growing out already, rests around her ears in a short, cropped bob. Cal likes the way it frames her face.

The duke and duchess have gone to bed, with orders to be awakened when the ambassador arrives.

"I can't go to breakfast; I will stay up here while you make excuses for me," he tells her.

"What?" she asks, pinching her nose.

"I've caught some kind of fever, some kind of terrible disease from Argonia," he instructs.

"But then I have to go down and meet him?" she says, obviously panicked.

"Shadow."

"Listen, I'm pretty certain I've met him before as well. He bought honey from my aunts. I can't see him! He'll know I'm Renovian!"

Cal is firm. "The ambassador isn't going to remember you simply because you met him once. He meets quite a few people."

"What if we've both fallen ill? That way it's more believable, especially if we've caught something on our travels," she says triumphantly.

Cal relents. "That's fine. We're both ill, then. I'll tell the maid to bring up toast and tea. But we need to be able to go on the royal hunt somehow. The king himself invited us."

If he's suspicious about her anxiety regarding the Renovian ambassador, he chalks it up to her general inexperience and forgets about it soon enough.

CHAPTER THIRTY-THREE

Shadow

THE DUCHESS IS HEARTBROKEN THAT we'll miss her extravagant breakfast, but when the maid says we might be contagious and have both been revisited by our dinners—thanks to a hefty dose of ipecac syrup I found in the drawer of the vanity—she backs down and wishes us a speedy recovery.

We can't play sick for too long, or else the duchess will fetch a doctor, and he'll know we're not truly ill.

After the maid delivers my tea and toast, Cal calls me to his room to discuss the situation. I am wracked with guilt. This valuable "missing art" Nhicol is searching for in Montrice is sure to be me. My mother is quite well positioned at court and has surely alerted the authorities to begin their search. I can't let him find me. I can't.

"I've been thinking," Cal announces as soon as I enter the room and shut the door. "These royal hunts are always so big. We can probably avoid Nhicol altogether if we're careful." He's standing by the window, looking out at the grounds of the Girt estate.

"I thought of that too. But—what if we're not careful enough? What then?" I can just imagine the scene: the ambassador recognizes us as Renovian and unmasks our true nationality to the king, who decides we are spies and sends us to the dungeons, or worse, the gallows. Or worse, my mother discovers exactly where I am and what I'm up to.

Cal paces back and forth a couple times. "How do we know he isn't already aware that we're here or who we really are? Maybe this is part of the queen's plan."

"But why would she send him here without sending word?" I ask.

"The question isn't whether she would send word, the question is would she send him here without telling *him* that we're here." Cal takes a sip of tea and grimaces. "Or is he here for his own reasons?"

"I have no idea. But until we know, we have to stay away. As you mentioned earlier, he can easily be an Aphrasian spy, or a double agent. We don't know. We need to find out what he's doing here before we let him see us."

We hear footsteps in the hallway. Cal takes charge. "The maids are on their way to tidy up. You need to go back to your room. Here's the plan: We're going to feel better, but be a bit late, so we'll join the party at its tail end. The ambassador will be up near the front with the Girts and the king. Once the hunt begins, it's just a matter of avoiding them."

"Okay. And what about after? How long is Nhicol going to be here?"

"We'll figure that out later. Let's just get through this first."

A FEW HOURS LATER, I'm laced into Montrician hunting garb, which basically amounts to a riding habit with puffy sleeves, embroidered with the yellow rose of Argonia. The Montricians hunt in full formal gear, so I have a large white wig on my head as well.

Cal knocks on my door. When I answer, he's holding up two white eye masks. "I just remembered this is one of those strange Argonian hunting customs."

"Brilliant," I say. "With that, and the ridiculous curly white wig you're wearing, your own mother wouldn't recognize you." I cringe. "I'm sorry. I . . ."

Cal is looking out the window at the gardens below. He doesn't acknowledge my awkward comment about his late mother.

I put on the mask and powder my nose again.

Cal is staring at me.

"What?" I ask him.

"You just—you looked like someone just now," he says.

"Who?"

He shakes his head and doesn't say, although I have an inkling of who it might be. "They're getting lined up. Showtime, Lady Lila." On our way out the door, he knocks on the wood trim. Aunt Moriah used to do the same thing for good luck. She would like him just for that.

We step into line as King Hansen's trumpeter announces it's time to begin. The procession starts forward from the gardens toward the woods. The couple in front of us, two older people donning parasols and lace finery not intended for actual hunting, smile politely.

Seconds after we start, a handsome young man, a bit older than us and wearing a sharp black hunting costume, jogs up behind us. "Have I missed the boring part?" he says to Cal. Then: "Haven't had the pleasure. I am Lord Mathieu." He holds out his hand.

Cal shakes it. "Lord Holton," Cal says, then gestures toward me. "My sister, Lady Lila."

Cal and I catch each other's eye. This is the ambassador's husband. My pulse is racing even though he doesn't know me. I decide paying as little attention to him as possible is the best strategy, so I simply bow slightly and then walk forward. Cal isn't as lucky.

"To be quite honest, I've never been to one of these things. Spouses typically stay behind, but I insisted on coming along. Montrice has the finest silks and I'm hoping to buy a few dozen bolts to bring back to Renovia. I own drapers' shops there."

When the king's party reaches the edge of the woods, everyone stops. The trumpeter blows the horn to get our attention before making an announcement. He stands on a little wooden stool and shouts: "His Royal Majesty King Hansen and the distinguished Ambassador of Renovia have joined together in the spirit of friendship to offer a generous prize for today's royal hunt: one thousand coins of silver to whoever fells the largest prey. The horn will blow to announce the end of the hunt, wherein all shall gather here with their conquest."

"I could win, easy," Cal whispers to me.

"Don't be so sure," I reply. "I'm here."

He scoffs playfully at that. "In any case, we aren't going to win that silver because we aren't drawing attention to ourselves, remember?"

The horn blows. The king and his servants, carrying his extra arrows and swords and daggers, head off down the trail into the darkness of the forest. Ambassador Nhicol follows, and then all the rest of the Montrician nobility after him. Cal and I hold back a bit, waiting for the crowd to disperse among the trees and pathways of the duke's property. He does have some of the greatest grounds of any estate I've ever seen.

"I'm going to catch up with my husband," Lord Mathieu tells us.

"It was a pleasure making your acquaintance. I'm sure we'll see one another at dinner."

"The honor was ours," Cal says, and I repeat the same.

When he's out of earshot, Cal frowns. "A friendly joint prize between King Hansen and the ambassador?"

I nod. "We need to find out what's going on here."

We venture into the woods off the path so we can watch the others.

Dogs bark in the distance. A man shouts. Leaves crunch under feet; a lady lets out a high-pitched shriek, then giggles. We won't find the answer to the question of how the ambassador became so friendly with the king in the fields. "This is pointless. We should just go back," I say to Cal. He doesn't respond. "Cal?" I look around.

"Over here," he says in a loud whisper.

I follow his voice behind a tall shrub. "What are you doing?"

"Look." He points at something on the ground.

I lean closer. There's a bit of glass—something shiny. I reach out to touch it. Cal grabs my arm. "Don't touch it!" he says. "It might be dangerous!"

The dark glass swirls.

"It's the shield!" I exclaim. "That's what the Aphrasian guard was wearing on his chest, but bigger."

"I had a feeling."

"How did you find it?" I ask.

"I saw something glittery, thought it might be lost jewelry at first. There were a few shards of whatever that is. It led me here. Looks like it broke off, maybe?"

As I reach for it, a twig snaps.

"Leave it for now." Cal grabs on to my arm and pulls me low

to the ground with him. About ten feet away from us, Duke Girt appears to be tracking an animal. He hasn't seen us. He draws his bow back. Aims.

The trumpeter's horn blasts through the air.

The duke lowers his bow and misses. I hear a small animal escaping into the forest. The horn scared it off.

We watch it run away while the duke heads in the opposite direction. When he is gone, we join the rest of the hunting party gathered in the field. To our surprise, Duke Girt is being crowned the winner of the royal hunt. A dead stag lies at his feet, and I feel a frisson of wrongness. Why am I seeing a pile of wooden branches? I blink my eyes again, and I see the stag once more.

Magic, I think. The duke has somehow ensorcelled the branches to look like a dead deer. I tell Cal as much. "The duke is a mage," I whisper. "That's not a stag."

Cal frowns, watching as the duke takes his bows.

"Pure luck!" he tells the crowd. "Thank you, thank you."

Is the duke an Aphrasian? Have we unwittingly stumbled into the conspirator's home? The Duke of Girt is clearly a liar and a cheat, but could he also be part of the enemy order that has plotted the death of the Renovian dynasty?

Someone touches my shoulder. I look to my right. Ambassador Nhicol is standing there with his hand extended. "We haven't been introduced," he says. I open my mouth to speak, but nothing comes out. My mind is spinning—

"Apologies, she is terribly shy," Cal says, deepening his voice. "May I introduce you to my sister, Lady Lila Holton. Pleased to make your acquaintance."

"And this is my brother, Lord Callum," I say weakly.

"Ambassador Nhicol of Renovia, on behalf of Queen Lilianna. What brings you to Montrice, Lord Holton?"

"Merely passing through."

"Is that so?"

"Traveling to claim our late grandfather's estate," Cal says smoothly.

The ambassador nods. "Very nice." He claps for something the king said about the prize money.

"If you don't mind," Cal says. "Aren't Renovia and Montrice . . . ? I'm curious how this arrangement came about?"

"Well, you know how it goes. If I told you, then I'd have to kill you," the ambassador says, grinning.

Cal puts his hands up. "Understood."

"And . . . if you don't mind *me* asking, why the masks?"

"Well . . . I suppose the same answer applies." Cal smiles broadly.

The ambassador slaps his arm. "Funny!" he says to Cal.

"It's an Argonian custom," Cal explains.

"Back to the house for food and libations!" Duke Girt announces.

"That's my cue," Ambassador Nhicol says. "Looking forward to speaking with both of you more tonight."

"Likewise," Cal says. I simply curtsy. I feel sweat pooling under my wig. Now I'm certain I've met the ambassador before. I can't place him. The voice, I know it from somewhere, I'm sure of it. Why do I think I heard it in Deersia? But that's not possible. Perhaps I wasn't fibbing when I said he'd purchased honeycomb at the marketplace. As soon as he walks away, I exhale a breath I didn't even realize I was holding. How are we going to make it through this visit? We can't wear masks the entire time.

We step in line and begin the procession back to the house for the resting period before dinner. Behind us, servants load the dead stag onto a cart. They'll bring it to the taxidermist to be stuffed and mounted on a plaque. I wonder if all the duke's hunting trophies are phonies.

When it's our turn to file into the duke's great hall, I step through the door to find King Hansen standing there. I curtsy; Cal bows. "Your Majesty."

"I'm sorry to have missed you at the hunt," he says to me, as a beautiful courtier behind him sneers in my direction.

I curtsy once again. He's holding a bouquet of wildflowers, which he hands me. "I picked them myself."

"Thank you, Your Majesty." I'm supposed to flirt with him, but all I want to do is run upstairs.

"They reminded me of you. Wild and beautiful," he says, his voice thick.

"Thank you, Your Majesty," I repeat, taking them from him and keeping my eyes on the floor.

The king exits abruptly after that, his personal servants trailing after him.

I turn to see Cal watching me. He raises an eyebrow but doesn't say anything.

Chapter Thirty-Four

Caledon

"WE NEED TO PROVE OUR suspicions," Cal says. "About the duke being the mage and the hidden conspirator."

"Yes, but how?" Shadow asks. They're convening in Shadow's room while the rest of the guests are napping before dinner.

The two of them have changed from their hunting outfits into daywear, though Cal hardly finds it comfortable. If this is the life of a nobleman, they can have it. The land and title and prestige come with too many conditions and obligations.

Shadow bites her thumbnail. "We have maybe, I don't know, until the fourth bell? I need time to get ready for tonight."

"Not a lot of time. How about the duke's office?"

"That's the most logical place. But how can we be sure he isn't there?"

"We'll just have to take our chances. If he is, I'll make up something. Say I want to buy some land."

Cal peeks out the door. It's clear. He and Shadow start down the hallway and tiptoe down the wide staircase to the first floor.

Cautiously, they head toward the room where they first met the duke when they arrived.

The door is closed. Shadow sidles against it and places her ear on the wood. She nods and Cal pushes the door open. They slip inside and close the door behind them.

The library is stuffy and masculine, lined floor to ceiling in dark walnut bookcases on three sides. The fourth wall, where they entered, is covered in oil portraits of the duke's predecessors. Heavy red leather chairs flank a circular table in the middle of the room. There's a writing desk in the corner. "I'll start with the desk. You see if there's anything in the cabinets . . . or in a book. Could be a false book, maybe. Check everything," Shadow says. She crosses the room and begins opening desk drawers and riffling through papers.

Cal stands in front of the bookcases, a little irritated at being told how to do his job, but holds his tongue and methodically begins to search. He opens a cabinet door at the bottom of the bookshelf. Nothing but candles, lined in rows. The next one holds more books; the third, newspapers bound with twine. He walks around the room opening cabinets but none offers anything promising.

Rows upon rows of books stare him down. Impossible to check through them all. Not a single one is out of place or gives any indication that it has been read or looked at recently.

Shadow has a handful of envelopes. She flips through them quickly and places them back in the drawer, then moves on to the next one.

"Find anything?" he asks her.

"Just old invitations, notices . . . well, wait. This is strange." She holds up an envelope. Cal walks over. It's addressed to *TRH The Grand Duke and Duchess of Girt*.

"What is it?"

"A letter. From Renovia."

"What does it say?"

I hold it up to the light. "It's a letter from King Esban, thanking the duke and duchess for their kindness to his brother."

"Alast?"

"No, Almon. The older brother, who was supposed to be king, except he died young," says Shadow.

Cal frowns. He knows his history. "Almon was killed during a hunt with a grand duke in Montrice. At first it appeared as if Montrice had conspired against Renovia, but suspicion fell to his brother Esban instead. The Aphrasians started the rumor that he had poisoned his own brother. His legacy was always tainted by this doubt until he died heroically in the battle of Baer Abbey."

"Esban would never do such a thing! And neither would Alast. The three of them were close, that's what my aunts told me. They were never rivals. They all had the same goal—to bring down the Aphrasians," says Shadow. "Do you think this is the same duke who hosted King Almon?"

"Could be," Cal replies. "It was only twenty years ago."

"But the duchess is younger than that," says Shadow.

"Maybe he remarried," says Cal.

"Maybe," Shadow agrees.

"Anyway, we already know the duke is suspicious. The question is whether he's involved with the Aphrasians, and if they are the source of that black shard we found."

"Do you think it was his?"

"Possibly, and more likely than not. But the shard could have been from anyone. There were dozens of people in the woods today alone. We don't know how long it's been there, either. Maybe two weeks, maybe two years."

Chimes announce the second bell. Shadow shoves the letters back in the drawer and slides it shut. "We're running out of time."

Cal turns and his eyes rest on the paintings on the far wall. One in particular catches his attention: It's slightly askew. Only slightly, yet noticeable next to the precision of the others. Perfect place to hide something. Fixed to the back of a painting, he guesses. He hopes.

He reaches out to pull it away from the wall.

The door flies open. He yanks his hand back.

It's Duchess Girt.

"I've been looking all over for you. What are you doing in here?" she says, eyes narrowing.

Cal turns his head toward Shadow but she's gone. "And *you* are exactly who I am looking for," he tells the duchess.

Though she still looks suspicious, her face softens some. She shuts the door. "Why is that?"

"Why do you think?" he asks, his eyes hooded from practice. He should have done this sooner. He needs to distract her, and fast. Make her forget that it's strange to find him here, standing in her husband's private office.

"Oh, I thought you'd never—" the duchess says, but she doesn't finish because Cal has already pulled her toward him.

"Never do this?" he asks. He brushes a hand on her cheek and lowers his face to hers. When he kisses her, she's ready for him, and returns his kiss with fervor.

He grimaces, but continues to kiss her, wrapping his hands around her waist as she digs her nails into his scalp to pull him closer.

"Lord Callum!" The duchess gasps, coming up for air.

"Yes, My Grace?" From the corner of his eye, he catches Shadow watching him from under the desk.

Her glare could melt steel.

CHAPTER THIRTY-FIVE

Shadow

I'M SEATED AT THE FAR end of a long table in the most formal of Duke Girt's three dining rooms. As visiting guests of honor, Ambassador Nhicol and his husband are near the head of the table, where King Hansen took the duke's place, being of the highest rank. The duke sits to the king's left, the duchess beside him. Ambassador Nhicol to the king's right. Cal and I are on the same side of the table as the Renovian ambassador. There are candles lit, but the light is dim and yellow, so if I keep the long tendrils of white wig around the sides of my face, I hope I can avoid the ambassador's attention. With so many seats between us, it shouldn't be difficult. Not to mention, I'm wearing so much kohl and rouge that my own mother would probably walk in the room and look right past me. As for Cal, he wears an elaborate white wig as well, along with a pair of gold spectacles. Between that and the outlandish Montrician high-necked, lace-collared frilly shirt he's wearing, I almost don't recognize him.

Plate after plate of exquisite dishes are delivered to the table, but having recently watched Cal in a clench with the duchess, I have absolutely no desire for food. Especially as I have to sit next to him while she flirts with him and he flirts back. There he is now, raising one eyebrow at her suggestively when she wraps her lips around a thick piece of steak. How much of it is an act, I have no idea.

Why do I even care? He clearly doesn't.

"Nauseating," I hiss when the duchess winks at him.

"Jealous, are you?" he whispers.

I sit up straight. No! Of course not. If he wants to kiss her, it's no concern of mine! "Not jealous, just revolted by how easy this is for you," I say. Perhaps that explained the closeness between us in the woods and in the inn; perhaps I was just another mark.

Cal takes a long sip of wine.

Duchess Girt taps her fork against the side of her goblet and the chatter dies down. All faces at the table look her way. "I would like to take a moment to share some good news with you. An important guest of ours is engaged to be married." She raises her goblet and looks directly at us. "A toast to the happy couple."

At first I panic, but then I remember the lie I spun about Cal's engagement. Of course the duchess would bring that up. She wants to see if it's true, and if it is, if it's still happening. I finish off the rest of my champagne and pick up the wineglass next to it.

"Are they not brother and sister?" the old woman who stood in front of us at the hunt asks loudly. She looks to her husband, face scrunched in confusion. He shrugs and takes a sip of wine.

The duchess giggles. "Oh yes, Lady Helena. My apologies. I meant to say that Lord Holton is himself betrothed, but unfortunately the lady in question is not with us tonight."

"I see," Lady Helena says. "Who are they again?" she says about us.

"Excellent question, Lady Helena. For those who have not been properly introduced, the duke and I have had the privilege of hosting Lord and Lady Holton of Argonia." People clap lightly; some of them nod in our direction. The duchess sips her champagne and puts it down, dabs the corners of her mouth with a white napkin. "Lady Lila, what was the name of your ancestral estate again?"

"On our maternal grandfather's side, that would be Backley Hall, in Stavin," I tell her with a false smile, annoyed that she has placed the spotlight on us, and worried about catching the attention of the ambassador. People on the opposite end of the table lean back in their chairs to get a look at the strange girl. I glance down, letting the wig obscure my face.

"Backley Hall," says one of the courtiers near the king. "I don't think I've heard of it."

"Oh, the vizier can tell you all about it," says the duchess. "I hear he has a personal connection. Maybe he'd be willing to share?" The duchess leans forward, making the diamond earrings that hang to her shoulders swing and glitter in the light. I'm suddenly self-conscious of my own naked ears.

I hate to admit it, but the duchess is very, very pretty. She's all rosy cheeks and gold hair, and so small and feminine and soft. Maybe Cal even enjoyed kissing her. I take another long draft of my wine.

"My pleasure!" The vizier begins to stand. A footman rushes forward to pull the ornate golden chair out for him. He launches into the same story he told the other day, about Lord Holton the Elder leaving him an emerald ring.

"Are you all right?" Cal asks worriedly when I almost tip over the finger bowl.

"I'm fine. I'm sorry I can't be more elegant, like your gorgeous girlfriend, Duchess Flirt." I'm practically snarling. And probably being far too loud. I don't even care.

"More champagne, lord, lady?" A footman leans forward between us.

I hold out my empty flute.

Cal shakes his head. Then he puts his hand out to the waiter, stopping him from pouring any more into my glass. "My sister has had quite enough."

"Don't listen to my brother," I growl. "Pour."

I drink from my newly full glass.

Cal sighs. "What's going on? You *are* jealous. I had to kiss her! Or we would have been discovered!" he argues.

"No choice, did you? Well, from what I saw, you seemed to be enjoying it." I wish I'd never helped him escape from Deersia; I should have let him rot there.

"Everything all right down there?" the duchess calls across the table.

"Absolutely," Cal says. "My sister is chastising me for continuing to feast."

"Nonsense," the duchess says. "Who doesn't like a man with a bit of meat on his bones?"

The ambassador raises his hand, and his husband smacks it down. "You're terrible!" he says, laughing.

Lady Helena adds: "A gentleman should eat as much as he pleases, unlike a lady. Though I believe Lady Holton knows that already." She looks approvingly at my full plate.

"It's been a long day and the wine is strong," King Hansen says. It's the first he's spoken during the entire meal. "Leave the poor girl alone."

At least someone is sticking up for me. The duchess takes exception to that. "Just a bit of fun, Your Majesty, no harm meant." She bats her eyelashes at him but he isn't paying any attention to her whatsoever. The king looks directly at me. Like he can see straight through the makeup . . . the wig . . . the gown . . .

I turn away from his gaze. Servants are placing dessert in front of us. This ordeal is almost at an end, and then I can go lock myself upstairs, wipe this paint off my face, and continue our search for the duke's true allegiances.

A tall chocolate confection arrives, dusted with powdered sugar and a dollop of fluffy sweet cream. I pick up my fork and skim a bit off the side. I'm aware of tension in the room but don't want to look up. I just pick at my cake. The table has become awfully quiet. I glance up and see that the king is still watching me. Everyone else is aware of it too, but they're pretending they aren't.

"Lady Lila," King Hansen says. "Have you received an invitation to the Small Ball?"

I blink a few times. "Er, no, Your Majesty."

He looks at the vizier. "You haven't invited Lady Lila—and her brother—to the Small Ball?"

The vizier shifts uncomfortably.

"Issue the invitation at once." The king returns to his cake, as if the matter is settled.

"May I ask a question?" Cal says. "Why is it the 'Small Ball'?"

"Because we are a small group, of course," the vizier says, looking baffled. "Are you not familiar with the tradition?"

"No, I'm not. In Argonia we only have large balls," he says with a straight face.

I thwack Cal's shin with my pointy-toed shoe. He doesn't even flinch.

"In any case," the vizier says, "I was under the impression that the

Holtons were going to depart by then; otherwise I would surely have sent them an invitation. Allow me to set this right, Lord Holton?"

"We would be honored to attend," Cal says.

"Then it is done, and, Renovia, are you staying for the event?" asks the king.

"It is our distinct pleasure to be able to," says Ambassador Nhicol as Mathieu beams at his side. "You are too kind, Your Majesty."

Please no. Please no. Please no. I can't do this all over again.

Duchess Girt claps her hands. "It's settled! Everyone's coming to the party!"

❧

CHAPTER THIRTY-SIX

Caledon

THE VIZIER SHOWS UP FIRST thing in the morning to fret over their wardrobes. He visits Cal's closet first. "Oh, but what will you wear?" The vizier sighs, flicking through the various shirts and jackets and pants Cal has collected during his stay. "We have, let's see, one . . . two . . . three days! Three days. We can come up with something in three days, I think. We'll get started right away." He shuts the closet door decisively.

Next they walk down the hall so the vizier can tackle Shadow's closet. The duchess follows him around, taking mental notes for the tailor. He pulls each gown from the oak wardrobe and tosses it onto the bed until there's a gigantic rainbow of silk and lace toppling over onto the floor. A maid picks them up, replaces the hangers, and places them over a chair, waiting for the vizier to leave so she can hang them back up. "Something . . . let's see . . . no . . . no . . . absolutely not . . . what's your favorite color, dear?"

"Red," Shadow says.

"No. Blue for him, darker blue for her," the vizier tells the duchess. She nods solemnly. "Agree completely."

"In fact, we should get out there right away." He turns to address his footman, who stands patiently in the hall outside the door. "Get the coach ready." The footman bows and leaves. The vizier sighs and rolls his eyes, as if to suggest the staff is a bother, rather than people doing him a great service.

"Tea for the drive?" the vizier asks Duchess Girt. He doesn't wait for her response, which will of course be yes. He leaves the room. As she follows, she brushes suggestively against Cal. *Later,* she mouths to him. She runs her manicured nail across his lips.

Once she's gone, the swoosh of her gown fading into the house somewhere, Shadow says, "Do you need something?" She is standing by the window with her arms crossed.

Cal's taken aback. "I thought we would talk about—" He is about to say "the duke" but he doesn't get a chance.

"There's nothing to talk about," she snaps.

He runs his hands over his face and hair in frustration. "Why are you so upset with me? Don't we have more important things to worry about?"

She looks out the window.

"I already told you . . ." He pauses to collect his thoughts. He thinks she could be jealous but he can't be sure. Besides, if Shadow cares for him, wouldn't she say something? It's not as if she's shy, like he keeps telling people. "All I did was kiss a girl I didn't particularly want to kiss, but I did it, for us."

"For me? You kissed her for me?" Shadow whips from the window. "Should I be grateful? Should I kiss the king too? For you?"

"If it comes down to it, if it helps us uncover the conspiracy," he says. He wants her to understand this is all for the greater good. "We are here for the queen. So can we please do what we're here to do?"

Shadow rubs her forehead. "Yes. Of course. I think I'm just tired. And overwhelmed."

Hooves clack on cobblestones outside the window. They see the carriage bringing the vizier and duchess to town. Shadow pulls the velvet curtain halfway across the window. "There, they're out of our hair now. Where's the duke? Did he ever mention where he was going to be today?"

Cal scans his memory, trying to recall if Duke Girt said anything at breakfast. "Not that I recall. Let's go find out."

They go down to the breakfast room, the smallest of the estate's dining spaces, to ask for fresh tea and something light to eat. Cal picks up that morning's discarded news and scans the headings.

QUEEN OF RENOVIA TO VISIT MONTRICE,
CROWN PRINCESS TO ACCOMPANY HER

Cal wonders if the queen has come to Montrice to check on his work, if she will send a message somehow.

A few minutes later, a maid arrives with a tea service, a bowl of fruit, and an assortment of breads and pastries. Cal thanks her and says, "Miss, do you happen to know where we can find the duke?"

"Oh, he's gone to town, to the solicitor's office, my lord," the maid responds.

"Any idea when he'll return?"

"Usually when the duke goes to town, he's gone until early evening, my lord. He left orders not to serve a full luncheon this afternoon. Do you need anything more?"

"No, thank you," Cal says.

As soon as she leaves the room, he and Shadow nod to each other.

Today they will make a much more thorough search of the duke's study. Cal hopes he won't have to kiss anybody to get out of it.

CAL LISTENS AT THE doorway like the last time. Nothing. Shadow turns the knob—it doesn't budge. Locked.

"Now what?" Shadow says. "I doubt we'll get another chance. We can't stay here forever. Maybe we can go outside, try to get in the window? It may even be open for air."

But Cal is already picking the lock with the sharp tip of his dagger. He jerks it to the side; there's a satisfying click. He returns the dagger to its sheath and turns the knob again. The door swings open. "Listen for anyone snooping around," he tells Shadow.

"Always."

Cal closes the door and locks it behind them. He checks the windows. If the duke comes back earlier than expected, they can climb out and drop down fairly easily. The drop is only about six feet. There are bushes, but if they fall in the right place they can avoid those.

He didn't notice the first time, but the duke's office is filthy with dust. The maids must not be allowed in very often. There are stacks of papers on the desk, some discarded drafts with large inkblots marring the words, some with lines of text crossed out. All of them appear to be real estate and tax transactions or household expense logs, receipts, records of staff payment. Cal is careful not to move anything out of place—he knows that even if it appears to be a reckless mess, the duke almost certainly has a method, and will be able to tell if something is amiss.

Shadow scans the shelves on the wall. There's far too much to go through in detail, row upon row of old ledgers and saved papers stored in leather boxes, lined up by size. She takes one of the boxes off the shelf and lifts the lid. "Nothing," she says. "Same as what's on the desk."

The desk has drawers on each side. Cal opens them one by one as Shadow had the first time they were in the study. Papers. A book of Montrician history going back to the time of the ancients. Quills. An old, stained inkstand. Empty ink bottles. Full ink bottles.

"This is odd." Shadow had stood on a stool and taken one of the boxes from the top shelf. It's opened on a petite round side table next to a reading chair. She holds up a piece of paper. "Look."

Cal takes the paper from her and reads it.

BILL OF MORTALITY

A REPORT MADE TO THE KING'S MOST EXCELLENT MAJESTY
By the company of the parish clerks of the capital of Montrice
Does hereby declare the mortal deaths of Their Royal Highnesses,
The Grand Duke and Duchess of Girt

It is dated twenty years ago, a few months before the letter from King Esban, thanking the duke for his hospitality to his late brother. But how could the duke host King Almon if he was already dead?

Cal hands the paper back to her. "Are you thinking what I'm thinking?"

She nods. "The real Duke and Duchess of Girt are dead. They've been dead for over twenty years."

"So who are these imposters?" asks Cal.

"Their murderers," Shadow says, shuddering.

"Except the duchess is our age," says Cal.

"Or she only looks like she is," says Shadow. "She could be a witch, or some kind of shapeshifter."

Cal is about to agree when she holds up a hand. She hears something. They stand still as stone. Seconds later they hear walking in the hallway right outside the door.

Cal places his fingers around his dagger. His window plan seems silly now—they can't get to the window; it's on the other side of the room.

They stand there, waiting, a box full of the duke's personal papers spread out in front of them.

The footsteps continue past the study door.

Shadow lets out a huge sigh of relief. Cal relaxes, tension leaving his neck and shoulders. "Must have been a maid," he says.

"Good thing it wasn't the duchess. I don't think I could handle such a vulgar display a second time," she says archly.

"And how do you think I felt? I'm the one who had to do it." He expects her to laugh or make a snide comment back, but Shadow is silent. "Would it make you feel better if I kissed you too?" he teases. "Then you won't feel left out."

"Don't patronize me," she says, a hurt tone in her voice.

"I'm sorry. The fact is, sometimes part of being a spy is making someone *believe* you want them when you don't."

She stares at him, still annoyed.

"Not unlike pretending to be the heir to a Stavinish estate. Would you like a lesson in the art of espionage, my lady?"

She doesn't answer directly, but that draws a smile and short laugh from her.

"Here," Cal says. "Let me teach you." He steps closer to Shadow and takes her hand in his, pulling her toward him. She won't look him in the eye, but she allows him to bring her close and put his arms around her.

He softly touches her cheek, leans down, and brings his mouth to hers.

It is supposed to be a lesson in spycraft. But when he feels her skin against his, it is the furthest thing from his mind.

Though he only intended to give her a brief kiss, once he's started, he finds he doesn't want to stop. Shadow doesn't either, and her hands twine around his neck, urging him closer. He presses himself against her as she opens herself to him, and her mouth is soft, and sweet, and he is lost in her, in this.

Yes, this. This is what kissing the duchess was not. Kissing Shadow is everything—it is more than everything—it is as if he were sleepwalking, and now he is awake, all his senses, his entire being, his soul, alive and singing.

Then suddenly, just as the kiss deepens, his hand in her hair and her arms around his neck, it's over.

Shadow jerks back.

Cal is left alone, stunned. "Do you hear something?"

She shakes her head. Quickly, she dumps the papers back in the leather box, replaces the lid, and slides it back onto the shelf. "Thanks for the lesson," she says. "You're a wonderful teacher and an even better actor."

"What? No . . . wait! That's not . . ."

But she doesn't answer. She runs out the door, leaving him alone in the duke's study.

CHAPTER THIRTY-SEVEN

Shadow

THE SMALL BALL IS TOMORROW night. Cal is undertaking a dress rehearsal with the costumes that have been made for us. "I look like a fool," he says, frowning at his clothing.

We are easy with each other, having entered into an unspoken agreement never to discuss what happened between us the other day—the "lesson"—and me running away from it. He was making a point about espionage, nothing more. I have to stop thinking about his kiss. Obviously, he's more than forgotten about it.

As for the true identities of our hosts, we have agreed to keep a wary eye on them but decided it is safer to stay at the estate than to tip them off to our suspicions by leaving.

So the Small Ball it is.

"Oh, stop pouting," I tease him. "You look rather elegant, if I do say so." I smile, thinking of the Queen's Assassin fretting over a dancing costume.

"I'm not pouting. Consider the practicality. Look, I can't move my arms"—he demonstrates by lifting his arms to show me how confining the metal breastplate is—"and the cape is so heavy. It will slow me down if we encounter any problems." He fusses with it, yanking the front tie down. "And it's choking me!"

I laugh and reach out to help him tie a better knot. "You had it too tight." We haven't stood so close together since the kiss. I finish quickly and back away. "There. Is that better?"

He nods but continues to fuss with it. "The king's upcoming engagement will most likely be announced at the Small Ball. A marriage to a princess of Argonia or Stavin will strengthen his army and forge a greater alliance against Renovia. The royal houses of Argonia and Stavin are already unified through a great-grandmother. Only Renovia remains apart."

"Or maybe he'll marry our Crown Princess Lilac," I say. "Wouldn't that be something."

"I'm sure the queen has considered it," says Cal. "It would be a pathway to peace between the kingdoms."

"Poor Princess Lilac," I say.

"Is Hansen so unappealing?" Cal asks.

I shrug. "King Hansen is fine, a little pompous and a little vain, and our enemy of course, but he seems harmless. I just meant how sad not to be able to choose whom to marry, even as a princess."

"We all have our duty to fulfill," he says, continuing to fidget in his formalwear.

A thought occurs to me. Cal's nervous. I've never seen him this way before. "You don't know how to dance, do you?"

"I know how to dance," he says indignantly. Then reconsiders. "Generally speaking. But the Guild does not offer their assassins formal training in the art, no."

I laugh. Growing up I learned all the court dances from village fairs and festivals. Plus all the lessons from Missus Kingstone over the years. "It's easy. Believe me—they can't do anything too complicated in those wigs." I look at his chest. "Or that armor. I'll teach you."

"There's no need. I can stand in the corner with my sword and cape."

"Unacceptable. Nobody will believe you're Lord Holton of . . . oh, what is it? It's been called so many things by so many people I don't know what's right anymore."

"Backley Hold," he says.

"Exactly. Listen—nobody will believe you're Lord Holton of Backley Hold if you don't dance. All highborn men of the realm know how to dance. They *love* dancing. So let's get started." I hold my arms up. I wait for him to come toward me but he just stands there. "Come on. You need to be a lot closer to me than that," I say.

He takes a few reluctant steps forward. "Really, this feels entirely unnecessary. I'll have you know I've gotten by just fine all these years without dance lessons."

"But it is necessary if we are going to uncover what's truly going on here in Montrice. Remember what you said? 'Espionage is an art. You must have a wide range of skills.' Skills include dancing."

"Fine." He takes my hand and puts his other on my waist. I try not to focus on that. "Now what?"

"Let's start with the basic steps. Put your feet like this. Perfect. You're mostly moving in a square; think of it that way. Like this." I lead him through the steps. He picks it up right away. "Excellent! Now, you lead."

Cal relaxes a bit. After leading me through a few more short steps, our actions become more fluid, less halting and deliberate. I relax and forget about the movements so much and become aware of the feel of his hand in mine, the other warm against the small of my back.

I break away. He looks stunned, briefly, but wipes the expression off his face.

"See?" I say, perhaps a little too cheerfully. "You're a natural. It's a bit like sword fighting, except nicer. You didn't even step on my foot. Now let's try something a bit more complicated. I'm going to spin as you let go of my hand, then you bring me back to you again. Okay?"

Cal catches on right away. As I turn, he reaches out and takes my right hand, and we come back together flawlessly. As if we've practiced this many times.

We do that a few more times, melding the twirl with the other steps. He's agile and light on his feet, which isn't surprising, considering his training. He has excellent posture and instinctively understands the way to make our bodies move in sync together. But I do my best not to get distracted by that. Probably more of his acting at work, and the thought spoils the magic for me.

"You just need to memorize the steps to the different dances. That should come easily. You might be better than me already," I tell him. He shrugs, but doesn't reject the compliment.

"Your father never took you to court? Or to a village fair?" I ask when we're finished.

Cal pulls the cape off and tosses it aside. He plops down into the chair. "The truth is I barely knew my father. I mean, I remember him, of course. But even before he died, he was gone a lot. Working. So I didn't know him the way I should have. And no, he never took me to court or to fairs; there wasn't much time."

He must see the concern on my face because he goes on. "Don't get me wrong. I know he loved me. But I don't think he knew how to be a father. I don't think he expected to raise a child alone. He taught me things, sure. He told me stories. Stories he learned from my mother."

"What happened to her?" I have been too afraid to ask before.

He looks down at his hands and fiddles with his sword pommel. "I know almost nothing about her. My father didn't want to talk about her—it hurt him too much. She died not long after I was born. Her name was Medan. She grew up on a farm and had a younger sister, he said. She was a Guild healer. She taught my father about herbs and using Deian magic to cure people. That's how I knew what to do for your arm.

"She didn't think the monks should be the only ones with magic. She caused a lot of trouble, teaching magic—small magic, what she referred to as 'kitchen magic,' nothing that would ever be a threat to anyone, but still—someone could report her, and the Aphrasians would come for her, and that could put the Guild at risk. My father wanted her to stop. For her own safety. Even if many agreed with her. Well, he was right.

"One night a villager called for my mother to care for their sick daughter. She'd just had a baby herself, but my father said that only made her more determined to go help. She left me home with the neighbor and headed across town. She was there all night, nursing their daughter. She did her best, but for some things, there is just no cure. The girl died a few days later. The parents blamed my mother. Claimed she was evil, a witch, using Aphrasian secrets nefariously, for her own gain somehow. That she'd stolen their daughter's lifeblood. A mob came to the house while my father was away on a mission for Queen Lilianna. Broke down the door. Tied her to a pole. Set her on fire."

I want to comfort him, but I don't know what to say. "I'm so sorry, Cal. That's . . . it's . . ."

"I know," he says. "But I don't remember anything. I was just a baby. The mob left me sleeping in the cottage. Luckily she still had at least one friend left—a neighbor who stole me away from the house and kept me until my father could return to collect me.

"When my father died, an old blacksmith took me in as an apprentice and left me the shop in his will. It's a good cover while I'm bound to service by the oath my father made. I'm the Queen's Assassin, and if not that, I'm a blacksmith."

I grab his hand. "Cal—you're more of a prince than any I've ever met." The words fly from my mouth before I can stop to think about what I'm saying. He looks at me with surprise, and his eyes soften. Maybe he's thinking of the kiss, maybe even considering another. Because I am.

I feel my heart pound in the silence between us. But he does nothing. I was right, he forgot about it and gives it no further thought. He's probably kissed dozens of girls.

I drop his hand.

"Everything will be fine tomorrow," I say to smooth things over and move on. "Get your dancing shoes ready."

✦

CHAPTER THIRTY-EIGHT

Caledon

UNBEKNOWNST TO HIS TRAVELING COMPANION, Cal has not forgotten about the kiss. It is all he can think of when he is not trying to remember where he has seen the duke before. He knows it is important, but for the life of him he cannot recall. He is almost certain the duke is the conspirator against the Renovian crown, but he cannot act until he is certain.

As for the kiss, since it appears Shadow has given it no further thought, and is cheerful and friendly toward him once more, he is careful not to show his feelings. They are friends again, and that is all that matters. But images and sensations keep returning to his mind—her soft, sweet mouth, and the way their bodies moved together, fluid and graceful, during the impromptu dance lesson.

He almost kissed her again, after telling her about his family. It is a good thing she pulled away. Whatever is happening between them has to stop.

On the night of the Small Ball he leaves his room and heads downstairs to meet her in the entry hall, conscious of keeping his stupid cape from getting underfoot.

As he descends the wide staircase, he sees Shadow standing near the door.

She doesn't see him yet, but it's clear that she's waiting for him, and the sight of her takes his breath away.

Her gown is deepest midnight blue, slightly shimmering, with delicate floral embroidery across the bottom of the skirt. A golden sash is tied around her tiny waist, and he makes a silent offer of gratitude to Montrician aristocrats for their preference for incredibly low necklines. Instead of wearing the traditional headpiece, a large conical shape with a sheer veil, she wears her hair pulled up under a blooming crown of flowers to match the embroidery.

His cape is the same shade of blue, with a red dahlia at his breast like the ones on her dress and in her hair.

Her eyes sparkle when she finally catches sight of him. "Cal! How handsome you look!" she says, even though she saw him in it yesterday.

"And you, my lady, will have a dozen proposals before the night is through," Cal says, bowing to her.

She laughs. "I hope not!" *So do I,* Cal thinks as he offers his arm to escort her.

The duke and duchess join them in the entry hall. The duchess is flustered. She fans herself frantically with her right hand, balancing her tiny puppy in her left. "The ambassador has taken ill," she exclaims. She looks at her husband. "Is it contagious, do you suppose?"

"I told you, dear, the doctor assured me it is not," he says calmly.

The fan shakes even faster. "Oh dear. I do hope it's not . . . foul play . . ."

"People do get ill," the duke says, dismissing her.

"I suppose you're right. Terribly disappointing." The duchess hands her yapping pup over to a footman and brushes hair off the front of her gown.

"Honestly, don't you know better by now?" the duke says to her.

"Oh, hush," she says. "Let's go or we'll be late!" She takes a long look at Cal. "Well, don't you make a fine knight in shining armor, oh my!" She pats his shoulder with her fan on her way past him to the door. "And, Lady Lila, you look positively . . . interesting."

The couple exits ahead of Cal and Shadow and climbs into the first waiting coach.

Once they're settled in their own carriage and the clopping of hooves covers their voices better, Shadow whispers: "What do you think about the ambassador?"

"Certainly suspicious."

"Do you think he was poisoned?"

"It's possible. But I think it's more likely he's using illness as an excuse, like we did. Maybe he thinks it will be easily believed because it will seem like he caught it from us."

"Not sure what to make of 'the doctor assures me it's not contagious.'"

Cal shrugs. "We don't have enough information. And right now, it isn't our concern. You need to get King Hansen to talk. Dance with him. See what you can find out, who is close to him. I think he'll like dancing with you a lot more than me."

"I'm not so sure about that. You look awfully dapper tonight, Lord Callum. I think you could loosen anyone's lips."

"Even yours?" he asks.

She turns toward the window, pink spreading across her cheeks.

THEIR CARRIAGE DRIVES UP the lane leading to King Hansen's castle. It's illuminated by torches all the way up to the curved approach in front of the entry. They pull up behind other carriages and wait their turn to exit and go inside. Footmen rush to open carriage doors, while royal guards stand outside the doorway. Yellow light spills out onto the front steps.

Finally, it's their turn. A footman opens the coach door and Cal steps out. He turns and offers his gloved hand to Shadow. As she emerges, people stop to stare, dazzled by her beauty. Shadow seems not to notice, but Cal does, feeling a surge of pride at being her escort. *She is mine,* he thinks, before he can stop it.

The palace has been transformed since the last time they were there for the weekly audience. For one thing, it's much more crowded, though Cal can't tell if there are more people or if the elaborate gowns and capes are taking up all the space. There are thick green flowered garlands strung over every window and doorway. Tables are covered in shimmering white tablecloths that are accented in thin gold and silver thread. Urns of flowers are set up in every corner and at every table, along with gold candelabras holding bright white tapered candles. Blazing chandeliers are suspended from the ceiling, and hanging gems glitter in the firelight. A fire roars in the giant hearth. Musicians wearing green and white play merry tunes while guests dance or gather in groups, talking and laughing over plates heaped with food. A chef carves fresh meats from a spit in an adjoining room while footmen pour bottles of the finest Argonian wine into long-stemmed glasses.

King Hansen, in head to toe gold brocade and white lace, glides across the dance floor with a flaxen-haired maiden in a flouncy mint-green gown, one of the higher-ranked noblemen's eligible daughters. "I wonder if that's her," Shadow says to Cal. "The one he's meant to marry?"

He shakes his head and points to a line forming on the other side of the dance floor. At least a dozen similar-looking aristocratic young women stand there, waiting for a chance to dance with the king. It's already clear they can't get near Hansen. "Every woman in Mont wants a turn with him," Shadow says. "So which one is the one?"

"Does it matter? Once he sees you looking like that, I have a feeling he'll let you skip to the front of the queue," Cal says.

Shadow looks at him out of the corner of her eye.

"What?" he says.

"Nothing," she answers.

"Tell me," he insists.

"You are full of compliments tonight."

"Is that a bad thing?"

"No, it's just . . . you've never noticed before. How I look."

How could I not? Every man in here does. "That's not true," he says. "It's just that you look different this evening."

"Just different?" But there is a teasing lilt to her tone and not the hostility from the other day.

"You look very pretty," he admits finally.

"I'll accept it," she says with a smug smile.

A nobleman in an outfit like Cal's comes toward them. "Uh-oh. Here we go," Shadow mutters to Cal.

The man holds out his hand to Shadow. "May I have this dance?"

She accepts his hand. He leads her to the dance floor. She looks back at Cal with a pleading expression. He puts his hands up. *What can I do?* he mouths. She rolls her eyes and shakes her head at him just as the nobleman swings her around and sweeps her away into the crowd.

Cal moves to the edges of the room and stays in the shadows, as far from the dance floor as he can while still observing the guests. His gaze sweeps the room and settles on two men in the opposite corner, deep in conversation. He follows their gaze toward King Hansen. He must get closer to them, but it's almost impossible to concentrate on them when he's so distracted.

Shadow twirls by, holding her skirt up so that it billows out even farther, led by another member of Montrice's lesser nobility. This one appears to be respecting her space, at least. She is smiling politely but keeps looking around the room. Another nobleman cuts in. She isn't going to have a moment alone at this rate—they all want her attention, however brief. And who can blame them? She's practically glowing tonight.

Her face is fresh, natural, and she holds herself with a charming forthrightness. No one would ever guess she's a beekeeper's ward, let alone an apprentice assassin.

Shadow glides by again, with a new dance partner. More are waiting at the sidelines, itching to step in. They all think they're wooing the titled heiress to a substantial foreign estate. Cal's amused at the thought of them finding out who she really is.

The vizier spots Cal and rushes over to him, his loyal footman close behind. "Lord Holton! I have found you at last. Here, come with me. You must dance with the finest ladies of Montrice! I know, I know, you said you are already betrothed, but you never know, do you? And there's nothing wrong with having some fun, is there?"

Cal resists, trying to beg the vizier off, make him go away. "Grand Vizier, you are too kind, but I have just arrived and would like to get my bearings."

Although if he's being honest, the only person he wants to dance with is Shadow. The vizier is correct, there are many beautiful young ladies attending the ball, but he only sees one.

The room feels suffocating, spinning. It's too hot and there are too many people; too many faces appraising him, ready and willing to pounce. He's hardly been here a week and he's overwhelmed with all of it, especially the petty intrigues and social demands. He wishes he were back in the mountains with Shadow. Even when they argued or struggled, at least he felt alive. In control of himself. He doesn't feel that way now. He feels empty. He needs to finish the task that has been ordered of him: Uncover the conspiracy and continue his search for the scrolls. He's not here for parties and feasting and social intrigue, and he's not here to fall in love either.

But it's far too late for that.

He is mad for her, anyone could see that—does she? Does she feel the same way? The way she kissed him in the duke's study . . . and her jealousy that he had kissed the duchess . . . the way they held each other those cold nights in the mountains, that one night at the inn . . . it gives him a sliver of hope that maybe, just maybe, she shares his feelings.

All the more reason to make quick work of why he is in Montrice in the first place. After he uncovers the conspirator and returns the scrolls to the queen, he will be released from his father's vow. He will be free.

Free to speak the truth of his heart. Free to be with her, to pledge his troth, free to make a family at last. Perhaps she would reconsider her desires as well. Perhaps he could persuade her to stay with him. The thought is so sweet that he is filled with ache and longing.

He will do whatever it takes.

CHAPTER THIRTY-NINE

Caledon

CAL SENSES AN OPENING AS the music fades to silence. He slides past one of the hopeful suitors and offers his hand to Shadow. "May I have this dance?"

Smiling, she accepts. The orchestra begins to play again, a fast and merry tune. They twirl across the marble dance floor, looping around all the others in perfect harmony, until finally the rest of the couples begin migrating to the edges, toward the watching crowd, giving Cal and Shadow room to show off their new skills.

"Keep in mind, you're my brother," Shadow whispers to him.

"Thanks for reminding me. I almost forgot," he says, a mischievous twinkle in his eye. "That would certainly give them something to gossip about, wouldn't it?"

Shadow stifles a laugh.

The sound of it almost makes him want to kiss her again, right then and there, but he is a man of restraint. The song comes to its end. All the guests clap for the orchestra. "I suppose I have to let someone else dance with you now?" he asks, although it's the last thing he wants to do.

Shadow shakes her head with a smile. "Let's not."

A footman is making rounds. As he passes, Cal reaches out and takes two glasses of champagne. He hands one to Shadow. "To not."

"I don't want to dance," she says. "But I would like to see more of the palace."

"Let's promenade," he decides. "Perhaps we might stumble upon something interesting."

Guests are lingering at the grand hallway, admiring the portraits of King Hansen's ancestors and the suits of armor worn by past monarchs, including a smaller set that Shadow immediately approaches. It's roughly her size. The portrait behind it shows a girl of about fifteen or sixteen years, looking back directly at the viewer, wearing a simple cream tunic dress under chain mail. Shadow reads the plaque underneath: PRINCESS ALESSIA OF MONTRICE, DAUGHTER OF THE FIRST KING.

"She looks like trouble," Cal says.

"'Led the king's troops at the Battle of Caravan, 1000 ED (Era of Deia),'" Shadow reads. "I think she sounds amazing."

So are you, Cal wants to say. But he doesn't. They continue on, stopping at various portraits to read about the nobles who once walked these same halls. Cal is so caught up in it he almost forgets these are Renovia's long-established enemies.

"Ready for another?" Cal asks, holding up his empty glass. He wants to leave the exhibit. Nothing of use here, and they need to stay on track.

Shadow says, "Sure," even though he knows she's enjoying the portraits.

Since they're so close to the end of the hall, Cal keeps walking rather than go all the way back from where they came. It's darker that way, fewer candles lit, but he saw some people go in that direction. He's sure either passage leads back to the ballroom.

They turn the corner and find a wrinkled elderly woman sitting at a cloth-covered table in the hall. Her frizzy gray hair is tucked under a black cap and she wears a shapeless black cape and sack-like dress, so it looks a bit like her head is emerging from a pile of bedclothes. She is shuffling a deck of cards with long, gnarled fingers tipped with bold red nails. Others are fanned out in front of her, facedown. The cards' backs are plain black except for the triple eternity circle etched in gold.

He has the sudden urge to turn back, but his pride won't allow him to do that. It would look cowardly. He wonders why he finds the old woman so unsettling. *Keep walking. Look straight ahead. Don't make eye contact.*

"My lady," the old woman says, lowering her head when Shadow passes.

Shadow stops. "What are you playing?" she asks the old woman. Cal frowns. Why did she have to stop? Nothing good can come of this. Phony fortune-tellers just prey on vulnerabilities and draw out people's fears, and that's the last distraction Shadow needs with so much at stake. He's seen plenty of these women; they target people who seem friendly, malleable. They take advantage of the fervent desire people have to reclaim magic, to control their own fate. Also, he has to admit he's a bit superstitious, even if he doesn't believe in it.

"It is no game, my lady," the old woman says. "It is destiny."

"No, thank you," Cal says, trying to move them away. He hates hearing that; fate has had its way with him too much already.

He'd rather avoid hearing anyone's destiny, especially Shadow's.

The old woman doesn't acknowledge him. She stares at Shadow. "For others, I charge. For you, nothing. Your soul is calling to me. You have questions. Doubts. I have answers."

"Come on, Shadow. Everyone has questions and doubts. We have business to attend to, remember?"

"My aunts could do this. Or something like it. They used rocks. With symbols."

"Ah yes. The Seeing Stones. Come here, my lady," says the crone.

Cal stands back, powerless to stop Shadow. He relents. What's the harm? The crone will give her a vague reading and that will be the end of it. He'd wager a gold coin that as soon as it's done, she will advise Shadow to meet with her elsewhere, except not for free.

She hands the deck to Shadow. While she shuffles it, the old woman says, "Let your energy mingle with the cards. The more you think, the more they know."

Shadow hands them back to her. She cuts them in three piles. "Stack them," the fortune-teller orders. Shadow does as she says. Then the woman pulls six cards, placing them facedown in a diamond pattern, with one in the middle. The last one, she lays across the bottom card.

"Are you ready to see your destiny?" the old woman says.

Shadow nods.

She flips over the first card. "Ah. The Empress. This represents you, the fertile young maiden. You find peace in nature, yes. Yet you also hold the crown and the scepter with grace and authority. Let's see what hovers over you." She turns the card at the top of the diamond. "The Queen of Wands. An older woman in your life. Your mother? Your aunt? She possesses great power, and believes in peace. And yet . . . the black cat sits at her feet. She holds a secret, a darker side. Something hidden. On either side of you . . ." She turns the cards to the left and right of the Empress. "The King of Pentacles and the Knight of Swords. One holds power and a large gold coin in offering, the other—strength. Protection. Loyalty. A choice. At your feet is the path you walk . . . which will you choose?" She turns the card below the Empress. She gasps.

"What is it?" Shadow cries out.

Cal rolls his eyes. Here's the hook. Though he admits he's ever so slightly worried about the cards—they seemed strangely . . . accurate. *You're falling for it too*, he tells himself. He looks at the card the woman turned over.

"The Tower," the old woman says. "A disaster. Crisis."

"What does that mean?" Shadow says. "What will happen?"

"Let's turn the last card, your destiny." She turns it, then sits back and crosses her arms. Satisfied. "See? All is well. After the storm, the sun."

Cal looks at the calligraphy at the bottom of the card: *The Wheel of Fortune*.

"Fate," the old woman says, "always wins."

CHAPTER FORTY

Shadow

WE'RE SITTING AT BREAKFAST THE next morning, back at the duke's estate, Cal with a strangely foul mood about him. He seems irritated, but I don't recall having said or done anything to upset him last night, nor do I remember anyone else causing concern.

A footman arrives to deliver a pot of fresh tea to the table. "Excuse me," I say to him. "But could you possibly bring me a sprig of peppermint from the kitchen?"

"Lady Lila, if you require anything, please feel free to come to me first. I *am* your hostess," the duchess says. She reaches for a slice of toasted bread, muttering, "Directly addressing the staff, imagine . . ."

"Maybe *that's* your major disaster," Cal says to me out of the corner of his mouth.

Ah, so it was the fortune-teller—after that he went from having a wonderful time to wanting to leave and go to bed. Except he didn't even believe she was a real wise woman, and besides that, nothing she said was terrible—I can't remember every card exactly, but I do remember she said all would be well in the end. Though I suppose she *could* say that to anyone? I'm not certain how that type of thing is supposed to go. I've only had my fortune read once.

On my thirteenth birthday, when I was finally old enough to practice some magic, my aunts cast Seeing Stones for me, as they had done when they turned thirteen. At the time I thought they were the most beautiful things I'd ever seen: translucent rose quartz, polished smooth, with carved symbols accented in gold leaf. Moments after they were thrown, from a pouch Aunt Mesha's great-grandmother had made, into a circle drawn with coal, Aunt Moriah gathered them back up and shoved them in the bag.

"What happened? Why did you do that?" I asked her.

"It was a mistake" is all she would say. Whenever I asked them to throw the Seeing Stones for me after that, they made excuses or outright refused. Which is why I was insistent on having my fortune read last night; a part of me was dying to know what the fates had in store.

A knock at the door. One of the footmen opens it. The butler walks in carrying a silver tray with a single white envelope on it, along with some peppermint leaves on a tiny porcelain plate. "A message arrived for Lady Lila," he announces.

"For me?" Who could possibly send something to me here? He lowers the tray next to me so I can take the letter. It's sealed with a plain, red-wax circle. No royal stamp, no identifying monogram or crest. It's deceptively simple—exactly why the Guild uses it for secret correspondence. So no matter what's inside, you know where it truly came from.

Cal is studying the envelope and I know he knows too.

I release the wax and take out the folded parchment. Everybody is staring, watching me. "Oh, I'm sure it's nothing," I say as I scan the paper. My stomach lurches. This shouldn't surprise me. Of course they would know where I am.

It's a short letter. Only a few lines. The less said, the better, they taught me. Always. Because you never know who else might read it.

Dearest Child,

The ambassador will send a carriage for you this evening. Make certain you and your brother are on it.

All my love,
Mother

"Bad news?" the duchess asks me.

"My brother and I have to see to our mother." As soon as the words leave my mouth, Cal throws his napkin down on the table as if he's ready to leave this moment. "Not an emergency, brother," I say, holding up my hand to stop him. "Mother isn't feeling well, but that could mean anything."

The duchess looks as if she's about to cry or have a tantrum or both. "B-but . . . what about the ball?"

The duke shakes his head slightly but says nothing to his wife.

"We just went to the ball?" I say, confused.

"Not that one, the other one. There's another. Fine—I wasn't supposed to say anything. But . . . but we are planning one in your honor."

Oh, of course. This is Montrice; there's always another excuse to throw a party. The never-ending displays of wealth, the competition, the fake friendships and backstabbing and constant nonsense. There's an entire world outside their door they know nothing about—I haven't heard a single mention of the general hardship of the townspeople since we arrived at the Girt estate. I think of the destitute children I saw when we first arrived.

Why has my mother summoned me? How does she know I am here? What is she going to tell me? She is furious, I am sure.

"When are you planning to host this next ball?" Cal asks the duchess. I want to kick him in the shins. I know he's being polite, but he doesn't understand he's only encouraging her.

"Next week," she says hopefully. "It was supposed to be a surprise, but now I've gone and ruined it." She stares down at the table and fixes her mouth into an exaggerated pout. Then she perks up as if something has occurred to her and leans across the table toward us, though really she's addressing Cal. "But you understand why I had to, don't you? We can't exactly have a ball in your honor if you're not there! Will you be gone long?"

"We are not sure," I say, because I am not. I am not certain we will even be allowed to return.

"I'm sure we will make it back in time," Cal says smoothly.

"Oh!" The duchess claps her hands. One of the dogs yelps and jumps off her lap onto the floor. "Of course! And when you return, I dare say you could stay forever if you wanted to!"

"Calm down, Aggie," the duke says from behind his newspaper. I start, as all of us have forgotten he is at the table.

She ignores him. "Promise?" she says to Cal.

"I can't make any promises." *He's already burdened with too many promises.*

With that, she frowns dramatically.

"But we shall do our best," he says, ever the consummate guest, the perfect spy.

———·———

I TELL CAL THAT my mother has called for us, but has not said why. I'm irritated and upset, so instead of telling him anything of substance, I confront him about what happened at breakfast.

As soon as he opens the door, I push past him and without waiting for the usual pleasantries, I blurt, "Why do you treat her that way? Like she's a puppy or a child to indulge."

"What is that supposed to mean?"

"Telling her we'll be back. Giving her hope. Leading her on." I pause. "I'm beginning to think you've maybe indulged in more than just her attentions." The insult leaves me feeling triumphant. Why should I be afraid to say what I feel?

He looks genuinely shocked. "No!" He shakes his head. "Do you think I would . . . and then . . . never mind. You do understand it is in our best interest to maintain good relations with her in case we require her assistance in the future?"

Okay, maybe I *should* be afraid to say everything I'm feeling. Or at least think it over a little more before I let it fly out of my mouth. "I'm sorry. It's just . . . why did you give in to her tantrum like that?" No matter that we have more pressing issues to discuss.

"Because I want her to want us to come back, just in case we need to. Neither one of us knows what's going to happen. You said yourself it's a Guild missive; it might even have come from the queen."

My arms are crossed. "Fair enough." I know he's right, which embarrasses me more. I should have left well enough alone. The duchess shouldn't even have the power to bother me right now. My mother has called for me, and she's no doubt furious about what I've done.

He looks at me with his head cocked sideways. "And what makes you so certain we aren't coming back? We haven't finished here. We know the duke and duchess are imposters, but not who they really are or what they are after. But if you want to go home, nobody is stopping you."

Somehow, I had forgotten that he is the Queen's Assassin and I am merely Shadow from the Honey Glade.

Cal frowns and rakes a hand through his messy hair. "I'm not holding you here. I can handle this quite well on my own."

"Clearly," I say as I leave the room. "Good luck with the duchess when you return."

CHAPTER FORTY-ONE

Caledon

AN UNASSUMING BLACK CARRIAGE ARRIVES for Shadow and Cal that evening to take them to a manor outside the city where the ambassador from Renovia has traditionally made his home in Montrice. On the short journey, Cal reflects on the bizarre twists and turns his life has taken in just a few months—prison, escape, the hunt for the conspiracy's mastermind, all with a beautiful and headstrong girl by his side.

When they arrive at the ambassador's estate, two women come running as the carriage pulls up the gravel road to the main house, arms waving in the air. They're plump, of middling age, both with wild curls—one blond and fair, the other brunet and olive-toned; the blonde's hair is longer—and both are wrapped in layers of colorful skirts hitched up into their belts, their bodices loosely tied. They each wear tall laced-up boots; the blonde wears black leather and the dark-haired one wears brown.

The ambassador and his husband stand behind them.

The manor is grand but simple, made of stone and timber, with paned windows and paneled doors. Cal already feels more comfortable here than he did at the Girt estate and he hasn't even been out of the carriage yet. Like all Renovian holdfasts, there is a lush garden, chock-full of vegetables and herbs, and beyond that the barn and the fields.

Shadow can hardly wait for the carriage to halt completely before throwing the door wide-open and leaping from it, nearly tripping on her own skirts while doing so. "Auntie! Auntie!"

They meet at the edge of the road, the three of them embracing and laughing. At first this scene makes Cal feel happy for Shadow, but that happiness turns quickly to sadness—he has nothing like this, and maybe never will. His parents both dead, and no other family. Does Shadow know how lucky she is?

They break apart. The dark-haired aunt notices Cal standing awkwardly near the carriage and calls out to him. "The infamous Caledon Holt!"

He nods. She waves him over. "Well, what are you waiting for? Come give us a hug!"

Cal walks up the path toward the house. The fair-haired woman grabs him and gives him a warm hug. "I don't know if you remember us. You were just a wee thing last we laid eyes on you. I'm Moriah, Shadow's aunt. This is Mesha."

The dark-haired aunt steps over and hugs him for a long time. "I haven't seen you since you were a small lad. Do you remember me?"

She does look somewhat familiar, but Cal shakes his head. He wishes he did. He instantly sees why Shadow talks of them so often. They are full of warmth and genuine affection.

"Let's go inside and get you two something to eat. You must be famished!" Aunt Moriah says.

"Yes, let's go. We have lots to talk about," Aunt Mesha says. Then she calls out to the footmen at the carriage. "Thank you; we will call on you again when it's time." She points to the chimney.

Ambassador Nhicol and Lord Mathieu greet them as well. "Moriah, Mesha, we will take our leave for the evening," Nhicol says, as the two of them disappear up the stairs to give Shadow's family some privacy.

But where is Shadow's mother, who arranged this meeting?

CAL WANTS TO KNOW more but neither of the aunts offers to explain, and he figures they will tell him soon enough. The ambassador's abode is Renovian in every way, with cozy chairs, colorful rope rugs, and bright paintings hung on every inch of available wall. It is a relief after all the artifice of Montrice.

There's a woman in the sitting room, on a tufted rocking chair in the corner, partially obscured by darkness. She's dressed shabbily, in dingy brown-and-tan peasant skirts and clunky wooden clogs on her feet. She wears a linen cap on her head and opaque spectacles— the type worn by those without sight.

"Mother!" Shadow says. She immediately kneels before the shabby woman who wears an ornate emerald ring on her finger.

Mother? This is Shadow's mother? The Guild spy?

"I'm terribly sorry for everything," Shadow says.

Shadow's mother's voice is as cold as any Cal has heard. "We will discuss your insubordination later. For the time being there are more important things to discuss than your running away."

Running away? Cal is confused but doesn't say anything. Wasn't Shadow sent to him on orders from the queen?

"Come, eat, child," says Moriah, ushering her and Cal to the formal dining table, where they all gather. All except for Shadow's mother, who remains silent in the rocking chair. Moriah passes out bowls of thick beef stew. "There's a fresh loaf of bread on the table, and fresh butter too."

Cal doesn't wait for bread or even for the stew to cool off; he takes a bite immediately. It's too hot but he doesn't care. "Delicious," he says, mouth full.

Moriah chuckles. "Glad you like it!"

"It's been so long since I had food like this," he tells her. He hasn't eaten anything but prison gruel or aristocrat nonsense in many weeks. When's the last time he had a hearty home-cooked meal? He can't recall.

Moriah claps her hands. "Excellent! Now that that's settled, let's get to it. Where to start?"

"So I take it the ambassador recognized me," says Shadow.

Shadow's mother coughs. Aunt Mesha glances in her direction. Aunt Moriah nods. "Yes, he was at the party to confirm your presence. We had alerted the Guild the very day you disappeared. And it goes without saying that we threw a locus spell straightaway.

"It didn't take too long for them to discover that you'd made your way into Deersia—at least we assumed it was you, considering that Caledon was also missing, sprung from prison ahead of schedule, by a novice stable hand no less, and then appeared in Montrice with a sister matching your description. I mean, honestly, Shadow, hardly subtle. Ambassador Nhicol sent a messenger immediately to let us know what he'd found. We called you here because no other correspondence is safe, and it is imperative that you know what we're facing immediately."

It takes a few seconds for Cal to absorb everything that's been said. He blinks a few times and puts a hand up to halt the conversation. "My apologies, but I was under the impression that Shadow was sent to Deersia by Queen Lilianna, in order to serve as my apprentice." Now that he's spoken it aloud, he doesn't know why he ever believed her. That was, of course, ridiculous. He was so eager to leave that cell, and so distracted with his orders from the queen, that he didn't think.

There is silence around the table.

Shadow can't quite meet his eye.

It is Moriah who answers. "You were supposed to be freed by Ambassador Nhicol, who arrived at the prison undercover, as a Montrician spy. But a few days after he arrived, you were gone."

"Ambassador Nhicol was the Montrician spy! I thought I recognized him; I certainly recognized his voice!" says Shadow.

Cal is stunned.

"Wrongdoing aside, I, for one, am rather impressed by how far you got," Mesha says, motioning her head toward her niece. "She has no formal training whatsoever."

"Yes, well, we will sort this all out later," Moriah says. "We need to stay focused on what's ahead, not behind."

Mesha walks up, holding a small box in her hand. "This is why you're both here." She opens the small case. Its pillowed interior is lined with dark red satin. On that sits a small shard of iridescent black glass.

Shadow's eyes widen. "Where did you get that?" She looks from one of the women to the other.

"The Aphrasians have been mining it at Baer Abbey."

"What is it?" asks Cal. "We found some in the woods at Duke Girt's estate."

"And we had a bit of trouble with it on the road, when we ran into a group of monks."

"You've seen this before?" Aunt Moriah asks.

"Yes," Shadow says. "We had a scuffle with some—well, we thought they were Deersia guards—but it turned out they were Aphrasians. They captured us when we were fleeing Deersia."

Shadow's mother stirs from her perch in the sitting room.

"And while we were trying to escape, I used some of the energy conjuring you taught me . . ." She is speaking so fast she nearly trips over her words.

The aunts look at each other and smile proudly.

"But it ricocheted back at me. Knocked me out. When I came to, I noticed the guard had some kind of shield sewn into his vest. But it wasn't normal, not made of metal. It looked almost liquid, except it was definitely solid. It looked exactly like that." She points to the box.

Now the aunts exchange a wide-eyed look of alarm.

"We were hunting with the duke when we found another piece," Cal adds. He examines the shard in its case.

"It is obsidian," says Aunt Moriah. "An ancient and very powerful substance. It can do many things—strengthen the magic of the one who wields it, and keep one safe from outside magical forces."

"And the Aphrasians have it," says Shadow, her face paling.

"So that's what they were doing back at the abbey," says Cal.

"Exactly, and this also explains why they've suddenly gained so much power after lying dormant for so long. We think the ore was discovered there, possibly when they were building a new vault or something of that nature. The Guild believes the hills at Baer are full of it. Only exactly how deep or where or even how to extract it, we don't know. Yet."

Shadow sips her tea. "When I was at Baer," she says, taking time with her words, "something odd happened. It happened once there, and again when I touched the floor of the great hall at Deersia."

"When were you at Baer?" Moriah asks, almost shouting. She stops herself, takes a breath. "You know what, never mind." She waves her hand in the air.

"What happened, child?" asks Mesha.

Shadow looks at her aunts. "I had a vision—but it was more than a vision—it seemed like I was actually transported. The first incident was at the tree . . . I went back in time and witnessed the end of the Battle of Baer."

Cal sits back and crosses his arms. Why didn't she tell him this before? The aunts gasp. Shadow's mother inhales loudly, as if bracing herself.

"The second, at Deersia, wasn't nearly as disturbing, but I saw it when it was brand-new, a thousand years ago. Omin of Oylahn appeared to me."

Aunt Moriah turns to the sitting room and nods to Shadow's mother, a look passing between them.

"Did the mage say anything to you?"

"'Follow your path,'" says Shadow.

They are all silent for a moment.

Cal breaks the silence. "So the Aphrasians not only possess the scrolls, but it appears they now have a powerful magical weapon as well."

"Exactly. It is even more vital we uncover the Montrician

conspirator and eliminate the threat," Aunt Moriah says. "What have you found so far?"

"The duke and duchess are imposters," says Cal. "We believe that they murdered the real duke and duchess more than twenty years ago. Or at least, the duke did; the duchess is quite young . . . or merely looks it."

The aunts nod, and Shadow's mother leans forward. So this is the great Guild spy Shadow told him about.

"We have no evidence that the duke is working against the Renovian crown. However, we do believe the duke is a mage," he says. "But is he Aphrasian? That we do not yet know."

Everyone gathered at the table ruminates on this information. Shadow looks nervously at her family; Cal can tell she's worried that they won't allow her to help him finish their work. But her aunts only sigh, and make no move to reprimand or order her to stay.

"There is a plot to assassinate Princess Lilac," Shadow's mother says finally. "The princess is in Montrice with the queen, and she is not safe. The two of you must discover the truth about the duke as soon as possible. The queen herself orders this."

"Where are the princess and the queen now?" asks Cal.

"All I can tell you is that they are safe in Montrice," says Shadow's mother.

Shadow perks up. "I am given this assignment as well?"

Shadow's mother studies her for a long time, then nods.

The princess has always been a target, Cal knows. His own father told him this. The Aphrasians will stop at nothing to render her death.

Aunt Mesha bustles at the table. "Would anyone like more to eat?" They all decline. Cal wishes he could fit more away, but he just can't. He stands and clears the table for his hostesses.

Once the table is clear and the dishes are done, Aunt Mesha takes Cal by the arm and walks with him to the front door. "Darling, would you mind terribly if we have a moment alone with Shadow?"

"Of course." She puts him off guard by giving him a quick hug before walking back inside. He decides to admire the gardens while Shadow speaks with her aunts and mother.

Though he's some distance from the house, he hears everyone talking before it falls eerily silent again. A minute or two later he hears stomping and shouting, then Shadow bursts out the door. Cal sees she's changed. Agitated. She heads straight to the road without looking at him. Her aunts follow after her. Moriah's eyes are red and puffy. She holds on to Mesha for support. Shadow's mother does not come out of the house.

"Is everything all right?" Cal calls out. None of them pay attention to him—they seem to be lost in their own world—unaware he's there anymore. They just walk past him, toward Shadow.

He watches them from afar as they argue, or rather, as Shadow does, her arms flailing around. The aunts seem to be trying to calm her down. Cal stands around near the house, unsure what he should do. Should he go inside, talk to Shadow's mother maybe?

Finally, Aunt Mesha walks back toward him. "The coach will return in a little while and bring you back to the Girt estate. There is little time to spare. If the Aphrasians have a way to deflect magic and strengthen their own, then even the Guild does not stand a chance against them. We don't know how much time we have before the enemy strikes. You must uncover the conspirator before they reach the princess. Lilac must live."

"I understand," Cal tells her.

"I'm not sure you do. But we believe in you. Both of you." She smiles at him. "Find the Montrician conspirator and take care of them, by whatever means necessary."

Cal nods.

She pauses, then continues. "There's not a lot we can do to assist you, but we'll do what we can. For now, we'd like to bestow a protection charm upon both of you, if you are agreeable to it. From that, we can give you each a talisman to carry."

He's never experienced something like that, but he doesn't see how it can hurt. "Thank you," he says. "I would be grateful."

CAL WALKS OUT TO the back field with Mesha to meet Shadow and Aunt Moriah in an open space behind the barn.

They join hands around a small stone fire pit. Shadow stares blankly into the flames. He is eager to know what happened in the house. For now he'll have to wait.

The women begin chanting in unison: "Deia, hear our call; please assist these dear souls as they fight to do right, mend what's been broken, and restore the rightful ways of the world."

The flames flicker. A soft breeze blows past them. The aunts exchange a knowing smile. "Now you two may join hands so the spell can be sealed," Mesha says.

Cal takes Shadow's hands in his. She keeps her eyes down. The aunts walk around them, spreading salt and dried herbs from tiny drawstring pouches they've pulled from their belts. They continue the chant: "Deia, hear our call; please assist these dear souls as they fight to do right, mend what's been broken, and restore the rightful ways of the world."

Cal feels a tug, an invisible rope, wrap around them as the aunts walk and chant. Shadow closes her eyes, so he does as well. The sensation grows so that he swears he can actually feel it, physically, the warmth around his legs and torso and arms, extending between the two of them and all around them, an undetectable shield.

And then his hands, holding hers, begin to feel hot, and he feels the same sensation fastening their hands together, and he wonders if he's merely imagining it or if it's happening to her too.

CHAPTER FORTY-TWO

Caledon

THE NEXT MORNING, SHADOW IS uncommonly pale and tight-lipped the entire trip back to Montrice. Cal asks her, only once, what happened while he waited outside. She tells him—forcefully—that she doesn't want to talk about it, but that she will when the time comes.

He wishes they could have stayed at the ambassador's manor for longer. Despite whatever upset Shadow so much before they left, he had a good feeling about the kindhearted women who raised her, although her mother gave him a bit of a chill.

Shadow's aunts gave them each a drawstring pouch, and instructed them to keep the charmed talismans on their person at all times. It was the closest thing to parental affection Cal had experienced since his father passed. Perhaps they could tell how he felt, though, because while they waited for the carriage, Mesha and Moriah told him stories about Cordyn from their days at the Guild. They said he was one of the top students, and also one of the most mischievous, often reprimanded by the training council for his pranks and rule-breaking.

While they were telling him this, it almost seemed that Cordyn was with them. Cal felt the familiar presence, the spirit of his father. Who knows? He might have been there. Cal is willing to believe in many more things than he used to.

THE ENTIRE RIDE BACK to Mont is somber. The butler informs them that the duke and duchess have gone out of town and to their country estate, as the duke had to take care of some unexpected business. That's fine with Cal and Shadow, better even. They retreat to their rooms without fanfare and take the rest of the day's meals there.

By all accounts the party to honor them is set to carry on as planned—that much is clear enough in the hustle and bustle of the staff as they dash from one wing of the house to another carrying chairs and vases and glassware. They leave them alone, and Shadow retreats to her room without inviting him, and so Cal takes the time to puzzle out the pieces of the conspiracy.

The black glass they'd discovered during the hunt, the same substance that the monks were mining in Baer Abbey, had to be recently found, he decides, if they had only started excavating. Since it was on the duke's estate, then all signs point to the Duke of Girt as the conspirator. Cal blinks and wonders why he didn't feel as confident before. It was right in front of him. It's as if he was in a fog, and now his mind is clear.

Shadow's aunts and mother didn't know why Princess Lilac was in Montrice, only that the Aphrasians are set to assassinate her. He hopes that, wherever she is, the princess is safe for now. Is the princess in Montrice to marry King Hansen maybe?

And if the King of Montrice does not marry the Princess of Renovia, then which kingdom has been chosen? Stavin has the fiercer army, but Argonia commands an armada. Montrice will show its hand soon, and Renovia must be ready.

Cal feels the pressure of his task on his neck, on his chest. He will keep the princess safe; he will unmask the conspirator before they can hurt the royal family. If he fails, the princess will die. So he must not fail.

As for his dreams of a different life, of one with Shadow—if she feels the same way about him—then he must earn his freedom as soon as possible. But he needs to know her heart. He has hope, but not certainty, and her sudden coldness is not promising.

THEY SPEND TWO DAYS this way, avoiding each other—or rather, with Shadow avoiding him. He respects her need for privacy, but as the days pass, he worries more and more about what upset her so greatly, and if it could be related to him in some way. Perhaps her mother saw into his heart and deemed him unworthy of her daughter.

Eventually, the morning before the party, they bump into each other in the main entry hall: Shadow, carrying a straw basket filled with fresh flowers, on her way inside from the market; Cal, just back from a final fitting with the tailor.

"Have I done something to offend you?" Cal blurts out.

She startles, then answers softly, "No. I am not upset with you. I am not upset with you at all." Her eyes well up with tears.

"Would it help to talk about it?" he asks.

"I . . ."

The front door flies open and bangs against a column near the doorway. Duchess Girt descends upon them like a hurricane of hoopskirts, making Cal feel stifled even though they're standing in such a cavernous space. Forget the hurricane, she reminds him of an enormous confection, piled with frosting, her hat the cake topper. That's all he can picture now: a talking dessert.

"Hello, hello!" she calls. "Did you miss me?"

"Very much!" he says smoothly. "How was your trip?"

"Oh! Don't ask. The country is so boring. Nobody who is anybody was there at all! The duke spent all his time in stuffy meetings and I sat around doing needlepoint, of all things. I missed an opera, a night at the theater, and the king had another reception, I'm told." She puts the dog she has been holding down. It runs off into the house, probably to chew up Cal's boot again.

Cal's suspicions are raised doubly. The aristocracy descends on the countryside only after the fall social season is over, so whatever drew the duke away must have been important. And if the duke is the conspirator . . . ? Cal glances at Shadow and wonders if she has the same thought as he does, but she is only watching the dog as it scampers down the hallway.

Duke Girt walks in, followed by a team of footmen overloaded with luggage. He walks right past them without saying hello, disappearing down the hall. They hear the door to his study shut and lock.

"That all goes up to my room," the duchess says about the luggage. The staff begins marching up the stairs with all of it.

Another footman enters, holding a single trunk. "That goes in the duke's room," Duchess Girt tells him.

"Yes, my lady," he says, following the others.

"Everything ready for the party, I hope?" she asks, while smoothing out the wrinkles in her skirt from traveling. She looks them both up and down and grimaces. Without her influence, they both reverted back to their own simpler wardrobes.

"Yes indeed," Shadow says. "Cal saw the tailor this morning, before you came back. Isn't that right?" She looks at him.

"That's right," he says. The tone of her voice . . . something is peculiar about it. Or maybe it is just the mood. It's odd hearing her sound so distant.

"Excellent," the duchess says, clapping her hands together. "What are you planning to do tonight, Lord Holton?" She looks at him expectantly.

"I was up very early this morning; I'm afraid I'm already incredibly tired. I was planning to go to bed."

She tsks. "That's too bad. Of course, now that I think of it, I'm tuckered out myself. Traveling does that, doesn't it? In any case, we should save our energy for the party—there will be no sleep that night! Isn't that right, Lady Lila?"

Shadow smiles sweetly at the duchess. "Yes, my lady, no sleep at all."

CAL DECIDES TO ASK Shadow directly what is the matter. If he hasn't done anything wrong, why does he feel as if he's being punished? Why did she go from being his friend, his partner, *kissing* him, to ignoring him? If she's decided she wants him out of her life and for him to have nothing to do with her, fine. But he has to know.

He takes a deep breath and raises his hand. Lowers it. Turns to walk away. *No—you need to know.* Before he loses his nerve he knocks on the door.

No response.

He knows she's in there. And that she recognizes his knock. He tries again.

The door opens. A lady's maid stands there. "The lady is indisposed at the moment, my lord," she says.

Cal peeks into the room. Shadow is sitting on an upholstered chair in front of the mirrored vanity, wearing a floral-print satin robe, her short bobbed hair wrapped in tubes of various sizes. She locks eyes with him for a second before they dart away. She pinches the bridge of her nose. "It's all right, Cornylia. Let him in."

Let him in. As if she'll merely tolerate him. That, of all things this past week, hurts the most.

She puts on rouge in the mirror while he waits, clasping his hands in front of him, to be addressed. Then she puts down the feathered puff on the vanity tray and looks up at him.

"Shall we have the first dance? Surely as guests of honor, we can claim that?" he says with a smile, trying to lighten the mood.

He waits for her customary quip. Instead she says, "I don't think that's a good idea."

The sadness in her voice is like a punch in the stomach. "Why?"

"I can't say. Not yet."

"Then when?" This is agony. He lowers his voice. "What am I to do? How do I continue, not knowing what's happening with you?"

Shadow's expression remains impassive, but a tear slides down her cheek. She quickly wipes it away. Takes a deep breath. "Your orders haven't changed, Cal, but mine have."

"And you can't share them with me?"

She looks down at her lap. "No," she says so quietly that he almost can't hear.

The silence between them stretches for an age. Shadow won't look him in the eye, and Cal feels dread in his heart and a temporary weakness in his knees. All his dreams turn to ashes in his mouth. There is no future here; she has withdrawn from him. She is a closed door and he is out in the cold.

Without another word, he walks out, the door swinging closed behind him. "Excuse me, sir!" the lady's maid exclaims when he passes, despite the fact that he bumped into her and not the other way around. She hurries back into the room as he walks away.

His first thought: *I'm not attending this party.* His second thought: *Of course I am. I'm Caledon Holt. I am the Queen's Assassin.* He feels particularly murderous tonight.

His third thought: *This is why I vowed never to fall in love.*

CAL WAITS UNTIL THE revelry is in full swing—and he's had a few drinks—before making his appearance. It's not as grand as the Small Ball at the palace, but it's impressive nonetheless, and the crowd is substantial. He'll give Duchess Girt credit for that. She knows how to throw a party. And the Montrician nobles know how to show up.

Speaking of Duchess Girt . . . He spots her standing near a table of sweets, talking to some of her friends, other aristocratic women donning the same elaborate costumes and garish makeup—white faces, bright red mouths, pink rouge, sharp eyebrows.

He takes a glass of champagne from a passing tray. Across the room, he sees Shadow. Just as beautiful as the last time. She's wearing the same dark blue dress, but her hair is styled differently—worn naturally, without a wig, her short hair sleek against her forehead.

Shadow is dancing with King Hansen. A slow waltz. Too slow. Cal hates the sight of them together—he has to stop himself from pulling them apart. *That's not gentlemanly behavior,* he tells himself. And Shadow is doing what he asked of her. Becoming closer to the king, trying to gain his favor. He resists the urge to interfere.

Not only is she dancing, but laughing and smiling, too. He hasn't seen her that way in days.

The song ends and Cal is thankful, but now she's dancing with one of Montrice's young lords, Earl Something-or-Another. Cal can't keep their names straight.

Cal makes a beeline for the duchess. "Excuse me, may I have this dance?"

She is shocked, but thrilled. She hands her glass to one of her friends and grabs Cal's hand. "Yes, of course," she coos.

He spins her out to the dance floor and she melts into shrieks and giggles. People begin talking about them behind their fans, which only encourages him. He pulls her in tighter. "Oh my," she says breathlessly.

By tomorrow morning everyone in Montrice will believe he's sleeping with Duchess Girt. He scans the crowd, looking to see if he's being watched by the only person who is his intended audience tonight.

Finally, he spots her, being led in a passionless dance with that priggish earl. Shadow catches his eye but turns away, her gaze stony.

Good. That's what he wants. He feels petty. Vengeful. And maybe, possibly, just a little bit drunk. He looks right at Shadow as he twirls the duchess.

Shadow narrows her eyes at Cal, then gives the hopeless sap

she's dancing with her most seductive gaze. The earl is smitten, and Shadow snaps her fan open and closed at him.

Cal flushes bright red to the tips of his ears, his heart pounding with fury.

The song ends. Dancing couples pull apart to clap for the orchestra. Cal turns to look at Shadow, but her dance partner is clapping alone. She's already gone.

CHAPTER FORTY-THREE

Shadow

THE APHRASIAN CONSPIRATOR IS HERE. I can feel it. It's overwhelming, almost suffocating. As if the air is too dense. There's someone at the party working with dark and malevolent magic. The talisman from my aunts is tucked into a pocket of my underskirt, and it's been humming all evening, growing hot, then cold, then hot again.

While the duke and duchess were away, I slipped from the house with a shopping basket, as if I were going to the market in town; instead I combed the woods where the hunt had taken place to see if I could find more obsidian shards.

The sun was high in the sky when I found a tiny shard. I swept that onto a leaf and put it in the pouch. I feel it grow hot and then cold again against the outside of my thigh. Sometimes it gets so hot, I'm afraid it's going to burn me, but somehow it doesn't. It's responding to a dark mage, I'm sure of it.

Duke Girt is the obvious culprit, but he came late to the party and the obsidian was humming even before he arrived. I've been making the rounds all night, dancing with everyone I can, to see how it reacts. It also gives me an excuse to stay away from Cal.

I can't think too much about him, lest my heart break any more than it already has. I can't think about what my mother has asked of me. But there is no going back now; there is only a way forward and there is no escape. I promised my aunts I wouldn't run away this time.

So I stay where I am, even if I can't bear to see the hurt on Cal's face. I have to tell him, but I am too afraid. There's also a small part of me that can't bring myself to tell Cal because it believes this won't be real until I do, that maybe it won't be true until I utter the words out loud.

An earl and a viscount and a marquess take turns twirling me around the dance floor. Young, old, and in between, it doesn't matter. A few of the boldest among them try to place a wandering hand in the wrong place without so much as a blush, or get their foul beer-tainted breath so close to my face I could faint. Or punch them in the teeth.

But I do neither. I plaster a phony smile on my face and keep it there. I am a spy, maybe not a Guild spy, but a spy nonetheless. I need someone to slip up and say something. The combination of too much spirits and the masculine desire to brag and impress a pretty face should work to my advantage, and I have Cal to thank for that lesson.

Still, I've had no luck so far. All I have to show for my efforts are cheeks that feel bruised from smiling.

I spot Caledon across the room. He looks so lost. It makes my stomach knot. I should just tell him. Why can't I? We are both here on the queen's orders now. Not that it matters. If only we had been able to speak our hearts to each other before the other night, if only we'd had a few more days of innocence. He must be nothing but Caledon Holt, Queen's Assassin, to me now.

I've been suffering with this for days, alone. But it is my burden to carry; he already has his own.

But then he walks right up to Duchess Girt and asks her to dance. Naturally, she jumps at the chance.

Fine, let him flirt with the duchess.

Did he kiss her the way he kissed me? I cannot help the hot blaze of fury that fills me at the thought. He kissed me like he wanted to become part of me—is that how it felt to her that day in the library? That his soul was in his kiss? And that he would love her forever?

The worst thought: Yes, of course it was the same. Because he's adept at acting. At *lying*. It's what he does. I have to remember there is nothing between us and never was; it never had a chance to flower. And he can always find other girls to kiss and dance with, of that I am certain.

"Lady Lila, is everything all right, my dear? You look a bit flushed." My dance partner, Lord—oh, I don't remember his name—asks me.

"I'm quite all right. I think I just need something to drink?"

"Say no more. You wait here. I'll return shortly." My eager suitor rushes off somewhere to fulfill my request, just as a footman appears with a tray of wineglasses.

I accept one and decide to flee the ballroom rather than watch Cal dance with the duchess. But when I turn the corner I run right into my suitor. "Oh," he says, looking at the wineglass in my hand and holding a similar one.

"I'm sorry, my lord, but I think I've broken my heel, and I'm off to . . ."

He kneels on the floor. Overeager, this one. "Let's have a look. I know a thing or two about shoes . . ." He grabs the bottom of my skirts and tries lifting them up.

I immediately slap the top of his head with my fan. He puts his hands over his head and stares up at me in surprise.

"Sir! A gentleman does not lift a lady's skirts!" I begin to fan myself frantically, as if I'm in need of smelling salts.

He blushes and jumps to his feet. "Please accept my apologies, my lady. I did not mean . . . I only meant to . . ."

"Well, I never!" I shout. I harrumph for emphasis and storm away. That should take care of him. He'll avoid me for the rest of the evening out of sheer humiliation.

I walk through the hall leading away from the ballroom, then stop to remove my tight heels so that I can continue. When I bend down, I feel the talisman knock against my upper thigh. I realize the metal hasn't reacted in a while. The farther I venture into the private areas of the house, the colder it gets.

Now that I've thwacked a nobleman on the head, I'm feeling bold.

Tiptoeing, shoes in my hand, I creep up the stairs toward the duke and duchess's private bedchambers.

I pause to listen. It's silent upstairs. I'm not sure what I'm doing or what I'm looking for. I don't have a plan, exactly. I just know that I'll know when I find it.

Each of my footsteps creaks on the wood floor. I'm positive I'm alerting everyone in the house to my actions, but of course that's silly, because there's a loud party going on in the ballroom and the entire household, including the staff, is there right now.

The duke's bedchamber is at the end of the hall. I run my finger along the striped wallpaper. It's textured, so the sensation is extra satisfying.

I realize maybe I had a little more champagne than I think I did. But then I am not alone.

The Duke of Girt appears in the hallway, and he does not look surprised to see me. "Why, Lady Lila," he says, cordial and friendly. He smells familiar somehow, underneath that perfume. "What brings you here?"

"I . . . I was looking to get some air," I say weakly, as the talisman hums.

"Shall we step out to the balcony?" the duke asks. "So we can see the fireworks?"

The obsidian is humming so hot it almost burns my skin, but there is only one answer I can give: "That would be lovely."

I realize where I smelled that scent before. It's from the forest, when I had a predator hunting me, the day I stumbled upon Baer Abbey. The unmistakable smell of rot and death. It smells like my would-be assassin.

Even so, I follow the duke to the private balcony outside his chambers, his hand on the small of my back, leading the way.

CHAPTER FORTY-FOUR

Caledon

SOMEHOW THE DUCHESS MANAGES TO find Cal after he thought he'd escaped her.

She comes up behind him while he's getting a glass of wine and something to eat, covers his eyes with her hands, and lets out a high-pitched giggle. "There's my little bunny rabbit," she coos.

"Oh, hello," Cal says. *Bunny rabbit?* The duchess is getting bolder by the moment. Good. Perhaps he will finally learn something from her.

This is what he should have been doing from the beginning, warming up the duchess, becoming her confidant. Why hadn't he? He was distracted, he realizes now; he was too concerned with Shadow. No longer.

"Shall we dance once more?" he offers.

"Oh! Yes, let's do that," she says.

It pains him to return to the dance floor, but it is the closest thing to intimacy in a public setting. The duchess is voluble and naïve, and he would like to know more about this mysterious duke and his business in the country.

He sees a flash of Shadow's dress across the ballroom and tries to ignore it.

The duchess leans in to whisper in his ear. "The duke is away so often, it gets terribly lonely, and cold. Even in the summer months, the house is so large and drafty, the nights are simply frigid. I shiver, all alone."

"He leaves you often?" Cal asks.

"Yes, and he goes *so* far away. He never pops back up unannounced, you know. No out-of-the-blue midnight arrivals back from Renovia, like some husbands like to do. Try to catch their wives at something naughty." She giggles. The sound stabs him in the ear. But she's finally said something interesting and so he twirls her back toward the center of the floor.

"You poor thing. What is so important in Renovia that could keep the duke away from his lovely wife?" he asks.

She tilts toward his ear; he gets a whiff of the alcohol on her breath. "My husband is a very important asset to the crown, bunny. He has many associations in Renovia."

"Is that so?" Cal says. "Friends? Family?"

"You could call them friends, I suppose. The grand prince was one," she says coyly. "A very good friend indeed."

"Is that so?"

"Oh yes, Alast was here on a hunt not too long ago," the duchess tells him.

"The duke does enjoy the hunt," says Cal politely. "He is so good at it."

The duchess laughs. "Oh! Nothing could be further from the truth! The duke loathes hunting. He's terrible! But it is a useful hobby, I suppose."

"I see," says Cal, who isn't sure he does. Not yet.

"Pity what happened to him, don't you think? The poor man, assassinated in cold blood by a lowly blacksmith!" the duchess says, as if she read his mind.

"Yes, a tragedy," says Cal. "But I suppose now the duke doesn't have to leave you for Renovia, since the grand prince has passed," he says to the duchess.

"Quite the contrary! He's leaving tonight."

"Tonight! Why so soon?" he asks, watching Shadow disappear into the crowd again. "What exactly does His Grace do in Renovia? Manage the grand prince's estate?"

"I suppose you could say that," the duchess says lightly.

Cal furrows his eyebrows, feigning confusion.

She goes on. "I will tell you a secret! He is leaving to make sure the insurrection continues as planned!"

"Insurrection? Against the queen?"

Duchess Girt laughs. "Don't tell me you're one of those Renovian sympathizers!"

He arranges his face to hide his pounding heart. "Of course not! What is the duke planning?"

"Oh, I can't say, but perhaps I will give you a hint. By tomorrow there will be *regime change*."

Regime change? The assassination of the princess? Of the queen? Is that what this nitwit duchess is talking about? Does the duke plan on killing the queen and the princess while they are in Montrice?

Cal feels a cold shock in his chest; he tries to ignore it and remain calm. "You don't say," he remarks, voice cracking a bit. Good thing she's oblivious, the state she's in.

"I'm so pleased you understand my predicament, about my husband's absences, I mean."

"Yes, I do. It's clear to me now."

She presses closer to him. "Then you know it's a terrible trial for me to stay all alone."

"I see that," Cal says.

"Anyway, let's talk a little more on when you'll join me when the duke is away," says the duchess.

Cal agrees, and continues to flirt with the duchess while his mind is elsewhere. The duke is leaving tonight, for Renovia, where if the Aphrasians are successful there will be regime change. Is the duke headed to take the Renovian throne while the queen and the princess are in Montrice? In any event, the plot against the princess is underway. He has to stop it. He has to find the duke.

But first he has to go find Shadow.

CHAPTER FORTY-FIVE

Caledon

CAL SWINGS THE DUCHESS BACK toward the edge of the dance floor, where an older gentleman stands alone. "My dear," he says to the duchess. "I have monopolized your company too long." Before she can protest, he leaves her and heads into the crowd to find Shadow.

The rooms are so packed and the women's hats and hairpieces are so monstrous that he can barely see beyond what's right in front of him.

There is no sign of Shadow or her blue dress anywhere, not in the large ballroom nor the small one, nor in any of the receiving chambers or hallways. Did she leave the party because he was dancing too close to the duchess? He shakes his head. Of course not. She wants to discover the plot against the princess as much as he does. So where is she?

He conducts a few more rounds through the party but there is no sign of her. The sound of booming cannons signals the start of the fireworks, and he follows the crowd out to the balcony. He bumps into the earl that she was dancing with earlier, but he is alone.

"Have you seen Lady Lila?" he asks.

The earl looks mortified. "Did she tell you what happened?"

"What happened?!" asks Cal, alarmed.

"Oh, nothing, nothing! I only meant to help with her broken heel," the earl says. "It was innocent!"

Cal pats the man on the back. "Of course, of course. A broken heel, did you say? She must have gone back to her room to change."

"Yes, she went off that way," the earl tells him as he points to the south wing of the house instead of the stairs.

Cal narrows his eyes as he heads toward the south hallway. These are the duke's private quarters. What is Shadow doing here? He is starting to really worry. If the duke is the conspirator, then no one is safe, not just the princess, but Shadow as well.

He runs to the door that leads to the duke's bedchamber and opens it. Nothing. No one. Just the bed, tapestries, and a roaring fire. Cal is about to leave when he sees movement out on the balcony.

The duke has his back turned. He is wearing a gray evening suit with a black cape around his shoulders. Gray and black, the traditional colors of the Aphrasians, a code indicating his allegiances. Cal has been a fool, more concerned with romance than conspiracy.

But now his mind works overtime. The duke is an Aphrasian conspirator. Grand Prince Alast was definitely in Montrice with the duke a few months before he was killed . . . so he *was* conspiring against the queen, his sister-in-law. The truth is a bitter pill, even though there is no alternative.

Except Cal is thinking of the papers they found in the duke's study. The bill of mortality. The deaths of the real duke and duchess. The letter from King Esban thanking the duke for hosting his brother. King Almon died here during a hunt, and Grand Prince Alast visited the duke for a hunt before being killed himself.

The duke loathes hunting but finds it a useful hobby . . .

CAL STORMS OUT TO the balcony and opens the patio doors, but the duke does not even turn around. Instead he removes a silver cigar case from his inside coat pocket and flips it open. "Ah, just the man I was looking for," he says. The inky ring on his finger shines in the dark, and when it catches the moonlight, Cal notices that its stone is made from the same liquid glass as the fragment the aunts showed him and Shadow the other evening. Obsidian. The duke wears an obsidian ring.

The duke addresses him, his back still turned. "So, Lord Holton, if that's what you're calling yourself these days, you have come to confront me at last?"

"Your Grace?"

The duke steps away from the railing and turns to face Cal.

Cal can't believe what he's seeing. He blinks a few times. *Alast?* It's the grand prince, the one he killed at Baer Abbey. Alive. But how? And why is he here?

"What have you done with the duke?" It's a ridiculous thing to say, but he does so without thinking.

"*I* am the duke," the man with Alast's face says. "Or do you prefer this face?" he asks, and shifts again, so that it changes to that of the leader of the group of monks who ambushed them in the forest.

The truth hits Cal like a flash of lightning. Grand Prince Alast was a guest of the Duke of Girt a month before he died. The duke killed him on a hunt and took his form. The grand prince was never a traitor; instead, he came too close to discovering the truth of the Aphrasians and died for it. But Alast was no longer useful after Cal killed "him" at Baer Abbey. So the duke went back to this form, the one that wears the face of the Duke of Girt.

"Who are you? Who do you work for? The king?" Cal demands.

"King Hansen?" the duke sneers. "The king is a shallow, stupid boy, nothing more." Now the duke laughs. "Oh, my young assassin, you are very young indeed. The better question is, what am I?"

"A shapeshifter," says Cal. With the obsidian ring and the blood of his victims, the duke can take on any form he chooses.

"At last we understand each other," says the duke.

Enough is enough. Cal must act now, while he still has a chance. Cal slips the dagger from his sleeve into his hand. But before he can strike, the duke shakes his head. "I wouldn't do that if I were you."

The duke motions to the far side of the balcony. Cal turns to see Shadow standing in the corner. She is bound by an invisible force, trapped by a collar she wears around her neck—one made of pure obsidian.

"A wave of my fingers and the collar will slice right through her pretty neck. A pity, don't you think? But then it also stops her from talking, which is an advantage if you ask me," the duke drawls.

Shadow's eyes are wide with fear. She cannot move. He can almost hear her thoughts in his head. If only he could make out what she's trying to tell him.

"Let her go," says Cal, his mind racing. All is not lost, not yet.

What is Shadow trying to tell him? He can't quite make out the words.

The duke laughs. "It's over, Holt. By tomorrow Renovia will be mine again. I tire of this conversation. Jander, take care of him."

Another, smaller figure comes into the light. The young, mute stable boy from Deersia. Jander walks closer to Cal, his mouth set in a grim line.

He raises his blade, but instead of striking Cal, he turns quickly and slashes at the duke, cleaving the finger that wears the obsidian ring.

The ring. Cal realizes now that was what Shadow was trying to tell him. *Get the ring.*

Jander had heard her instead.

The duke roars and sends Jander flying across the balcony, slamming the boy's body against the wall so that Cal can hear bones break. The small body falls to the ground with a thud. But the duke's hold is broken. Shadow wrenches the obsidian collar from her neck and collapses.

Now the duke turns to her, raising his hand and sending a powerful force to obliterate her, just as he did Jander, but Shadow recovers and holds her hands high, sending the shock force back to the duke.

"Cal!" she screams. "Now!"

The duke staggers back but recovers quickly and raises his arms once more. Yet he is not quick enough. Cal doesn't hesitate. He is fast and deadly and merciless. He has his dagger drawn. He stabs the duke once, twice, three times, straight through the heart.

He is the Queen's Assassin, the protector of Renovia, and his blade is swift and true. The duke falls to the ground, dead.

Cal runs to check on Shadow, who shakes him off. "I'm all right. My aunts' talisman slowed the duke down a little. But Jander—help Jander."

Jander lies prostrate on the floor. Cal puts his fingers to the boy's neck. There is a pulse. "Stay with me, Jander." He tries to keep him present. "Fight it."

But Cal knows that in truth, the boy is mortally wounded.

"I have lived long enough," Jander says. His voice is as raspy as an old man's. His face begins to waver, change. He grabs Cal's shirt. "Listen to me."

"I'm listening," Cal tells him.

"Duke Girt. Whatever he calls himself now."

"Yes?"

"You have to burn his mortal flesh."

Cal nods. "Because he is a shapeshifter."

Jander shakes his head impatiently. "No. No . . . Caledon, he is more than that. You must burn his body with the fire of Deia. Or he'll return. He always comes back."

Cal's body goes strangely still. A chill runs up his back, and gooseflesh, along with an overwhelming vertigo. He wants to say something, anything, but nothing comes out of his mouth. The duke is not just a shapeshifter, but the return of the immortal demon, a monster of legend, a monster who has stalked Avantine for centuries.

"Yes," he promises. He will burn the duke's body with the white fire of Deia. It is the only way. But right now he wants to keep Jander here, alive, with him, though he can tell the boy—is he really a boy?—is being pulled away toward Deia.

"Who are you really?" Cal asks, then realizes that is the wrong question once more. "What are you?"

"Cursed," answers Jander sadly. "I was cursed by the king long ago. But if you burn his body I will be free." He grabs Cal's shirt and tries to pull himself up somewhat, into more of a sitting position.

"Hurry. Take the body, burn it." He starts coughing, hacking blood. Specks of red splatter on the glass doors.

Shadow comes to kneel by them, puts a hand on Cal's shoulder. They huddle together, Cal holding Jander's body in his arms, when a scream pierces the air.

Duchess Girt is standing at the doorway, shaking, mouth open in a now-silent shriek, along with a growing pack of onlookers vying for a glance at what's happening outside.

The duchess finds her voice and screams again, this time shoving people aside to get inside. As she goes, she yells, "They've killed the duke! Murderers! Lord and Lady Holton are assassins!"

"Caledon!" Jander spits out. He grabs him one last time and yanks him close. "The scrolls! He has the scrolls."

It is the last thing Cal remembers before they are taken away.

CHAPTER FORTY-SIX

Caledon

ANOTHER CELL. ANOTHER DIRT FLOOR. The room spins, hazy; objects waver in and out of focus; voices are loud, then quiet and back again. Searing pain slices through his head. He reaches up to touch the source—he has a massive swollen lump on his head.

Someone yanks him by the collar and drags him across the floor. He kicks and tries to pull the shirt away from his neck. They drop him. He coughs, spits, catches his breath. His head is throbbing. Everything hurts, everywhere. Did they beat him while he was passed out? More important, what happened to the duke's body? And Jander? And Shadow? Where is she?

Two men lift him, one at each arm, and begin pulling him. He tries to walk. His legs feel numb, asleep; they collapse under him.

Everything around him is a blur—there are shapes, people, doorways, loud clanging noises, what sounds like scraping objects across walls.

A large door opens in front of him. Bright light blinds him— he squeezes his eyes shut against its onslaught. The guards stop abruptly and let him go. He opens his eyes, grabs on to a rail in front of him for support. Once his vision adjusts, he sees dozens of Montrician nobles around him, and in the middle of them, directly across from him, sits King Hansen.

Cal is standing in a partitioned space with waist-high wood rails keeping him away from the rest of the people in the room. He's in a court chamber. The only way out is the way he came in, and multiple guards stand behind him.

More commotion behind him. Doors open again and other guards escort Shadow into the prisoner space alongside him. Shadow doesn't say a word to him or look at him. He knows they can't speak to each other but he wants her to at least look at him, so he can find some kind of comfort in her eyes. She keeps her face firmly forward.

Duchess Girt stands up in the audience and begins shouting and pointing at them: "Lowborn murderers! Assassins!" Another woman goes to her side and quiets her. The duchess allows herself to be directed back to her seat, but she is careful to ensure that the entire room hears her mournful wails.

Phony, Cal thinks. King Hansen watches her; even he looks impatient with the spectacle.

"Please," Shadow says to the room. "Let us explain—"

"Silence!" the king roars. His lips twist into a snarl. "You trespassed in my country, gained entry under false pretenses, and murdered a man of noble birth who was a member of my court. What else is there to understand?"

I will not be able to come to your aid if you are caught, the queen had warned. He unmasked the Aphrasian conspirator and killed him. But he will die for his duty, and he has failed his father and his friend. Shadow will die as well, because of him.

Cal cannot even bear to look at her now.

As they're led away, the vizier, wringing his hands, approaches them in the hall outside the chamber. "Why? Why did you do it?" he wails. "Now I too am under suspicion!"

Cal doesn't answer his question. "When is our actual trial?"

"Oh dear. Don't you understand? That *was* the trial. You live or die at the king's command. And he is displeased, very displeased, indeed."

Cal watches as Shadow is led away. He tried to save her, he tried to save Jander, he tried to save Renovia. He hopes the princess and the queen are safe. He hopes it wasn't all for naught. But the thought of Shadow hanging because of him is too much to bear.

Cal lunges against the guards, but there are too many of them. They throw him to the ground and begin kicking and punching him until he's spitting blood—and a tooth?—and feels himself slipping in and out of consciousness, the world fading.

He's dragged back to his cell, barely aware of anything around him. The king announces that they will be executed in the morning, as enemies of the crown. There is no reprieve, no escape.

There's nothing he can do to save himself or—even worse—to save Shadow.

Chapter Forty-Seven

Caledon

DAWN. CAL WAKES SLOWLY. HIS mouth is bone-dry. There's an aching throb in his neck and head. He looks down at the bruises on his arms and legs—they're already yellowing. Can't be from yesterday. He's disoriented, unsure how many days he's slept. He must have had a concussion.

There is very little light in his cell; the only window is a narrow slit near the top of the wall, set deep inside the brick. There's no slot in the door here, like there was at Deersia. They don't expect to keep anyone in this place for very long. There's a water jug on the floor, but the water smells a bit like rotten egg, so he decides not to chance it yet. No use in getting ill on top of everything else.

He hears loud banging outside, but he looks around the tiny room and finds nothing he can stand on to see out the window. Sounds like hammers hitting wood—something is being built out in the courtyard. Gallows. That's all it can be. What else?

He knows now that the last time he'll ever see Shadow is right before the executioner puts a hood over their heads, right before they swing to their deaths. And that's if he's lucky—if he can call it that. They may go to the gallows separately, which means he'll actually never see her again.

The duke must have known all along; he was just biding his time. He must have recognized them from the beginning. They had fallen into a trap, and it had just snapped shut.

Cal has killed him three times already—as the fake Grand Prince, as the Aphrasian monk on the Deersian road, and as the duke, but until his body is burnt, the shapeshifter will return. Cal has wounded the insurgency, but no doubt they will rise again. The Aphrasians have the Deian Scrolls and are mining obsidian at Baer. Soon their army will be unstoppable.

There is no hope. As she warned, the queen will not come to his aid. There will be no interference from Renovia. He was supposed to be acting on his own, in secret. An acknowledgment that she sent her assassin to Montrice would only spark a war.

CAL LIES ON THE floor, curled up on his side. He aches so much, both from the guard's rough treatment and the pain of his failure, that even breathing hurts. If he could just tell Shadow he's sorry. He stays with that thought, imagining what he would say. *Shadow, this is all my fault. I'm sorry. I failed.* Or, *Shadow, please forgive me for what I've done, and for not telling you what is in my heart when I had the chance.*

So much remains undone. And he doesn't leave anything undone. Why is he accepting this? He is Caledon Holt, son of Cordyn Holt, the Queen's Assassin. He hasn't come this far to fail.

He jumps up and goes over to the wall under the window. There's nowhere to get a decent toehold, but he tries to reach up and grab on to a tiny lip on one of the stones. It's not enough—his fingertips can't even get a grip. He tries again, but only manages to scratch his right fingers against the jagged edge. Another stone a bit farther to the left looks more promising, so he tries that one, and this time he actually grasps the rim. He pulls his body weight up, rooting his feet around for a toehold, but finds nothing to support him. Within seconds he falls back to his feet.

It's useless.

Cal has a disturbing thought—the stones are so smooth and poor for climbing because so many in the past have tried that they've been worn down.

Just then the cell door swings open. Cal twists toward it, fists up, ready to take down anyone he has to in order to escape—or at least try. He's not going to the scaffold willingly, or easily.

The person standing at the door is not a guard, not even a person of the temple sent to comfort him in his last moments. It's the vizier, swathed in all his flowing robes and ridiculous furs, a ring squashed onto every stout finger. *Why is he here?* Cal wonders. *Does he want to unburden his conscience about something?*

The vizier bows. "My deepest apologies for the events which transpired yesterday. I pray you will accept my request for forgiveness, as it was an unfortunate misunderstanding."

What? What misunderstanding? Cal can't even speak; words won't come out of his mouth. He can't figure out how to respond to that—an apology?

The vizier stands up straight. "If you will, please, follow me." He begins to leave the room. Cal doesn't move. The vizier looks behind him, waiting.

Is this a trick? A trap? He isn't sure what to do. *What if this is just a way to make me go without a fight?*

"I assure you, there's been an error since rectified," the vizier says. But Cal can still hear the commotion outside. He closes his eyes.

What should I do?

He hears his father's voice inside him: "Go."

Cal's eyes snap open. The command was clear, as if he's standing right next to him. He decides to listen. One way or the other, there is no option but forward. Perhaps following the vizier will lead him to a better opportunity to flee, even.

He nods at the vizier and follows behind him, but keeps a safe distance in case he's about to be ambushed. The deeper they walk into the building, the less he can hear, until eventually the sawing and hammering fades away altogether. Now all he hears is their footsteps.

They are deep in the dungeons. A man screams from somewhere within the lower levels of the catacombs. Cal startles. The vizier, without looking back or pausing, says, "Ignore that."

They take winding steps up a tall tower. There are long skinny windows in the tower staircase; he can finally see what's being built in the courtyard, and it's not gallows, but something even more puzzling: a stage and rows of seating, as if a joust were to take place. The stands are being decorated with the green of Montrice on one side and purple for Renovia on the other.

He'd heard of this before, though never outside of Argonia: public combat. That's what he's going to have to do. Fight a Montrician knight, probably to the death, for the crowd's—and King Hansen's—entertainment.

Fine with Cal. He is willing to fight for his life, and fight it will be. He has no doubt he can win, and when he does, he is determined to find the Deian Scrolls, and finally, freedom. There is some hope after all. Silently, Cal thanks his father for the message. He's glad he didn't try to take the vizier down at the cell, because he might not have made it out, and even if he'd survived an attempt to run, he wouldn't have this chance again.

At the top of the steps they enter a tower room. Cal is stunned to see it's more than just a room; it's a sumptuous bedchamber outfitted for someone of extremely high rank.

"What is this?" he asks the vizier.

"A token of our regrets," he says. "You'll find new clothing laid out for you on the bed, and a freshly drawn bath."

"Where's my sister?" Cal asks. This unexpected development makes him more suspicious than anything else.

The vizier's face changes but he answers. "You'll see her a bit later, when we return to bring you to the great hall. I pray you like the clothing chosen for you. If the bathwater is too hot, or not hot enough, please call." He motions to a large silver bell on the bedside table. "In fact, should you need anything at all, please call. A personal servant will hear." He bows and then says, "Oh! And food is arriving shortly. Again, all my deepest, most sincere apologies." He bows again. Then he scurries from the room.

What in the name of Deia is going on around here? No reason to worry about the fight; he's done that before. As a little boy, when he was first introduced to training through joust, he thought it was great fun. He *is* worried about Shadow, however. Why must he wait to see her? Where are they keeping her? Is she in another room like this one, or—and this thought chills him deep into his soul—are they making her the prize? Is she a hostage?

What will happen in the great hall?

CHAPTER FORTY-EIGHT

Caledon

As PROMISED, THE VIZIER DOES indeed return to the tower chamber to collect Caledon and bring him downstairs to the great hall. As before, he bows, apologizes profusely, and seems afraid to look Cal in the eye. *Does he feel guilty for what he's about to do? Or what he's already done?* Cal can't tell.

He was grateful enough for the bath, never mind that the water was tepid; he was not about to ring the bell. Who knows who would come? He's wary of everything that's happening. The new clothes fit perfectly, and are nothing like the absurd getup he had to wear to the Small Ball, either—they'd sent him loose black pants, a crisp white shirt, and a fine leather vest and boots, all in the Renovian style and exactly his size, which means they must have consulted the tailor he'd used before. He is happy to have familiar clothes again, but this has strengthened his belief that he'll be representing his homeland in a joust or duel of some sort. Otherwise, why would they go to the trouble?

As Cal follows the vizier down the ancient tower stairs, he peeks again at the growing excitement outside. There are bunches of flowers, green and white or purple and white for each kingdom's colors, being placed along the sides of the stands with the banners. Montrice spares no expense for their tournaments.

Rather than going back into the dungeons, the vizier takes him through a separate door, down a long corridor, and through yet another door into the great hall. Cal's heart pounds with the anticipation of seeing Shadow again. He crosses his fingers at his side, hoping that she's in good care and that he won't be expected to fight for her life or something equally heinous—he's heard of such things in far-flung kingdoms, and at this point he isn't ruling anything out. A Grand Duke of Montrice died at his hand. The only thing that could be worse is if Cal had been caught assassinating the king himself.

The great hall is packed wall to wall with people, dressed only slightly less formally than they were for the ball. They're all smiling, laughing, chatting, prepared for a party. Not a solemn event—at least, not for them.

King Hansen sits in his throne on the dais as he did the day Cal first met him, but instead of looking bored, today he has a weak smile on his face.

The vizier stops short of the dais and puts his hand up to indicate that Cal should stop as well. Cal scans the crowd for Shadow's familiar face, but he doesn't see her anywhere. His stomach turns; this all feels off somehow. Like some kind of sick game.

Trumpeters step forward; their instruments begin blaring. The noise startles Cal again. He is really on edge. Not good; he has to regain control over himself. This is exactly what gets novice assassins killed—he has to try to stay above his physical feelings, his emotional responses.

There's a hush across the room.

All faces turn toward the grand doors as they glide open, pulled by white-gloved guards in brand-new green-and-purple attire. Cal almost expects lions to emerge, and though he's wrong about that, it's not a terrible guess.

A procession of Renovian aristocrats marches through the open doorway, led by the most important of them all, the Duke of Devan, who walks in with the ambassador and his husband. As they enter, they form two rows, one on each side of the door, creating a kind of path. One by one, Cal recognizes all the nobles arriving from Renovia. Are they here for the show? That's right—last he knew, he was a traitor to them.

Finally, they are all inside. There's a pause. The trumpets blast again. King Hansen stands up.

Queen Lilianna emerges from the door, head to toe in vibrant purple, the first time she's been out of mourning garb since King Esban's death. As she passes through, the Renovians bow to her. Cal does the same. She walks, head high, shoulders back, straight up the steps to stand on the dais next to her young Montrician rival. She hasn't even glanced in Cal's direction.

The vizier stands at the bottom step and bellows through the hall: "Queen Lilianna of Renovia!"

Those gathered bow or curtsy respectfully, even if she is not their sovereign. Queen Lilianna steps forward and speaks. "From this day until my last day, I am no longer the Queen Regent of Renovia."

There is an audible gasp, including from Cal. *Regime change.* Did the Aphrasians take control of the kingdom even though he killed the duke?

"I choose to step aside and pass the crown to my daughter, heir to the crown and only child of King Esban the Second of House Dellafiore. She will henceforth be joined in marriage to King Hansen the Third of House Opel. Our two kingdoms will no longer be rivals, but allies, one joint kingdom, vast and prosperous."

The crowd applauds.

Princess Lilac? Why this? Why now?

The queen sweeps the room with her serene glance. "Your Majesty, my lords, ladies, and gentlemen. This marriage is our thanks to the Kingdom of Montrice for uncovering a terrible conspiracy against my kingdom, and for keeping my daughter safe."

Cal is stunned. The queen is thanking Montrice for keeping the princess safe? And marrying her off to the enemy?

The grand doors open again. Queen Lilianna's daughter steps into the great hall, veiled and wearing a dazzling lavender gown with a long train. She walks toward the dais as her mother did, and those around her bow. Like her mother, she also keeps her chin up, determined, exuding confidence she may or may not actually be feeling.

But where is Shadow? Cal strains to search the crowd, but finds her nowhere. And then a thought dawns on him, and he wonders why he did not see it before. Why did he not question it all sooner— the Argonian emeralds, her perfect manners and knowledge of court life? He had buried his suspicions because he did not want them to be true. There was an assassination plot against Princess Lilac, and he had been tasked to keep her safe. And he did. He cannot bear to look at the princess. He knows. He knows.

For when the princess reaches the queen, Queen Lilianna takes her by the shoulders and turns her to face the crowd. "I present Princess Lilac, soon to be Queen Lilac of Renovia-Montrice." She steps in front of the princess and pinches the edges of the veil between her fingers, then lifts it, draping it behind her head. Finally, Queen Lilianna steps away, revealing her daughter to the crowd.

Cal's heart stops, even if he already knew in his heart what he is now seeing before him.

It is Shadow. Shadow is Queen Lilianna's daughter, Princess Lilac. Shadow is heir to the Renovian throne.

And she is betrothed to King Hansen.

EXCERPT FROM THE SCROLL OF DELLAFIORE, 2.4:

A Comprehensive History of Avantine

The Story of Esban and Lilianna

IN RENOVIA IT IS SAID that a young warrior queen and an Other-worldly mage fell in love and founded the Dellafiore dynasty, each eldest child inheriting the mage's magical blood. [Scroll of Omin, 1.2] It is said that Omin appears to his kin at times of need.

The Dellafiores ruled peacefully for generations. Until one day when the ruling Dellafiore king was assassinated by his jealous cousin. Phras stole the throne by force, surrounding himself with a mighty army, cementing his position by sending his minions out into the kingdom to collect and destroy all written magical works, making it illegal for commoners to practice magic. His loyal followers, the Aphrasians, were rewarded with Baer Abbey. They hoarded the sacred texts of magical knowledge and the history of Avantine in a document known as the Deian Scrolls, becoming gatekeepers of religious and political power.

Thereby the Dellafiores vanished. During this time the Hearthstone Guild is formed in order to resist the Aphrasians. Their primary function is to protect the Dellafiores and retain as much of the Old Ways as possible. As such they train as warriors as well as lower mages, both for *their own protection and for the inevitable clash with the Aphrasians, which has been foreseen through the Seeing Stones by one of their seers.*

Again, generations pass as the Guild develops into a notorious society of underground assassins and spies.

One day the Tyrant King's descendant, Prince Esban, soon-to-be crowned king in the wake of his brother's untimely death, travels to the neighboring Kingdom of Montrice—Renovia's perpetual rival—for a royal ball.

It is there that Prince Esban is introduced to a young noblewoman named Lady Lilianna. Much to the chagrin of the other eligible nobles, after only one dance, he falls madly in love with her. But Lady Lilianna is meant to marry the Crown Prince of Montrice, in a marriage ordained by the king himself.

Instead Lady Lilianna elopes with Prince Esban. Soon they are crowned King and Queen of Renovia.

However, the queen has a secret. Her birth name is Lilianna Dellafiore, and she is a direct descendant of the mage Omin and Queen Alphonia, a bloodline hidden from the Tyrant King for centuries upon centuries.

Lilianna tells Esban the truth of her lineage the night he proposes. The past has no bearing on the present, he tells her. And in any case he intends to keep her birthright a secret, to keep her safe.

Only Deia Herself knows whether Lilianna was as taken with Esban as he with her. Chroniclers of Later Times will doubtless debate this point—did the sole Dellafiore survivor truly love the dashing young prince, or was the match orchestrated by the Guild to restore the bloodline to its rightful place on the throne of Renovia?

But secrets don't remain secrets for long, and the Aphrasians, suspicious of Lilianna from the very start, soon discover exactly who, and what, she is. A Dellafiore back on the Renovian throne is the utmost threat to their very existence.

When Esban announces the impending arrival of their first child, the Aphrasian monks take it upon themselves to eliminate the usurper and her progeny. An assassination on the queen is attempted, but fails, and the perpetrator is caught by the queen's personal bodyguard, a Guild assassin named Cordyn Holt.

The guilty man is revealed to be an Aphrasian. In response, a furious King Esban orders the scrolls returned to the royal family. The Aphrasians resist, for none relinquish power without strife. They commit high treason, taking up arms against their king. All pretense of being his loyal servants is gone; they have long grown accustomed to power in their own right.

And so the king decides to bring his army to Baer Abbey, to finish the Aphrasian order once and for all. The king's army emerges victorious, if weakened. King Esban is killed, leaving his widow and newborn baby.

With her father's death, Princess Lilac becomes Queen of Renovia.

The Deian Scrolls are never found.

But a Dellafiore once again sits on the Renovian throne.

— III —

ASSASSIN & QUEEN

CHAPTER FORTY-NINE

Shadow

THE ENGAGEMENT RECEPTION, HELD IN the grand marble ballroom, is everything a bride could possibly dream of: hundreds of friends and well-wishers, inside a gorgeous castle decorated with the fullest, most vivid blooms to be found for miles around, excellent food prepared by royal chefs, free-flowing champagne, a beautiful dress. And the future groom? A powerful young king.

But the bride is me, and I am miserable.

And I can hear people whispering, buzzing about the coming wedding. I could try to ignore it, but I'm also trying to listen for word of Caledon's whereabouts, so I have to endure the chatter.

So far he's nowhere to be found. I need to speak with him, desperately. I need to explain, but he vanished after the engagement was announced. I couldn't even look at him while it was happening, but it was the only way to save us. To save both of us. My mother made that clear.

His pardon was my one condition for going through with the marriage to Hansen.

The queen—*my mother*—floats toward me.

My mother is the Queen of Renovia. I have known this for my entire life. And I have been in denial about this truth my entire life. For my own safety, I do not speak of it, let alone think of it. When I was little, my aunts cast a spell to keep me from the truth. When I was older, I learned to guard my words on my own. In my mind, my mother is merely a high-ranking member of the Guild who serves at the palace.

Royal bodyguards follow me everywhere I go. They have always followed me, but I learned to shake them early in my childhood.

I liked to pretend I was merely a maiden of Nir, a farm girl from the Honey Glade. But I have always known who I am. The day I was running in the forest, I was running away from the truth, because I had told my aunts and my mother I wanted to join the Guild and they forbade it. My place was as a princess, not a spy, they argued. I had a royal duty to fulfill.

I am Princess Lilac, hidden away to ensure my safety, given to the greatest assassins of the Guild, Moriah Devan and her wife, Mesha Abad. When my mother summoned me to the palace, when the trunks arrived, the jewels given to me were the crown jewels.

I didn't want to be the princess, so I disobeyed the queen and ran away to become Cal's apprentice. I wanted to show them I could be as dangerous and deadly as they were. I wanted to show them I had the strength. Instead I put myself and my country in danger. If Cal hadn't been so quick with a blade, if the duke had had enough time, he would have been able to kill me and his duchess would have taken my form. Duchess Girt wasn't as dumb as she looked; she was actually a witch.

The Aphrasians would have taken the crown once more.

But they didn't, because Cal is good at his job.

Now the queen is right in front of me, her eyes hooded as they have always been. I cannot read her thoughts or emotions. I have never truly known my mother.

When she called me to the ambassador's house, it was to tell me I was betrothed to King Hansen. I refused to comply and fought with her and my aunts that night. There had to be some other way to bring peace to the land. They allowed me to return to Girt only because there was no safer place in the country than at the side of the Queen's Assassin. They knew that Cal would keep me safe. They were right.

I told them that night that I would never marry King Hansen. Yet here we are. Funny how things work out like that.

"Selling me to Montrice was part of the plan all along, wasn't it?" I ask my mother.

Her back stiffens. "What a foolish thing to say," she tells me. But it is not an answer.

When the ambassador found out that Cal and I were to be executed for the duke's murder, the queen was already in Mont.

She was too late to stop the trial, but she was able to negotiate our release and force the king to accept me as a bride in return for not sparking a war between our kingdoms. She threatened to tell the neighboring kingdoms of Montrice's betrayal, how they had harbored Aphrasian rebels in order to frame Cal and me for the duke's murder. By funding the Aphrasian resistance in Renovia, Montrice had broken the treaty between the former nations of Avantine. Renovia could make an alliance with Argonia and Stavin instead, but the queen preferred Montrice and its highly defensible fortresses. Besides, it appeared Montrice and Renovia were owed an engagement.

The king accepted her offer. It helped that he already found me beguiling, he told my mother.

Viscountess Karine walks over to me and curtsies. "My greatest wishes on your auspicious engagement, Your Highness," she says, beaming.

"Thank you," I say, and nothing more. I don't want to encourage conversation. Lucky for me, she curtsies again and departs. There are some benefits to royalty, I discover. People don't impose themselves on you as much. They keep their distance.

When I turn back to the queen, she motions to me. "Come here, child."

"You're hardly my mother," I say, feeling bolder by the second. "You shipped me off to be raised by the Guild, and only appeared when you felt like it."

"You have no idea what you speak of," she says. She looks stricken. But it was her decision to send me away, to ensure that we were estranged.

"If I hadn't asked for his pardon, you would have left Cal in that prison cell! He uncovered the conspiracy and found the enemy's true face! You had no qualms about leaving him to rot, when he was only following your orders! That was cruel, *Mother*."

She opens her mouth, but she's interrupted by a tinkling sound from across the room, then more noises joining in. People are tapping their crystal goblets with their rings, spoons, anything they have at hand.

The king stands at the front of the room. He puts his hands up to quiet everyone first, then looks at Queen Lilianna and me, holds his hands out toward us, and says, "My future queen!"

He's inviting me to sit at the front of the room alongside him, a visual display of our combined power. The people want to see us together. Want to believe in a love match, the symbol of a new peaceful future for our two kingdoms. That's fine. I'd rather sit there with a fake smile plastered on my face than continue to talk to my mother.

I do my best impersonation of an elegant stroll to assume my place next to my fiancé. Once I'm there, footmen begin their service.

Queen Lilianna takes her leave, nodding to Hansen and me. The rest of the party returns to their gossip and wine and food, and my betrothed returns to ignoring me, leaning his body as far from mine as possible to speak to the beautiful courtier next to him. The one who looked at me with so much disdain when he handed me some wildflowers not too long ago.

I am alone in a foreign court, and the whereabouts of my only friend are a mystery to me.

CHAPTER FIFTY

Caledon

CAL MUST SPEAK TO SHADOW but he can't bear to attend the engagement party. He slips away in the wave of people migrating from the great hall to the grand ballroom and retires to his room in the tower instead, where he lies on his bed and listens to the hum of revelers below, their flits of laughter drifting up to him from outside on the balconies.

He doesn't want to see Shadow—Princess Lilac—no, *Queen* Lilac—with King Hansen, and he's already had so many shocks that morning, he doesn't think he can handle any more. None of it seems real. He's gone from certain death by hanging to uncertain death by battle to . . . well, practically wishing the first had come true so that he won't have to witness Shadow's union to another.

He's alive and may return to his home in Renovia, but he must return without the only thing he cares about. He must leave Shadow behind.

The vizier told Cal that King Hansen would want to winter here in Montrice and set out to Renovia in spring, to summer there. The king has never even been to Renovia. Now, along with Shadow, he will rule it. He will be Cal's sovereign.

The duke's body has been spirited away to the catacombs, and there is no sign of Jander. If Cal is to burn the body, he must do it soon, but how?

There is a knock on the door.

The door opens. Queen Lilianna walks inside. Cal leaps off the bed and bows quickly. "Your Majesty."

She nods in greeting. "Caledon Holt, you uncovered—and eliminated—the Aphrasian spy, and more important, you brought my daughter to Montrice safely. Without you, this alliance would never have been possible. Our two kingdoms no longer need live under constant threat of warfare and strife."

Cal bows reluctantly. "Thank you, Your Majesty."

"Caledon Holt, the greatest assassin of our time, it is I who must thank you for your service. There has been a plot against my daughter's life since before she was born. My spies told me they would strike before her eighteenth birthday, so I called her to the palace for her safety. But I knew she would never come to court willingly, and that she would seek you out in Deersia. She has idolized you since she was a child."

Cal is startled. Unbeknownst to Shadow, her lies were made of truth. "After all, there is no place safer for the princess than with the Queen's Assassin."

He bows, even as he has chills all over his body.

But the queen is not finished. "Love is useful, is it not?" she asks.

"Pardon?"

"She refused to marry King Hansen, even when I told her it was her duty to the kingdom. But you made the choice for her when she learned the only way to save you was to marry him. We were able to broker peace without war or bloodshed. All it took was a spark between two young people, and the kingdom is saved. She could not bear to see you die in prison. Her love for you is the kingdom's gain."

Cal's mind is reeling.

Shadow is marrying Hansen to save his life.

Her love for him has saved him and the kingdom, but doomed herself.

They have been betrayed. They are pawns in the queen's game, caught in a trap they willingly walked into, both of them. Their heroics and bravery only led them to a gilded cage.

Yet Renovia has no need of heroes; Renovia needs peace, and his sworn duty and loyalty lie in what is best for the kingdom. He is the Queen's Assassin and he will do his job best by murdering what is in his heart.

"Your Majesty, the duke—the Aphrasian—or whoever he is—he is more than a shapeshifter. His body must be burned with the fire of Deia," he tells her. "There is little time to waste."

She shakes her head. "It would be wrong to draw so much attention to yourself or to alarm our Montrician hosts. Regardless of his treachery, the duke lies in state in his chapel and to take the body now would be unseemly. See that it is done on the morrow."

"As you wish, my queen."

"When you have fulfilled your duty and returned the scrolls, I have set aside some land for you near Serrone. A barony would suit, don't you agree?" the queen asks.

He bows his head. "You are too kind, Your Majesty."

"A word to the wise. Forget my daughter. Let her find some happiness in this marriage, which will be impossible if you remain in her thoughts. When you reclaim the scrolls, you will be titled and landed and can live the rest of your life in our peaceful countryside."

"Thank you, Your Majesty," says Cal.

Fireworks burst into the sky over the castle. They both look out the window to see them light up against the black night, green and purple of course, intended to represent the joy of the union, but instead it mirrors the breaking heart inside his chest.

"Time for me to return to the festivities," Queen Lilianna says. He nods and bows, looking down at the floor, glad that he will soon be alone with his sorrow again.

As she reaches the doorway, she turns and lifts her chin into the air. "Shadow is a princess. Even if she was not betrothed to Hansen, she could never marry you. It was never meant to be, my son." The queen's eyes soften. "Perhaps you will meet another maiden, marry, and have children of your own. You are the son of my husband's greatest and most loyal friend, and I wish you nothing but happiness and contentment."

"My deepest gratitude, Your Majesty." He bows again.

She nods curtly. "Good." With that, Queen Lilianna floats out of the room, the folds of her gown billowing around her.

The door clicks behind her. Outside, an enormous purple heart erupts in the night sky, followed by a green arrow that shoots up and pierces it right before it falls apart and turns to ash on the ground.

CHAPTER FIFTY-ONE

Shadow

"CAL." I SHAKE HIS SHOULDER gently. "Wake up. It's me. It's Shadow."

I crouch at the side of the bed and nudge him again, but Cal's sound asleep, his mouth hanging open, brown hair tousled every which way. He looks adorable. I almost don't want to disturb him—I wish I could just climb into bed with him and go to sleep. Like we did at the inn, which now feels like a lifetime ago. Knowing what I know now, I'd do so many things differently. We had so little time together. Tomorrow I will be wed to Hansen. This is our last chance.

"Cal, it's me," I whisper once more. I am terrified of being found in his room, and yet I cannot leave. I must tell him everything. I must explain.

This time his eyes fly open, and when he sits up there is a dagger at my neck.

I jerk away to avoid accidentally getting hurt. Once he's awake, he's immediately the Queen's Assassin.

"Shadow?" he says as his vision adjusts. "Is that you, or am I dreaming?" He's still holding the dagger.

"It's me. Really me." I lean back and pull my cream robe tighter, embarrassed; coming here seemed like a better idea before Cal actually woke up. What if he doesn't want to listen? What if he no longer cares for me, if he ever did?

"Shadow," he murmurs, not quite awake, and as if he can't quite believe I'm here.

"Yes. Can you put your blade away? I'm sorry I woke you." I'm sorry for so much more than that.

He sits up, completely clear-eyed now, and sheathes his weapon. "Don't be. I'm glad you're here." He almost reaches his hand out to me, as if he wants me to grasp it, but he hesitates.

That makes me feel better. But I wish he had taken my hand. "I had to sneak away. This was the only time I could see you before—"

"Yes," he says, cutting me off. It's almost as if he can't bear to hear the words.

There's an awkward silence between us for a few seconds. Then we both begin to speak at the same time:

"Let me explain . . ."

"Why did you lie to me?"

His question stops me short. My initial instinct is to deny that I did, but I'm through with all that. There can be no more concealed between us. "I thought if you knew who I really was, you would keep your distance," I confess. "And you certainly wouldn't bring me to Montrice with you."

"It was all a story, then, wanting to join the Guild, wanting to be my apprentice?"

"Just because it's a story doesn't mean it's not true," I say.

"Do I even know anything real about you?"

That hurt. Although he did not know my true identity, he knew my soul. But I understand his pain, for it is mine as well. "To be honest, I feel like I don't quite know myself."

"You are Princess Lilac," he says. "Were you there? That day in court? When the queen gave me my orders?"

I nod. "Yes, it was me. I ran to the palace to tell the queen that you'd saved me from the grand prince, so you would not be punished for killing him."

"You looked like that, the day we went hunting, with the white wig and the mask. I almost recognized you," he says.

"I know," I say. "When my mother sent you to Deersia, I was shocked, so I changed out of my costume and ran out to try to see you before you were taken away."

"And pretended to be a merchant's daughter," he says. "When you were the princess all along."

I nod. "I accompany my mother to some of the royal ceremonies; the people must see the princess once in a while to know I am alive. But mostly I live with my aunts. I told them from the beginning that I wanted to join the Guild. I was convinced I could do my royal duty that way. What better weapon than a royal assassin, after all? No one would suspect a princess, would they?"

He shakes his head.

"But my mother disagreed and my aunts had to comply. That's when I ran away the first time, to Baer Abbey. My life has never been my own, either."

I sigh. "You saved my life. But I had to go back to my aunts. I didn't want them to worry. I was sent to them as a baby, right after the Battle of Baer. It was your father who insisted upon it. My aunts were his trusted friends from the Guild. Well, my aunt Moriah was a friend. My aunt Mesha . . ." This is the hardest part.

"My aunt Mesha is your mother's younger sister. But she couldn't tell you. She had to forsake her family if she was to be mine. Your father insisted on it, that no one could know the truth, not even his own son."

Cal rubs his hands down the sides of his face and stares at the floor, but he doesn't speak.

I decide we can return to that when he's ready. "Well, I was lucky; they were wonderful. And they knew a thing or two about natural magic too. They taught me as much as they could. As for my mother—well, she came to visit once in a while."

Telling him this story makes me think that maybe I am a little too harsh with the queen. She had to send away her only child, in the midst of chaos and the loss of her husband. I regret my harsh words, when all she did was out of love for me, and the safety of the kingdom. Just like me, her life has always been bound to Renovia. She is a Dellafiore, as am I.

"Then I was summoned back to the palace, to take my place next to my mother's side. I could no longer be Shadow; I had to be Lilac. But when I saw you being carted off to Deersia, I knew I had to intervene. You'd saved my life; I owed you. And . . ." This part is excruciating to admit. "I thought it was the perfect opportunity to get what I wanted. To show them I was worthy of Guild training. So I forged a work order to get into Deersia and set you free. And then you took me on, so we came here. I'm sorry that I couldn't tell you the truth earlier."

Cal doesn't respond. It is like he is made of stone.

"Anyway, I brought you something." I uncover a heavy square box, wrapped in midnight-blue velvet, embroidered with the sacred symbol of Deia.

He leans over to look more closely.

I remove the cover and unlatch the box. "This may help you fulfill your vow." I open the lid.

Inside the box is a piece of obsidian, shaped like a key.

His eyes widen. "A key to the scrolls. It has to be."

"It was found among Duke Girt's things, hidden behind a painting. All his worldly possessions revert to the king. Duchess Girt—or Gertie or whoever she is—has apparently abandoned her title and fled the kingdom before she could be apprehended. All Hansen cares about is horses, wine, and gambling. Nothing is really important to him, not even the scrolls, as incredible as that might seem. So I was able to take this for myself."

Cal gazes at the key, transfixed.

I continue. "Honestly, he didn't even notice. I suspect he just wanted to return to his dice games. I am lucky. I can only hope his hobbies will keep his attention elsewhere."

Cal still does not speak.

"Use the key, find the scrolls, return them to Renovia, and claim your freedom," I tell him. "The future is yours."

"And what about your future?" he asks at last. "You can't do this, Shadow." Cal puts his face in his hands. Shakes his head. "You can't give your life to him."

If only I'd understood his feelings earlier, when we had more time alone. "I'm doing it for you."

"I don't need it," he says. "I would rather remain in a cell for the rest of my life than see you throw your life away."

"It is mine to do with as I wish," I say softly. "Here." I push the box closer to him. "Please, take it. Find the scrolls. You're almost free. Isn't that what you've always wanted?"

"I am not free, not without my love," he says, and this time, when he looks at me, I don't look away.

My love. How do I answer that? There has always been so much unspoken between us. And yet now that we're together, now that he's saying the words I've so longed to hear, it is hopeless. Our fate is already sealed.

"Leave with me. We can run away; we've done it before. We can find the scrolls together," he says, taking my hands in his. "Shadow. Be with me. Always. I am yours. Be mine."

Oh, my heart. I cannot breathe and my entire body is aflame.

He is everything I never knew I always wanted.

Caledon Holt.

The Queen's Assassin.

He is mine.

I can see it so easily. We could don servants' garb and slip away in the night. Hansen would not look for me, at least not at first. But then my mother would wonder where I am at breakfast. An alarm would sound. Cal would be accused of kidnapping the princess, and the king's bride. We would be hunted for the rest of our lives. If we were caught, he would be executed. I could never risk that. And there is more to think about than our fate.

I shake my head. "No, if we leave together, there'd be another war. Hansen has been placated by the promise of expanding his kingdom. If I disappear, he will blame the queen for his humiliation and he will invade Renovia. I can't have that on my head."

"But you can have it in your bed," he says bitterly.

I flinch at his words. But he looks more resigned than angry.

"I have no choice. As you have been bound by an impossible vow, I, too, am tethered to a fate—but one that will never let me be free. But this is larger than you or me. I'm simply a vessel for an heir who will inherit two kingdoms. Our child will be wed to the heir of Argonia and Stavin. It is my mother's plan to unite all the kingdoms of Avantine once more, through blood and marriage; to start a new Dellafiore dynasty."

That silences him.

But I am not here to talk about Avantine history. I must go back to my chamber, and yet I am here, in my robe and nightshift. I need to ask something of him, and if I don't do this now, I will never have the courage again.

"Cal, listen to me." I reach for his hands. Mine are shaking. "Hansen will have my name and my kingdom. But he will never have my heart. That remains with you, my love, forever."

In answer, Cal pulls me toward him and puts his hands on the sides of my face. "You will always be Shadow to me," he says softly.

"Cal." I want to say more, but soon there are no words between us. He puts his soft, warm mouth over mine, hesitant at first, then eager as I respond in kind, and somehow, none of this matters anymore. He breathes into me as his strong arms circle my waist, and I slide my own around his back, pulling him closer.

"We might not have tomorrow, but we have tonight," I whisper.

At that, he pulls me down to the bed. We shed our clothing and slip under the covers. He kisses me all over so I can barely breathe.

The world narrows to the two of us in this room, our bodies fitting together as one. I pull him closer, closer, until he's on top of me, and we move in sync as if dancing.

Our bodies joined as our hearts, we soar to the skies.

We are free.

CHAPTER FIFTY-TWO

Shadow

"COME BACK TO ME." IT'S the earliest hours of morning; the sun is barely peeking over the horizon. I've spent the last few hours wrapped up with Caledon in his sheets, our legs and arms entwined, as if we cannot bear to be parted, and the truth is, we cannot.

"I wish I could," he mumbles into the pillow.

"I can order you to return." The truth is, I am his sovereign; I could make him do as I wish. A thought occurs to me.

He turns over so that I rest my head on his bare chest. This is how we slept in the cave, in the inn; this is where I am meant to be all my life. I cannot bear to let him go. I cannot bear for him to leave me. He must come back to me. This cannot be the end of us.

"Please," I say.

"What are you saying?" he asks.

What *am* I saying?

The queen may have her plans, but I can make my own. I think of the story we spun not too long ago, the one about Cal and his Renovian fiancée. I can see him now, speaking the words to me like a vow . . . *To be unmarried to each other, but together, forever.* I think I can keep that promise.

"You could not be my husband, but you wouldn't have to be," I say. "There is a room off Hansen's bedchamber, for his favorite." For his mistress. I have seen her at court these past few days, a beautiful girl who gazes at me with barely concealed contempt.

Thankfully, my future husband has many distractions.

"But there is a room off mine as well," I tell Cal. "No one would know. You could return to me, there. When you come to Montrice, when you come back to see me."

He doesn't respond, but I am seized by the idea and cannot hide the hope and joy in my voice. "You can come back, to be by my side, in between your journeys. Come back to me—come back to Montrice. We can steal time together, you and I. We will find a way. You will not be my husband, but I will be yours forever."

Cal shakes his head. He gets up from the bed, pulling on a pair of pants that were strewn on the floor. I watch him out of the corner of my eye, trying to pretend I'm not. He looks out the window at the encroaching light. "You should go."

He's not wrong. My new ladies-in-waiting will show up soon to dress me for the day, and they would be quick to report my absence. "Where will you go?" I ask him. My hands fist the sheets, rumpling them.

He doesn't answer.

"I ask too much," I say. Of course he will not return to me. I am to marry another, and being the queen's consort is beneath him. He would be under constant threat of discovery, and with little more status than one of my servants. Once he has fulfilled his vow, he has a barony in his future, land, riches, freedom to marry, to have children of his own.

"You ask so little," he says. "But that is not the reason." He takes my hand and presses it to his lips.

Outside, mourning doves coo. Roosters crow. The sun peeks out from beyond the mountains.

"You will not return, then," I say as I leave the bed. My heart is shattering, but I will not cry. I will be brave for him.

Cal keeps his back turned, which I find endearing—he's shy about looking at me while I put my nightclothes back on too.

"Will I see you again before you go?" I ask when I am dressed.

"I don't know." He is standing by the window, his back to me, shirtless, his hands shoved in his pockets. I try to etch the picture of him that way into my mind so I'll have the memory always. My handsome, dangerous assassin.

He turns around and it seems as though he's about to come toward me, but he hesitates, so I go to him and throw my arms around his neck. He folds his arms around me and squeezes tight. I pull my head back and look at him, our faces nearly touching. He runs his hands up my back and then grabs on to my hair and kisses me again, long and hard and possessive. Soon we will need to return to bed.

But he draws back suddenly. I feel the wrenching as if he'd taken a piece of my soul. "Goodbye, Lilac." It is the first time he has called me by my real name. He smiles, but his eyes do not.

The sounds of morning are more insistent now. I have but a short while before the ladies come knocking.

I will not run away with him and he will not return to me.

Love is not enough.

I walk to the door and place my hand on the knob. Before opening it to leave, I look at Cal one more time. I want to tell him how much I love him, but I can see that he already knows.

I walk out and shut the door behind me.

⚜

CHAPTER FIFTY-THREE

Caledon

WHEN THE DOOR CLOSES, CAL feels a profound emptiness. Grief overtakes him, the same as when his father died. He is entirely alone in the world. Again. His heart feels like lead, weighing him down so that he can't even bring himself to get up from the windowsill to watch her go down the steps.

He does not intend to be in Montrice when she and Hansen exchange vows. The mere thought of it makes him ill. He will leave by sunset.

Then he sees something he hadn't noticed before. There's a light purple handkerchief on the pillow. He picks it up. It is made of the purest silk, embroidered with a monogram: *HRH, LD*. Her Royal Highness, Lilac Dellafiore.

Just like the one she gave him in Serrone, it smells of perfume as well. Only this time, he recognizes the scent of freshly pressed lilac.

❧

CHAPTER FIFTY-FOUR

Caledon

OUTSIDE, CAL SEES THE WEDDING party preparations going up—green and purple cloth banners and huge canopies, upholstered chairs being carried in by a parade of workers, silver torches being installed to line the property for the evening reception.

He wonders what Shadow is doing at that very moment. Is she looking out her window at this scene, too? Does she wonder where he is?

Cal watches from the window as workers install the stage where the marriage ceremony will take place. Where Shadow will become King Hansen's wife. How can he let her do this? How can he let her go?

No one questions him as he makes his way through the palace down to the catacombs; they are too busy with wedding preparations to bother with another Renovian in their midst. The steps down to the dungeons are damp and slimy, and Cal takes a torch from the wall to light his way. Even if the duke was unmasked as a conspirator, he was still an aristocrat, and Cal counts on his body being entombed underneath the castle along with other dead nobles. There are statues depicting their former visages: kings, queens, dukes, duchesses, earls of every stripe. Knights buried with their swords.

He walks between the tombs, reading names, looking for the final resting place of the evil duke.

"He's not here," a small voice says.

Cal swings the torch over and sees a boy hunched over by an empty tomb. "Jander?" he asks, startled.

The boy nods. "You can call me that for now."

"Where is he?"

"We were too late," Jander tells him. "The sun went down. So he came back. As did I."

Cal sighs. "He was the one who cursed you, didn't he?"

Jander nods. "A long time ago."

A very long time ago, Cal knows now. For he finally remembers where he's seen the duke before, in a painting at the royal palace when he was called to see the queen. The hawkish visage, the angry eyes. The duke is none other than the Tyrant King himself, King Phras of Avantine.

"I found this," he says, showing Jander the obsidian key. "Any idea where the lock may be?"

"I might," says Jander. He stands up.

It's time to go then. They leave the catacombs together; Cal stops at his room to gather his things. He packs lightly, and finds a few things for Jander on the road. But there's only one thing from Montrice he wants to keep. The lilac handkerchief. He tucks it into his back pocket alongside the other one.

Jander picks up a satchel and follows him out.

Cal smiles. He has lost an apprentice, only to gain a new one.

They leave the palace as musicians rehearse the wedding march. He doesn't look back.

Queen Lilac

QUEEN LILAC IS ALONE IN her bedchamber yet again, though she's not complaining. For all her husband's avowed attraction to her, they have yet to consummate their marriage. Hansen leaves her alone, and for that, she is truly grateful. He spends his nights with his favorite.

Her ladies-in-waiting have been dismissed for the night. The king's apartments are far away from the queen's, per the royal custom in Montrice; they are practically on the opposite sides of the castle. Hansen keeps late nights, while she prefers waking early to have a light breakfast of ginger tea and toast on the back veranda by the gardens, where she can watch her swans at the pond.

This schedule leaves the two of them with very few opportunities to be together. That's a good thing. She knows it could be worse. Hansen may be vain and pompous, but he is not unkind. They are simply disinterested in each other, their marriage a political alliance and nothing more. At least their kingdoms are at peace.

In the afternoons, she trains with a Guild master. She is a queen now, and no one can tell her she cannot. She will follow her own path; she will turn the wheel of fate on her own terms.

She picks up one of the newly bound books she ordered from the royal printer. This one she'd had made especially for herself: an illustrated collection of Renovian legends, hand-drawn and accented with gold leaf.

Tomorrow morning she will write to Aunt Moriah and Aunt Mesha. She hopes they will visit the palace soon; she misses them dearly. She has forgiven them their part in this, for like her, they had no choice. Somehow, she has forgiven her mother as well. Now that she is queen, she understands her responsibilities to her people and the need for peace throughout the land.

All is serene as usual in the palace; a cat meows somewhere outside; feathers rustle in the dovecote. A horse whinnies softly in the stables. The kitchen maids throw old dishwater into the garden sluice and refill their pails at the well for tomorrow's washing.

Lilac's thoughts wander to Cal, as they often do in moments like this. She wonders where he is. Whether he'll ever return. Whether she'll ever see him again. Most likely she will, but only as a servant to the throne. He is still the Queen's Assassin, and she is his queen.

She opens the book and carries it with her toward the bed. She's looking forward to falling asleep with the fairy tales of Omin of Oylahn and Queen Alphonia. She, too, needs distractions.

Lilac is almost asleep when she hears a soft knock.

It is coming from the small door, the one that leads to the room next to her bedchamber.

Another knock, a little louder this time.

Her heart seizes. She can barely breathe. But hope springs to her chest before she can stop it.

She thinks back to her last moments with Cal, her desperate request of him.

You can come back, to be by my side . . . You will not be my husband, but I will be yours forever.

Lilac runs to open the door, her heart beating wildly in her chest, filled with fear and hope and love.

There it is again. A knock from the little room just off her bedchamber, the one that will be known in history as the Queen's Secret.

ACKNOWLEDGMENTS

THANK YOU TO ALL MY amazing editors and queens: Jen Besser, who believed in the story, Kate Meltzer, who helped shape and guide it, and Ari Lewin, who polished it to perfection. Thank you to Anne Heausler, who has copyedited all my Penguin books and keeps my mistakes off the finished work. Thank you to the queens of Penguin: Jen Loja and Jen Klonsky. Thank you to PR queen Elyse Marshall, who keeps my books in the press and my tours always fun! Thank you to my marketing and sales queens: Emily Romero, Erin Berger, and Felicia Frazer.

Thank you always to my assassins: Richard Abate and Rachel Kim, my 3Arts family. Thank you to Ellen Goldsmith-Vein and Eddie Gamarra, my Gotham Group family.

Thank you to my Spilled Ink family.

Thank you to my DLC and Johnston families, my family of friends, and my family-family. Mike and Mattie, everything is for you.

Thank you to my family of readers.

I love you all. Thank you so much.

TURN THE PAGE FOR A SNEAK PEEK
AT THE COMPANION NOVEL!

❧

Caledon

HE CAN'T TAKE HIS EYES off her. The royal procession—
newlywed king and queen on horseback, trailed by courtiers on
their own steeds, marching guards, and a tootling band squeezed
into a decorated wagon—is out for another jaunt into the countryside surrounding the capital of Mont.

Cal has positioned his assassins throughout the procession, to
stay alert to any threats from within as well as among the gaggles
of farmers and villagers thronging the road. He's sent Jander to
ride at the front, along with the scouts and the royal crier. Cal will
never get used to the lilting sound of the Montrice accent. Better
the flat tones of Renovia, where everything—people and geography
both—lacks pretension. There's an ostentation to Montrice, and its
court, that he doesn't like. Even this procession is ostentatious—
thirty courtiers and twice as many guards.

The distant mountains are capped with snow above the tree line,
but here in the lowlands it's still autumn. Since their marriage several months ago, King Hansen and Queen Lilac have ridden out

like this at least twice a week, to visit hamlets and villages, and to preside over harvest celebrations.

Queen Lilac. His friend Shadow's true identity, revealed to the world. It has taken some getting used to, even if he has accepted it, accepted her, for who she is. He watches her up ahead, a slim and graceful figure on her horse, cloak thrown over her shoulder because the day is so fine. Hansen, her husband, leans toward her and says something; Lilac laughs. She lifts her face to the light, but Cal's behind her and can't read her expression. A spark of jealousy shoots through him, painful and sharp. The king is handsome in the bland, expected way of titled monarchs, but handsome nonetheless, sitting regally on his majestic steed, waving to the crowd.

The Kingdoms of Montrice and Renovia are united: Look at the happy young king and queen—so beautiful, so well dressed— delighted to be meeting grubby country folk in their muddy villages. It's all designed to dispel rumors that the marriage is one of mere political expedience.

Lilac might be Hansen's queen in public, but at night, in private, thanks to the secret room and passageway adjacent to her own, she is still his Shadow. Just this morning they were entwined in each other's arms. But now she rides next to the king while Cal remains on the fringes, watching for danger.

The fact that Cal shares the queen's bed, while the king sleeps with his own rotating array of favorites, is nobody's business but their respective royal Majesties. Hansen and Lilac are cordial, distant. If the king is unnerved about his wife's curiously close friendship with the royal assassin, he has made no indication of it.

"Long live the king!" people shout from their perches on hedgerows, or from stations along stone walls and tumbling wooden fences. A few cheer for the queen as well, the local maidens and lasses the loudest in their admiration. Lilac is young, energetic, and vibrant—an equal to their handsome king—and her blood hails from the old and storied line of Avantine's ancient rulers. Not only that: Everyone knows that she's brought Renovian bounty to the Montrician coffers.

There aren't as many people out today, Cal observes, reining in his horse and falling farther back. It's later in autumn now, and most of the harvest festivals and rituals are over. Lilac will miss the outings, Cal suspects, though she always complains afterward about being forced to ride alongside Hansen and pretend his conversation is sparkling. She finds him exceedingly dull, and Hansen has been chafing about having to visit villages rather than riding to hound out in the forest. Every cold day reminds the king that hunting season is underway, and he wants to get back to his usual pursuits.

A village looms, one of several the procession will pass this morning on its way to the town of Sancton. Cal gallops to the front, whipping a glance at Lilac as he passes. She's smiling, but it looks strained. At least the village visit will cheer her up. During these autumn processions, in every hamlet and village, every tiny settlement and every town, Cal has seen lilac-colored ribbons tied to window latches and branches of trees. The people of Montrice are welcoming Lilac as their queen. In the towns, small girls present her with bouquets of autumn leaves and flowers. Hansen is asked to drink a symbolic draft from a horn of plenty, and he makes the same joke every time about wishing for ale rather than well water. Everyone laughs, he plants an awkward kiss on Lilac's cheek, and then the entire royal procession moves on.

Today should be no different, but Cal feels uneasy. He rides up alongside Jander and nods at his slight, frowning apprentice. Some people are surprised that the Chief Assassin trusts and relies on a skinny boy, but they don't know that Jander is more than just a humble stable hand, and older than everyone in the entire kingdom.

"It's quiet on the road," Jander observes in his low, rasping voice.

"Too quiet?"

He gives the slightest of shrugs. But Cal trusts Jander's instincts, and his own. Something *isn't* right today. Perhaps the news from Stur has already reached this village. He had urged the king not to make this trip, but Hansen insisted. Behind Cal, a few people are cheering for the king, but with less gusto than usual. The country folk lined up to watch are craning to get a glimpse of Lilac, but they're not smiling or cheering. The village that lies ahead looks the same as so many others in this part of Montrice—while the capital city, Mont, is rich and dazzling, the countryside is full of thatched roofs, daub-and-wattle walls, penned goats and sheep, water troughs, a makeshift shelter over the well where chickens peck around in the dirt, and a donkey or two tied to a post. Cal has seen dozens of these over the past few weeks. The only difference among them is the general dirtiness of the populace, and whether the tree of life grows in the middle of the road or in an overgrown village green.

"Long live the king!" bellows the crier from Castle Mont, in his green-and-white livery, his beard as rusty as the leaves drifting from trees. "Long live the queen!"

"Long live the children of Stur," a voice in the crowd says. So they do know about Stur. The speaker is a young man, maybe, but when Cal tries to single him out, it's impossible. There's a sour look to the people assembled here; they seem discontent, which is understandable.

In a moment the villagers have all taken up the cry. "Long live the children of Stur! Deia bless the children of Stur! May we never forget the children of Stur!"

Cal looks around. There are no lilac ribbons tied anywhere, not a single one.

"Pray for the souls of the children of Stur!" shouts one old woman, her voice high-pitched and cracking. "Deia damn the evil magic that killed them!"

Cal trots back toward Lilac and Hansen, scrutinizing their expressions. Both have heard the shouts of the villagers. Hansen looks ill at ease, as though he's ready to turn his horse and gallop home. Lilac appears serene and untroubled: That's her aunts' assassin training at work, Cal thinks. Give nothing away with your face or your body language. Make no rushed gestures. Let no enemy perceive you as nervous, startled, unprepared. Afraid.

"Deia damn the witch who killed them!" a man shouts, and Hansen's horse rears a little, unnerved by the noise. Cal doesn't like this. The witch—who do they mean? He glances around. They all seem to be looking in one place. At one person, anyway. The queen.

The lilac-frosted ice.

"Boo! Boo!" The sound is all around them, men's and women's voices, sour and angry.

That's it. Cal has to stop this, right now.

"Your Majesty," he says, drawing his horse close to Hansen's. "I believe we must return to the capital."

"What's going on?" Hansen asks, bewildered. "They're upsetting my horse."

"The terrible news from Stur has upset our people," Lilac says in a loud, clear voice, no doubt aware that her words will carry. "That's to be expected. We should have canceled this visit today as I suggested. It is . . . unseemly at such a sad time."

"I don't know why they're angry with *us*," Hansen complains, frowning at Lilac. "Hang this. We're in the dark like everyone else, and news of Stur arrived just this morning. I saw no reason to change course. This is still my kingdom."

"Quite," says Cal, keen to end the conversation. The booing intensifies, the crowd growing more brazen. He holds up an arm to summon the assassins, and they gallop up, circling the monarchs.

"Rally to the king and queen," he mutters. "Follow me."

"What on earth is going on here?"

It's the Duke of Auvigne, his face even ruddier than usual. "What is all this to-do? These subjects need a good thrashing, if you ask me. I've never heard such disrespectful nonsense."

"We're returning to the castle, Your Grace," Cal tells him. "At once."

"Very well, but the guards should arrest some of these louts and make an example of them."

"That won't be necessary." Once again, Lilac sounds calm and firm, though Cal knows that she must be in turmoil. When he looks into her dark eyes, there's no sparkle. "We should make haste."

At a nod from Cal, Jander takes off toward the back of the procession, to spread the word of an about-face. In an instant, they're on their way, retracing their progress along the road to Mont. The city is visible on its hilltop in the distance, and Cal wants to set a quicker pace than their journey out.

The countryside isn't a happy place anymore, and it's not a safe place. *Deia damn the witch who killed them.*

In the minds of the people of Montrice—so adoring last week— has everything changed so utterly? Is Lilac the "witch" they fear? Cal is troubled, but for now he needs to get Lilac back behind the city wall and into the castle, where she will be safe from her people.

✣

CHAPTER TWO

Lilac

IT'S BEEN THREE DAYS SINCE our last attempted journey, and for the time being no one is allowed out of the royal castle. People here in Mont call it a palace, but it's more like a fortress, the moat a weed-infested gully strewn with iron spikes to deter invaders. At nightfall the heavy portcullis clangs shut and the drawbridge rises. We're all trapped in here, for our own safety. These are dangerous times, and I fear the danger will only grow.

Aside from an emergency meeting of the Small Council, I haven't seen Hansen. He has always had the love of his people, and I don't think he's taken our recent reception well. Maybe he thinks it's my fault. In fact, I'm sure he thinks it's my fault.

The weather has turned chilly and wintry, and it's been decided that we should suspend further excursions around Montrice until . . . until what? Until spring? No. Until the rumors die down, and the anger.

The day drags, and then at last, night falls. I sink into my vast bed, its brocade curtains drawn around me before my ladies depart, fussing with their candles and competing to be the last to wish me good night.

"Sleep well, Your Majesty," they say, though their faces are anxious, and I doubt any of us are sleeping well right now. All the talk is of the terrible news from Stur and the people who died there. The *children* who died there. My ladies are careful not to say anything directly to me, but the men in the Small Council are less circumspect. Anyway, I knew—as soon as I saw their faces and heard their displeasure when Hansen and I rode out the other day. They hate me. They blame me.

The lilac-colored frost over the pond. A curse from the Renovian witch. It is easier to blame the devil they know—the foreign queen—than the one they don't, the demons who walk among us once more. The King of Stavin is convinced the Aphrasians have returned, and who am I to dispute this? Stavin is right: We *have* been slow to act. The problem is that the king does not even know where to start looking for perpetrators. The Aphrasians seem to have disappeared into thin air. I have pushed Hansen to send soldiers to Baer Abbey, but the king does not listen to me. And my mother is still, for all intents and purposes, the leader of Renovia.

I lie in my vast bed, propped up on my pillows, listening to the soft night sounds of the castle, waiting.

Hansen, in his own apartments at the far end of the hall keep, may be hosting his usual revelries—drinking, gambling—games that might be raucous or debauched. All with his favorites and his dogs. I actually have no idea. He could be brushing up on the scrolls and drinking tea, but I doubt it.

He's kept his distance from me since our marriage, which is a great relief.

He hasn't insisted on my presence at any of his evening entertainments or once tried to join me in my bed, or summon me to his.

This is a marriage of political expedience for both of us, after all. A political disaster right now, especially since the people blame or suspect me for the terrible things that have happened lately.

The guards call to one another across the battlements, and an owl hoots from a distant perch. Sometimes, if there's no wind, I think I can hear whinnying from the stables, when the horses board for the night, though maybe this is my imagination. I'm longing for the castle to settle, and for the business of the day to be over.

Because that is when Cal will come to me, through the secret door in the hall's cellars, all the way up the narrow stone staircase, to the tiny antechamber we call the Queen's Secret. I'm waiting for his knock on the door. Waiting, waiting, waiting.

It has been three days since the ill-fated trip to the village, three days since he has visited. I can never acknowledge our friendship in public, but I saw the alarm in his eyes when the crowd turned ugly. I want to tell him I'm all right, that I can take care of myself, that he doesn't need to worry so. But I also, selfishly, just want to be with him.

The fire in the grate is low now, no longer spitting and hissing. The taper by my bed is still lit, but it throws little light, and I can't see into the recesses of the large room. I just need to wait, and to listen.

Tap-tap-tap.

I fling myself out of bed and snatch the key from its hiding place, inside the bound edition of Renovian legends that I keep on a high table, within arm's reach of my pillow. Then I scamper into the room's darkest corner, not bothering to fetch the taper. I know the path by heart, know every chair and footstool to avoid. Cal will have made his way up the stairs in darkness as well, slipping through the recesses of the cellars in stealth to make his way here. To reveal the door, I must pull aside the tapestry and trace the oak panel down to the lock.

With a click it's open, and just knowing he's there is intoxicating. I can sense his tall, broad form before me, even before he says a word. All I have to do is reach out a hand and touch his chest, so firm and broad, and I am weak at the knees, swooning.

"Lilac," he says, his voice low and soft, loving, and he steps into the room, swallowing me in an embrace before we close the door. I don't want to let him go. I burrow into his neck, breathing in his particular scent that's impossible to describe. There's a musk to it, and the subtle hawthorn aroma of the soap we make in Renovia. Cal smells like home to me, in every way.

"I missed you." I hadn't realized the strain of keeping up a false front all day. "Where have you been?"

"Interrogating the messenger from Stur, and sending our own people down there to ask more questions," Cal says, and he draws my head back and kisses me gently. "I need to know what's true and what is just fear and rumor."

"And did the messenger tell you anything we didn't know?" I ask. Cal shakes his head, and I see how tired he looks—the dark rims under his eyes, his hollow cheeks, rough with stubble. It's no surprise that he's exhausted: Since the parade, the capital has swarmed with spies from Argonia and Stavin, their embassies merely public fronts, the ambassadors entertaining the rich and mighty of Montrice while their spies sneak and snoop behind our backs.

"Too many stories," he says. "Half of it from legends and old crones' tales."

I put my hands on his temples and massage. If I could take his burden, I would. He is more husband to me than my own.

He leans back, his olive skin against the crisp white linen sheets, his eyes glinting in the flickering light of the taper. "The villagers swear the pond went black with dark magic, and then lilac. And news has leaked of the letter from Stavin—"

"Which no one cared about until now," I interrupt. "Even Hansen thought Goran was merely a warmonger looking for an excuse to invade us. But now it's different. People are scared."

Cal sighs, tracing a hand over my hair. His touch is pure comfort and I have to resist the urge to close my eyes. "Fear is contagious," he says, "especially where the Aphrasians are concerned. But we need to know more. It's possible the story is exaggerated."

"Tell that to the people booing me in the countryside. Maybe Hansen is right for a change, and we can't trust Goran. Stavin has never been one to shy from a conflict or a chance to expand its borders."

"Part of the issue," Cal says in a deliberate way, choosing his words carefully, "is that this happened in Montrice, not Renovia. It reminds everyone that you're Renovian."

I lean against him, trying to draw on his strength. "But why would I do something so cruel, and then leave a sign that blatant?"

"No one who knew you would ever believe it," says Cal.

"But they don't know me at all," I say in despair. It suddenly dawns on me that my position here is as flimsy as my marriage.

"I will never let anything happen to you," says Cal, his gaze steady. He puts his arms around me and I feel my heartbeat slowing.

"The Montricians associate the Aphrasians and their dark magic with Renovia," I say. "It's only fair, I suppose. The Aphrasian king ruled Renovia, and since that time our kingdom has failed to defeat or contain his followers. And now here I am, married to the King of Montrice."

Cal winces, as he often does at the mention of my marriage and my husband. He would rather we had run away than see me as another man's wife. The life we have eked for ourselves in secret, in shadow, wears on him. I begged him to make this sacrifice, but it does not come without heartache.

For now, however, we both must push our feelings aside. I clear my throat. "So I'm the evil queen," I say, my voice low. "They believe I'm in league with the Aphrasians. But why?"

"With Aphrasian magic at your disposal," Cal reasons, "you plague Stavin until it's weak enough to annex. Then you undermine Montrice in a campaign of magical terror. Next target is Argonia, I suppose. Everywhere would be subject to the Kingdom of Renovia and its Dellafiore queen. The Avantine Empire intact once more."

"All hail Avantine," I say, unable to suppress my bitterness.

"All hail the queen," Cal says, with a raised eyebrow. I know he's teasing, trying to make me feel better about this absurd theory. This plan I would never want. I never wanted to be a princess, let alone a queen. That is my mother's plan, my mother's wish, but it is not mine.

"Just last week they loved us," I tell him, pulling away from his embrace. "Hansen and me, I mean. They all wanted us to visit their manor houses and villages and harvest festivals. The groveling, the declarations of fealty. How quickly things change."

"The kingdoms may be united in name," Cal says, "but suspicion persists toward Renovia. Everything about this situation is new for the people here. Montrician queens are meant to be consorts, not joint rulers."

"I may as well be a consort," I say, unable to shake my dark mood. "No one listens to me in court. And my mother doesn't seem to need my help back at home."

"You'll never be a consort." Cal's face softens and he smiles at me. "You're a born leader. And a wild Renovian. That's why they're scared of you."